THE MOST DANGEROUS SPECIES

Book II

Mar Preston

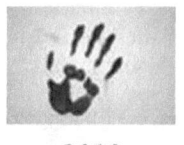

2016

ISBN: 0984495282
ISBN 13: 9780984495283

DEDICATION

To Lily

ACKNOWLEDGEMENTS

My editor, Jenny Jenson, made this a much better book than the first draft I sent off to her. She was able to find in its imperfect beginnings the book I really meant to write. My proofreader, Mary Goss, found every possible error. If any errors remain, it's because I fussed around with the manuscript after she'd signed off. Writers are never done fussing with it.

I may have put the words together to make this book, but many people helped me, whether they knew it or not. Patrice Stimpson, my fellow animal lover, who patrols the mean streets of Pine Mountain Club, is the prototype for Holly Seabright. Dex Stafford and the other characters are wholly imaginary.

My beta readers, Nancy Cole Silverman, Kate Thornton, Clark Lohr, and especially Candy Posson, offered invaluable comments on the first best draft I could manage. And thank you also to Gregg Miller, LAPD retired, who caught out the worst of police procedural errors. I truly value the support, guidance, and encouragement that I've received from Judith Cassis, my friend and mentor.

I offer apologies to the residents of my village on which this novel and its predecessor, *Payback*, is loosely based. The O'Malleys and other villainous characters, are created entirely from my imagination rather than being based on actual people.

In my view, only fine people live here in the village. I also offer apologies to my friends in Bakersfield, which is filled with interesting people and fun places to go. Its misfortune is that it sits at the lower end of California's San Joaquin Valley where all the noxious smog collects at the base of the mountains. Please forget all the terrible things I've written about it.

The Most Dangerous Species is Book II in the Dex
Stafford and Holly Seabright Series

CHAPTER ONE

The neighbors called security, so Holly Seabright showed up in the patrol Jeep. They'd watched this old fool who'd just gotten his final divorce papers dig holes in front of his cabin with his Bobcat, roaring back and forth. One tree to plant and so far had dug twenty-one holes. First he'd dig a hole. Then he'd have a drink and go back and fill in the hole, and then dig a new one.

Holly listened to his sad story for a while, then persuaded him to park his machine for the night and go to bed. If she hadn't read in the local weekly that he'd dragged his ex-wife's couch out on the deck of the cabin she'd moved into and taken an axe to it, she'd have felt sorry for him. He'd left his wife's half of the couch on the deck. Set fire to his half. That got security patrol and the deputies there in a hurry. The forest was so dry after four years of drought in California that Sierra Mountain Village would have gone up like a rocket.

Holly shook her head, driving away. People! Don't you just wonder sometimes?

Around 8 p.m. on a spring evening. Friday.

Wearing the hated black battle dress uniform that made any woman look like a bag of potatoes tied in the middle, Holly Seabright showed up to her village patrol job, 5 ft. 10", underpaid and unappreciated. Coming into work tonight, careful not to show up looking blissed out and yawning, she basked in the afterglow of the first weekend she'd spent with Dex Stafford in a month. Between his schedule and hers they'd had damn little time for any hot monkey sex, or even much kissy-face-tickle. The boss gave her the eye when she came in but didn't say anything. Things were tense between them. By now Stafford would be half way back to Bakersfield, curling down the black mountain roads towards California's Central Valley. He was the first real boyfriend Holly had in a while, and remembering his big hands on her, she really wanted to hang on to him. She left the office at town hall and got into the Jeep patrol vehicle. The radio crackled. She took the call, hearing the yips of a nearby pack of coyotes.

"Sierra Mountain Village Patrol. Go ahead, please," she said, thumbing on the mobile radio.

"Holly? Holly? Is that you?"

"Sierra Mountain Village Patrol. Go ahead, please." Not recognizing the voice, she didn't break radio protocol. Too many people listened in to radio calls for something to charge up the monotony of a long evening in a sleepy mountain town. They monitored the radio, hoping something terrible was happening to the neighbors. That would be interesting.

"It's Peach. Come over. I need help. Please. Get here as fast as you can. Something terrible…" her voice high-pitched and panicked.

"On my way." Holly thumbed the radio off and climbed into the patrol Jeep. Was Peach crying?

She headed towards Paws at the opposite end of Sierra Mountain Village. Peach Bryson operated a first-rate cat rescue sanctuary like a precision machine. Hitting the gas hard, she sped through the quiet village center, past real estate offices, gift shops, and the town's few restaurants. Everything normal there.

She pulled the Jeep into the graveled parking lot of Paws, scattering a trio of cats who fled into the shadows. Their eyes shone green in the headlights. Cats outside the fence? More cats skittered out of her way as she shone the Maglite around, mounting the steps that led to the walkway separating the house and the cattery buildings. A coyote howled at the scent of prey, and she heard other yips and barking. For the coyotes, cats running loose were like opening a free lunch counter to the public. Not good. Not good at all.

No motion sensor lights came on. Odd. The 150 or so cats wandered freely among the room-size kennels and outbuildings they called cottages filled with cat trees and climbing structures, with alcoves and hidey-holes for nervous cats. Ordinarily none of them ran loose outside the ten-acre, fenced property. The cattery's old dog, Lily, shambled over to sniff Holly's pants.

Peach Bryson stumbled into the walkway from the cattery. She fell into Holly's arms as Holly stood at the top of the stairs, taking a moment to figure out what was going on. Peach's Humpty-Dumpty body was squashy and boneless, and she was crying hard.

"Oh, thank God you're here, Holly. I went back to the house to get another can of kitten formula…" Hunched over, her face heart-attack red, she looked as if she would pass out from hyperventilation,

"Slow down, slow down. Here, sit." Half carrying her, she led her over to a forty-pound pail of cat litter and forced her to sit down on it. "What's going on?"

"I think Don's dead. I can't go back there…."

Holly found this hard to believe, but they were both in their 70's. "You think he's dead? Where is he?"

"He's in the treatment room. Oh God, oh my God. I think somebody killed him. He's just lying there and the blood on his shirt…vaccines all smashed on the floor."

"Killed him? Peach, how do you know somebody killed him?"

"Because I saw him."

Somebody killing Peach's boyfriend was pretty unlikely. Holly left Peach and stepped carefully down the dark hallway of the main building of the cattery. She flicked on the light switch and nothing happened. But there were lights on in the house. Darkness and the silence made it eerie. The clock mounted by the door of the treatment room ticked loudly. She heard the coyotes again and sensed cats swarming underfoot. The hair prickled on the back of her neck.

With the Maglite in hand, she stepped carefully, heading past the kennel enclosures that lined both sides of a central corridor, shining the light ahead. She wished suddenly she had a weapon other than pepper spray and a baton. Worth calling the Sheriff's deputies for backup? No. First of all, she couldn't believe anybody killed mild-mannered, sweet old Don Farrow. Secondly, the guys stationed at the substation 18 miles away could be anywhere patrolling their 640-square mile coverage area.

Don Farrow could even be alive.

All the doors of the six 12 x 12 rooms in the main building were wide open. Cats were everywhere—tabbies, marmalades, calicos, tuxedos, cats of every color and description: cats fleeing from her, cats winding around her feet in the dark. The meowing, hissing, and claws skittering on the linoleum floor were broken by the hard sobbing of the old woman. The air around her buzzed like a neon sign. At the far end of the hallway, the loading dock door framed a rectangle of moonlight.

Training kicked in. Stop to listen. Size up the situation. Take deep breaths. Observe and report. Slow down. Heart jackhammering in her chest. Maglite held ready as a club, Holly paused at the door of the treatment room.

A dark shadow pooled on the floor by the table where the staff mixed up vaccinations, prepared kitten formula, and treated minor injuries. One look in the powerful beam of the flashlight told Holly this wasn't a heart attack. Way too much blood. A struggle had taken place that had knocked over a tall gooseneck lamp and a tray of vaccines and syringes. The Mag beam flitted over his face and Holly froze. Eyes wide and still, vacant but for a hint of surprise. Dead.

A thought stabbed her brain like a shard of glass. Get the hell out of here.

━━◆━◆━━

Bursting with questions, Holly backed out fast.

Don was Peach's new boyfriend, if that was the correct term for a newly-in-love couple in their seventies. Peach found the man of her dreams, and then this. Whatever it was. Murders took place somewhere else, not here.

Peach stood up in the darkness as Holly approached. Her teeth were chattering with anxiety.

Holly put her hands on Peach's shoulders and felt her shaking. "You called 911?"

"Holly, could he still be alive? Is it possible?"

A quick look at the blood told her there wasn't much chance of that, but if something could be done, a nice guy like Don deserved it. "Make the call. I'll wait here."

Peach stumbled off into the house. Peach lived in a four-bedroom, two-story log structure set near the road that dead-ended at the edge of town. Sierra Mountain Village had a lot of nice homes, a sprinkling of McMansions, and one neighborhood limited to manufactured, and mobile homes. Peach Bryson's house was one of the nice ones, but nothing compared to the house she'd left in Beverly Hills. Holly couldn't sit still and resisted the impulse to start rounding up the cats streaming all over the place.

She heard the kitchen door slam and Peach's quick steps down the hallway. "They're coming. Don shouldn't be alone, Holly. We should go out and sit with him."

Holly pulled her close. "No, Peach. We should leave things like they are so that..."

"Do you think it means your Dex will be coming?"

Detective Dex Stafford was hardly *her* Dex. He was a very different guy on the job.

Holly led her back into the kitchen to wait. Peach's face was white with shock, her pupils dilated wide with fear, her cotton top stiff with drying blood.

Ooooooh, Holly thought: *What's this?*

CHAPTER TWO

Sirens approached, their howls long and dramatic in the still night. Headlight beams stabbing the roadside stands of Jeffrey and piñon pines, red and blue lights spinning on top of Kern County Sheriff's vehicles. Behind them the Fire Department and paramedics from the substation pulled into the parking lot in front of the cattery. Holly knew what was coming next.

Peach twisted away from her and grabbed a cordless phone, punching in a phone number with shaking fingers.

"Who are you calling, Peach?"

"Brenda. We've got to get the cats back."

Brenda of the stop-light red hair and solid pound-age. Competent Brenda. If anybody could wrangle the cats it would be the cattery manager Brenda. They'd never get the feral cats back, but at least they were fixed and had their shots. Some of the cats ready for adoption would return once they got hungry and thirsty—if the coyotes didn't get them.

Words spilled out of Peach. "I...I can't believe anybody would kill Don. I can't believe it"

A picture flashed in Holly's mind of last summer's high tea fundraiser. Peach invited her old friends from Beverly Hills and Actors for Animals pals from Hollywood, casting a net far and wide in the animal community to support the cattery. She loved parties and people loved her parties. And she made raising money look easy, making donors think that pressing a big check into her hands was their own idea.

"Oh, we've been arguing a bit lately," Peach said, her white curls bobbing around her face. "Don says he wants to live like normal people, whatever that is. You know the housing development people are badgering me to sell my land?"

"I heard that."

She walked over to the kitchen stove where she straightened a tea towel. "I wish my son was here. No, I don't. You know how he is."

Holly knew. "Do you want me to call your daughter to come over?"

"No, no. The cats…she never liked the cats and… she has her children and that husband. She can't just pick up and leave them…."

"But she lives in town, Peach. It would take her five minutes to get here."

The sound of heavy boots came across the deck. Holly opened the kitchen door. "In here," she called out.

Bill Madison. Everybody on security patrol knew and liked Madison. The Sarge ran the substation in Frazier Oaks, a town down the road close to the Interstate that ran north and south connecting Mexico to Canada. Madison was pushing Holly's application to join the Kern County Sheriff's Department.

"Hey there, Seabright. Heard the call," he said. "Hello, Mrs. Bryson." The blood on the front of her cotton top registered on his face. He frowned and shot Holly a quick look over Peach's head. She shrugged.

"Sorry to hear about this. Holly, did you take a look?"

"From the doorway." She picked up a white cat and held him close for comfort. The cat squirmed to be let down. Peach burst into a fresh flood of tears.

Madison gripped her shoulder and mumbled a few kind words. He went off to convene with his guys. "Stay here with Mrs. Bryson, Holly."

The deputies were excited but quiet about it, out of respect for Peach. Unexplained death was uncommon, even with the aging residents that made up much of the population of the town. Violent death was even rarer in the scattered villages that lined the one road in and out of the mountain towns, and news about it would spread quickly. Meth, heroin, domestic abuse, identity theft, yes. At this point, though, murder seemed unlikely. Holly got Peach settled with a cup of chamomile tea and a plate of Fig Newtons along with a promise to stay put. It was hard to ignore the blood that stained her black-and-white cotton top.

"I know this is tough, Peach. Try to be patient."

Peach hugged herself, rocking back and forth in one of the chairs in a corner of the big kitchen. From there she could look out the windows into the well-lit parking lot in front.

Holly stepped outside and called Ed Bradley, her boss at Sierra Mountain Village Patrol. She whispered to him Don Farrow had died under suspicious circumstances and filled him in on what little she knew. Ed decided to call in Pete, the new guy, for backup and leave her at the scene. Any calls after this Pete could handle. Probably.

"Think she did it?" Madison broke away from his deputies to ask Holly. He jerked his head toward Peach who was still in the kitchen.

"Absolutely not," she said.

He lifted a skeptical eyebrow. "You go in there for a look see?"

"No way. I went to the doorway of the room and then backed out." She glanced back at the house, drawing Madison aside. "Think Stafford will be assigned to this one?"

"Depends on who's up." Dex Stafford knew the territory, the people. But the Kern County Sheriff's Department had their own logic and both of them knew it.

"Paramedics need to pronounce death just in case. There's no electricity back there. Power's out?"

"It was like that when I got here," Holly said. "Wait. I'll ask Peach."

She darted in the house to find Peach with her head tilted back in a chintz-covered easy chair in a corner of the airy kitchen, tears flowing down her cheeks. She smoothed the fur of a cat in her lap. *All our cats, our beautiful cats.* Holly thought of the coyotes and shuddered. Peach's old dog Lily slept at her feet.

"Peach, what's wrong with the lights in the cattery?"

She took a moment to answer. "There were lights on when Don and I were out there working. Something must have …" She trailed off.

Holly took the news back to Madison outside. "Lights were fine she says. There's a circuit board around…here it is. Look. The main breaker's off. Somebody tripped it."

"We gotta have light," Madison said, making a note. He reached over with a gloved hand to flip the master switch to the on position. Light flooded the corridor and lit the treatment area where Don Farrow's body lay. They walked down the middle of the corridor and stood there at the door.

"You think *that* happened by itself?" Holly said.

"Not likely." Madison called in the paramedics who edged their way through the crime scene into the treatment room, kneeling by the body and sharing a look. They officially pronounced Don Farrow dead.

Holly couldn't wait any longer. She went back in the house and sat down at the kitchen table. "Peach. What happened out there?"

Peach got up and put on a pot of coffee and turned to her. "It's all so crazy. Don and I were bottle-feeding a litter of four-week old feral kittens because I couldn't find a foster for them. Don wanted me to close the cattery and we were fighting." She held a hand over her mouth and hunched her shoulders. "I screamed at him, Holly. I screamed at him just like a shrew. He died after we had a fight and we never made it up."

Holly flinched at the raw grief on her face. She got up and put her arms around her, blinking hard, breathing hard through her nose, a trick she'd learn to stop from crying.

"He's dead, isn't he?"

Holly nodded.

"I knew it anyway." She said nothing for a long time. "He was so good with the animals, but they got hair all over him and he didn't like that. He was kind of a dandy, you know," she said looking up at her through tears. "I shouldn't say that, but he was. So careful about his dress. Oh, I'm going to miss him…" Her shoulders crumpled.

Holly kept nodding and yupping as Peach repeated herself, all of the big questions still unanswered. Her ears were tuned outside waiting until the detectives assigned to the case arrived. She saw from the window the police scanner ghouls were already there, parking behind the line of official cars trying to persuade a deputy to tell them something, anything juicy.

"Did Lily bark?" Holly asked.

Peach thought for a minute. "Yes, I think so, but I can't remember. I just can't think straight right now."

CHAPTER THREE

A half hour later Holly looked out the kitchen window and saw Dex Stafford get out of the Kern County Sheriff's vehicle and reach in the back for his murder kit. Nice butt. Stafford was taller than she was and that was important to her. His crisp brown hair shone in the lights that illuminated the parking lot. He looked around. Harry Price, his old partner, got out of the vehicle on the passenger side. Shanko, his current partner, could get on somebody else's nerves for a while. Dex called Shanko a LOP—in Department parlance a lazy cop.

Stafford looked up, saw her in the window and smiled. A report of a fresh body could mean anything from natural causes to suicide to homicide. When she first met Dex Stafford a couple of months ago, his good looks had created a sensation among the unclaimed treasures of Sierra Mountain Village single ladies. She could see now he wasn't as pretty as she'd first thought. Something about the nose flawed perfect good looks, but how important is a nose, she asked herself?

She watched as a cluster of deputies surrounded Stafford, the fire guys and paramedics drifting closer. One of the deputies asked Dex a question and he started giving orders to process the scene. What looked like confusion wasn't. Everybody knew what to do. She came outside to say hello.

Sgt. Madison thundered down the stairs to meet Stafford and Price. "Criminalists are already in Arvin, so they'll be here soon," Holly heard Stafford tell Madison.

Arvin was a spread-out town on the flats about 45 minutes away from here, home to air quality rivaling that of Beijing and New Delhi. The noxious yellow haze of pollutants blown from the north was trapped at the end of the San Joaquin Valley, circled by a ring of mountains. Holly took a big breath at the top of the Grapevine Summit and tried not to breathe every time she hit the flatlands in Bakersfield.

If it was any of the other detectives in the department, they'd take her statement and send her home like the peon she was. Holly didn't think Stafford or Harry would do that. Dex knew she was on the board of directors in the Paws operation and involved in all its politics. He also knew she was a curious cat herself and would have a hard time keeping her nose out of the investigation.

Dex's partner Harry Price had just returned from an around-the-world-trip, the gossips said unchanged. Harry wore his grey hair in a regulation flat top, beefier, a little wider in the ass, still all business. His face was so tanned he looked like an English walnut. Only a winter spent on the South Sea Island Cruise in a yacht gave you a tan like that. How could he be unchanged after everything that had happened to him?

County cars now lined the road on both sides, red and blue lights spinning on the light bars, the deputies milling around. The village was home to about 1500 people on a blustery winter afternoon in February, and doubled on a glorious holiday weekend in July when the air was full of crickets and bird song. Half of the three thousand properties were second homes owned by well-off people who lived in Bakersfield or the Los Angeles sprawl, their mountain vacation homes unoccupied much of the year. Looking out for empty houses was one of the priorities of the patrol department.

Sgt. Bill Madison who commanded the nearby Sheriff's Department substation stood at the top of the stairs leading to the parking lot outside Peach's home. He and two deputies descended the stairs to meet Harry and Dex. The long, low addition housing the cattery buildings stretched away into the shadows. The Coroner's Death investigator was on his way and he would begin the process of determining mode, manner, and cause of death.

Harry ordered the deputies to check in at the top of the hour so nothing got missed. Every murder investigation piled up reams of paper, reports, field investigation notes, photos and all the etcetera of preparing a trail leading to a suspect and a court case. Holly stood at the edge of the group, while all the *hey, how the hell are ya's* were happening. She edged down the central hallway inside until she reached an alcove opposite the treatment room where she'd have a good view. *I'm going to stay here, dammit, until somebody turfs me out.*

She watched from the shadowed alcove while Dex and Harry worked their way down the hall toward her. Neither one of them spotted her as they did their initial walk-through. The two detectives stood talking inside the room, looking around, four feet away from the body, trying to put together what happened. She could hear them talking.

"No surveillance cameras by any chance?" Harry said, looking around.

Dex laughed. "To watch hanky-panky between cats?"

"Looks like a doctor's office," Harry said peering around the treatment room.

"This is where they do simple stuff like injections. I know they have a vet and vet techs who come in all the time."

"Lotta equipment. This is a nice house," Harry said. "There's money around."

They stepped closer, hunkering down by the body.

"She's putting all her money into the cats. Holly volunteers here," Dex muttered.

"Hmmpf. Why were the lights cut?"

"I don't know. Create confusion. Make a delay. Sneak up on the guy? When did the power go off? Before or after they got him down?"

Harry's low rumble of a voice. "What makes you think there was more than one? He looks like a little old guy. What would it take? Must have got him from behind. Doesn't look like there was much of a struggle, except for this."

Price pointed to a tray of instruments and vials of vaccination fluid crashed to the floor, a standing lamp knocked over. He peered at the body, moving the edge of the cotton golf shirt upward with a ballpoint pen. The front of Farrow's shirt was a stiff carpet of dried blood.

"Ooooh, ugly," Dex said. "Knife. See it anywhere?" He got to his feet and pivoted, making a quick survey of the room.

"Nope. I think I can see three blade entries. Got it in good and twisted it up hard to make sure he hit the heart."

"Damn. Victim's wearing gloves. No epithelial cells under the fingernails."

Harry Price considered the wounds, squatted down by the body. "Froth of blood on the lips so he got a lung too. Wish he'd left the weapon for us."

"Takes skill to hit the heart with a blade, training."

"Or luck. Like it's somebody he knew. If he came up behind him like in a surprise, the angle would be different."

Price gave Dex a look. "Better not let Gorman hear you speculating. He'll get all pissy if he thinks you want his job."

Dex laughed. The laugh ripped through the room. Gallows humor.

They studied the body and the wounds on Don Farrow's chest without more conversation. Stafford had told Holly last week they had new lab techniques for DNA analysis. Their own DNA could be contaminating the scene even without contact with the body, no matter how careful they were. Breathing near the victim was enough. That's how sensitive DNA testing had become. And defense attorneys knew it too.

"Maybe it's PETA nuts, wanting to free the animals. Maybe Farrow caught them and then…" Harry said.

Holly gritted her teeth. Oh, no. Not PETA. Please, no.

"Cats? These aren't chimps. I don't know about cats," Stafford said. "I think people like this place. It's popular. That's what Holly tells me."

"Nuts are nuts, remember? We can't discount that."

"But why wouldn't they kill Peach Bryson then? She's the one that runs the place."

"Who the hell knows? Let's get a preliminary statement from her before the coroner's guy gets here."

Holly slipped out the loading dock door while they were still talking and went back in the house.

CHAPTER FOUR

Stafford and Price had come back into the kitchen and ordered Peach outside while the search took place inside the house. Holly was surprised it had taken them that long to remove her from the scene. The question was where to put her. A different neighborhood, and they'd shove her in the back of a police car to wait. Here it was cold at night, even in summer.

Outside the fence there was a redwood picnic table in a small enclosure where potential adopters could get to know a cat they might like to take home. It was lit with fairy lights which cast just enough illumination to page through a photo album Peach had brought outside with her. A deputy kept watch just out of earshot and didn't object when Holly sat down across the table. Peach held out the album, turning a page for Holly to see. Happier times. She and Don stood on the deck in front of the sign saying Paws. Don was slightly taller than Peach with soft, white hair, blue-green eyes, and a tan. The look of love on his face as he gazed at Peach shone from the photo.

"I just think of Don alone out there," Peach glanced up at the main cattery building, her brow furrowed with anxiety. "It just doesn't seem right."

Holly watched deputies going into the outbuildings where they housed geriatrics and cats with feline AIDS and leukemia. She did her best to sit on her hands, imagining what was going on, wishing she were part of it. She grabbed a Maine Coon cat who had edged out of the scrub oak bushes. She liked the skinny old guy who was on his last legs.

Time passed slowly, Peach shivering. When she heard voices approach, she stood up to greet Harry Price and Dex. Up close Dex looked tired, purple shadows under his green eyes. How could Harry Price still look the same?

Peach got to her feet with an arthritic jerk at the table to pull herself upright. She had cried herself into a sodden grief that was hard to witness. She nodded vaguely at Dex as he introduced Harry Price. Dex spotted Holly who gave him a nod, all the electricity between them tamped down tight.

Plenty of detectives at a crime scene would have gotten rid of her, a mere security patrol officer. Detectives often suffered from the *Cop God Syndrome,* given all that power and authority to have people snap to at their bidding. Stafford wasn't like that, at least she hadn't seen that in him so far. Shanko, his partner while Harry had been gone? Oh yes. All cops could be assholes sometimes.

"Do you think Mrs. Bryson could go inside? It's really cold out here," she said to Dex.

Dex looked at Price. "They're probably done in the kitchen."

"Okay," Price nodded.

"I need to have Holly with me. I can't do this alone."

"For a few minutes then," Price agreed. He led the way into the kitchen. Holly tucked herself into a window seat. Peach sank into a kitchen chair, and waved them to sit down.

"You tell them. I can't do it again…I can't. I just can't." Holly saw Stafford and Price take in the blood on Peach's top and the wordless comment that passed between them.

"The victim is Don Farrow, Ms. Bryson's, um, boyfriend," Holly said when it became clear Peach wasn't able to speak. She walked over to the table and sat down, letting the Maine Coon down on the floor.

"Ms. Bryson called me at 8:03 and I went to the door of the room Mr. Farrow is in with a flashlight to look, but I didn't enter. The victim was on the floor on his back in what we call the treatment room. The electricity was out at the breaker panel when I got here. Sgt. Madison threw the main breaker switch so we could see. Nobody entered the treatment room except Sgt. Madison and the paramedics. None of the deputies."

Price nodded. Stafford reached across the table and gave Peach Bryson's hand a squeeze. "I'm sorry for your loss," he said. "Tell us what happened."

"Just give me a minute." Peach pulled herself together with effort.

"Did Mr. Farrow live here?"

"No, no. He had a rental cabin here in the village and a house in Taft." She gave them the two addresses.

"Do you have a key to the houses?" Stafford asked.

"No, no. I can't imagine what happened," she said, looking frightened. "Everybody liked Don."

They all said that. To the family of victims, their loved one was always much loved and innocent.

"The photo guy will need to get shots of your blouse and then we'll have a lot more questions."

Peach looked down at herself and shuddered.

This wasn't the same vibrant woman Stafford remembered hosting a recent fundraiser to pay for vet care for the cat sanctuary. At the party, Peach moved confidently from group to group, the well-groomed Beverly Hills matron. Now everything about her had crumpled and faded. He gazed around the big kitchen, noting all the cats in the room silently watching him. Cats draped over a window sill, on a gate-leg table which held about twenty figurines of cats, in boxes and beds and climbing trees around the edges of the room. A sharp ring tone sounded and he stood up to take the call out in the hallway. The white forensics van pulled in.

"Yeah, Shanko. What have you got?"

The hallway was lined with framed photos of cats who had been adopted into good homes. He went silent, listening. Swiping the phone closed, he called Harry Price to come outside. Holly followed him. Price put a deputy back inside to watch Peach.

"Hey there, Seabright. How you doin', Holly?" Price said once they were out of the kitchen and the door closed behind them. He swept her up in a big hug and she hugged him back.

They chatted for a moment as Stafford's impatience built.

Finally Harry got down to business. "Yeah, yeah, Stafford. Chill out. What have you got so far?"

"No criminal record on the victim for a start. Looks like your upstanding John Q. Public. Donald Andrew Farrow, age 73. Drives this year's Lexus and has a Range Rover registered too. Shanko found a couple of speeding tickets."

"Anything else?" Price asked, heading back to the kitchen door.

"Belongs to a lot of scientific organizations. Shanko's started on the phone records. The banks. Lexis-Nexis. All that."

You never knew what surprises turned up. Practically nobody was who he said he was.

Price opened the kitchen door and stuck his head inside.

"We'll be back, Ms. Bryson. You mind waiting inside for us, Holly? " Holly nodded, as though she expected this. Peach didn't look up from the contemplation of her coffee cup as Holly took a seat at the table with her.

Stafford and Price walked back down the short corridor that connected the house to the cattery.

"Make sure you print the circuit board box," Harry said, calling back over his shoulder to the forensics team. "You see the blood on her shirt?"

"Yeah, I did," Stafford answered.

The short Latina who headed the forensics team stepped in with her bag of magic dust and tricks. Stafford examined the floor for prints. Might be something useful, though he knew from Holly that volunteers and potential adopters and the three paid staff were in and out of here all the time.

Dex took his new laser measuring device off his belt to get started mapping the scene, leaving the body where it was. The laser replaced the old metal tapes that folded up in the middle and generally made scene mapping a pain in the ass. The laser cut down on hours at the scene, if there was a lot to document. What he really wanted was a 3D scanner on a tripod that would process a crime scene in 15 minutes. He loved the new technology, just not having to explain and justify all his cool toys five times to the dinosaurs in the command structure. With the dip in oil revenues, Kern County was even more strapped for resources. He'd wait a long time for a 3D scanner.

CHAPTER FIVE

Half an hour later, Peach came out and beckoned to Holly as she stood talking to one of the deputies in front of the cattery. "Please. I need to talk to you," she said, beckoning Holly into the kitchen.

Normally Peach moved and talked briskly, directing, persuading, jollying volunteers along, making things happen. Now she was in slow mo and appeared to have trouble concentrating enough to make it to the end of a sentence. She sank into a chair at the table and held her head in her hands. Holly pulled out a chair opposite her at the long table where the cattery board meetings were held. Everybody gave Peach cat figurines and plates, photos, and amateur paintings of cats, and everybody's gifts were lovingly displayed on the walls and a double row of plate rails near the ceiling.

"We're in trouble," Peach said.

"What kind of trouble?" Holly said carefully.

"The County. Don warned me. Now all these people are here and he—your boyfriend—he's going to find out."

"Peach, if you know anything about how Don died, you shouldn't be telling me. You should tell Detectives Stafford and Price."

"I can't. They'll close us down."

"What, Peach?" Holly took her hand, fearing what she'd hear. "What's going on?"

"You know the free spay/neuter days for ferals the county puts on in Bakersfield?"

"Sure, I know, Peach." Holly nodded. "I do transporting for you, remember?"

"Well, I sometimes put friendlies in the traps and say they're ferals to save money. Don told me not to do that and I did it anyway. He said it was cheating. And if I had…maybe if I'd listened to him, maybe he'd be alive…" Her eyes pleaded for absolution.

"Peach, that's not why Don died. How can you think that? Somebody was angry enough to kill him," Holly said with so much force that it came out too loud. "It can't be about the cats. That isn't reasonable. It must be something else."

"But that's not all. The Conditional Use Permit I got from the county says we can only have 150 cats, and I don't know how it happened. People leave litters of kittens on the doorstep. I know I said we have 158, but we're closer to 170 and..."

"That's what you're worried about? The number of cats?" Holly gripped her hands tightly, leaning across the table. Peach's cornflower blue eyes were huge with panic.

"Do you think the Sheriff's Department is going to count cats?" Holly said as softly as she could, restraining a giggle of nervousness forcing its way upward.

"Look at them. Those men are outside poking their nose into everything," she said, pulling her hands away. "That man, he..."

"You mean Dex? Detective Stafford? Peach, listen to me. Just listen." Holly waited until she got Peach's wobbly attention. "I can absolutely guarantee you the detectives won't be counting cats unless they're related to Don's death. And they're not, are they?"

She shook her head slowly, then let it slump forward. "They dig into everything when something bad happens. I know that. They're awful."

"I don't think you need to tell them about the cats unless it comes up, Peach." Holly's giggle of nervousness threatened to bubble over.

Peach got up to put on another pot of coffee. Doing something seemed to make her feel better. The air was still thick with tension, both of them straining to hear what was going on. All the outside lights were on, and the deputies were in and out of the buildings in the back.

"Try not to worry," Holly said. "Everything's going to be alright."

That sounded empty and stupid. She thought of the times of trouble in her own life when a well-wisher had told her everything was going to be alright.

It hadn't turned out that way for her. Nor did Peach appear comforted.

Stafford watched as the Coroner's investigator arrived, breathing hard as he hauled his equipment out of the car. Butch Gorman was ready once he had a suck on his inhaler. Bakersfield had the worst air quality in California. It seemed like everybody had an inhaler, mostly, kids. Gorman wore a white shirt, blue windbreaker, and a John Deere feed cap. He had a bald head ringed with frowsy white hair and glasses not in fashion at any point in her lifetime. Taking his time and puffing hard after climbing five stairs, Gorman looked around with a pained expression. Holly stood next to him, trying to look as though she had some official function.

"What the hell is this place?" he asked Dex.

"They save cats," Dex said, leading Gorman toward the treatment room.

"What the hell for?" Dex shot Holly a smile.

"Who's she?" Gorman said, pointing at Holly. He regarded her with cool eyes, starting from the ugly combat boots, up the black pants and uniform blouse.

"She's okay," Stafford said.

"Oh, yeah?" He looked her over head to toe. Dex led him past her down the hall. After a minute Holly followed them and stood in the door of the treatment room, well out of the path of the criminalists. The burly investigator smoothed on latex gloves and hunkered down next to the body. The butcher shop smell of fresh blood filled the air.

"Goddamn it, cat hair everywhere." He looked back at Holly. "Get her out of here. I don't want civilians in my scene."

Holly raised an eyebrow and shot a look at Dex. He shrugged. It wasn't a surprise to either of them. The criminalists kept out of Gorman's way as well, marking evidence with pup tent numbered markers. They were also grousing about the animal hair. Farrow lay on his back, both arms back behind his head as though he was still trying to ward off blows.

"I need better light," the death investigator growled. He crab-walked around the evidence markers with a great deal of puffing and blowing.

The criminalists tilted the big lights this way and that until Gorman nodded. Stafford watched the painstaking routine, careful to appear eager. Gorman unlatched a side pocket of his kit and took out a pair of ordinary nail scissors, careful to dip them in RNASE Away, a substance that removed all previous DNA. Next he snipped hair samples and placed them in his Decedent Hair kit envelope. All this took about twenty minutes while the criminalists waited in silence. Only then did he signal to Dex he was ready to do the body exam. All this time he squatted next to the body, his big stomach making his breathing even more labored.

Gorman located a rib and slid in the slender probe that looked like a dipstick just above the waist. Then he withdrew it and regarded it carefully. Some departments didn't do a liver temperature reading, considering it worthwhile only for exclusion purposes. Too many factors influenced internal body temperature. Kern County still did them.

A cat hiding behind the treatment table burst out and skittered across the floor through bloody footprints, ping ponging back and forth between Stafford and Price who jumped out of the way.

Gorman shouted. "Goddamit. Now what?"

He yanked his kit out of the way and began a long rant about how one cat could jeopardize crime scene integrity. It wasn't funny, but Stafford still had a hard time keeping a straight face. One of the criminalists snickered behind him. Gorman was a stickler for procedure and this wasn't the first rant and pant they'd heard. But who could he blame? The cat? He went back to his careful examination of the body.

Don Farrow stuck to the floor with congealed blood that had run down his sides. The floor released the body with a suck Stafford hoped he wouldn't remember. Bruises on his arms and hands, but no cuts. Gorman pointed at Farrow's neck.

"See this?"

"Yeah, what is it? Looks like bruises across his throat," Dex answered obediently.

"Hunh," Gorman grunted.

Gorman liked his detectives to play stupid. Dex wouldn't be pushed into speculating with the bad-tempered investigator. Gorman liked the new guys who knew everything and leaped to conclusions. Oh, he liked them a lot. He'd really enjoyed slamming Shanko, Dex's former partner, to the ground.

"Could be. Might have been choked out to get him down." Gorman swiveled his head around again. "Look at your blood spatter. Killer was a lot taller than the victim and he lifted him up and back. Looks to me like he knew what he was doing."

He shoved a criminalist studying footprints out of the way. She turned to snarl at him, but he was oblivious.

"Got a good one, sir," the stocky criminalist with a purple streak in her hair said to Stafford. She pointed to the photographer circling the print, snapping it from every angle.

"And there's this. Somebody bled all over a light-weight hoodie like the ones thc Search and Rescue guys wear. Anyway it's got a label on it says Search and Rescue. That helped." The square-shaped criminalist logged it in as evidence.

Gorman puttered around for a while but eventually placed all his goodies back in his cases, rose painfully from a pivot point of his right knee and teetered a bit. Respectfully, Dex looked away as he clambered to his feet.

Gorman passed a plain white cotton sheet and what looked like a painter's drop cloth to one of the deputies. Body bags were expensive and not reusable. "Help me bag him."

He grumbled and complained as they trundled Farrow down the hall.

CHAPTER SIX

The detectives had gravitated to the break room, turning it into an impromptu operations area. Stafford called Holly in to take her statement formally. They were alone for the moment until Harry Price arrived. In public, she and Dex were as careful of their hands and glances as nuns in a medieval convent.

"Hey, babe, how are you?" Dex said, his hand almost touching her shoulder.

"I'm so damn sorry for Peach is what I am."

"What do you know about Don Farrow?"

Holly leaned back against the unlit woodstove. Dex eased into an armchair, taking out his notebook.

"A genuinely nice guy and I knew him pretty well. He was here a lot and always treated the volunteers right. When he started cleaning out his house in Taft, he donated a lot of good stuff to the thrift store. You know about the thrift store Paws runs?"

Dex nodded. "See any tension between him and Peach?"

"None. It was really sweet. Don was old-fashioned— brought Peach flowers, chocolates, things you don't see much anymore." She sensed a glimmer of tears and her throat choked up. She recalled old training. You are a stone statue, hard and cold. A stone statue. The tears dried. "He didn't talk about himself much, come to think of it."

"I take it he had money too. What did he do for a living?"

"He invented some type of glass thingy process the military uses in planes. Apparently he made a ton of money off that, and then some refinements on the original idea. He lived over in Taft and met Peach at one of her fundraisers. That woman knows how to put on a party. Remember the fundraiser she did here this summer?"

"I might have met the guy," Dex said, paging back in his memory bank," but I don't remember him."

"No, you wouldn't. He was more a listener than a big talker. I think that's why people liked him so much. He wasn't always running his mouth about *me, me, me.* Anyway, before long he rented a cabin over here. Peach told me he thought it didn't look right for him to stay over at her house."

Harry came in and sat heavily in a recliner, making notes on his recorder, ignoring them.

"Married?"

"No. Divorced a long time ago, I guess. We were working out here one time and he asked me if I was married. Chatting like you do when you're getting to know people. I said that was one thing I hadn't tried, and then I asked him if he'd ever been married. He gives me this funny look and says, 'It takes more than a pretty face to stay married.' I got the *shut up now* signal. Peach said his life was always pretty much his shop. He'd lost interest in his inventions, so helping her run things here at the cattery made him feel good. You have no idea what she had to do to push the cattery through. She hired a law firm finally to help her. It wasn't Peach," Holly insisted. "I know how you think, so just get it out of your head Peach killed him. She loved the guy."

"You know how I think, do you?" Stafford laughed, glancing at Harry. If women only knew how men thought. "Plenty of people kill somebody they love."

Harry's phone rang and he got up to take the call, walking out of earshot.

"Must be nice to have money," Dex observed, looking around.

"I wouldn't know. If I had money I'd rip up that disgusting cat piss carpet in my living room and put down linoleum."

"Yeah, that would be nice." He hesitated, then asked. "You think I could come back to your place to get a few hours of sleep when we're done here? Save the county a buck? We're looking at hours here at least. That way I won't have to do a 65-mile trip to my place in Bakersfield and drive back in the morning."

They got to spend so little time together it came out sounding tentative.

"Of course," she said.

⚔️

Pushing grieving relatives in the moments following the worst thing that had ever happened to them was hard, but it had to be done. The kitchen was available and despite the late hour, Peach Bryson bustled around setting coffee and cookies out for Price and Stafford on the flowered tablecloth. Three fat calico cats lounged on the kitchen counter, watching them. The kitchen smelled of coffee, cats, and grief.

Peach Bryson was as soft and lovely as a ripe Georgia peach, even at this late hour. She had surrendered the clothes she wore without protest, and put on a pink blouse and filmy skirt, with magenta sandals showing manicured toenails lacquered turquoise. She

41

had the soft southern accent Paula Deen's cooking shows made famous. Her blue eyes were red-rimmed and swollen, and unlike many of her former Beverly Hills neighbors, her face was untouched by the scalpel.

This was the first opportunity to get a detailed statement from her. Price finished his routine family-of-the-victim speech of condolence. Stafford snapped on the recorder and opened his tablet to take notes. He smiled, munched a cookie, and tried to look mild and encouraging.

"Let's start with you telling us about your day yesterday, Ms. Bryson. Was Mr. Farrow with you all day?" Harry began, tapping his pen on the side of his old fashioned reporter's notebook and turning his chair toward her.

"Please call me Peach. In my mind, Mrs. Bryson is still my mother-in-law." The old woman tried a smile, the smile that brought in the big donations to the cattery. "Where do I start? Don and I spent a couple of days in Santa Clarita doing errands, visiting donors, and taking a little R & R. We got back about 3 o'clock, I think. I checked in with Brenda, the cattery manager, and Doreen, the manager at the thrift shop. I had a crew of workers out in back, and I went out to see how they were getting along." She thought a moment. "I spent the afternoon straightening out problems, and Don and I made dinner together and we went out into the cattery to do the last check of the day. Maybe 6:30 or so."

"Who else was there at that point?"

"The manager and the volunteers all left around 5:00 o'clock. I didn't notice when the outside workers left. Don and I were medicating a new litter of kittens. I left him in the treatment room where we do all that. I went in the house to get another can of kitten formula and the phone rang."

"So what time was this?"

"Oh, I don't know. Around 7 maybe. I didn't look."

Stafford rummaged through his notes. Where were they at in the process of getting the phone records?

"Oh, and I talked to my daughter a while, and then I remembered Don was out there working while I was chattering away. I no sooner put the phone down than it rang again with a potential adopter on the line. You have to spend time with people when it's an adoption. I must have been gone a good while, but I thought I heard Don talking to somebody."

"Do you know who it was? Did you recognize the voice?" Dex said, hitching his chair closer.

"The TV news was on pretty loud. I think it was a man's voice, though. You can't hear really well from in here. I was on the phone with this woman who wanted to adopt two kittens from the same litter, and it sounded like such a good home for the cats, oh, I just wasn't paying attention." She gripped the edge of the table hard. "I feel so bad. I might have been able to do something. Poor Don."

"Don't be so hard on yourself. If you'd gone out there maybe something bad would have happened to you too." This realization must have struck Peach as well as she turned away and blew her nose hard.

"So what happened then?" Harry said.

"I thought I heard raised voices, so I got this woman off the phone and hustled out there with the can of kitten formula. It was dark out back. I tried all the lights and kept calling Don. I got scared when he didn't answer me. I heard somebody running out the back door, I think." She paused. "I can't be sure. So I grabbed a flashlight. We leave them in all the rooms because we have power outages up here. That's when I noticed all the gates in the fence were open and the cats were outside all over the place. I was frantic calling for Don and stuffing cats back inside. That's when I went into the treatment room and saw him."

"Did you touch him?"

"Of course I did. I loved him. But then I saw all the blood."

Harry and Dex looked at each other. Damn. She had to go lovin' on him and mess up the evidence. People did it every time. Still, it would explain the blood all over her. But had she done it deliberately? Had she been the one to kill him?

Peach saw their look and it dawned on her through the fog of grief they were regarding her suspiciously. She collected herself and sat straighter in her chair.

"I know what you're thinking, but I loved Don and I would never hurt him."

"And then?" Stafford prompted.

She stopped and thought. "When I found him–I went crazy, I think. I must have. I ran around in circles in and out of the house after I saw him, trying to think of what to do, and then I thought of Holly." Her voice faded away to nothing. "I depend on her so much. I called her and then you got here." She put her face in her hands.

"What was Don's mood in the last few weeks?" Harry said, changing the subject.

"We were both happy. The only bad thing was... well, the cats. And my children. There are problems."

Price lifted his eyebrows.

"Well, what I mean is...Don wanted me to close the cattery. He wanted me all to himself, and he wanted to travel."

"He have any kids?"

"No. He had one marriage but it was unhappy and didn't last long. He didn't like to talk about it."

"We need to get a list of Don's family and friends from you, ask some questions about his life and so forth. Can you help me with that?" Price asked.

"I have to, don't I? I keep all that stuff on my computer in the office upstairs. Let's get it over with."

"You go ahead," Stafford said, taking a pull from his coffee cup, and trying to get a read on this. Unlike most of his cases where he walked into a stranger's life at the moment of terrible crisis, he knew something about Peach Bryson and this setup. He knew from Holly that Peach sailed into town, made friends among the animal rescuers, and began giving out free litter and kibble for cats and dogs. Almost everybody on the mountain had a dog and a cat or two. Families strapped for cash gave up their animals to the shelter in Bakersfield, where the solution to the overpopulation was euthanasia. Paws made it possible to keep pets by giving out free food and supplies, and picking up the cost of spay/neuter procedures. Sierra Mountain Village looked prosperous on the surface, but there were people living here who were hanging on to solvency by their fingernails. Pensions, and county checks got spent at the town's one grocery store, which stocked as much liquor and wine as everyday convenience store items.

Peach Bryson made a difference.

CHAPTER SEVEN

Holly tried to persuade Peach to rest before she left to drive home, but she knew Peach wouldn't sleep. This was only the beginning. She hurried home to her cabin on the other side of Sierra Mountain Village. Before Dex got there, she vacuumed hard and stuffed the cats in the spare bedroom. With her part-time business of dog grooming, it was impossible to keep the place clean enough for somebody who had allergies. The fur got right up Dex's nose and made him sneeze.

He slid into bed with her late, late in the night as the setting moon lightened the rectangle of window that looked out across the valley to the mountains. She had the fleeting thought this might be what it was like if they lived together, Dex coming home late at night smelling of death. She fell back to sleep thinking it was way too soon to allow herself living together thoughts.

Would she really like him being here all the time?

He was gone when she woke up a few hours later, her animals clamoring for breakfast. First things first. Open cans and pour out kibble with meowing cats twining around her. Keep the pigs away from the slow eaters. Separate the ones with special diets and feed them in the bathroom. Medications. Clean the litter boxes. She fretted about her own pressing investigation into the destruction of the shrine as she went about the routine. It would have to wait. Peach was on her mind, even in the dreams she half-remembered.

Stafford and Price met with the deputies to resume the search outside Paws in the daylight. At 8:00 a.m. they knocked on Bryson's kitchen door. Peach had made breakfast for them, which irritated Stafford. They weren't visitors, or guests.

"Oh, please," she said. "Making breakfast took my mind off Don. We can talk while you're eating." Again, tears filled her eyes.

How could you say no to this nice old lady? So he sat down with Price and ate bacon and pancakes, with cats padding around his feet. Peach went around the table filling cups, not that anybody needed more coffee. The kitchen was quiet with just the occasional chatter from their radios and a TV morning show playing softly in the next room. Dex shoved away his empty plate and took out his notebook.

"Let's go over the list of names you gave us. People important in Mr. Farrow's life," he said, putting serious business into his tone. "He'd been married before?"

"Yes, but he never talked about her. They were only married a few years as I understand it."

"When were they divorced?"

The kitchen door opened and a big burly man stormed in, bent, and hugged Peach. "Sorry to hear about this, Mom," he said, giving them a scowl over the top of her head. She reached up to hug him.

"Oh, this is my son Skip. These are detectives, um, this is Mr. Stafford, and...um..." she said vaguely. "They want to talk to me. About Don, you know. Your sister must have called you. I tried and tried and you didn't pick up."

"Sorry, the charge on my phone ran down. I only saw the messages this morning."

Both detectives got up and shook hands, introducing themselves to Skip Bryson. The son wore a camo vest over a T-shirt that said Search & Rescue, shorts with lots of pockets, and sunglasses shoved up into thick sandy hair.

"I'd like a word alone with my mother," the son said. He didn't ask permission. He led her into the adjacent living room and closed the door. They could hear the low growl of his voice and her protests. A few moments later, they returned. Peach Bryson looked even more shaken. The old woman perched on the edge of a chair and patted the chair next to her to indicate where she'd like her son to sit.

Stafford noted his Search and Rescue T-shirt. So did Price.

"He can stay, can't he? I'd like him to stay. He should know what's going on."

Instead, Skip Bryson took a seat at the opposite end of the table from her, glowering at them.

"Oh, I forgot something." Peach went to the counter and began opening and closing drawers and cabinets, mumbling to herself. Then she went into the living room. She had a short attention span. Stress? Age? Just the way she was? Or was it a pretense to avoid hard scrutiny?

Stafford was getting used to cats underfoot, displaying themselves everywhere. One jumped off the counter onto the empty chair next to him. He quickly put a finger under his nose and pressed up hard to stop himself from sneezing.

"Oh, kick them away if they bother you," Skip Bryson said out of his mother's hearing. None of the cats went near him, Dex noticed.

Bryson pointed toward the recording device on the table, then tilted his chair back and gave both of them a long considering look from narrowed eyes.

"Why do you want to record what my mother says? Is she under suspicion?"

"We record everything now, Mr. Bryson," Dex said. "People forget. Hey, we forget too. And everybody gets interviewed who's involved in a case like this."

Skip Bryson stood up to wash his hands at the sink, ready to go belligerent.

"A case like this, huh? As long as you remember we're American citizens and we have rights."

He ground that in with a tight smile, amping up the testosterone quotient in the air. So Skip Bryson was the steely-jawed hero in a stand against police brutality in defense of truth, justice, and the American way.

"I'm not likely to forget, Mr. Bryson, especially with you reminding me," Harry Price said. Price was now Bad Cop. Dex would be the Nice Guy. Human nature made it work every single time.

Peach returned to the table with a Ziploc bag filled with chocolate chip cookies she scattered onto a plate on the table. "Please help yourselves. Maybe I should take some to the gentlemen outside?"

"They're fine," Price said. "Don't worry about them."

"This is a terrible thing, Don dying like that. Gunshot?" Skip Bryson looked at Stafford and Price's frozen faces, set to give nothing away. "How did he die?"

"We're not ready to say yet," Price said, looking down at his notes.

"Did he put up a fight?" Bryson leaned back against the counter in his chair, big Doc Martens unlaced, showing powerful bare legs with a pelt of brown fur. "Look at my mother. You can't think she killed him?"

"We don't think anything yet, sir," Price said.

"Like, did they find anything under his fingernails? Did you check for that?"

"He had gloves on. Besides, that's up to the coroner's office and the pathologist, not my scope of operation," Harry Price said.

If the guy didn't shut up, they'd have to get rid of him.

"We're pretty Big City down there in Bakersfield, you know," Price said. "We watch the crime shows too."

This brought a big burst of laughter from Bryson, and he crashed his chair back down on the floor and slapped the table. "Yeah, I thought about being a cop like you guys. Then I heard you didn't do much chasing bad guys down alleys and I like action."

"Hey, Price, you remember the last bad guy you chased down an alley?"

"Not since I worked patrol," Harry said with a smile. "I've been giving the old adrenaline a rest lately."

"You guys look like you work out," Bryson said. "They got a gym there at the station?"

Immediately Stafford marked Bryson down as a people-pleasing liar. Nobody in their right mind would say Harry Price looked as though he worked out. Nearing retirement age, Harry had spread out so that a gap appeared in the midsection of his shirt where a button was stretched beyond its capability. Too much cruise ship food and soft living lately. Stafford was surprised his wife Rosalie let him out of the house with that shirt on. Maybe she didn't care anymore.

"Yeah, yeah, we've got all that stuff. Problem is nobody laces up your shoes, shoves you inside, and locks the door," Dex said with a smile toward Harry.

"Oh, man, I couldn't live without exercise. You guys know what I do, huh?" He didn't sound devastated to learn Don Farrow was dead, or in any hurry to offer comfort to his mother. He ignored her in favor of worming his own way into the spotlight.

"We're kinda busy here," Price said, letting his impatience show.

"I'm head of the PE Department and football coach at the high school. You've heard of us. Winning team. Didn't you know that?"

"No shit," Stafford said, for something to say. The vibe in the room could be simply that Bryson enjoyed the attention. Big stuff, being involved in a murder investigation.

"Yeah, no shit. We've beat every high school team in Bakersfield. Wait here. Mom keeps all this stuff." Bryson launched himself up and disappeared into the living room.

Dex and Harry looked at each other. Time was passing. Peach saw the look and said quickly, "Oh, it will just take a minute. I'm sorry. He …."

Bryson reappeared with a scrapbook, his brag collection. "Yeah, the whole town comes to our games." His mother looked on, her face wary.

"Everybody loves a winning team," Harry commented, taking the scrapbook from him. They schmoozed around a bit, part of the process of getting the guy sized up. Price could bullshit all day long, Man of a Thousand Faces, and get the job done at the same time. Bryson finally gathered his stuff together, disappointed his *I Love Me* session had ended.

Harry Price turned in his chair toward Peach, getting serious. "Let's get back to yesterday, Ms. Bryson."

The old woman swallowed hard. By nature Peach Bryson was a nurturer and a fusser, wanting to serve coffee, make tea, bring juice. It got on Dex's nerves because it reminded him of his mother, who still lived with him. The date she was moving out had come and gone many times.

"Tell them about that guy, mom," Skip Bryson said with a hurry up wave of his hand.

Peach looked perplexed. "What guy?"

"That guy with the tattoos you hired. The parolee?"

"Oh, Felix, you mean. Well, tattoos don't mean anything. Look at you."

Stafford had already noted the ink on Bryson's beefy arms. "What guy?"

"I've got all his paperwork somewhere. He did the heavy cleaning that the girls, the volunteers—I call them all "girls" though most of them are middle-aged ladies. Silly, I know." She slid a fork back and forth on a desert plate, mashing crumbs of coffee cake. "Some things are just man's work and when Felix came around I had him clean up the store room. We'd had a big delivery of kibble and litter, and he did a good job. He came once. No twice, he came," she said, touching a finger to her forehead as an aid to memory.

Price stood up and stretched his back. "How did you know he was a parolee?"

"Because he told me."

"And that was okay with you?" Stafford said, thinking of the mean-ass motherfucker parolees he knew who would rampage through this old woman's life and destroy everything she had just for kicks.

She sat up smartly, showing the steel inside the velvet gloves. "I'm a good judge of character, Detective Stafford. I wasn't always a cat lady."

"I told her. I told her something like this would happen. If I'd been here," Skip Bryson said, putting himself in the picture again, "I could have saved Don."

"Where were you?" Price said, turning to Skip Bryson. "Just for the record."

"Last night?" Bryson chortled, as though they were kidding. "I did a Mud Run till noon then I dropped in here around 2 o'clock to see if Mom was back yet. Then I had business to take care of at the high school. You know Mud Runs?"

Stafford nodded. He was too familiar with the obstacle course challenges, which held no appeal for him. His sometime partner Shanko was the one who needed to prove himself doing Mud Runs. Shanko was working the case from back at the station in Bakersfield, coordinating reports and backgrounders, pulling financial and phone records on the victim, putting together the book.

"Talk to anybody while you were here?"

"Yeah, Brenda." He jerked a thumb outside. "She runs things outside. Like I say, around two."

"How long were you here?"

"Oh, ten minutes. Then I went to my office at the school. Yeah, I stopped in at the thrift shop to see how things were going. I got home around six o'clock, maybe. I was in all night. My wife will vouch for me."

"Oh, yeah?" Price said. Harry had a talent for showing interest, even if he was bored rigid, filled to the brim with contempt, or ready to go for somebody's throat.

"You can check," Bryson insisted, standing up and sitting down again backward, leaning his forearms on the back of the chair. "You should be looking at the people who work here and all those volunteers. Not me or my mother."

"We'll be doing that," Price said.

Stafford sat back watching. Him first or his mother? The workers could wait.

CHAPTER EIGHT

Stafford and Price detailed Peach Bryson's and Farrow's movements the previous day. Her story was consistent with what she'd already told them. They got contact details on the workers, and anybody who had reason to be around her operation. Outside they compared notes leaning against the county vehicle parked in the lot. Bryson came thundering down the stairs and swaggered toward them.

"My mother is a wonderful woman but she's naïve." Bryson had a high reedy voice for a big guy. "I wish you'd talk to her about these people she hires."

"Oh, yeah?" Stafford said noncommittally. Peach Bryson didn't look naïve to Stafford, but in the early stages of an investigation, you tried to listen to everything with an open mind. He regarded Bryson squinting into the sunshine, rocking back and forth on his Doc Martens.

"Especially these wetbacks." He shook his head. "She's got all these people traipsing through her life, even the women who work for her and all the volunteers. All of them got a hard- luck story and she's a sucker. You know. Tell her she's putting herself in danger."

"Right now we're looking at Don Farrow, Mr. Bryson." *Then you.*

Bryson watched him, fingering the stubble on his heavy jaw. "Go easy on her is all I'm sayin'."

Stafford shrugged. "Were you wearing those boots here yesterday?"

Bryson nodded.

"We need to take a look at them for purposes of elimination. We'll be looking at anybody who had any reason to be back there."

"Oh, yeah. Really?" Bryson looked down at his feet in scuffed Doc Martens.

"Routine. Just routine." To find out if there's any blood embedded in the sole. That's why. "You mind taking them off for me?"

"You want me to go home barefoot?" The swagger and the sneer again.

"I'll get a deputy to drive you home so you can get some new footwear, if you like," Stafford said.

Bryson snorted, looking as though he might make a big deal of it. Then he sat down on the steps and took off his boots and handed them over. "Nah, I don't need a ride."

Stafford took the boots over to his vehicle, put them in a plastic evidence bag and shut the door. "If you think of anything else that might help, would you let us know?" He flipped a card to Bryson who looked at it and then tucked it away in one of the many pockets of his camo survival jacket.

"Robbery maybe. Don sometimes carried a lot of cash on him," Bryson said with a lift of his eyebrow. "You know we had a burglary here a few months ago. Stupid vandalism. Most likely those lowlifes across the street."

Stafford kept nodding, but made a note to look for Farrow's wallet. "We'll be looking into that too."

"My mother's not healthy, you know. She's got this lung disease, COPD, and a heart condition. I'm worried about what this will do to her."

Price took a phone call from the coroner's office and began issuing orders. Stafford ignored Bryson, dictating notes into his recorder while he still remembered details. Bryson finally stopped talking and stomped back into his mother's kitchen in his sock feet.

The deputies brought the news Don Farrow's wallet had been found near the back steps. Sixty dollars in twenties. The credit cards were still there. His cellphone hadn't turned up yet. Maybe they'd get lucky and find fingerprints on the wallet.

Yeah, right, Stafford thought. Right.

Like this one is going to be easy.

━━╪┼╪━━

Holly scanned the sky as she left her cabin. Drought got everybody's hopes up. Rain was predicted, but once again it was the disappointment of sunshine and blue sky. Her shift didn't start until early evening and she'd planned on checking the shrine, see if there'd been any new developments; but the events of last night, which didn't seem real in the harsh light of day, were more important. Why would anyone want to kill Don Farrow? And Peach…oh, Peach.

Knowing that Dex and the crime scene techs would still have the scene cordoned off Holly decided to stick to her plan and hit the shrine first. She climbed into her truck and hoped that by the time she got to Paws, Dex would have wrapped up and she could actually accomplish something.

Tucked back into a stand of scrub oaks near the road, Holly got out of her truck, prepared to hike up to the shrine. A dog walker wearing sweats and a big sun hat approached her, a grim look on her face. Holly recognized her as one of the occasional volunteers at Paws.

"What's up, Carol?" Holly said, hoping this wasn't going to take long.

"You know us church people had nothing to do with that thing up there in the meadow, that shrine thing everybody's talking about," she said. "Buddy, get back here. Now sit." She pushed down the scruffy dog's hindquarters.

"I'm not listening to rumors, Carol."

"You can try not listening," she said triumphantly, "but people are still talking. Not just about Peach's boyfriend getting killed, but that shrine place up there. I'm telling you. And I'll tell you something else," she huffed. "We never put up those flyers. That's crazy. Who do you think it is?" she said leaning forward, prepared for a confidence. The boss beat it into them: *keep your pie hole shut about what goes on.* Carol's eyes sparkled with anticipation of a juicy piece of gossip to transmit to the little groups who gathered at the transfer site or the post office.

"Now you want me to spread rumors? C'mon."

"Those women were up here running around in robes and worshipping goddesses. Everyone knows they have orgies. I don't know how Betty Anne Armbruster can show her face in town."

"Who were they having orgies with? Men like your husband?" *That dried-up old stick?*

"Don't be disgusting, Holly. And that bonfire in May. We heard about that."

Holly squeezed her eyes closed in an effort to keep her mouth shut. "You mean the Beltane celebration?"

"Whatever, that heathen thing," she said hotly. "I was raised in the church. The Pope says all this women's religion stuff is an abomination and he's right."

Holly started the truck and revved the engine. The new Pope or the old one? She liked the new Pope.

Carol put a hand on the door to stop her leaving. "I think those Sierra Club people destroyed the shrine. That's what I think."

"Pffft. You have any proof?"

"I just know." She looked at Holly as though that proved it. "Everybody knows you're doing an investigation."

Holly laughed out loud. "Investigation? Oh, please. I've got no standing, no jurisdiction, no nothing. Please, Carol, people have got to let this go before it gets any crazier. Look, I have a really busy day, and I want to go up to the shrine and then over to Paws to help Peach out. I gotta go."

Holly headed for the trailhead, leaving the good church lady behind, disappointment reddening her face.

◄═╬═►

With Peach still on her mind, Holly hiked toward the shrine. Two days ago Betty Anne Armbruster dragged her up here, yelling at her to do something. The grave of Holly's poor old cat, Princess Nasty Bitch, had been dug up, along with other desecrations of a site people considered sacred. Holly had marched down the hillside to pick up her cat's grave marker, but the pink satin she'd wrapped the body in was strewn across the rocky hillside covered with rabbit brush, chamisa, and sage. The coyotes had carried her bones away.

People called the Seven Sisters a shrine. Mt. Pinos, a nearby peak, was sacred to the Chumash Indians who lived here peacefully for hundreds of years and believed the mountain peaks around Mt. Pinos were the center of the world. That was how the shrine got started near the top of a long meadow, a slow climb up a dusty path. New Age believers hung dream catchers, ribbons, and spiritual ornaments on the branches of the pines in the grove. The shrine sisters started gatherings up there: drum circles, meditation retreats, solstice rituals, memorial services, ceremonies, and animal burials. A summer festival in town called itself The Center of the World. Holly was on the edge of the group as one of the animal people.

A few days ago vandals pulled everything down off the trees, scattering the stones in the fire circle and digging up the graves of beloved pets. The shrine's destruction seriously pissed Holly off—and a lot of others as well. The shrine sisters complained to the town council, but it was on Forest Service land way beyond town limits. Nothing the council could do. The sisters and their friends kept up a barrage of complaints and fired off letters to the local weekly. Debate raged among the community Facebook groups.

Working patrol, Holly had a pretty good idea of who the lowlife elements on the mountain were: the speeders, the drunks, the druggies, the wife beaters, and petty criminals. But the vandals had to be somebody with a grudge against the New Agers, the tree huggers, and the nature worshippers. She'd been sticking her nose in people's faces asking questions, but still hadn't any idea which sonofabitch to dime out to the sheriff's guys. The Town Council commiserated with the believers, sure. What could they do?

It wasn't really a crime, as crime gets defined. The bureaucrats at the Forest Service Ranger station said they couldn't do anything because the shrine was illegal. Taking the complaint to the Board of Supervisors in Bakersfield was laughable. Like they cared what people in a remote corner of the county thought? The Sarge who ran the substation down the hill threw his hands up in the air when Holly told him about the destruction of the shrine. His deputies were all over illegal grows and busting up meth labs, doing whatever they could about identity theft and petty street crime.

The boss told Holly to figure out who did it and get the sheriff's guys to go after them. *Get these women shut up and things back to normal.* She had investigative experience and was the only one on patrol who cared deeply about the shrine. It had become a personal vendetta and then Don Farrow was murdered. Were the two things connected? She couldn't see how. Why was it up to her to figure out? That was one of those perplexing questions that had got her in trouble before. But she would try.

Holly whipped out her cell phone camera and pivoted in the middle of the path to document the orange-needled pines, mostly pinions and Jeffreys bordering the path. When the needles turned orange. the trees were in their death throes, killed by the bark beetles. She would post it on her Facebook page to show the water hogs the drought was real. Breathing faster when she reached the upper meadow on the shoulder of the mountain, she approached the shrine sisters sitting around the fire circle sharing pastries. She glanced up to take in the sight of the 8,800 foot mountains across the valley where Sierra Mountain Village lay, horizon after horizon, all the way to Mount Pinos, ridged purple and blue in the distance. Below on the meadow she saw three coyotes running, tails up, playing in the warm sunshine.

She glanced into the semi-circle of pinion pines forming the Seven Sisters shrine. People were drifting back now, hanging mementos on the lower branches of the trees. Dream catchers and crystals shimmered in a shaft of sunlight, along with feathers, and strips of tinsel, pagan symbols embroidered on strips of bright fabrics, and a few Mass cards. The circle of stones had been rebuilt inside the shadowy center of the pines. Something that looked like a witch box lay on a square of purple satin. Before long the shrine would be weird and wonderful again.

Betty Anne Armbruster waved to Holly, her upper arm wobbling under her red T-shirt. Unpacking a picnic basket, she wore denim coveralls and combat boots. "Come have some muffins."

Bonnie Johns of course wasn't eating. Skeletally-thin, Bonnie aspired to live on air and dreams of world peace. Roger, the only man who sat vigil with the women preoccupied himself with a complicated knitting pattern that looked like a sleeve of an Icelandic sweater. Suzanne was showing off, her legs scissored in the full lotus meditation pose. Betty Anne's daughter Chloe polished her drums with a cloth and looked up with a smile as Holly approached. Ah, Chloe, one of the Paws volunteers, and so sweetly simple.

"Anything new?" Holly said, hunkering down to grab a carrot muffin.

Betty Anne smacked a page-sized flyer in her hand, smirking with glee. It read: *Devil Worshippers. We know who you are.*

"Wow." Holly read it, shocked; here was the flyer Carol mentioned.

"Now do you see what we're up against?" Betty Anne hollered. She had a funny way of talking. Every sentence started in a normal tone of voice and then towards the end her voice would blare out at a high volume, often cracking on the last word.

"Who did this?"

"I don't know. Somebody nailed them to the trees on the path on the way up."

"Poor trees," Chloe murmured. Chloe was a little simple. Holly knew she shouldn't say *simple*, but there were worse words. Chloe had been hired at the grocery store in town but the cash register operation was beyond her. She was sweet: but all the time? Holly figured she might be sweet with a flamethrower at her back to keep her in line.

"What does this even mean?" she said, looking around, reading it over and over.

"Well, isn't it obvious?" Betty Anne said. "The Christian Taliban told people they think all of us up here are witches. The shrine is supposed to be where the coven meets. At least somebody had the nerve to say it to my face at the post office. Instead of this!" She waved the flyer in Holly's face.

Holly rolled her eyes. "What Christian Taliban? You just can't go making accusations like that, Betty Anne."

"Oh, piffle." Betty Anne blew out a snort of air from pinched nostrils to show her disdain.

"You're still staying up here all night on watch?"

Betty Anne had a wild, high-pitched cackle as well as the peculiar volume control setting. "Some of us maybe," she said looking cagey. Betty Ann liked being known as the Keeper of Great Secrets. "Look, Suzanne's husband's ashes were in a silver box and now it's gone. Along with the bones of the kid's hamsters. I'm staying to protect what's left. Maybe those assholes will come back."

"But nobody's up here alone, are they?" Holly looked around. She wasn't afraid of the dark or animals—well, bears and mountain lions, yes. People sure as hell spooked her though. "That's not a good idea."

Betty Anne pulled up her T-shirt and Holly saw the butt of a pistol.

"And a gun is really a terrible idea, Betty Anne. Do you even know how to use it?"

"You want to find out?" She pulled the pistol out and Holly recognized a Glock 23, the weapon she was issued when she'd been on the police force in Park City, Utah. The other women looked away, pained. They were the non-violents, yoked to Betty Anne only because of the shrine.

"See that rock down there, the one some slimeball put yellow paint on?"

The shot rang out and a hunk of rock flew.

"Geez, Betty Anne," Holly said, alarmed. "You're going to have the Forest Service crawling all over you."

"Those Do Nothings," Betty Anne hollered, her face red with outrage.

"Some things rise above man's laws," Suzanne murmured from her full lotus position.

Holly gave Betty Anne a sharp look, getting to her feet. "I really don't like this." She would never convince them, she realized looking around at the hard faces pinched in expressions of outraged self-righteousness.

"I wish you'd rethink this, Betty Ann," she said, spanking her pants for ticks. Dealing with Betty Anne on other issues was wasting her breath. She would be more useful at the cattery giving Peach whatever comfort she could.

"Yeah, yeah, we know what you think. Don't you care they dug up Bear's grave?"

The memory of her old dog Bear hit Holly with a pang. She'd pushed all 55 pounds of him up here in a wheelbarrow to bury him the night he died, sobbing every step of the way.

"I care. You know I do, but I don't like the way this is going. Somebody's gonna get hurt."

The wind blew high and wild here at night. The moon was nearly full. She could picture it skidding across the sky, lighting the valley, the coyotes howling. Enough light to shoot somebody.

Stafford's phone rang and he snatched it off his belt, dropping his pen and clipboard on the walkway joining Bryson's house and the cattery. They had to figure out who had the authority to decide things. Farrow's backgrounder said no kids. Peach Bryson didn't have a power of attorney or know anything about his will. A name appeared on the screen, one of Madison's deputies from the substation in Frazier Oaks. He called the deputy back.

"We're at the victim's rental cabin on the other side of town, sir." Deputy Jackson's rumble of a voice came over the phone line.

"Yeah, Jackson. What?"

"Somebody beat us to it and tossed the place. I mean, that's what it looks like at least."

"Aw, shit. I'll be over as soon as we release the scene here." Stafford finished checking over the evidence log, making sure everything got nailed down correctly for court, and then headed over to Farrow's rental cabin.

The cabin lay up a hill, past the wood-sided building housing the post office and the upstairs gym. As usual, there were groups of retirees chitchatting outside, blocking the road. Everybody turned to look at him as he passed in the county vehicle, and then the conversations started up again. Doubtless they were discussing the murder.

Deputy Jackson waited for him on the small deck of Don Farrow's cabin looking out over a dry creek ravine filled with chaparral and scrub oak.

"You can go now, Jackson. Thanks."

"Yeah, I got calls stacked up."

Stafford shoved the cabin door open with effort. Everything in the kitchen had been dumped higgeldy-piggeldy on the floor. He picked his way carefully through the contents of upended kitchen drawers and cabinets. Cutlery and kitchen implements lay all over the place, the cupboards empty, pots and pans on the floor.

"Oh, shit." He stood in the kitchen looking around. The windows looking out into the forest were clean, windowsills dusted. Despite the havoc the place smelled clean and earthy from a basil plant upended in the sink. He turned as he heard a vehicle crunch into the drive-way, recognizing the bull engine of a county Crown Vic. He leaned against the counter at the sink until Harry breezed in dressed in one of his fancy Italian suits and silk ties, checking his cell phone.

"Hunh," Harry said, stopping abruptly to look around.

"Yup." Dex grinned at Harry, whose face had fallen seeing this mess. "Doesn't look as though he lived like this, though. He was an engineer, right? Those guys are neat all the way into compulsive lunatic territory.

Think somebody went through this place looking for something?"

Stafford reached in his pockets and pulled out a set of blue latex gloves.

"Search me," Harry scowled.

"Yeah, right." Dex paused at the door to the living room. "Same thing here." He saw a filing cabinet through the door of the living room off in a den kind of room. The drawers were open, manila files strewn all over the floor. A desktop computer and a cell phone charger sat on the desk. No cell phone. No laptop, which Peach Bryson said went with Farrow everywhere.

Harry righted a nice-looking mission chair, perched on one of the wide arms and took another phone call. Stafford picked his way through the other rooms of the cabin, muttering and shaking his head.

"Guess what?" Price's grin split his brown face as he swiped the phone closed.

Stafford noticed he'd had work done on his teeth lately.

"Your lily-white Peach Bryson. She killed her first husband."

"No shit," Dex said, wheeling around, a file folder in his hand. He huffed out a breath of astonishment. "She charged? Convicted? She do time?"

"Nope. This is Beverly Hills. Bet there's a story there."

"Funny she never mentioned it, huh? When was this?"

Harry read off a date and then calculated backward. "I found it when I ran her through the system. She was young, 34, long time ago. The husband was a downtown corporate attorney. Came from a well-off family, left her everything. She shot him and said it was an accident."

"Accident?" Stafford screwed up his face. "Accident? Aw, shit."

"They couldn't prove there was any setup between Bryson and the housekeeper who was the only witness, so they couldn't file charges."

"But they must have thought there was something hinky," Stafford said, setting a pile of manila folders on the desk to paw through. He sat down in Farrow's desk chair.

"Nothing they could prove. So there it is."

"So," Stafford said, leaning back against the chair, swiveling it around and steepling his fingers. "That's where her money came from."

"Not all. Peach went into real estate and made money herself. She owns the cat place outright and a piece of land adjacent. Healthy brokerage account balance. Credit score 740."

"What's this give us?"

"So we'd be looking hard at Don Farrow's will, wouldn't we? See who he left his money to. Does she inherit? Maybe Farrow was another *mistake*."

"Nah, I can't see it. This kill's different."

"I've been thinking about that. Most knifings are frenzied attacks. This one's way different. Efficient."

"Skilled…somebody with training…"

"…Yeah, like the guy knew what he was doing. Gets behind Farrow with a sleeper hold, cuts off his air, chokes him out till he loses consciousness. He's going down and then the guy gets him with the knife…" Stafford said, getting into it.

"Right-handed cuts…" Price said.

"Knows how to come up from below, gets the knife in good and twists it up and around so he's sure he hits the heart…"

"Efficient..."

"Which means," Price interrupted again,"…Farrow knew the guy. Would you let somebody with a knife get around behind you? Or even somebody you sensed was a little off…a stranger?"

"Nobody would. That's not even a cop thing. Maybe she hired somebody," Stafford said. "One of the Mexicans on the work crew. They like knives." All the air went out of him thinking the world was even closer to hitting bottom when nice ladies like Peach Bryson went around hiring hit men.

Price slapped his thighs and launched himself off the arm of the chair. "We need to see what's in the will for her now Farrow's dead. Maybe she *was* after his money. She's our best suspect so far—if the son's alibi pans out."

"She's a hero to all these animal people around here. I'd hate for it to be Peach. As for the son, he's definitely guilty of being an asshole."

Harry looked at him closely. "Nah, I like him. You're not going to get all sentimental on me, are you? I can talk to the Sarge, get you assigned to another case."

Stafford reared back. "Hell, no. If she did it, I want her ears pinned to the wall. She did it once before."

Then he thought how the news would affect Holly.

CHAPTER NINE

A group of volunteers captured and returned yowling cats to a row of carriers stacked three cats high in the parking lot of Paws. Cats of every size and description. Cat fur complicated everything. The forensics teams were still bitching about it. Stafford got out of his vehicle and stood a moment checking his email to see what else had come in. A cluster of women steamed over towards him, looking grim and impatient. People thought it took an hour to process a scene—like on CSI.

"When will you be finished here? We have to get the cats back inside." A tall woman with red hair and the broad-shouldered build of a swimmer took the lead.

"Sorry, ma'am, I can't tell you," he answered, putting away his phone. "And who are you? I'm Detective Stafford."

"Brenda Viglen. I'm the cattery manager." She stuck out a hand to shake. "Peach called me to get the cats back and settled down."

"We're not done yet. Maybe a few more hours." He smiled at her, but she was too focused on her task to smile back.

"Couldn't we put some of the cats inside in the kennels? Please. They get anxious in carriers. They can injure themselves."

Stafford shook his head and looked around. "Can't do that. We need you to stay clear until we're done."

"See, today is our regular adoption day," Viglen insisted. "The whole point here is to find them homes."

"I know that." Stafford bent down and peered into a carrier that held a black and white tuxedo cat recoiled as far back in the carrier as it could squash itself. "I wish I could give you access but I can't. Not yet." He stood up and then sneezed four times in a row.

Brenda Viglen massaged her temples, muttering to the other volunteers who drifted away with her. A hot buzz of anger and impatience fizzled in the air as he ran up the steps and turned toward the crime scene. The Kern County Sheriff's Department wasn't popular this morning, but that was nothing new. A car filled with looky-loos wanting to rubberneck and be part of the excitement tried to edge past the deputy into the parking lot, pointing to the *Adoptions Today* sign. The reporter from the local weekly paper darted from group to group with her mic interviewing volunteers. Bakersfield media was there as well. Artillery fire couldn't keep the media away from a good murder.

Stafford didn't need telling they should look hard at the person who reported the discovery of the body. He pictured Peach Bryson. She barely made five feet, soft in the middle and the keister, with no muscle tone in her arms. He'd taken a good look at those arms in the black and white, short-sleeved blouse she wore last night. No defensive wounds or broken fingernails. That didn't mean it hadn't happened. Farrow would have fought back, but he was in his seventies and didn't look muscle-bound himself.

Peach Bryson was definitely a person of interest, even if Holly said she was a saint walking the earth.

⪥ ⪤

CHAPTER TEN

Holly pulled into the lot at Paws and got out of her old red 4 x 4 truck, looking around. The deputy with the sign in log had gone, but the county cars and the forensics van were still there. She could hear Skip Bryson shouting as she went up the stairs to the deck and the kitchen door of Peach's house. She raised her hand to knock, and stepped back as Skip came barreling out and gave her the death stare. He shoved past her, his face red, testosterone coming off him in waves. She watched him thump down the stairs wearing only socks on his feet, yank open the door of his fat-ass SUV and get in, spinning gravel as he gunned the vehicle out onto the road. She hesitated before she knocked again on the door. She'd seen him go from zero to ballistic before. What now?

"Holly! Holly!"

She turned to see Brenda Viglen, waving from the redwood picnic table under the oaks.

"C'mere. C'mere. I want to talk to you," Brenda hissed.

"What's up?"

"Here. Sit down. You mean besides Don getting killed? Besides Skip going crazy? Besides that? Geez, you're a cool one."

"What set Skip off this time?"

"Who knows? I heard him screaming at Peach, her crying."

"What a sonofabitch to pick on her now."

Holly looked up to see cats watching them from the branches of the pines inside the fence. Three of them were curled together at the base of another tree. The cats were free to roam the fenced 10-acre enclosure, living a cat life as close to ideal as possible. Long red hair trailed down the back of Brenda's flannel shirt, sweat-soaked under the arms. She stomped ahead of Holly down the path that led to a shed beyond the outer fence that served as an all-purpose junk storage room with a microwave, a fridge and thrift shop easy chairs for the workers and volunteers to rest. In the corner of the old shed sat a small woodstove they'd scrounged from a construction site. It scented the air with the smell of old fires.

Up here in the mountains it got cold in winter. The cattery buildings had central heating for the cats during the hard weather; the woodstove made the shed tolerable for the workers in the winter.

Brenda collapsed down in one of the chairs. She supervised two other employees who did the hard work of feeding the cats, rudimentary vet care, emptying the many litter boxes and sterilizing all the equipment. Holly scanned the volunteer log. Volunteers helped, but couldn't be counted on, even though they loved Peach, and who didn't love kittens? The work was hard and dirty. She held down the spigot as cold water from the Sparkletts bottle gurgled into her glass. Hot outside today and getting hotter.

"So whaddya think?" Brenda asked. "You believe this? Don was such a sweet old guy. Peach told me you were here last night. So tell. What's your boyfriend say? Lucky you, what a hunk!" Brenda jumped up from the chair and went to the window to look out. "What does he say?"

"I don't know much more than you do, Bren. He's pretty close-mouthed with this stuff. He's not going to tell me much. What do you figure happened?" she said, sitting down.

Brenda laughed. "I was in the grocery store this morning and heard one of the O'Malleys and that trashy clerk saying the cats chewed on Don's body."

"That's crazy! I mean, he only died a few minutes before Peach found him," Holly spluttered.

"Oh, people. You know people," Brenda hooted. She fell silent as footsteps sounded on the path to the shed.

Mike Jarvis, the cremation guy, approached them. Jarvis wore his sunglasses on a strap twisted around to rest on the back of his neck, a Green Bay Packers T-shirt, and black jeans. Holly took a sip from her coffee, wondering what it was like driving around all day with dead animals in the back of your truck.

Brenda perked up seeing Mike Jarvis. She jumped to her feet, sucking in her gut and tucking her hair behind her ears, beaming like a 17-year-old girl. "Hi, Mike."

"They told me I've got a pickup." Mike carried a plastic cooler like you take to the beach.

"Yeah, I put him in that box there just inside the gate," Brenda said. "I loved that old guy. He just didn't make it with all the excitement around here." She pointed through the chain link fence. "See? That's him?"

The deputy working the log stepped forward to stop him as Mike moved toward the gate. "Where do you think you're going?"

Jarvis bristled. "Like she said. I take away dead animals for disposal."

"Nothing comes out of a crime scene. Nothing goes in," the deputy said.

Jarvis' head reared back. His chest went out. "Hey man, it's a dead cat."

"Come back later," the deputy said, turning his back on Jarvis.

"I'm just doin' my job."

"So am I," the deputy said over his shoulder. "How do I know what you got in there?"

"You could look," Brenda said to him. "It's just one of our cats."

The deputy sniffed. "Nothing goes in or out of the crime scene."

Brenda rolled her eyes and Jarvis spit in the dirt. He put an arm around Brenda's shoulders and pulled her away to sit down at the table again out of earshot of the deputy.

"Goddamn cops. They're all assholes." He was seriously mad.

"Oh, never mind them."

"Yeah, but now I gotta make a trip back here."

"Would that be so bad?" Brenda said with a big grin. "You get to see me?" She curled one shoulder forward and tossed her red hair back.

Holly stared at the amazing transformation that took place in a woman in front of a man she liked. We're all still in high school, she thought.

"Terrible thing what happened here," Mike Jarvis said, holding out a bottle of cold water for both of them. "It's hot out there, girls. Have some water. Do they know who did it?"

"Nope. They don't tell you anything. Eh, Holly?"

Holly nodded, distracted by seeing the two detectives enter the storage shed where they kept the landscaping equipment. What were they looking for there?

"Hey, Bren, did I leave my nice hat here?" Jarvis said.

"Nope," she said, smiling brightly.

"You keep your chin up, babe. I'll give you a call later. See how you're doing."

"Sure, I'll be home tonight right after five. Come for dinner."

"Well, I can't say for sure, but yeah, maybe I could...I don't know..."

Jarvis got up, giving the deputy the stink eye as he passed, heading out to the road where he'd parked his truck. Brenda grabbed Holly by the shoulders and jumped up and down.

"He's coming for dinner, Holly. Did you hear? He's coming for dinner. Oh, what will I fix? I've got no food in the house."

Holly hadn't heard that at all. *Oh, please, Brenda.* She wished she could protect every one of her friends from hurt.

"I wonder if he eats meat. I need to ask him." Brenda hurried out after Jarvis. Holly followed her past the main building, sneaking peeks through the fence at the forensics people packing up their equipment. Mike Jarvis had already pulled out onto the road. He looked okay but was he also going to break her heart too? Any new men on the mountain were pretty thoroughly checked out. The gossip was this one wasn't married. At least there was that.

"Damn," Brenda said, sweeping up a cat which had ventured out from the junipers that edged the parking lot. "Oh well, I'll call him."

"Mike's such a good guy, Holly. Yesterday he came over and fixed my water heater and he loves the cats. He's taken Boz in to live with him to get the kid away from the gangs in Bakersfield."

Mike's grandson Boz waved to Holly from the passenger side of the truck. Boz didn't look like a banger to Holly, all upholstered up with tats, swaggering around the village wearing the uniform of hoodie and bags. In fact he looked like a geek, pale, as though he spent a lot of time inside playing computer games. There weren't that many young people up here to hang with. She'd seen him talking to the O'Malleys at Basecamp café about computer games one day. Bad company, the O'Malleys, who lived across the road from Paws.

Holly looked up to see Dex Stafford beckoning to her. "Hey, Holly. Can I see you a minute?"

Stafford led her to a shed behind the cattery where they stored the grounds equipment.

"Hey, you. How's it going?" she said, keeping her hands to herself with effort.

"I'm beat. But I'm glad Harry's back. Maybe that'll be the end of working with Shanko. That's good news."

"I'll bet. Harry say anything to you about Rosalie? Are they still married?"

"I'm afraid to ask," Dex said with a laugh.

Holly wanted to grab him, but this was hardly the time or place. He looked too tired to fool around anyway. She reached out to pat him on the shoulder as he slumped against the wall.

"So what's the deal?" she said. "Somebody knifed Don. You know how the deputies talk. That's what they're saying."

"Don't push me, Holly, okay?" he said, frowning.

"Sorry, I'm just asking. I knew Don. I liked him."

He rubbed his face with both hands. "I need to interview Brenda Viglen, the manager here."

"Mind if I sit in?" She tried her most winsome smile on him.

He frowned and looked at her hard from under his eyebrows. "This whole interview thing is screwed up. You know we like to interview people at the station where we have control...but logistically we're stuck doing it here. Let me do the talking. Right?"

"Sure, boss, you betcha. Yowsa." She gave him a good-humored salute.

Brenda shot Holly a look of trepidation as she came in with Dex and sat down in the break room. Holly made herself as small as possible, tucked into a beat-up old chair in the corner. Dex settled Brenda down asking her about her job, made a few comments about the cats, and complimented her on getting the rest of the cats rounded up. Rapport-building.

"Will this take long? I really should be getting back outside," Brenda said, "see how the volunteers are doing getting the rest of the cats back."

"Wish they could tell us what they saw," Dex said with an easy smile. "So tell me about yesterday, Brenda? Start from the beginning."

"The beginning." She got up, rummaged around on the desk and found a clipboard with loose pages she handed to Stafford. "The sign-in sheet says we had three volunteers yesterday and the last one went home at 4 o'clock. I logged out at 5."

"Did you see anybody hanging around when you left? Anything unusual happen?"

Brenda scratched her red topknot with a pencil. She twisted up one side of her mouth and looked at the ceiling. "Nope. The cleaning crew of Mexicans was still out in back sterilizing boxes. I don't know when they left. Peach and Don got home about three o'clock and we went over everything that had happened while they'd been gone. Them coming home was the only thing out of the ordinary. Except for…"

Brenda shot a look at her. Holly threw up her hands with a *Tell Him* gesture. "Her son. You know, Skip? The high school football coach?"

"What about him?"

"He was here making a big stink."

"Yeah? About what?"

"Look, Detective. I need this job. Skip likes to come in and bother me. He wants to look at the books, to see what we take in for adoption fees, what we spend on vet care. I tell him to ask Peach but he gets mad… he scares me. And he didn't like Mr. Farrow."

Stafford made a note, letting the silence bubble.

"I'm a single mother and there's damn few jobs in Sierra Mountain Village that pay a living wage," she burst out, "and fewer even that offer health insurance. Peach is good to me."

"Don't you think she'd want you to do anything you can to figure out what happened to Don? What you tell me stays in confidence," Dex said, his big green eyes disarming.

Yeah, unless he needs you in court, Holly thought to herself.

"Give me a hand here, Brenda. I'll find out anyway. When did the thing with Skip Bryson take place? Yesterday?"

"Yes, but he left around two o'clock before Don and Peach came back. Doreen from the thrift shop called me and said Skip came over there later to get ugly with her. I don't know anything about Don," she said. "When I left at 5 o'clock, everything was peaceful."

"You have any idea why somebody would kill Mr. Farrow?"

"I don't have a thought in my head about that. Everybody liked him."

Stafford gazed at her for a long moment, then put his notebook away and checked his phone, giving her time. He would come back later to question Brenda when he had something to push her on. He, for sure, wouldn't overlook Skip Bryson as a suspect. Bryson was big and ugly and mean, but a killer?

It took a lot to kill somebody up close. For real, that is. Not like in books.

CHAPTER ELEVEN

Stafford re-read the email from his Sarge informing him Shanko would be assigned to them for a few days. Stafford swung his arm up in the air prepared to smash his cell phone to the ground, then thought better of it, catching Harry Price's look. He and his partner stood in front of the cattery updating Sgt. Bill Madison. Shanko had married Harry Price's daughter Lauren, who had been for a brief time Stafford's girlfriend. Shanko was a devotee of The Tough Mudders, ten to twelve-mile obstacle courses. Stafford was sick to death hearing Shanko bragging about the fire pits, dropping from intimidating heights, the Arctic Enema and the Live Wire Shock Field. Doubtless Lauren would be there screaming from the sidelines, holding their baby. Unless she stayed home under the covers sucking her thumb. Usually the Lieutenant didn't pair Harry Price with his son-in-law, but it was vacation season and they were short-handed.

A blowsy, grey-haired woman who had been watching everything from the deck of a house across the street marched toward Stafford, beckoning with a finger.

"Hey, you. You the one in charge here?" She crossed the road wearing a stained white tank top showing off a bobbling shelf of mammaries. Wide in the middle on skinny legs, she picked her way across the pavement daintily, her hand up to her green sun hat.

"You. I want to talk to you," she said to Stafford, pointing at him. He met her at the edge of the road. The street audience rustled with anticipation.

"So what happened over here?" she said, jerking her thumb towards the cattery as though he would be itchy to share all the blood and gore with her.

"You live there, ma'am?" He tilted his head in that direction. Good witness possibility here along a dead-end road that didn't have many neighbors.

"For thirty years. My husband grew up in that dinkshit shack. Born, battered, and bred there. So we got a murderer running loose, way we hear it?"

Dex heard Sgt. Bill Madison calling him. "Hey, Stafford, I need to talk to you."

"Never mind him." The woman grabbed Dex by the arm and attempted to turn him away from Bill Madison. Dex reared back from her. "I'm Beatrice O'Malley. There's things I could tell you about that place…"

"Hey, Stafford. I need you," Madison shouted.

"Ma'am, I'll get back to you." Stafford left her still grabbing at him and talking loud. Two punks who had been standing on the porch of her house started walking across the road to join her. He heard them talking loud, making sure he heard them.

"Hey, Mister, you wanna know about them people, ask me."

"Tell her I'm gonna shoot me some cats."

A deputy left the Sarge's side, and passing Stafford, pushed the neighbors back across the road. He bellowed. "No shooting within Sierra Mountain Village limits. You know that."

Sgt. Madison had a funny smirk on his face, watching Stafford walk toward him.

"You know them?" Stafford asked.

The deputy returned to stand by the Sarge, his back facing the street. He busted out laughing. "It's been war between old Beatrice and Ms. Bryson since day one over the cats. One of her good-for-nothing sons shoots one of the cats every so often. I get called. Animal Control gets called." He threw up his hands. "What can we do? Peach wants us to run a ballistic analysis on the rounds that got the cat. She even offered to pay for it when I talk about the budget, but what am I gonna do? Like the DA's office is gonna prosecute a cat murder when everybody in Bakersfield is killing each other? The cat place isn't going anywhere, far as I can see. Stan O'Malley's looking for a slip and fall so he doesn't even have to make a pretense of working. And Leroy and Dwayne, the kids aren't any better." He paused to spit in the dirt.

"Like that, huh?" Dex nodded. "So have we got a statement from her?"

"Sure, but just the initial late last night," Bill Madison said. "We gotta do it formal like today. You should do it, Stafford. The old girl likes your pretty face."

Dex shuddered. "Yeah, okay. Heard we got Shanko for a few days. You could put him on it."

"He don't have your sweet ways with the women," the Sarge said, looking innocent. Stafford was too tired to tell if he was kidding or not.

"O'Malley say they saw anything?"

"Saw a wetback running away around the right time," the deputy said, his hands on his duty belt.

"You kidding me?" Stafford said, narrowing his eyes to look at him.

"That's exactly what she said," Deputy Jackson said, flipping through the pages of his notebook to stab a spot on one page. "Her exact words."

⊨═ ═⊨

Stafford and Price reviewed what needed to be done, leaning on the wooden deck railing outside the main building of Paws, watching the frantic cat recovery activity in the parking lot. Cats who had been already captured were yowling from inside a row of carriers covered with old towels. Every volunteer Peach Bryson could chase up, Holly among them, was working the neighborhood, trying to entice the cats back.

Stafford spotted Holly coming across the yard lugging a cat carrier in each hand. She piled the heavy carriers on top of the stack that held the feral cats in long wire traps, grabbed an old towel to cover the newcomers, and wiped sweat off her brow. Brenda checked the returnees off on a list. Stafford gave Holly a small wave. He liked the jaunty way she walked, the way her hair smelled. But those cats. Everywhere he turned—cats. He watched her filling bags with kibble the volunteers were placing in spots the cats were likely to visit, along with bowls of water.

Harry Price checked on emails, turning to Stafford with a loud snort. "Oh, ho, our Skip Bryson is up to his ears in debt, and there are three bankruptcies in his record."

"Farrow had money. He needed money. You think?"

"But how was killing him going to get it?"

"Gimme a minute. I'll figure it out." Stafford scratched his stubbly jaw. He had found a pink razor blade in Holly's bathroom cabinet, but he suspected she'd been using it since God invented trees. He listed the people he needed to see: Farrow's lawyer to check where he'd left his money to; the O'Malleys across the street; and the criminalists to see if they'd got anything yet; and go back to Farrow's cabin to see what the deputies doing the search had uncovered; and interview Skip Bryson again and check his alibi. For starters. Each step of an investigation spun off a thousand details. Harry Price would follow the body so Stafford would be spared the autopsy. The criminalists were finished inside. The temptation was always to dog them, but it didn't do any damn good. Their work was slow and meticulous, work that would drive him crazy.

Alexandra Esquivel, the team leader, emerged from the crime scene, blinking at the sunshine outside. She wheeled out her cart of equipment with a black duffel bag on top. He caught her eye and walked over.

"Anything good?" Stafford said.

"A few good boot prints. Maybe." She tried to push past him.

"Fingerprints?" He danced with impatience.

"Oh yeah. Too many to run here at the scene. DNA maybe. You gonna get out of my way, Stafford?"

"Sure. Sure. Sorry."

"You know it's a myth you always get something from forensics, don't you? You do know that?"

"Yeah, I know that, but can I just see the hoodie? I never got a chance to look at it."

"What's it gonna tell you?"

"Give me an estimate of the size then. Can I see your evidence log? Just that?" He gave her his best smile.

With a huff, she opened the duffel bag and pulled out a clipboard. Quickly Stafford scanned it.

Orange. Size XXL.

Bryson? He was definitely the hard-bodied type for S & R. And he'd been wearing the S & R T-shirt. Could it be this easy?

CHAPTER TWELVE

Madison's deputies were canvassing the neighborhood doing knock-and-talks to turn up witnesses. Stafford had learned to trust the deputies—within limits. In a rural mountain area like this, deputies had investigative experience. They knew who was selling, buying, manufacturing meth, who was in rehab, needed rehab, and when to call Children's Services. The detectives only showed up for major crimes.

Sgt. Madison ambled across the yard toward him along with a deputy. The Sarge was an affable guy with a good line of chat for the civilians. Deputy Frederickson looked Minnesotan: blond with a florid face, white eyelashes, and pale-blue eyes. Mason knew him from encounters at the Central Receiving area of the downtown Bakersfield jail.

"What happened to you?" Stafford said, gesturing at his bandaged arm.

"Biker chick came at me with a shovel," the deputy said with a snort.

"Oh man, women," Dex said, shaking his head. "They're the dangerous ones. So what have you got?"

The deputy jerked a thumb across the street. "Neighbor, Beatrice O'Malley, says she saw a man running away right before Bryson made the call, carrying something." He checked his notebook. "You already met her. Five feet tall, all mouth, and filled up to the brim with hate. Mexicans are the reason blah, blah, blah. Her son and his girlfriend and the baby are living in the garage. This cat place here had a burglary a couple months ago. The O'Malleys probably, but try proving it. And yadda yadda. Baby crying the whole time I'm tryin' a interview her."

"A burglary, huh?" Stafford said. He made a note to see what was taken; Paws was hardly a burglary target full of items worth stealing. Bryson's house and furnishing included nice things. Why wasn't the house hit?

"Get a description of the runner?"

"An old green truck with a bad muffler waited on the road for him. The guy was wearing a white T-shirt and jeans."

"That'll help a lot," Stafford said, disgusted.

"There's always more with somebody like Beatrice. The husband will be home later. He took his son and the girlfriend down to the outlet stores at the bottom of the Grapevine. She's hoping they can get jobs and get the hell out of her garage."

"Okay. I'll go over later, talk to old man O'Malley. Her boys."

"Beatrice hates this place, all the cats. They get out, she says, and wander the neighborhood. Says her husband takes potshots at them for fun with his B-B gun. Claims that doesn't hurt them."

That would make the O'Malleys real popular with the Paws ladies.

"Where do you want to go for lunch?" Stafford asked. The downside to small towns was that there was usually only one good restaurant. Here it was Silva Bella and they weren't open for lunch. The old standby was La Leña, the good Mexican place on Sierra Mountain Village's two-block-long main street.

"I don't care," Stafford said, putting away his notebook. "We better ask Shanko."

Harry frowned.

"Shanko," Stafford hollered over his shoulder.

Shanko came out of the cattery yanking off his blue gloves and throwing them in the wastebin. He looked away from his father-in-law's tight face. Harry had won an astonishing amount of money playing the lottery. Everybody badgered him for so-called loans or capital to start up a new business venture. Shanko had gone on his dependents' list when he'd married his daughter.

Fifteen minutes later they were eating sandwiches, kicking around a theory of the case. Shanko put a leg over the bench of the picnic table outside the grocery store under the tall Jeffrey pines. He slid in next to Harry who moved away from him.

"Like he came prepared to kill Farrow," Shanko said talking with his mouth full. Shanko, of course, had an opinion. The mouth on him never quit and he was impervious to other people's opinions. "And was either lucky or knew what he was doing."

"And the cat hair," Stafford laughed. "The disgusting scenes those criminalists process? And they're complaining about cat hair?"

"We'll see how much forensics gets if our guy was smart. This isn't TV," Harry said, examining his sandwich skeptically.

"And we gotta get a DNA sample on both the Brysons," Stafford said, picking the tomato out of his own sandwich.

Harry picked up his car keys with the NRA tag and spun them around his finger. "What did Farrow do that made her so mad she'd hire a hit man? If she did him."

"He had money. We know that," Shanko said. "Maybe she wanted money and he said no."

Stafford made a face. "She was going to marry him."

"But maybe he planned to leave his money to the Sierra Club or some damn thing like that. We don't know until we see his will, which we don't have yet. Or do we, Stafford?" There was an edge to Shanko's voice.

Stafford kept his face wooden. "You see me Googling myself? Practicing my golf swing? What the fuck you think I've been doing, Shanko?"

Harry put both hands on the table and stared pointedly at both of them.

Everything Shanko did irritated Stafford. At times he had a fleeting pity for Shanko who wore the dead-tired, wrung-out look on his face Dex recognized from the brief time he'd been involved with Harry's bipolar daughter, Lauren. Harry paid for a nanny and a housekeeper for their infant. Lauren had nothing to do now except sit around and be crazy. Having somebody else take care of their baby was a good thing.

"She looks like she's got a fair bit of money herself," Harry said, as the silence settled.

"Who ever has enough?" Shanko said.

Harry gazed out over the juniper bushes toward the road and made no comment. Across SMV's main street were cutesy plywood cuts of cowboys and Indian maidens you could stick your face in and have your picture taken. Very non-PC. Tourists loved them.

"But he gave away money all the time," Stafford said before Shanko started talking again. "Sounds like if you asked him he'd give you the shirt off his back."

"Yeah, but maybe our killer asked for too much, or maybe Don was tired of giving him money," Shanko said.

"Blackmail?"

"We haven't turned anything up yet worth blackmailing him over," Stafford said.

"Points back to Bryson then, doesn't it?" Harry asked.

"The son or the old lady?" Stafford said.

"I'm liking her," Shanko said. "Not him."

"Who else did you find he was giving money to when you went through his financials, Stafford?"

"The Rotary. The Lion's Club. Stuff like that. $5,000 to Peach when she had the fundraiser last summer. But I don't see Peach...." Stafford said.

"We been over that fifty times," Shanko said. "She coulda done it. She coulda."

"Yeah, prove it," Stafford said, taking a huge bite of his sandwich. Get it down fast and he could get away from Shanko. He finished his sandwich and tossed the brown paper bag into the bear-proof trashcan, still chewing and ready to go.

Harry was still on the fence about Peach. At least one of them was keeping an open mind about it.

CHAPTER THIRTEEN

Peach Bryson looked between them as Stafford and Price sat down at the kitchen table a little later, a plate of cookies on the flowered tablecloth. She wore a black skirt and top and looked brittle and exhausted. "Once a month I hired a crew of *jornaleros*. You know what that means, don't you?"

"Day workers. Where did you get them?"

"I do my errands and big shopping in Bakersfield and stop in at Home Depot. The workers wait at the exits where the contractors stop to pick them up for a day's work. I always looked for Carlos or a couple of his cousins from their village in Mexico. I'd write down a date, and four of them would go through the place doing heavy cleaning. We have to keep this place really clean, Detective. Disease and epidemics, you know. "

Her eyes filled with a readiness to instruct them on cat sanitation, but Harry cut her off. "Any paperwork on them?"

She shook her head. "They sign an invoice for our records, but it's pretty informal. They've got so little English, I never got to know them."

"So you don't have an address or a phone number?"

Again she shook her head. "They do yardwork for people up here in SMV sometimes. I've seen their truck packed tight with branches. I couldn't tell you what kind of truck it was though, other than it was green and it was old."

"An old green truck. Well, it's something," Stafford said to make her feel better. That confirmed Mama O'Malley's report at least.

"One of your neighbors said she saw somebody running away, somebody that looked like one of your day workers, right before you called 911."

"Oh?" She pinched her face into puzzlement. She stopped and smoothed her hand over the table cloth. "But I heard them leave before…"

"When?"

"I don't remember. I wasn't paying attention to the time." Recognition flared across her face. "I bet it was Beatrice O'Malley across the road. That woman's reported me so many times to Animal Control. They come up here and I show them around and it all blows over. I haven't had one citation from the County. Not one. She's just hateful."

Stafford spaced out, thinking his own thoughts, while Harry took a phone call from the coroner's death investigator. Peach got up to put on another pot of coffee. He didn't much like cats, an opinion he kept to himself because he wanted to get along with Holly. One or even two was fine, though. He thought about his mother living with him. When he got home and wanted to crash at the end of the day, BeeBee was there, full of bright chitchat. When was she moving out? He'd brought up the subject, and she'd bit his nose off. His parents were back together again. BeeBee was making his dad pay for running off with a blond bimbo during a late middle-age crisis. She lived at Dex's condo and acted like a girl of seventeen insisting on being courted. He waited for Harry Price, who was still on the phone with the coroner's office.

If Holly was accepted by the Sheriff's department and stationed in Bakersfield, what about all her cats? He stirred uncomfortably in his chair, thinking of life with Seabright and her twelve cats, him sneezing his head off. Sometimes it was nice to come home and see his parents in his living room peacefully watching TV. BeeBee couldn't watch TV at his Dad's place. Apparently *that woman* had once lived there and BeeBee refused to set foot in the house. They were looking at a new housing development on a golf course. It was weird, all-around weird. Dex loved his mother but he didn't love the fat Persian cat that sneaked into his room and slept on his bed. As soon as he lay down, he started sneezing. Her Jack Russell, the bark machine, hated him and Dex hated him back. But with her there, his laundry got done and there were always sandwich makings and leftovers in the fridge. He was an only child and used to his parents' attention.

"We need to talk to the day workers," Harry said, swiping the phone closed and giving Dex a sharp look. "You got them from the Home Depot on Ming?"

"I have no idea where they live. They know how to work, though. I only had to show them once. They're smart, you know, they just don't speak English."

"You don't have any photos, do you?"

"Oh no. They wouldn't like that." Bryson's eyes looked concerned. "You're not going to call Immigration?"

"No, no, just talk," Harry said. "I don't interfere in Immigration. Me and Stafford, hell, we got enough problems."

Skip Bryson waited outside for them when they wound it up with Peach Bryson. The guy was clean, you had to say that for him. Freshly shaved and smelling like Dial soap, he sported lots of muscle and beef in the shoulders and chest. Dex glanced at his feet and grinned. His Doc Martens' had been replaced with a pair of old blue high tops. That didn't affect his breezy manner or the presumptive confidence, taking for granted he was the superior in every situation.

"So you ready to make an arrest?" Bryson said.

"Man, you're watching too much TV," Stafford said, walking past him to the County vehicle. Dex sensed his eyes following him.

They'd hit him for the DNA sample when the time was right. Hit both Brysons. Peach could have been wearing the hoodie as well, though it would hang down to her knees.

Holly stopped in at Basecamp, Sierra Mountain Village's internet café, housed in a real estate office. The biggest business in town was real estate—selling second homes nowadays. Visitors came up in summer and never thought about snow or heating costs when they bought a vacation cabin with four bedrooms, spa, and greenhouse. Dwayne O'Malley's old Celica drove off, farting a cloud of black smoke. Holly watched him go, wishing she could nail his ass to the mess at the

Seven Sisters shrine. She was asking questions, trying to stir something up, find somebody who would tell her something about the vandalism. Somebody had to know something.

Pete, the new guy, was leaving, too, and climbed into his patrol Jeep carrying a takeout coffee. He gave Holly a look over his shoulder, thinking his smoldering gaze would make her drop to her knees in desire for him. Pete had two ideas in his head and they were both the same. The cremation guy's grandson Boz sat on the deck outside Basecamp drinking one of the café's handmade sodas. There were few summer jobs around for teenagers. The town used to hire them as lifeguards at the pool in summer, but then the council had decided to cancel the lifeguards as a cost-cutting measure. So far nobody had died, so it must have been a good decision? Right?

Were Boz, Pete and Dwayne O'Malley meeting? Holly sauntered past Boz, who stopped her.

"Hey there, officer, got a minute?"

She looked down at him. Good-looking kid, if you liked that white-blonde-pink-Nordic look. He was slight and thin and to her unattractive, a permanent smirk carved into his face. The lives and thinking processes of teenage kids were an anthropological mystery to her.

"You think I should worry about bears, officer? I walk my dog out in the forest."

"Whereabouts?" Holly asked, looking over his shoulder to see who was inside the café: Chloe whom she'd last seen at the shrine, wearing a flowered sundress and painting her toenails blue.

"The paths around town," Boz Jarvis said.

"Lot of bears around. Some with cubs," she said, registering something smarmy about him. He also had those ridiculous gauges in his ears that stretch out the lobes. Ick. She must be getting old that this stuff bothered her.

"I can handle a bear," he said.

Holly laughed in his face and let the door slap shut behind her. She knew Brenda didn't like Boz. She also heard Chloe, one of the Shrine Sisters, had a boyfriend. Chloe and Boz? Chloe and the younger O'Malley, Leroy? Eeek. Chloe and Pete?

Who was she to say? Everybody liked sex. She wished she got a more regular supply.

The big TV inside Basecamp played a home sales show on low volume. Billie must be somewhere in back cooking up something good. A crippled-up old rodeo rider who dragged himself in every day perched over a table working on his photos, his walker close by. Another regular was updating his website. Couple of tourists. Normal. She grabbed up a Bear Aware flyer and took it outside to Mike Jarvis' grandson.

"Here you go, Boz. Lots of information about bears here."

"Thank you, officer. I surely do appreciate that."

Holly took a good look at the hickey on his neck as she passed.

CHAPTER FOURTEEN

Later that afternoon Holly ran down Pete, her fellow patrol officer, at the old gym in town with the stinky, rusted equipment. Pete didn't fit with the rest of the patrol staff. He thought he was a cop with a big swinging dick because he'd applied to the Kern County Sheriff's Department. Holly had been a cop, a for-real cop, and for a brief time made detective. Pete had been a roughneck in the oil field and got hurt—again like her. She'd gotten in trouble with alcohol, but that was in the past now. Pete had himself a serious porn addiction. She caught him once petting the peter in the office and even his lumpy, scarred, shaved head had blushed.

As usual he'd left the event log a mess at the end of his shift. She needed an address to follow up on a barking dog complaint. Holly banged on the door of the gym and he lunged over and yanked it open, hope lighting his face.

"Give it a rest, will'ya. I have a boyfriend. How many times do I have to tell you? These people up on Woodland." She shoved the report at him. "What's the address?"

"I don't know why you're so down on me. Didn't I put in the address?"

"Of course you didn't, Pete. That's the only reason I'm here."

"Lemme think," he said. He walked with the report back to the weight bench and sat down spread-legged. She looked away. The gym smelled like a dead fish in a sweat sock.

"Hey, I heard you were talking to people about that looney-tune thing up on the meadow," he said, handing his log sheet back to her. Holly turned to leave. Who needed a look at his sweaty package?

"The shrine? The Seven Sisters."

"What was the point of that place anyway?"

"It's somewhere people thought was sacred. Like I buried a dog up there and one of my favorite cats. You know anything about it, Pete? You hang out with the lowlifes. You must hear things."

"My friends aren't lowlifes," he said, puffing himself up indignantly. "People don't like you asking questions and stirring the shit in the pot, Holly."

"Eeeuw. Man, you got a way with words. Stirring the shit in the pot?"

Holly grabbed the log from him and burned rubber peeling out of the parking lot of the old gym. Whoops. Abuse of a patrol vehicle, and Ed might get a complaint. Homeowners thought they owned you.

Stafford and Price might still be around so she called Dex. "Hey, handsome, it's that hot babe. Remember me? What are you up to?"

"Holly, Holly, Holly," Dex said. "I'm so busy I have to make an appointment with myself to scratch my ass."

"Oh, nice talk. So when do I get to see you?"

"We've got to check evidence in, so I'll be heading down to Bakersfield in a couple of hours. Any chance you could come over here? We've got a couple of questions for you."

"Sure. The call on deck right now is this ditzy, meth-trash whore who thinks there's a mouse in her closet. Or maybe it's the murderer who's wandering around town. You better catch him soon. You hear?"

Stafford laughed. She liked making him laugh.

Stafford stood alone in the parking lot of Paws when Holly Seabright drove up and got out of the patrol Jeep. He turned, hearing the crunch of gravel. The cat carriers were empty now and stacked shoulder high in a row on the pavement surface, only a few cats in sight. He walked over to her as she got out of the Jeep.

"How are things going?" she asked, looking around. Nobody in sight so he pressed her close against the Jeep and kissed her thoroughly.

"You feel so good, Stafford," she said, leaning against him with her full length. "Hot damn."

Harry Price thundered down the steps and pulled Stafford aside. "Get a room, you guys. Catch you in a few minutes, Holly?"

"Sure, I'll visit Peach." She ran up the stairs into the house and Stafford took a moment to appreciate the rear view.

Price was all business. "Okay, let's line up the interviews we need to get in the book." Harry ticked them off: DNA samples on the Brysons, neighbors, Peach's daughter, financials and phone records on everybody, the boot prints, backgrounders on Don..."

"Check out the son's alibi with the wife—what's her name?" Stafford asked.

Harry rummaged in his notes for an answer. "Arielle."

"Get the shoe impressions of the paramedics?" Dex asked, consulting his own notes.

"Yeah. Who's got keys to Farrow's place in Taft? You get that?" Price stuck in.

"Not yet." Stafford looked around.

Just then a Hummer blew into the yard, followed by a Land Rover. A small square woman flung open the door of the Hummer and hit the ground ready to fight, her black eyebrows pulled together in a V of outrage. She screamed, "Where's Stafford?"

"I'm Stafford," Dex announced, stepping forward.

A big hairy dog tumbled out of the Hummer, followed by two yipping terriers. The dogs spied a cat and shot across the parking lot after it. The back doors on both sides of the Hummer opened and two little kids shot out after the dogs. A volunteer saw the dogs coming and screamed. The driver of the Hummer looked over her shoulder, saw the chaos the dogs were creating and ignored it.

"I heard about Don Farrow. Why didn't you call me?" she said, huffing with outrage.

A man in a grey business suit eased out of the Land Rover and two pit bulls jumped out behind him and streaked across the pavement after the cats.

"Donald Farrow is my father. I heard he got killed here," she shouted.

"Tone it down, lady."

"This is where it happened, isn't it?"

Stafford nodded, taking a step forward. Harry stood by watching. "There's nothing to see here, ma'am. Who are you?"

"Andrea Posner. This is my husband Jerry. He's a lawyer." Jerry stuck out his hand.

Behind them Peach had come out the door to see what all the screaming and barking was about. Andrea Posner saw her and turned her back on Peach to face Stafford.

"Your father was already taken to the morgue in Bakersfield," Stafford said.

"This is that crazy woman's place, isn't it? The cat lady?" The dogs were barking, cats skittering up the pine trees and up the chain link. Volunteers streamed out of the cattery, yelling at the dogs' owners.

"Call off your dogs, ma'am. Right now," Stafford shouted.

She turned and snapped at her husband. "Jerry, do something," she hollered at Stafford. "Have you arrested her yet? You know she killed him to get her hands on my Dad's money."

"How do you know that?"

"Because I know her."

Peach Bryson staggered down the stairs and stood firm at the bottom holding onto the newel post. "You don't know me, Andrea. I only met you once, and Don wasn't your father. How can you say that?"

"You got him to marry you, didn't you? You were only after his money."

Stafford was more used to watching women with tattooed necks go at each other, swinging and clawing.

"Andrea, what are you talking about? We weren't married. And Don wasn't your father."

The sigh of relief that escaped Andrea Posner could have powered a hydroelectric generator. "So he didn't marry her," she said to her husband, who stood at her side watching. Breathing hard. "He must have come to his senses then."

"So was he your father then or wasn't he?" Stafford said, loudly enough to be heard over the dogs barking and the volunteers screaming.

"Well, not biologically, but he said he planned to leave everything to us kids. And I'm here to make sure that happens. There's eight of us kids. Barry's witchy wife called my husband because she saw it on the news. My brother and I don't speak."

Andrea Posner turned her back on him, finally noticing the chaos the pit bulls were causing behind her, and ignoring it. She marched toward Peach. "You got my father killed. Or you killed him."

"You have no reason to talk to me like that. And if he planned to leave everything to you, that's news to me. He never saw any of you unless you wanted money."

"Do something," Andrea snapped at her husband, who had gone to his Land Rover and taken out leashes. He stood there with the leashes in his hand watching the melee. The dogs had treed a couple of cats and were circling the spindly tree, barking hysterically. The volunteers were trying to pull them off. A kid climbed out of the Land Rover and tugged at his mother's arm.

"Mama, can we have a cat?"

"Get back in the car, damn you. You're not getting a cat."

Brenda Viglen charged out into the yard from the main cattery building, her red hair flying behind her. "Leash your goddamn dogs. Haven't you got an ounce of sense, woman?"

"How dare you? Jerry, do something!"

"What? Sue her."

"Oh, for god's sake." Andrea Posner grabbed two big pit bulls by the scruff of the neck, dragged them back to the Hummer, and stuffed them inside. She called over her shoulder to Stafford. "You tell that woman she hasn't heard the end of this yet."

"You want to talk to me, you make an appointment," Stafford shouted after her, flinging a card into the open window of the Hummer.

She backed the oversized vehicle up with a rooster-tail of gravel, roaring out of the lot coming close to knocking Peach down. Don Farrow's daughter, or whatever she was, gave Peach the finger as she drove out. The Land Rover followed her, her husband hunched behind the wheel having the grace to look embarrassed.

Stafford couldn't wait to meet the rest of the family. He figured this piece of work would head right over to Farrow's cabin to see what she could steal before anybody caught her. The deputies still searching the place would put a stop to that. Then he figured she'd be right back again to scream at him. No questions about her so-called father's body, how he had died, did he suffer? You just had to love people.

CHAPTER FIFTEEN

Holly rushed outside when she heard the shouting and the dogs barking and Brenda screaming. She heard the tail end of the conversation and put her arm around Peach to soothe her as they walked back into the kitchen. Harry and Dex came in, the question on their faces reflected in Holly's eyes.

"So what was all that about, Ms. Bryson?" Harry Price said in a gentle tone. He sat down at the table with Peach who picked up and then set down the set of cat salt and pepper shakers. She rearranged a stack of cat napkins, started to speak, then stopped.

"You had to know Don before any of that would make sense," Peach said, looking tired beyond endurance. "Andrea was the oldest of a bunch of rag-tail kids who lived next door to him. He felt sorry for their mother and helped them out a lot. They're not his biological children no matter what that awful woman says. Don kept saying we had to have a sit-down and straighten our estates out before we got married but we never got around to it." She looked up. "Well, certainly we were going to get married. Maybe even soon. As far as those kids, he thought they should be making it on their own now. Don was such a good man." She started laughing, an odd, braying laugh, and tears began running down her face. Holly moved over and put her hand on Peach's shoulder.

"Do you have any idea where we might get hold of his lawyer?" Harry asked.

"No, he never mentioned him by name...that I can recall."

Stafford gazed at her, trying to decide if her vagueness was pretense. Her eyes were clear and unwavering, but she had a tremor in her hands stroking the orange cat in her lap.

"We both had problems to straighten out before we got married. Don wanted me to close the cattery." She shot a look at Holly. "We were never free to travel and enjoy ourselves and Don wanted that. I did too. And, well. my son and daughter... They expect something when I die...I know that." Peach looked up and began poking at her white curls. "Skip, he's pestering me to find out what I'm leaving him. He's been so awful lately. If you knew Don, you'd know why we were so well-matched. Neither of us liked confrontations. Don would walk away and bottle it all up inside himself. My son says all I do is cry, but you have to understand the way he is. Things have happened in his life."

Stafford made his face wooden. Skip Bryson was probably born nasty. But the coach of a winning local high school was like a god around here. Holly'd told him it was common knowledge about the Social Darwinism that ruled the football field, training camp, and locker room. Bryson bullied the kids who didn't work hard enough to please him, but that was hardly a first in sports coaching.

"So as far as you know, he didn't write a will leaving everything to this woman," Harry said.

Tears ran down Peach Bryson's face. "I don't think so, but how can I know anything for sure?"

Dex and Harry went outside after Andrea Posner's exit. Stafford called Seabright out to join them. Holly looked delighted to be included, her eyes full of the joy and mischief of life.

"Wow. People, huh?"

Stafford patted a seat on the stairs beside him.

"You know anything about this woman?" Harry asked, nodding his head toward the parking lot where the scene with Andrea Posner still shimmered in the air.

"Not a thing. Don didn't have kids, wasn't married as far as I knew."

"You don't have any guesses at all about who did him, do you?"

"You've got a bead on Skip by now, I'd think. Big guy. Volatile." Holly scrunched her blond hair into a ponytail, twisting her mouth sideways. "I hate the guy."

Price looked surprised. "Really? Hate him?"

"Yeah, he's a bully."

Stafford knew lots of bullies and lots of cowards. Sometimes they were the same thing. Sometimes bullies were the real deal, living for the wild, soaring thrill of violence and destruction. Sometimes they were cops. Like Shanko.

Holly snorted. "Skip's tried to get his mother to close Paws. Every dime she spends on this place comes out of his inheritance. I stay away from him."

"Some people don't like Paws," Harry observed, leaning forward with his elbows on his thighs. He mopped at his bald head with a handkerchief. The sun was blistering today.

"And a lot of people do," Seabright said hotly, straightening. "Yeah, I know about the O'Malleys across the street and their riffraff sons and all their friends. They account for most of the crime around here. The Sheriff's guys will tell you that. But it's penny ante stuff. Not murder. But I wouldn't put the burglary here last summer beyond them. They hit the treatment room, looking for ketamine. That's an animal anesthetic the vet uses for surgeries when he comes here. The druggies get hallucinations, some sort of high from it. I wouldn't know. They wouldn't find ketamine or any other drugs here they could sell. We're smart about that stuff." Holly's face pinkened and her voice rose. "And I told you that the Seven Sisters shrine was destroyed, didn't I? What if they're connected?"

Stafford shrugged. "I don't see how yet, but for sure, we'll keep that in mind."

Holly's face went stony trying to judge whether he was blowing her off. "I wish you would because I'm turning myself inside out trying to get people to talk and if anybody knows anything, they won't tell me."

Holly went into the cattery to find Brenda after all the fuss had died down and Dex and Harry had left for Bakersfield. Brenda had finished sweeping out the birthing room where cats with newborn kittens were kept in cardboard boxes inside wire cages with the doors left open so the mamas could get away from the kittens when they needed to. She was disappointed not to find Brenda alone. Mike Jarvis, the cremation guy, had come back. Brenda was bouncing around, looking happy. She sat down with four calico kittens crawling over her, their eyes beginning to open. Holly took a couple of the fur balls from her and sat down on a pail of cat litter.

"Soooooo, tell. Who was that witch?" Brenda asked, all excited.

Holly didn't want to talk about Peach's business in front of Mike Jarvis. "I'll tell you later. It ended up to be nothing."

"Tell me now. Mike knows everything about what's going on here."

Oh yeah? Brenda was a good judge of character. She could pick out the volunteers who were going to be more work than what they got out of them. Except Chloe. Her judgment wasn't that good with men, though. And hers was better? Ha, ha, snort. Holly reminded herself about the guy she'd called Male Heroin back in Utah.

Holly gave Jarvis a long look. Big, heavy shoulders, a nice open smile. He had the same expression the church lady had. Gimme all the gory details. She didn't like that.

"So what do you think happened to Don? Did you know him?" Holly asked him.

"Why ask me?" Jarvis said, rearing back.

"I donno. Getting a fresh perspective." She couldn't help but be suspicious of everybody. It was a cop thing.

"I never even met the guy. I only know what's in the online paper this morning and what Bren tells me."

"Oh, don't mind her," Brenda said, getting a beer out of the fridge and handing it to Jarvis. Heineken. My, haven't we got fancy, Holly thought. Brenda trailed a hand over Jarvis' shoulders as she passed him.

"So who was that woman? C'mon," she urged.

Holly relented. "First she said Don was her father… then she admitted he was *like* a father to her."

"Weird," Jarvis commented.

"Mike says we should be looking for those Mexicans Peach hires. Knives are their thing," Brenda said brightly.

Duh. "I think they're doing that," Holly said.

"So who else are they suspecting? I betcha they think Peach did it. That's who it always is on the cop shows," Jarvis said.

"Mike and I watched a whole season of *Castle*. He always knows who it is. He's really smart," Brenda preened. "Did you know he was a Navy Seal?"

Really? The aching need in Brenda's face turned Holly's heart over in her chest. It wasn't that she didn't want her to have a boyfriend. Maybe this guy would be different. But she had things to do and all this drama and pheromones in the air were wearing her out.

"Guys, I have to check in at work."

"Oh, hey, yeah. Keep us posted," Brenda said, sinking onto Mike Jarvis' lap as Holly left.

⊨⊹ ⊹⊨

CHAPTER SIXTEEN

The next day, Sunday, Price and Stafford were back in Sierra Mountain Village at Don Farrow's rental cabin. Stafford rummaged through files thrown out of the filing cabin onto the floor of the den. Harry Price came in, running his hand over his bald spot and snapping on a pair of latex gloves. He smelled of expensive cologne these days instead of Right Guard.

Stafford looked up. "What?"

"The will?"

"Yeah? What?" He held up a sheaf of financial documents he'd found in the files. "The guy got a nice income off the patents. He sank money into a winery that's yet to pay off. I've heard investors buy into the lifestyle, the prestige of owning a piece of the action. Maybe he wasn't expecting much of a return."

Harry winced. "You must be talking about me. When Rosalie couldn't think of anything else to spend the money on, that's exactly what she did. You know she had herself done over. Cheek implants, porcelain veneers, everything lifted. She even talks different. You notice that?"

Dex rubbed his nose thoughtfully. "I've hardly seen her since you got back from that cruise."

"Neither have I. She's got all these new friends. People in LA, this interior design course she's taking. Now she's after me to get a personal trainer, get hair plugs."

"Harry, you've gone pussy-whipped." Stafford grinned.

Price's phone rang again and his face dropped the look of outrage, and went to blankness as he took the call. Stafford turned back to Don Farrow's desk, pulling out files and setting them aside as he read through them. *Keep your opinions on Rosalie to yourself.* Rosalie Price hated Dex anyway. Harry and Rosalie hoped Dex would be a settling influence on Lauren, but her meltdowns were way out of his league. He'd found out later he'd got Lauren on the rebound from Detective Shanko, who had been assigned as his partner when Harry took the leave of absence. Dex hoped Harry's money could keep her stuck together. Stafford tried to

cut Shanko slack because he remembered how drain-
ing Lauren could be. He tried. The guy was still an asshole, though. Shanko couldn't pass a mirror without
admiring himself.

He shoved the desk drawer in after going through
it looking for keys, notes, anything odd. He paused
when he found two folded sheets paper-clipped together: two IOUs made out by Don Farrow, signed by
Skip Bryson. One in the amount of $5000 and dated
10 months ago; the other more recent in the amount
of $12,000.

Harry got off the phone and stood up rubbing the
small of his back. Few cops got through the years on
patrol without back troubles.

"Look here," Stafford said. He handed over the
IOUs, which Harry studied, then looked up at him.

"Well, well," Harry said. "Wonder if these ever got
redeemed? You suppose Don ever pushed for repay-
ment?"

"Or whether his mother knew Don loaned him
money? I like this,' Stafford said, energized by a new
lead. "You want to take him on about this?"

"No, I'll keep looking for the will. Take Shanko.
Keep him out of trouble."

Stafford grimaced and Harry ignored it. Harry
was lead on the case. That was that.

"See Bryson's wife about his alibi. Then I want you
to interview that piece of work across the street, the

O'Malleys. Both Madison and Holly say they're worth a look. Let's check in with each other late afternoon."

"I might stay over with Holly tonight. See if I can get some mandolin practice in."

"You'll be practicing something," Harry said.

"Yeah, well, maybe," Dex said, smiling at the prospect.

⟞⟝ ⟞⟝

Holly, the boss, and Christy, Holly's best friend, talked over the destruction of the shrine while they ate breakfast at Basecamp Café. They'd decided hitting the O'Malleys head on wasn't the way to go. Besides, Stafford had warned Holly the night before to stay out of things. It was hardly the night of hot love Holly had been all wet and squirmy thinking about. In fact the air turned chilly when Holly asked one too many questions about the investigation. Dex turned away from her and was asleep in seconds. He snored.

Christy kicked Holly under the table when she brought up the O'Malley's probable involvement at the shrine. Christy used to date Dwayne, a fact she hated anybody to remind her of.

"Hey, it's a small town. There aren't many choices. Just because you're all hooked up," Christy said defensively.

"He snores," Holly said, pushing her chair out and standing up.

"So what?" Christy made big, wide eyes at her as she stood up. She picked her radio off the table, ready to go. She looked up at Holly, arms akimbo, all 5 foot 2 of her to Holly's 5 foot 10.

Ed eavesdropped on conversation at the next table in the busy café. People were talking about getting out their guns and oiling them to protect themselves, presumably from Don Farrow's murderer. Or had things reached the rumor stage where a serial killer was now roaming through town?

The boss rolled his eyes as he held the door open for Holly and Christy. The atmosphere was humid and still as the three patrol officers left Basecamp—tense, shimmering, the way it was before a thunderstorm hit.

Ed took a call, apparently from the Sheriff's substation. He listened, frowning.

"Gunfire up there at that so-called shrine last night. Those damn women," Ed Bradley said. He gestured to Holly and Christy to walk along the wooden deck with him away from the café.

"Nobody was hit, were they? Please tell me nobody was hit," Holly said fast.

"No, but you know it was one of those wackos doing whatever they're doing up there. You were going to get them out of there. Dammit, Holly."

"Look, let me talk to Betty Anne. Let me find out what happened," Holly said, angry at the stupid escalation of whatever was happening up there.

"Sgt. Madison's already reamed her out. She denied everything. I'm getting pressure from the General Manager to get those women out of there. Do something." He marched away from her, leaving Holly and Christy behind.

"Me? I told you. They don't pay any attention to me. I have no influence."

"Well, you're in with all those animal people," Ed Bradley said, giving the words an edge. "You're the best thing I got and people are getting squirrelly. I want updates on what you're doing to fix this."

He got into his Jeep with a huff, turning back to give her a sour look. Holly took a breath. *All those animal people.*

"Geez, he sounds pissed," Christy observed.

"The council could come down hard on Paws, stop us from picking up loose dogs, and close down the dog park."

"Yeah," Christy agreed. "What are you going to do?"

"Strangle Betty Anne." Holly took the switchbacks which led up and up toward the peaks with the best views of the sun dappled valley. Betty Anne hadn't returned her calls in the last two days. She would look for her at home first.

Betty Anne lined the hallway of the house she and her daughter Chloe shared with her prize-winning quilts. The door was open with only a screen between her and anydamnbody who wanted to shoot her or Chloe in the head and rob them, not that they had much of that up here. Until recently. Holly could hear the whirr of the sewing machine. When it stopped she called out to her. Betty Anne came down the hall, blinking, as if she'd been in another world and opened the door. Her shoulders were tense, her face wary as soon as she saw Holly.

"It wasn't me," she said coloring.

"Betty Anne, you're such a liar. Of course it was you."

"We were drumming, not bothering anybody. And then Pow!" Her voice escalated with crackling energy. "We were defending ourselves."

"From what? Rabbits? Coyotes? Somebody actually fired on you? How could you tell if you were drumming?"

Betty Anne marched through her living room and into the kitchen and Holly followed her. She could smell something sweet baking and hoped she would offer her a piece.

"Somebody snuck up on us. We all heard a shot." Betty Anne poured a cup of coffee and handed her a lumpy mug made during her ceramics phase. Chloe was removing a coffee cake from the oven. Holly set one haunch on a tall stool at the counter and made eyes at the cake.

Chloe turned around and glared at her mother, her blank, round face made up as if she were headed to a rave. Big eyes, way too much glittery blusher, lots of hiked-up cleavage.

"Where do you think you're going, missy?" Betty Anne shouted at her daughter. "If you think you're going out with that loser Boz, you can think again."

"You can't stop me!" Chloe shouted, her mouth a red-rimmed hole of hatefulness.

"Oh, yes, I can." Betty Anne grabbed her daughter by the shoulder and pushed her out of the kitchen. "You get upstairs. You're grounded and you know it."

Chloe struggled out of her grasp and screeched, "Don't touch me."

They were in the hallway now, wrestling, slaps and blows. Screams. Grunts. Holly leaned back on the stool to see them struggling. Chloe tore herself away, bursting out the front door, the screen slapping shut. Big silence.

Holly applied herself to cutting a piece of coffee cake. No sense wasting it. She'd never had fights like that with her mother. Betty Anne pulled herself together and charged back in the kitchen, ready to mix it up with Holly, who pretended she was deaf.

"Gunfire," she said mildly. "See, this is how people get hurt, Betty Anne. C'mon, call it quits with the vigil. Let the deputies figure it out."

"We'll be there until somebody tells us who did it," Betty Anne brayed at her.

"And then what are you going to do? You gonna take it to the Supreme Court? You'll never get anybody to admit it. And then what would you do anyhow?" Holly said. "Somebody shot at you, Betty Anne."

"Oh ratshit, trying to scare us off, that's all. The shots didn't come anywhere near us."

"How can you be sure of that?"

"'Cuz I know what small arms fire sounds like. Course, it scared off the lightweights. I don't think Roger's going to come back. Violence, you know," she said in a mocking sneer. "They don't like *violence*."

"I don't like this either, Betty Anne. Who do you think it was?"

"All the wingnuts have guns up here. You know that."

Right. All the wingnuts. The other wingnuts.

"You know those newspaper people will be up there sniffing around," Holly reminded her.

She blinked and screwed up her mouth. "Yeah, I know. I can handle them. Anyway, I gotta go rally the troops."

"Remember, you're not speaking for anybody but yourself. Don't you dare say anything about Paws."

Unsatisfied, Holly left to go back to the office to calm Ed Bradley down, hoping she wouldn't run into the General Manager or one of the town council people on the way in.

A dark feeling built inside her. Too many things were happening all at once.

CHAPTER SEVENTEEN

Stafford drove up to a recently painted, well-kept house on the other side of Sierra Mountain Village where the road switchbacked up and up. The views across the valley were an eyeful of scenery. Swatches of dead brown trees contrasted with the dark green hillsides. The purple lupines were done now, but the orange blossoms of California poppies danced in the breeze. He walked up the outer stairs of the house and peered through the screen door, which opened into a kitchen and open-plan living room. The sun sparkled off the windows. He saw a solid, handsome, serious-looking woman standing at the sink doing dishes. So this was Skip Bryson's wife, Peach's daughter-in-law.

"Detective Dex Stafford from the Kern County Sheriff's Department. Can I talk to you for a minute?" he called through the screen door.

She looked him over carefully and dried her hands on a tea towel. "Come in. I made coffee. Would you like some?" She gestured to a bar stool which sat at the granite island in the well-appointed kitchen, every large appliance stainless steel. Dex wondered what all these people would do when stainless steel went out of fashion.

"I guess you're here about Don Farrow, are you?"

Dex nodded. Caged birds twittered away somewhere in the house that smelled of toast and coffee.

Long sigh from Arielle Bryson as she sank onto a bar stool opposite him. "I can't tell you anything about his death."

"I just need background," Stafford said easily. "What was he like?"

"Just the sweetest guy. Everybody liked him, you know. What a damn shame. He must have been in the wrong place at the wrong time. Did somebody try to burgle them again? I don't know why they'd think there was any money there. I called Peach when I first heard, but all she could do was cry. I'm going over there later today."

"So how did you know Mr. Farrow?"

"I'm getting a Ph.D. in petroleum engineering, and Don helped me with the advanced statistics for my dissertation. We had these marathon tutoring sessions for me to stuff what I could learn into my head." She went on about his patience. His kindness. So far they hadn't turned up anybody who had a story to tell that took the shine off Don Farrow. "Who do you think killed him?"

Stafford gave nothing back this early in an investigation. "And the last time you saw him?"

"Two weeks ago. I've finished the statistical analysis, thanks to him." Her eyes were the cool blue of lake water. She swished her skirt across long, sturdy thighs.

"Did he ever mention somebody who didn't like him? Enemies? Anything like that?"

"Oh, Don wasn't the kind to have enemies." She thought a moment. "Well, this spring Peach had one of her big fundraisers. There was an awning, caterers, flowers, wine, a jazz combo. She'd invited those troublemaker O'Malleys from across the road. One of her lout sons got drunk and fell over the drum set. My husband and Don went over to tell Beatrice to take him home. There were words."

"Words?"

Arielle Bryson rose off the bar stool. She stood behind it, fingers gone white against the back of the stool. "Two minutes hostilities in a really nice party. Most people didn't even notice."

"You know we check alibis for everyone in an investigation," Stafford said. "When did Mr. Bryson get home Friday evening?"

She thought a minute. "Around 6 or 6:30?"

"He says he came home, had a shower and was in for the night watching TV. Can you confirm that for us?"

Arielle Bryson colored. "That's what he said, is it?" She looked down, smiled, and crumpled up a paper napkin next to a plate with toast crumbs on it. "Skip and I have separate lives." She pointed at the stairs. "He lives down there. We have a lot of issues, namely I can't have children and he wants to spread his seed to improve the gene pool." Now she laughed outright with a chilling timbre. "I heard his car drive up and the shower start up, that's true, around then, but I went out myself. I have a...friend, and Skip has a... friend as well."

"So you can't confirm he was home all night?"

She smiled. "Funny thing is, I thought I heard his car drive off right after that. He parks on the other side of the house so I never really know if he's there or not."

It wasn't the worst story he'd ever heard. One woman had told him her spirit guide could alibi her husband. He got Bryson's wife to repeat it a couple of times, but there was nothing more to shake loose. She had left Skip Bryson hanging by his fingernails on the end of the branch with his neck stuck way, way out.

"Surely you realize this makes us look hard at your husband. Why would he kill Don Farrow?"

"I can't think of any reason, and I know every thought that ever passed through Skip Bryson's empty head." She stood up and Stafford put down his coffee cup and walked with her to the screen door, which she held open for him.

"Did you know your husband borrowed $5000 from Don Farrow earlier this year? And then $12,000 two months ago?"

That seemed to shake her confidence. "No, I didn't."

"Any idea what that was for?"

"Damn him. He gets these crazy business ideas. Like starting a dry cleaner's up here that went broke in three months. Then a café. He either ordered too much and it spoiled, or too little. And he couldn't keep it open consistent hours, so people stopped coming. Besides, he didn't know anything about the restaurant business. Now he wants to move to New York and be an art dealer." She spread her palms wide.

"Art dealer? Really?"

"I know. It's crazy. Oh, Skip has his moments and his uses," she said. "I remember you from Bakersfield High School," she said, looking at him closely. "You were a year ahead of me. I guess which makes you about 32 now?" she said, her head tilted to one side. "I think you dated my friend Pamela Richardson."

The name of Pamela Richardson sent a chilly blast though Dex. "Yeah, I did. You keep up with her?"

Pamela Richardson. He did his level best never to think about her.

"She still talks about you."

Dex was startled. The past comes back to bite you.

"She says she saw you one time in an elevator in the courts building and you didn't even recognize her. Of course, she's gained a lot of weight."

"I didn't see her. Honest. Seems like everybody's gained a lot of weight since high school."

"You didn't gain weight," Arielle observed. "I didn't. You might check with Skip's girlfriend about Friday night. He's often over there." She scribbled down a name and address on a scrap of paper and handed it to him, her face giving nothing away.

"Oh?" Stafford said. He held her eyes for a moment, shook his head and descended the stairs. That would not be an easy woman to live with, he thought, but glad of the new lead. He was glad Pamela hadn't spoken up in the elevator. They had dated seriously for five years and parted, vowing they'd put the width of the country between them. So she was still in Bakersfield. They both were.

Nobody seemed to have a straight-forward love life.

══╬ ╬══

CHAPTER EIGHTEEN

Stafford leaned against his vehicle outside the Bryson residence. He called Price to update him on Skip Bryson's alibi.

"Yeah, I heard from the Sarge here about the girl-friend. Go see her now."

Kat McDonald was an elementary school teacher who lived in the manufactured home section of Sierra Mountain Village. If you could say any part of SMV was the transient part of town, this was it. A lot of rent-ers, hard-luck single mothers, and old people lived in those drafty old mobile homes. Stafford had seen the deputies out there knocking on doors, rousting peo-ple, and making small time drug busts as well.

Tanned and sturdy, Kat McDonald answered the door of a nicely kept place in shorts and a tank top, looking clear-eyed and fresh, smelling of sunscreen lotion. Stafford introduced himself and she cocked her head.

"Cops? What are you doing here?"

"You know about the murder that took place in town this weekend?"

"Sure, everybody in town knows. What's that to do with me?"

She beckoned Stafford into a living area strewn with sports equipment and children's books and toys, turning down the radio playing hard rock oldies. Photos displayed on every dusty surface showed McDonald on mountain tops and floating down rivers.

"We heard you were friends with Skip Bryson." Stafford perched on the edge of a futon, obviously her bed, while she settled on a folding metal chair facing him. "There's been a murder involving…"

Her head bobbed, her pony tail swished. "Yeah, I know. His crazy cat lady mother. Her boyfriend got killed."

"So we're asking around trying to figure out who was where, who was doing what about that time. We try to eliminate people. It would be Friday night we're interested in."

"You're asking me to give Skip an alibi? Is that it? Really? No kidding?" She laughed merrily.

"Yeah, that's it. Did you see him anytime on Friday in the late afternoon to the early evening?"

"Lemme think. Oh boy. See, I have this thing with time, even if I wear a watch. I get to work every day because I have two alarm clocks and my aide calls me in the morning."

"You do remember yesterday, don't you? Let's start from there."

"Sure. I came back from the Sespe Wilderness. Left before dawn on Saturday morning. So Friday night I guess I'd be getting my food and equipment together. Maps, you know. My crew was doing some climbing, so I was likely putting stuff together in the garage."

"And was Skip here?"

"He'd only get in the way. You get distracted and you forget something important."

"So he wasn't here from the late afternoon until early evening?" Stafford insisted.

"No, I don't think so. But I'll have to think about it." She paused. "Yeah, maybe for a while, but I was busy and I told him to take off."

"When was this?"

She screwed her face up to indicate deep thought. "I just don't remember."

How could people get through life like this, Stafford wondered.

"People think you're more than friends," Stafford said, hoping she wasn't going to be coy.

"People." Her face went still. "And who would that be?"

"His wife for one. She gave us your name and address."

"I know Arielle. So Skip, huh? You heard of fuck buddies? Friends with benefits?"

"Yeah, I know what you mean," Dex said, nodding. The idea and its practice wasn't new to him. Why couldn't all women be this tolerant?

"That's me and Skip. I don't want him, and Arielle knows that. She's got her boyfriend anyway. But Skip's always ready to backpack, hike, do a run, hit the sack—whatever I want. I don't want to put time into some big romance. So why have I got a cop here asking about him? You think he did it?"

"Like I said, we check everybody's alibi."

She was all sunny good health, beaming. "Hey, would it be better for him if I said he was here?"

"Why? You want to change your story?" Some alibi this would be if this went to court.

"Nah. Skip can take care of himself."

Harry wanted Stafford to meet him at the O'Malley's place, the people across the road from Paws who said they'd seen somebody running away at the time of the murder. Stafford left Skip Bryson's girlfriend's home and made his way up the sagging, unpainted steps of the O'Malley's two-story redwood siding house. In Sierra Mountain Village a weathered cabin could sit next to a well-kept show home. The lots were small and someone could trespass by yawning and stretch his arms into a neighboring lot. Judged by any standard, the O'Malley place showed indifference to what the neighbors thought. A washing machine sat on the front deck, along with empty cardboard boxes and a bucket filled with rakes and shovels. Two old junkers were parked on the street, another up on blocks in the dirt yard to the side of the house.

Stafford knocked on the door and was greeted by Beatrice O'Malley in another fashion triumph of black leggings and a short gauzy top that revealed a watermelon-sized stomach.

"Oh yeah, you. C'mon in. The other guy is talking to my husband."

Dex stepped inside. The place was chaos with the lid ripped off. Before his senses had time to take it all in, another big-bellied apparition shambled into the living space behind his mother wearing sweatpant bottoms and a stretched out T-shirt. The apparition was none too clean, bare-footed, unshaven, and bleating about coffee.

His mother said unsympathetically. "This is my son Dwayne. Here's the police come to wake you up so you don't lie in bed all day and hurt your back."

She jerked her head at Dex to follow her into the kitchen. Stafford ducked under the low ceilings and held his arms close to his sides to avoid touching anything. He stepped around a curl of dog shit on the shag rug. Penned-up dogs were barking from behind closed doors. The smell of dogs overcame the ammonia reek of cat piss. Beatrice pulled out a set of dentures from the pocket of her sweatpants and jammed them in her mouth, the better to articulate her malice and hostility. A smell of stale cigarettes, male sweat, and something unnamable emanated from piles of dirty laundry in the corner of the room. Dex hoped he didn't have to search the house. He wouldn't even take a shit in this place. Harry Price glowered at him from where he leaned against the kitchen sink filled with dishes. Apparently Harry didn't want to sit down either.

"Mrs. O'Malley signed her statement saying she saw a Latino workman running away and getting into a green truck and driving away around the time of Mr. Farrow's murder. No license plate," Price said, looking at his notes.

"Can anybody else confirm that?" Stafford said to the O'Malley parents who sat at the table. The apparition had found its way to the coffeepot where another lout of about the same age sat on top of the washing machine in the corner of the kitchen, round-eyed and jaw agape. This must be Dwayne's brother Leroy.

Leroy had a big chin, long bangs, and hair draping his shoulders. Somebody who looked as if he'd lost a few fights, as his nose wasn't quite on straight. An Old Testament beard that straggled down into his collar covered the rest of his face.

Beatrice O'Malley started talking again, taking her story from the top. "So like I was telling you...."

Stafford held up a hand to stop her and signal Harry he had a lead he wanted to explore. The spotlight had swung away from Beatrice and she didn't like it.

"I heard a story about words being exchanged between one of you." Stafford waved a finger like a windshield wiper between the two scions of the family, "and Don Farrow at a party across the road this summer. Which one of you was it?"

"Not me, not me," both of them said at the same time.

"Don't you even dare think one of my boys had anything to do with a murder. They're good boys."

Sgt. Madison came into the kitchen, his hands on his duty belt, scoffing. "Dwayne and Leroy here are boy scouts," Bill Madison said, "but I can print out a sheet here, Mama O'Malley, of all the trouble they've been in..."

"Juvenile, all juvenile," Beatrice O'Malley shrieked, launching herself across the room at him. The O'Malleys were on their feet now, howling out their innocence.

"I smell dope on you so don't give me attitude." Stafford got close to the older son, Dwayne. "Think I should toss your room? I could cuff you up tight and ride you down to Bakersfield in the back of my car. Or you can answer questions. What's it to be?"

Mama O'Malley was shouting again. The dogs behind the closed doors set up a cacophony of yipping and barking.

Price hollered above it all. "Enough. Enough craziness. I want all of you down at the substation in Frazier Oaks at 9 a.m. tomorrow morning. We talk to you one at a time. You hear me? No excuses. You be there."

Price held up a hand, palm out, to prevent Beatrice O'Malley from coming any closer.

"Understand?" he said, leaning toward her.

"Fuck you, cop," she said back, baring long yellow teeth. "I know my rights."

CHAPTER NINETEEN

Sgt. Madison joined Price and Stafford outside as they stood talking by the county vehicles parked along the road in front of the O'Malley house.

"Beatrice hates Peach Bryson because she won't hire her kids—and for damn good reason. I wouldn't let that pair near anything I wanted to keep," Madison said.

"Maybe she asked Don for money and he said no and she had another fit of temper," Stafford suggested.

"Could be. Could be," Harry said. "Let's bump her up to person of interest. Nothing from the other neighbors, though. Nobody saw her sneaking across the road about the right time." Harry scratched his bald spot and took a long pull at a cup of cold coffee from Basecamp.

"Not a lot of neighbors to see anything. Most of these houses are vacant—second homes. She's the one who saw a Mexican worker running away."

"And you only have her son Leroy's word to back her up, you notice?" Madison said.

"Yeah, I noticed. Still, it was around the right time, past quitting time for the day worker crew. We haven't been able to pin down when they left. Or find them."

"I interviewed Skip Bryson's wife, and she didn't exactly confirm his alibi," Stafford said, hitching at the body armor he wore under his shirt. Department regulations.

Madison snorted. "No love lost between those two, I hear."

"We need to confront Bryson again about the first husband," Harry said.

"I'll leave you to it," Madison said, heading toward his vehicle. "I have to live here and I like Mrs. Bryson. A lot of nice people live here, you know. They're not all like her."

"Yeah, but I don't get to meet them."

"Stick around with Holly then."

Stafford and Price had run Peach Bryson's financials and had them ready, along with a series of questions for her.

"Who do you think tossed Farrow's place?" Dex asked Harry as they walked across the road to Paws.

"Whoever was looking for something," Harry said, twisting the paper off a cough drop. "We don't know if they took anything. How you gonna tell in that mess?"

"Maybe we can get Peach over there and ask her to take a look around," Dex said.

"So it's *Peach*, is it? You've got a personal connection to this place and that ain't good, Stafford."

"I know that," Stafford snapped back.

"Maybe it was the local vandal Holly's been chasing," Stafford said.

"Happened once Peach shot somebody. Maybe she wanted Farrow out of the way too," Harry said, as they mounted the steps and knocked on the kitchen door of Paws. Wafting through the door came the warm scent of cinnamon and brown sugar.

"Why? I don't see any motive. Do you?" Stafford said, tamping down his feelings of empathy for a suspect he knew and liked.

Peach opened the door wearing a turquoise shift over a long gauzy shirt. She took in their faces with a glance and motioned them towards the kitchen table. This morning Stafford noticed the cat quilts, the cat curtains, the cat plates on the crown molding around the kitchen, the sparkling surfaces and clean smell.

"You found out, didn't you?" she said, weariness making her shoulders sag.

Price acknowledged this with a nod. "Of course, we did, Ms. Bryson."

"I was going to tell you last night but I was too tired to go through it all again."

"Why don't you sit down and tell us about it now," Price said, leading the interview.

She held a struggling Siamese cat in her arms. "Sometimes it seems like a horrible dream. Where do I even start? Benny—my husband—and I weren't getting along all that well, and his parents knew it. When it happened, they hoped I'd go to jail and they'd get the children away from me."

"So what happened?" Price said, leaning into her personal space. He pushed away an orange cat trying to climb his leg.

"Can't you read about it? There must be records you can look at." She looked back and forth between hard faces. The fridge ticked on beside them. "Okay then. Benny stayed out late a lot of times and came home drunk. Remember that Jack Nicholson movie where he's saying, "Honey, I'm home." You know the one in the big hotel in winter?"

Price nodded.

"He thought that was really funny so he always said it when he came in late, but this time he didn't. Maria, she was my housekeeper, my nanny, at the time. The noise downstairs woke her up too. I met her in the hallway outside Skip's room. We were both scared. Skip was crying. He was only six at the time. We hear this crashing around downstairs, glass breaking, and it didn't sound like Benny. He was always a happy drunk. We heard people talking, more than one person, and I thought he brought somebody home, but then there was shouting. You think about it later and wonder how both Maria and I could make a mistake like that, but we did. I ran back and got Benny's gun and called 911 and Maria got Marcy, my daughter, and we barricaded ourselves with the kids in Skippy's room."

Her eyes fluttered to the ceiling with the effort of recall. Her hands worked in her lap, washing each other. "We thought it was a home invasion like what had happened to the McGregors down the street. We heard somebody coming up the stairs and all the shouting downstairs was still so loud. The only thing I knew about guns was that the bullet came out the front end. My hands were shaking so hard we decided Maria had to fire the gun. But she dropped it. Then these people were crashing up against the bedroom door and I thought I was protecting the children. So I fired the gun at the door."

Long silence. "And it killed him?"

"Yes. It was the first and last time in my life I fired a gun. We didn't know all the noise downstairs was only my husband. When the police came, we were still barricaded inside the room. Maria and I didn't want to open the door even then. One of our neighbors had to come up the stairs and tell us it was really the police. Then I saw Benny lying on the floor in the hall. And so did Skip. And he's never forgiven me for killing his father." She twisted her hands together and put them between her thighs, leaning forward. "But this has nothing to do with Don."

She put her head in her hands. "I never loved any-body as much as I loved Don, even my awful children." Tears streamed down her face. "I thought I'd go to my grave without ever knowing the love of my life and now Don is dead."

"And who were the other people downstairs," Harry asked, unconvinced.

"It was just some cop show with a lot of scream-ing and yelling. I guess Benny turned on the TV for company when he got home because I was no fun anymore. TV—that was all it was. But how were we to know that?"

"Did you kill Mr. Farrow?" Harry asked.

"Of course I didn't kill him," she said, standing up suddenly as though the chair were confining her. "How could I have done that?"

Personally, Dex didn't think she had. Too much registered as genuine, not that he could spot a liar with 100% confidence the way Shanko bragged he could.

Other questions needed to be asked. Price let the silence cook and then asked, "You made a withdrawal of $10,000 cash a few weeks ago. What was that for?"

The question rattled her. Peach Bryson smoothed her hair and looked at the ceiling. Her face went tense, prepared. "I don't remember now. A payment to a vendor?"

"In cash? You're not still carrying around $10,000 in cash in your purse, are you?"

She looked away. "No, of course not."

"Mrs. Bryson, in a case like this we turn people's lives inside out." Stafford reached in a folder and pulled out a sheaf of printouts from her different bank accounts. "You do the books yourself?"

"No, I pay someone for that." She mentioned the name of a local bookkeeper.

"Care to call her up and get her to tell you where that $10,000 went? We're interested in that."

"Well, of course, I could. Do you mean now?" Her eyes went wary. "She's on vacation for a couple of weeks in the back country and she didn't take her phone. Why?"

"See, you do a lot of online banking, payments, payroll, transactions like that. But this was in cash. Now why would that be in cash?"

"I just don't remember," she said, her face sinking into the silk scarf she wore around her throat.

"You buy it," Price said, standing outside in the parking lot, his hand on the roof of the vehicle, a wide smile on his face. "I can tell by looking at you. You've gone soft, Stafford. A nice old lady tells you a story and you fall into it, hook, line, and sinker."

"Not yet, I haven't," Stafford said, turning red and sputtering in denial.

"Be careful, your nose is growing, Pinocchio. You believe her. I can see it."

"This is the first case I've worked where I had a personal connection," Dex admitted.

"Maybe you should let Shanko take over from here," Harry said.

"You want to work with him?" Dex was teasing. He knew how Harry felt about Shanko. His sniffing every ten seconds drove Harry crazy.

Harry made a disgusted sound. "Okay, Stafford, watch yourself. Let's hope there's no $10,000 slime trail to a hitman. We should have taken her down to the station and sweated her, but it's too damn far and the drive only wastes time. See whether she lawyered up."

"She'd only be smart to lawyer up. You know that. She does too. So we get the financials for both her and Farrow and his will and figure out who gets what. If he left her everything, I'm not going to be nearly so nice to that sweet old girl," Stafford swore. "Let's find out if the son has military background or martial arts training. We know the hoodie is probably his."

"Yeah, we know for sure, do we? Get going," Price said. "We hit him when the time is right."

The day ended eventually and Stafford needed sleep. Holly was working. His mother had left nicely folded and pressed shirts on his bed. Her Persian cat was sleeping on top of them. Couldn't she remember to close the door? Couldn't she do anything for him?

⏵⏴

CHAPTER TWENTY

A call came in to patrol complaining about loud music. Usually at night Sierra Mountain Village was pretty quiet. Nothing going on, so both Pete and Holly showed up on the call. Holly arrived, driving in from the west on Siskin Drive. Holly came from the east, parking nose to nose across from one of the town's two apartment buildings facing the park.

"Hey, isn't this where Mike Jarvis lives?" Holly said, holding her Maglite high in her left hand as she mounted the stairs. Pete was behind her, doubtless checking out her ass.

"Yeah," Pete said, looking around.

They could hear loud metalhead music. "Rock on, my friend." She expected to see long hair, a studded leather belt, and a Mastodon T-shirt. She didn't think it would be Mike, the cremation guy, Brenda's boyfriend. And it wasn't.

Boz Jarvis, his grandson, came out to the gate. From the front door wafted a haze of pot smoke, curling high into the night air. Pete and Holly were at the bottom of a landing looking up at Boz. Since her injury Holly hated looking up at somebody higher than she was. Inside she went dead still.

"You bring the pizza?" Boz said with a smirk. Chloe came out on the deck with him, tonight a pouty-faced little Pop-Tart hugging a pillow across her chest.

"Hi, Chloe." Holly waved. She kept her voice under tight control even though a trickle of sweat inched down from her armpit. Pete was backing her up. He was right behind her.

"Sir, we've had a complaint from the neighbors about loud music. You need to turn that down."

Holly heard something behind her and swiveled around. Leroy O'Malley stood at the bottom of the stairs boxing her in.

Pete had left and was strolling back to his Jeep. Boz smirked down at her from above. Adrenaline spike.

"Hey, Pete," Holly called after him, hearing her voice gone tight and scared. "I need you here."

Pete looked at her over his shoulder, grinned, and kept walking.

"Dude," Leroy said, taking a step closer into her space. She could smell him. He exuded a sense of menace from somewhere behind his Old Testament beard.

"Hello, Leroy," she said, forcing a smile, her back touching the wall. "You joining the party?"

Night. Darkness. A banger on the steps above. Muzzle flash and the bullet entering her shoulder, burning like a white-hot fireplace poker. Holly gripped herself tight. Don't let them smell fear.

"Hey, keep the music down, will'ya?" she growled and shoved past Leroy, hoping he wouldn't see her white face and trembling hands.

She headed to the patrol Jeep parked on the side of the road. Pete was already rounding the corner down by the fire station. The PTSD emerged from a part of her brain that she didn't yet have under control.

When she got home she called Dex, the cats twining around her. Leave a message. She thought of calling his mother's number, but she didn't want it to look as if she were checking up on him. All she wanted was to hear his voice and talk about the pressure at work, about the shrine. If the moment seemed right, she'd tell him about Pete and losing her nerve. But probably not. She didn't expect him to do anything. Or tell her anything about the investigation, although that would be nice. She only wanted to talk to him.

She stumbled up the stairs to share her bed with the blind calico, the three-legged Siamese, and four old tuxedos. Not the hot-bodied detective. But still, the sex, the lovely sex when they did get together. The kisses made her toes curl up and her nipples hard. Could be another long, stony patch of doing without. She also plain liked him.

The Deputy DA conferring with them on this case was a Dudley Do-Right Stafford disliked but had to respect. Price and Stafford took their turn at the end of a line of supplicants. The Sarge sat in on the session with the DDA where Price outlined their case, the evidence thus far, the time line, their theory the killer might have had military or martial arts training. They hadn't yet chased down the will. The DDA lifted his eyebrow at that. Their suspects were a sweet old lady who had once been arrested for murdering her husband, her volatile son, and the riffraff neighbors across the street. Witnesses were iffy.

The DDA explained the law in English and didn't run his mouth going off on tangents about what mighta or coulda. If you wanted a warrant, the dots had to connect: no fishing expeditions to find evidence to prop up a weak case. They respected him for it and also hated him a bit too, him in his Brooks Brothers suits and good haircuts.

He and Price knew they didn't have anything to hold Peach Bryson on, other than she had been the last person with the victim and was the person reporting the body. She couldn't give an explanation for the $10,000 nor could they find a trail from it leading anywhere.

"I got work to do," the DDA said, rising and leaving Harry, Dex and the Sarge looking at each other. "Let me know when you've got a case."

Dex gazed at the ceiling as he left the room, hoping to find words of encouragement written there.

"So look," the Sarge said, "take it from the top what you do have."

Stafford jumped up and went to the whiteboard. Persons of interest: Peach Bryson, Skip Bryson and the blood-stained hoodie, O'Malleys (weak). Andrea Posner and her eight siblings (weak). Leads: Latino seen running away by the O'Malleys, the parolee who worked at the cattery, the male talking with Don Farrow heard by Peach Bryson. Figure out who had tossed Don Farrow's cabin and what he was looking for. Peach Bryson's $10,000 withdrawal she'd gone skittish about explaining. Find somebody in the mix who knew how to use a knife. Nothing damning yet from forensics. Interview the ex-wife.

It wasn't a lot, but this wasn't television.

"You need to figure out Farrow's affairs and find out who he left his money to," the Sarge said, tapping his fist against his chin, studying the board. "Work it from there. Get on it. You know what to do."

Holly knew it was useless to say anything to Pete directly. But if she couldn't trust him to back her up, that meant trouble. Instead she called the boss outside to have a talk. She and Ed Bradley walked around the side of the town hall and sat on a boulder in the sunshine next to the pool filled with bobbing old ladies in a water aerobics class shrieking their heads off.

Ed looked apprehensive. "What's this about?"

Holly explained about the call but found a defensive edge had crept into her voice. "Pete. He left me, drove off..." she spluttered.

Ed Bradley took a good look at her. "So did you feel you were in imminent danger?"

"Well, not exactly..." Not even Christy, her best friend, knew how she seized up in the darkness with someone looking down at her from above.

"Did they threaten you?"

"Well, no, but the vibe was ugly...." That sounded feeble.

Ed didn't say anything, just looked at her until she looked away. "Pete mentioned he left because he saw a coyote near the volleyball court round about that time and took off after it."

"That's bullshit."

"Is this something personal between you and Pete?"

"No!"

"You sure?"

"I'm sure."

Ed stood up. "He thought you had it handled. Sounds to me like you did."

"Chasing a coyote. That's real useful." Holly was left with nothing to say except the truth about the old PTSD thing. "The O'Malleys and this Boz kid have something going. I know it."

Ed now thought she had it in for Pete. She didn't mention he gave her the creeps the way he looked at her. Ick. Ick. Ick. That sounded weak and foolish. She would manage that on her own, the way every woman did.

"You think they're the vandals then, the ones who brought down the shrine thing?" he said, peering at her from under bushy eyebrows.

"Yes. That's exactly what I think."

"Then bring me some proof. Your pals, the Sheriffs deps, they're too busy. Get me something."

Stafford worked on tracing the time line of Don Farrow's movements in the week before his murder. He headed out from the station listening to an Earl Scruggs CD played loud. Farrow's credit card trail led to Mimi's, a French-themed restaurant in Bakersfield. He pushed through the door and asked for the manager. The big-bellied man with the roseate nose of a drinker beckoned to the hostess, a slight, black-suited waif with a small triangular face. Smiling, she drifted across the busy restaurant towards him and took his card.

"I was on vacation last week. Ask Jilly here." The manager made the introduction and chugged off to reprimand a bus boy.

"Ooooh, a detective," Jilly Peters squealed. "I'm innocent. Honestly I am. This is so exciting."

"Yeah, a detective on a mission. Can we sit down for a minute?"

"Oh, anything I can do." She swayed across the room ahead of him to an empty table.

Stafford pegged her as a badge bunny. He put his strictly business face on as they sat down. He pushed a photo of Don Farrow across the table. She made a business of fingering it with long turquoise acrylic nails. Then she leaned forward, squishing the cleavage she kept on show and framed her face in her hands.

"Your job must be so exciting!" Jilly Peters trilled, wiggling in the high-backed booth.

Stafford leaned back. "Like yours. Routine 95% of the time. Mostly I write reports."

"Tell me what it's really like."

"What it's like?" he said. He tapped the photo of Don Farrow. "I need to know if you've seen this man and then I have to do 19 other things before I get to go home tonight. So if you could take a real good look…"

"I've seen him. Let me think a minute." Instead she re-examined Stafford's business card. "Dexter. That's an unusual name. Maybe you're a serial killer." All flirty now.

"When did you see him?" He sharpened his tone.

"Last week? You're rushing me." She fingered the edge of the silky shell worn under her black jacket to draw attention to her breasts. Stafford wasn't looking.

"Was he with anyone? Anything else you remember?"

She thought a long minute looking at him. "I think it was a party of two…No, I can't remember," she said finally.

He stood up. "Okay, I think I'll show it around to the wait staff. Thanks for your time."

"Oh really? Well, here's my card," she said, tucking it into his hand. "Call me." Then she flounced away looking fetchingly over her shoulder at him back to her podium and the lineup of patrons who had gathered.

Stafford buttonholed the manager again who took him around to the other workers in the restaurant. Nobody recognized Farrow in the photograph.

The hardware store where Farrow had bought a can of rust remover and furnace filters was a bust too. He relayed the news to Harry Price who shared the news of the autopsy, which confirmed everything the death investigator surmised and added nothing new. Three upward thrusts from a much taller assailant: the height determined from the angle of penetration and the blood spatter patterns. Bruises across the throat from the sleeper hold to render the victim unconscious. Done with considerable strength.

"So that makes the spotlight dim on Peach. And likely Farrow went down fast," Stafford concluded, pressing his cellphone tightly to his ear. "We already know he had no defensive wounds."

"Yeah," Harry interrupted, "but your killer would be covered in blood. It was twilight when he—or she—left the scene. And nobody saw him. How did he get away?"

"Harry, let me stop you right there. Me and the deputies covered that street twice to both ends of the road and the turnoff. No cars parked on the side. Nobody running. Nobody saw anything, 'cept the Mexican guy Mama O'Malley reported."

"Yeah. Look, I got another call. You coming back to the barn? Meet me for lunch."

The questions ping ponged around in Stafford's mind while he drove back to the station, making phone calls to shove ahead another case. Nobody so far had a motive to kill Don Farrow, which didn't make sense because knifing the old man took effort, plus the willingness to get in real close and nasty to finish the job.

Skip Bryson? By all accounts he resented any expenditure reducing the size of his inheritance, or turning off the spigot of money that ran freely from his mother. But Farrow had been lending (or giving) him money too. Why shut that off?

CHAPTER TWENTY-ONE

Skip Bryson had indeed been at the Tough Mudder event down at the foot of the Grapevine Pass as verified by the organizers. Bryson looked right for the crime, though he had a clean record. No calls to the house for domestic abuse. Martial arts training wasn't the kind of thing that showed up in a backgrounder. They'd have to dig for that.

Don had a rotary phone on the wall at his home in Taft and a prepaid cell phone that basically made and received calls. The cell phone hadn't been found, which closed off a promising line of inquiry. Stafford made a note to interview the ex-wife who also lived in Taft.

Stafford pulled into the parking lot at the station at shift change, personal vehicles coming and going, his mind still buzzing. He breezed inside to hit the vending machines. A Coke tumbling into the slot at the bottom of the machine would keep the buzz going.

He stood in front of the whiteboard in the squad room a moment to look for his case numbers. Forensics might have posted something in his absence. Nothing.

"You check Farrow's phone numbers, Stafford?" Harry Price said, leaning back in his chair to look at him around the edge of his cubicle.

Stafford was miles away, still thinking about Skip Bryson. He skidded over his office chair beside Price. "Yeah, they're all people Ms. Bryson identified as friends or business people."

"Since we're looking for a will, maybe Farrow asked one of those people for a referral to a lawyer to set it up for him." Price said. "Maybe you should call them all back and ask."

Stafford groaned. "Aw, Harry. Don't do this to me. Give it to Shanko. You saw the board this morning. We got other dead bodies and the Sarge is already getting antsy. Remember Peach said Farrow had taken a trip to LA and to Santa Clarita in the week preceding. He could have contacted a lawyer anywhere in the LA area."

"Which means thousands of possibilities," Price agreed. "Nothing's come in his mail yet either. And he's got no email setting up an appointment with an attorney in the week before he died."

The Sarge insisted they push their case on Peach Bryson. She had means — what was that ten thousand in cash for? And opportunity. But the county's district attorney didn't like to file any case he wasn't sure he'd win. The DDA they consulted reminded them it would be hard to make a case in court with a sympathetic perpetrator like Peach Bryson. Even one who had accidentally shot her husband long ago. So the move to file charges on Peach Bryson was slowly collapsing. Which left them what? The runaway Latino in the green truck?

The man arguing with Farrow? Skip Bryson? The O'Malleys?

Who else?

⟞⟊⟊⟝

Ed Bradley, Holly's boss, called her into the General Manager's office. Pete watched her go in, a smirk on his face she'd like to punch right into his skull.

Tall, skinny, and a nail biter, Van Doren was the first competent General Manger the town had kept in a while. He ushered her into his knotty pine office and swung into his executive chair behind his desk. She and Ed Bradley took seats across from him. No chitchat.

"Look, this thing with those women is a nightmare. It's got to stop."

"I'm trying," Holly protested. "People really care about the shrine—and I know about the gunfire last night. I talked to Betty Anne Armbruster this morning and she says someone shot at them first. She says she fired into the air." Holly knew how her face got red and all her emotions showed when her heart started going *whump, whump, whump.*

"I really haven't any idea who could have shot at them. I really don't," she said, trying to keep her hands still. "She insists it happened, but she couldn't produce any shell casings. Did the deputies back her up?"

He didn't answer her question. "This is a nightmare. It's a nightmare and I want it gone. You have influence over these women," the GM said, leaning forward. "Can't you tell them this is hurting the community?"

Holly shook her head. "I've lectured Betty Anne, especially about the gun stuff. You know how these gun nut people get. The deputies, Sgt. Madison, are the ones with the power. Can't they....?

Ed Bradley interrupted her. "They say Betty Anne denies she has a weapon."

"But she posts her pictures all over Facebook..." Holly spluttered. "I've seen the gun. That's ridiculous."

"She says she borrows guns for the photos."

"Nobody's going to believe that," Holly said, her voice rising.

"Right. That's why they're running a search warrant search on her house right now."

Holly drew in a breath, realizing she'd narrowly missed being there. She shot a glance at Ed, who knew how pig-headed Betty Anne was. "But what can I do about it?"

He lifted his eyebrows and shrugged.

"*I'm* supposed to get control of this? With what? Logic isn't going to work. I can't make bricks without straw. You can't send me up there to drag them down off the mountain when the Sheriff's guys and the Forest Service have already tried."

She looked at the GM. He gave her a flat-eyed stare.

"A nightmare," he said. "It's a nightmare."

The sun arced over the mountains to the east, dappling the tips of the pines golden. Holly drove around the loop in the center of town and parked near Basecamp. She peered into the windows of the internet café, which shared space with a realty office. Best coffee in town and fresh cookies. She knew a lot of people in town but not everybody. A shifting population of new home buyers discovered they hated the cold, and the cabin with the spectacular view they bought in August was costly to heat and the winter storms shut down the roads. So they sold and somebody new bought it.

Billie's bright smile of welcome had gone tight. Usually she and Holly had a chat about what was happening at Basecamp: open mic, storytelling, little theater, or a plain old salacious piece of gossip. Not today. As Holly passed through the tables in uniform she caught snippets of conversation. *Murdered. That cat place...First husband...killer.*

People she knew swiveled around to look at her. Oh, that's right. Security patrol was supposed to do something, no matter what the problem was. The atmosphere in the small space was oppressive. Thick and blaming. Lock your doors. Don't let your kids walk to the bus stop. This morning parents drove them, car engines running as though they might need to make a speedy getaway with their kid. A table of six was listening as a man Holly didn't know explained the irrefutable evidence of witchcraft and shapeshifting, linking it to the shrine. Incredibly, people Holly knew to be sensible and thoughtful were nodding.

She got her coffee, winked at Billie, and got out fast.

The cremation guy's grandson Boz leaned into the passenger window of a town Jeep talking to Pete, along with that creepoid Leroy O'Malley with his mullet and Old Testament beard. Holly pulled up alongside, her Jeep facing Pete's, suspicious of all of them. Pete didn't have the social skills for a patrol job. Their only weapon, except for pepper spray and a baton, was their calming line of chat. They were only supposed to use those weapons if they were bleeding out and lying there dying. And not on people. Liability rules the world.

"So wassup, Pete?" Holly said lightly, tapping her finger on the steering wheel.

Pete gunned the Jeep and shot past her with a scowl. Boz got into Leroy O'Malley's old Corolla and slammed the door, ignoring her. Mike thought he had removed this kid from bad influences? Holly got her phone out when she got back to Town Hall. For the hell of it, she sent a Facebook friend request to Boz Jarvis, Chloe Armbruster, and the O'Malleys. They all friended her back.

Idiots. Now she could see their posts, if they were dumb enough to brag about what they were up to.

On her lunch break she drove over to Paws, which was a sanctuary for her as well as the cats. She couldn't say or do much to help Peach feel better, but she could try. Peach was in the kitchen, vaccinating a litter of calico kittens, combining the two formulations and injecting it into the scruff of the neck. The kittens looked about six weeks old—darling fluff balls, their eyes beginning to open.

Peach looked haggard, every year of her seventh decade. She looked up at Holly when she came in and handed her a kitten. Holly baby talked to the tiny creature at arm's length, and then pulled him in close to fill her nose with the clean baby smell of a new animal.

"Did they tell you yet?" Peach said, standing straight as if she expected a blow.

"Tell me what?"

"That I killed my husband?"

Holly sank down into a chair, still holding the kitten. "What? I'm confused. Are you kidding me? Did you and Don get married? You killed him? I don't believe it."

"I thought everybody would know by now," Peach said, bitterness in every line of her face.

"No. What's this about?" This blasted the news of Betty Anne and the shrine out of her head. She put the kitten back in a box with the mama and grabbed a skinny old cat with a four- inch tail, which Peach allowed to live inside the house. Peach then told her this bizarre story of shooting her husband by mistake through the bedroom door.

"But you were never arrested? Charged? The case never went to trial, did it?"

"No, it was an accident but they put me through eight months of hell." She slid a mug emblazoned with the Paws logo in front of Holly who reached for the cream and sugar.

"This must have been a long time ago, though, wasn't it?"

"Sure. But everybody in Beverly Hills knew. Do you know how hard it was to establish myself in real estate after that? I worked, Holly, I learned how to work and

I built all of this by myself. I didn't kill Don. I didn't. I didn't. I loved him." Tears spilled down her cheeks.

Holly got up and went around the table to hug Peach, pulling her forward in a close embrace, smelling baby powder and hair spray.

"Pretty soon it will be in the local paper and everyone will know. All the volunteers will desert us," Peach wailed. "My daughter will say she's being disgraced all over again. Nobody will want to come here." She gulped, then sobbed hard. "And all my work for the cats will go for nothing."

Holly didn't know what to say. Maybe it was true. People were weird. She thought of the public shaming of speeders that flashed around the community Facebook groups. Or the vilification of some guy who cheated on the cords of wood he sold. The woman who pushed a lifeguard into the pool for disciplining her child.

"Listen, Peach, listen to me," Holly said. She waited until Peach looked up at her, tears running down her face. "None of this may happen. If they had anything on you about killing Don they would have charged you by now."

"They think because I was the last person to see him that I..."

"You weren't the last person to see him. The guy who killed him was. Everybody in town loves you. Look at what you've done. There's nobody down at the store giving away boxes of kittens anymore. You're giving away free kibble to people who have trouble feeding their kids. The kill rate's gone down at the Bakersfield shelter because of you. And maybe the editor won't print all that old stuff..."

"You think?" Peach said, her face full of hope.

"Anybody says anything around me and I'll bite their nose off, Peach," Holly said, a hoarse fierceness in her tone. "Why don't you pull in one of your rich actor friends to come up for a photo op? Maybe as a memorial to Don and his contribution to Paws?"

"Isn't it too soon after Don's death? I couldn't do that."

"Not a party. Maybe a celebrity to show support and adopt a few kittens. It would get your name and Don's in the paper in a positive way. We can think up an angle. We've got to try. And I gotta go back to work soon." Holly coaxed Peach along until she saw the old spark flicker into life.

Peach started making calls and persuaded one of the bright stars in the Hollywood firmament to do an event. Things were falling into place. Nobody could resist a celebrity. The paper would turn out.

She hoped.

CHAPTER TWENTY-TWO

Holly caught up to Stafford at the substation later on Monday when she drove down to Frazier Oaks to make the bank deposit. He came out the side door into the chain-linked parking lot filled with county vehicles.

"You look really discouraged," she said, sliding the window of the Jeep down. "Why don't you spend the night at my place and we'll work out some frustrations?"

"The Sarge wants an update at 4:30 today back at the station. You could drive down and spend the night at my place," Stafford said, giving her a wiggle of his eyebrows.

"With your mother in the next bedroom."

"She and my Dad are house-hunting. Honestly. As soon as they buy something we can dance naked at my place."

"As soon as…" she repeated. "Heard that one before. Why don't you ask her straight out, give her a deadline? They sure look like they have the money for her to move somewhere else."

"I can't do that." He looked away.

"Why not?"

"I just can't."

Hmmmph, she thought to herself. Interesting.

Stafford's next stop: the Paws thrift shop in Sierra Mountain Village. The manager, Doreen Stills, stood at a glass counter at the front of the store demonstrating some electrical gizmo to a customer wearing overalls, a metalhead T-shirt and flip flops. She smiled at Stafford as though she knew who he was.

"So, okay Red, here it is. You want it, it's yours for $5. I'm not gonna haggle anymore."

"C'mon outside," Doreen beckoned to Stafford. She led him out into the vacant lot behind the store littered with broken down furniture and black plastic bags filled with donations nobody had sorted through yet. She surveyed the mess, hands on the hips of her cutoff jeans, then looked at Stafford.

"You guys find out anything about Mr. Farrow, like who killed him? I sure liked him. And I wasn't there at the cattery on Friday, so I don't really know anything," she said holding her hands up, palms out. She kicked a cardboard box filled with kid's toys away and sat down on a milk crate, pushing one over for him to sit on.

"I know that. I wanted to ask you about Skip Bryson. Ms. Viglen says you have trouble with him."

Doreen's demeanor changed from cooperative to wary. She lifted one flap of a cardboard box with her sandal, then leaned forward to look inside. "You know Skip, right? As soon as Peach and Don left last week, he started throwing his weight around here at the store. I guess it was the day poor Don died. He picked a fight with me right in front of customers and the volunteers about the mess out here in back, and yelled at me that I was fired. Brenda screams right back at him, but I didn't want any more of a scene than we already had going. Tell you the truth, he scares me. I had an abusive husband, and I don't like men screaming at me."

She nipped at the chipped polish on her fingernails. "I told the volunteers to go home. We would straighten this out when Peach got back. I hate to leave without cashing out and locking up, but he's way too ugly for me to deal with. When I left, Skip was still there at the front desk going through my things. I drove by the store later and he'd put a sign on the door saying *Closed until Further Notice.*" She got up and paced around, pushing kid's car seats into a neat pile.

"Is he the boss when Ms. Bryson is away?" Stafford asked, checking out a stack of old tires.

"No. He's always interfering. He thinks we sell too cheap but I know our customers and he doesn't. He's got it in his head I steal from the cash register, that I take all the best donations home and sell them on Etsy and EBay."

"Any truth in that?"

Doreen's eyebrows shot up. "Why would I be living hand to mouth if I had all the money he claims I steal?"

"So when Peach and Mr. Farrow got back from their trip, you told Peach?"

"Sure I did, and she told me Skip has no authority over me. She told me I should open up the next day like usual and she would deal with him. So I did. It's not easy to ignore him when he comes in here huffing and puffing. And it's all about money with Skip."

Their old friend Money. So Skip had himself a busy day. A Tough Mudder, then make trouble for the women at the cattery and the thrift store, then he goes over to the high school. Then he pops in on the girlfriend. Or maybe he doesn't? Then what? His wife said he came home around 6:00 or 6:30, then maybe went out again. Or maybe he didn't?

It was a whole lot of nothing.

—⊱ ⊰—

Stafford checked in with Harry Price by phone, impatient because he didn't answer on the first ring. He cast a glance up and down the main street of SMV: the realty offices, the pizza restaurant, the gift stores that came and went, the good bakery.

"So what's the game plan for today, Harry?"

"I'm on the money trail, the outstanding IOUs for $17,000 between Bryson and Farrow."

"You know, I still have a hard time seeing Skip Bryson as a stone cold killer, Harry. These guys are usually trailing a long string of violent crimes."

"Money's a good motivator and Skip Bryson's in debt up to his ears, and he's got big ambitions. Take Shanko and interview Bryson's colleagues and Peach's daughter, Marcy. And get an update from Shanko on the crew of day laborers who were around. He should be there any minute. Gotta go."

Stafford swiped his phone closed, pushed off from the fence in front of the thrift shop where bicycles and kids' strollers were lined up, and looked around to see Shanko pull in behind his vehicle. Shanko had to get off his lazy ass first and look for the day workers. His sniffing every ten seconds had begun to bother him too.

Shanko got out of his car and slid in the passenger seat beside Stafford. They grunted at each other. Stafford headed the car downhill on the road leading through town down to the freeway. They passed rolling hills covered with blond waving grass and a stand of oaks here and there in a cleft of the hillside that marked out a trail of underground water. Driving a road set right on top of the San Andreas Fault made Stafford uneasy. The fault jiggled right through the town hall, community center, and golf course. He figured if you thought about this much you'd hide under the bed and never leave the house.

Shanko stared out the window at the black cows in a long valley where earthquake sag ponds dimpled the cow pasture, only a small green oval left now that rain fell so infrequently.

"How do you set yourself up as an art dealer in New York? That's what Bryson wants to do," Stafford said into the silence.

"You should ask Price." Sniff. Shanko broke off as his phone rang, allowing Stafford to think his own thoughts as they slowed to pass scattered houses, a gas station, a plastic-flower decorated cross and a bear figurine marking another highway death. Situated near the interstate, the high school bussed in kids from miles away. The school buildings themselves were old, showing a school district suffering declining enrollments because so many kids around here were home-schooled. He and Shanko checked in at the office. Bryson taught Civics as well as being the coach and head of the PE Department.

Classes were in session so the long, polished hallways were empty except for one kid outside the bathrooms. He wore the uniform of the imminent dropout: black hoodie, earbuds, black jeans, and T-shirt.

"Where's the PE coach's office?" Stafford asked.

"Huh?" He turned to look at them, mouth agape, eyes glazed.

"Football coach?"

The question seemed to defeat the kid. They swung past him. He slowly turned to follow their direction. Schools still smelled the same. They came upon a room that said *Teachers. Private.* They opened the door to introduce themselves and were welcomed by a chatty woman with an English accent who offered them a place to wait.

"Mr. Bryson always comes in at the start of the third period for a cup of coffee. You might as well stay here." She seemed about to say more when there was a hesitant knock on the door and a student entered. "Please, Mrs...my teacher says..."

"Get out, you horrible object. Get out," she shouted at the kid. "You probably can't read but the sign says private. Nobody knows what privacy means nowadays. It's lost and gone like every other civility. Now what was I saying? The PE teacher will be here in a minute."

The bell rang. Instant bedlam. When Bryson saw Stafford, he turned on his heel and pushed back through the throng of teachers surging forward for a break from the classroom. Dex and Shanko went after him, pushing their way through a crowd of students, high on being young and noisy.

"I hated high school. Worst time of my life," Shanko growled. Sniff. Sniff. He couldn't help pausing to stare at his image as they passed a mirror. Halfway down the hall they found Bryson slouched against the wall, waiting for them.

"Let's go to my office. I don't want to talk here."

He pushed through a door into the Athletic Department, unlocked the door of the office that said *Coach* and with his back to them he said, "What? What do you want? I told you everything I know." He perched one hip on his steel desk and took a basketball from a shelf and began to toss it back and forth between his hands. From the window in his office he could see out into the gym.

Stafford let Shanko do the bullshit routine of getting a baseline read on Bryson. It was like watching two gorillas face off, out-machoing each other. They immediately found their way to Tough Mudders, and

Dex watched for a few minutes, reviewing the questions he had for Bryson. When the amount of testosterone in the air made it difficult to breathe, Dex sat forward and shot out a question. Shanko was now Bryson's good buddy. Stafford could be bad cop and provoke him.

"So it turns out your alibi for the night of Mr. Farrow's murder is looser than you told us."

"Oh yeah? Why?" Bryson said.

"Your wife doesn't exactly confirm the story you told us. She says she heard your SUV go out again around the time of the murder. Where were you going, Mr. Bryson?"

"She's wrong. That stupid bitch doesn't know which way is up."

"The stupid bitch who's getting herself a Ph.D.? That the one you mean?"

"She wants to throw me in the fire. We're getting a divorce. I've got plans of my own and they don't include her and her boyfriend."

"We also interviewed Ms. McDonald."

"Yeah, so? Leave her out of this. She has nothing to do with anything."

"See, the wife can't confirm you were there all night like you say. The girlfriend can't remember if she saw you. You didn't exactly leave a strong impression there."

"She's a ditz," Bryson shot back.

"Want to revise your movements on the night of the murder?"

"No. I was in the rest of the night. Forget what Arielle said."

Stafford changed tacks. "You on the Search & Rescue team up here?"

"Yeah. So?"

Dex looked down a moment as though he was reviewing his notes. "Your mother said she heard a man talking out in back before she went out and discovered Don. That wouldn't be you, would it? I heard Don Farrow wasn't your greatest supporter. Bet he told you to quit sponging on your mother. Is that what he said to you?"

Bryson's knee did the jiggle dance, his feet pointed toward the door of the room.

"We found the IOUs in Don Farrow's desk. You ever settle up with him? Pay them off?"

Bryson licked his lips. "He's dead," he said with a sneer. He obviously thought that cancelled the debt.

"So now you owe the estate."

"Bullshit."

"Nope," Stafford said. "Whoever he left his money to is going to come after you for that debt."

The bell rang for the start of the next period. They heard a rush of boisterous teenage voices and the first bounce of the basketball out in the gym.

"Where did you go the night of the murder?" Stafford pushed.

Bryson got up from the desk, jaw clenched. "I didn't go anywhere and that's the truth. I have to go now."

"We'll be back for another friendly chat then about the truth," Stafford said, all smiles. When—and if—he had confirmation it was Bryson's hoodie covered in Don Farrow's blood. Next time he'd interview him at the station where he had control.

⇒⊢ ⊣⇐

CHAPTER
TWENTY-THREE

Price had gone through voluminous correspon-
dence with a patent attorney, Thomas Gaston,
found in Don Farrow's papers at his house in Taft.
Time to get a handle on Farrow's financial dealings.

Stafford, glad to be rid of Shanko, looked around
as they drove into the oil town of Taft. The biggest oil
gusher in California history took place here in 1910,
its force blowing the derrick into bits. A pool of crude
oil spread for an area of six square miles, poisoning
the land for more than a century. The only thing that
grew to the east of the town were saltbush in bare

dirt. From a distance the landscape, dotted with the gray-green shrubs and sand, was painted with a shimmering pointillistic brush. Pipelines in all directions connected the bobbing grasshopper pumps. The only living thing in the bare and hilly panorama were rattlesnakes and maintenance trucks winding through the oilfields.

Gaston's office was in a building in the newer part of Taft. The nameplate by the door read Sofranic, Gaston, and Bentley. Guy Sofranic, head of the firm, saw them right away. Affably, and with a two-handed handshake, he welcomed them in his office. His comb-over was loose on the left side, showing a lot of pink scalp.

"My partner Tom Gaston, Don's attorney of record, died a couple of years ago. But Tom and I worked closely together, and I've reviewed the files." He settled his well-fed bulk comfortably behind his desk. "Couldn't have met a nicer guy than Don Farrow," Sofranic said. "His head was up in the clouds about business and money, but he'd give you the shirt right off his back, that guy."

"That's what we've been hearing from everybody," Harry Price said.

"Sad thing is…" Sofranic said in the voice of the Rotary Club lunch, breezy and sure of itself… "I saw him go down and down when a guy he worked with sued him over the sole ownership of one of his patents.

They'd worked together, but the other guy got sick about a quarter of the way through the development of the idea and quit on it. Don filed as the sole developer of the patent as he was certainly entitled to do." The old lawyer patted his comb-over to make sure all was well. "Don sat right where you're sitting now and kept shaking his head. He couldn't believe anybody would sue him. He wanted to let it go and pay what the guy asked, but my partner told him it was a bullshit case and he should counter-sue. Huff and puff and the other guy would go away. It was a local guy too. But Don took it bad. He felt betrayed. Told you he was unworldly, didn't I?"

Sofranic took a call while Dex and Harry waited. "They were bleeding the guy for a win out of court, and then Don gave up. It just took the heart out of him, being sued. I watched a grown man lose his innocence about people. He gave him everything he asked for. Mind you he had other patents, other sources of income, but this particular thing put him into a real depression he never pulled out of until he met this woman you're telling me about."

"Give me some contact information about the guy that sued him, would you?"

Sofranic chuckled. "That would be the local cemetery. He got his money and then up and died. Irony, eh?"

Another lead went pop in front of Stafford's eyes. "So your partner's files would have a copy of the will then?"

The old lawyer looked surprised. "Oh, I wouldn't think so. He'd have another attorney for all his personal stuff. You don't have a will?"

"No."

"That's interesting."

"You know anything about some hard-luck kids who lived next door to him. One of them says Farrow had put them in his will." Stafford asked.

"Not a thing. But Don had a sizeable estate. You can be sure some lawyer will take the case on contingency," Sofranic said. "The people might end up getting some go-away money. You can sue anybody for anything nowadays." He was puffed up with self-righteousness, as if he had never done such a thing.

Really? Stafford wondered. Really? He'd never done that?

⚒⚒

After the session with the lawyer, they split up so Harry could search Don Farrow's house and Stafford could canvass the neighbors. Stafford found the address on a pleasant street on the west side of town farthest away from the desolate oil fields. Taft was a small town, everybody connected to the oil industry. The dying downtown held only a few small businesses hanging on, others boarded up long ago. On the outskirts of town sat a Kmart and dollar store, which explained the dead downtown. Don had a nice bungalow painted white with blue trim on a double lot in an older neighborhood. Beside the house was a two-story, grey metal shed. Farrow's next door neighbor was puttering in the flower beds that lined the fence between her tidy bungalow and Farrow's place. A cheerful sort of person, she looked like a retired librarian and was all too willing to talk.

"Ruthie Ormstead, that's me. Come sit on the porch out of the sun. I'll get us a drink." She settled Stafford into a comfy chair and hustled inside, the screen door slapping behind her. Stafford looked around at the pink and yellow flowers, wondering how anything grew in Taft. They'd been fracking here since the 1930s. He would rather die of thirst than drink the water that came out of the taps. Bad enough breathing the air in Bakersfield. Farrow's neighbor brought him a bottle of water instead of a glass and he relaxed, letting her lead the conversation into chitchat about her flowers and her volunteer work at the Oil Museum.

"'Course I knew Don. We were neighbors for more than 30 years. I been out in that place of his he calls his lab hundreds of times." She gestured to the grey metal shed. "It's all closed down now since he moved over to Sierra Mountain. I look over at his house now and it looks so empty, it makes me sad. I never met this woman, but he was sure crazy about her. We were always going to get together, the four of us, and then something would happen. I guess a *big* something happened to him," she said, pulling a hanky out of her sleeve and giving her nose a good blow. "You know who did that to him? It was all over the news. That's how I found out."

"We don't know yet. What can you tell me about Mr. Farrow?"

She hitched in her chair to get comfortable, kicking off her pink Crocs. "Nice fella. Good-hearted. Kind of a loner, I guess, with his head in the clouds about the stuff he fooled with in that lab of his. He deserved the best and didn't always get it. Isn't that life?" she said with a big laugh.

"When was the last time you saw him?"

"Oh, weeks ago. I was saying to Larry, that's my husband, the other day it had been a while. He was gonna give Don a call. Don't think he got around to it, though."

"Notice anybody around looking at his place? Anybody looked like he didn't belong?" Stafford asked, twisting the cap off the bottle of water and taking a swig.

She shook her head thoughtfully. "Nope. Can't say I did. Not much happens around here. I'd probably notice that. I always kept an eye out for Don's place."

"He ever say anything about anybody bothering him? Anything like that?"

"Nope."

"What can you tell me about his ex-wife?"

She set the bottle down on the glass table between them. Her plump cheeks creased in a merry laugh. "That I *can* tell you about. Tiffany was her name apparently, but she was determined people were going to call her Tingle." Ruthie Ormstead slapped her wide thighs. "Can you believe that one? Don always called her Tiffany and she hated it. Don could be a little fuddy-duddy sometimes, but c'mon? Tingle? Oh, she got to be the talk of the neighborhood, sunning herself out in the altogether, getting all the old geezers het up. She took off, oh must be eleven, twelve years ago. They were only married three, four years. I still see her around."

She paused to think it through, one of those people who had to nail down the exact day, the exact year, every trivial detail before she could go on. "She must have some sort of settlement from Don because she set herself up in this spa business in the back of the house she had before they got married. I hear from my girlfriends it's a place where they do hair and nails, exercises, and massages and so forth. Never been there myself."

"Did you know her well?"

She blew out a puff of air. "Well as you could know anybody so much younger than yourself. Don was an old fool marrying her. And still taking care of her years after she run off."

"How was he taking care of her?" Stafford asked. This could go somewhere.

"Things like he'd go with her when she bought new tires, advising her, stuff like that. Took her out to dinner now and then."

"So they were on pretty good terms even after she left?"

"Think so. No fool like an old fool, heh?"

Stafford's phone buzzed and he glanced down at it.

"Oh, go ahead," Ruth Ormstead said. "I'll get us more water."

Stafford took the call from someone he barely remembered in the press of trying to make every moment count. When she told him she was Jilly Peters, the hostess at Mimi's restaurant, her heart-shaped face zoomed into view, her eyebrows plucked to the width of a hairline fracture. He had run into her checking the places that appeared on Don Farrow's credit card in the two-week period before he and Peach had taken their few days of vacation.

She stumbled over her words. "You remember I told you that man you were asking about looked familiar? You remember me, don't you?"

He now remembered her flirty little ways, the light touches on his arm, her insistence he take her card and come back and have a free lunch. Hint, hint: call first so she'd be free. He remembered her all right.

"I told the girl who served them about meeting you," she said in a light voice.

Meeting me? You were an interview subject. Holly Seabright was all the woman he could deal with at one time.

"Yes," he said, giving nothing.

"She reminded me we had a big lunch party that day, an engagement, you know? I told you I sorta remembered the old man you were asking about, but I couldn't remember who he was sitting with. The tab you showed me said a party of two. Lucinda was serving them and they were seated right next to an engagement party who were really loud and noisy." She spoke fast. "And they were taking a lot of pictures, right? Everybody had their cell phones out. Well, the bride came in again yesterday and Lucinda recognized her. She told her all about how that man got killed. We watch crime shows, you know," she said.

Didn't everybody watch crime shows and think they could do his job?

"She has lot of pictures of her engagement party and she says she'll bring them in and you can look at them. Maybe you'll be able to find out who he was with that day."

"Can you give me her name and number and I'll take it from there." There was a silence. He knew what she was hoping.

"I suppose so," she said finally. "You could collect your free lunch. I'm off on Monday, though, next week."

"I'm sorry," he said, scratching his head. "I'm so busy up in Sierra Mountain Village I can't take the time. I'll ask her to email them to me."

"Oh, okay. Her name's Judith Cassill." She read off the phone number. Her voice went thick.

He ended the call and made a note never to go into Mimi's again. Man, if the women only knew what a prize he was, they wouldn't want him. He had the feeling Seabright was getting sick of him never being around. He hung up and called the bride-to-be and left a message.

Ruth Ormstead came back with two more bottles of chilled water. She remembered Andrea Posner and her siblings but they'd all scattered and she didn't keep in touch with any of them. They chatted a while longer, but she hadn't much to add, so Stafford thanked her and walked down the sidewalk to the street and next door to Don Farrow's place, entering through a gate set in the low picket fence. The front door was ajar and Stafford walked into an entryway with a rack of coats and boots showing someone with outdoor interests.

"Harry? Where are you?"

Price stuck his head out of the living room into the entryway. "In here."

"You getting anything?"

Price was going through Farrow's house that he'd lived in before he rented the cabin in SMV. For someone with a sizeable estate Farrow's home was frozen in the era of Ike and Mamie. That is, what Stafford could see of it. A tornado had swept through here.

CHAPTER TWENTY-FOUR

"Pigpen mess same as his cabin," Harry pronounced. "Somebody was looking for something here too."

"Break-in?" Stafford snapped on his gloves.

"Not that I can see, and I looked. Looks like a key entry, or he left the doors unlocked."

"Nah," Stafford said. "I can't see that." He made a note to find out who had keys. Cleaning lady? The neighbor? The ex-wife? He cast a glance around and sighed. "We need help here."

"I already called in a few deputies," Price said, squatting next to a mound of manila file folders. A motorcycle roared by outside, disturbing the hot, still air.

Stafford stuck his hands in his pockets and walked through the house, sighing. The Norman Rockwell artwork hadn't been disturbed: Hummel figurines left standing on shelves. Whoever burgled the place looked like he was interested in paper. No desktop computer. No laptop or tablet. Manila files, though, were strewn all over the living room and den. Stafford sank down on a flowered couch in the den, picked up a stack of folders thrown out of the filing cabinet and began to go through them. The room smelled musty. An ancient tube TV faced him.

The folders were labelled, but the contents were a dog's breakfast, a jumble of invoices, assay reports, warranties, and tax filings. Harry Price came in, and the stack of folders slipped off Stafford's lap. He picked them up, cursing.

"I took a look at his lab records in the office of that metal building next door," Price said. "They weren't fooled with, so his patents business isn't what our asshole is looking for. Probably it would take another scientist to figure out if anything's out of the usual."

"Yeah," Stafford replied, not looking up. "You never turned up the will then?"

"Nope, but I did find a separation agreement, dated four years ago." He passed the sheaf of paper to Stafford who scanned it.

"Well, well." The ex-wife's full name was Tiffany LuAnne Sanders Farrow with a local address. "You want her or should I take her?" Stafford said.

"You take her," Harry said.

Stafford followed Price out into the hot metal shed where Farrow had maintained his lab. Sweat beaded his brow within seconds as he passed through into the huge empty box.

"There's not much to see out here," Price commented. "Ms. Bryson told me he closed the lab and sold off the equipment over the summer." Metal shelves and tables were empty, the cement floor swept clean.

"Aw, shit."

⟞⟜ ⟞⟜

Stafford sank gratefully onto Farrow's couch—it was cooler in the house—and tapped out an email to Shanko.

What's happening with locating the Latino worker with the green slat-sided truck? You found him yet?

When he checked his email again, Shanko had answered.

I got a line on somebody. I'm working it.

Shanko was probably working it sitting across the street at the Starbucks. He opened another email from Shanko.

> Tracked down the parolee Bryson hired to work around the place. He alibis out. He went with the head of the group home on a grocery run. I got him on camera at Costco. He's out.

That left the guy in the green truck seen running away, though Stafford didn't put much stock in that going anywhere in a hurry while Shanko was assigned.

CHAPTER TWENTY-FIVE

At the corner of a rambling bungalow shaded by old eucalyptus trees in the new part of Taft, a sign hung crookedly read Calming Mind Day Spa. A pleasant path picked out by flagstones bordered with flowers led around to the back of the house where a redwood deck overlooked a hillside covered with blowing grasses and bobbing oil derricks. Wind chimes tinkled in the fresh breeze. Stafford peered through a lattice fence to see a turquoise pool shimmering in the sunshine. What went on in a day spa? His ex-girlfriend Lauren, Harry's daughter, and certainly his wife Rosalie, would know. Lauren had a taste for expensive things. He pressed a button at the door. The lace curtains shifted and one merry brown eye took him in.

"Yes? You're not my next appointment, are you? I couldn't be that lucky." She swung the door open and a mischievous grin lit a narrow, sun-tanned face. Her silver ponytail bounced.

Stafford introduced himself, and saw wariness.

"You're Tiffany Sanders Farrow, Don Farrow's ex-wife?"

"Yeah, yeah." She waved her hand as though she was chasing off a mosquito. "But I'm Tingle now instead of Tiffany and I go by Sanders. Call me Tingle."

Tingle? Was that really a name? Would he have to break the news about Don Farrow's death or would she already know?

"Can you wait five minutes? I'll be done with my client and we can talk. Oh, boy, I can't wait."

Stafford didn't often get a greeting with that much exuberance. He finished off a bottle of water and sat himself down and reviewed his notes. He'd like to have his own mind calmed, which danced between Holly, the future, other cases, a mandolin riff he couldn't get down, and when his mother would finally leave and his home wouldn't be filled with her incessant chat, Frank Sinatra CDs, and vacuuming. He fell into a daydream about being on a bandstand with a bluegrass band playing mandolin.

A client left looking relaxed, her hair wrapped in a towel. Tingle Sanders bounded out on the deck, and locked the door of the spa behind her.

"Hey, there. Is it about the parking ticket? I really meant to come in. Busy, busy, busy, you know. Gotta make that money while I can. Before I get old and grey. Hey, I'm already grey, aren't I?" This all said in a breathless rush, and loud!

She stepped close to Stafford, slapping him in the stomach. He automatically stepped back, not liking strangers touching him.

"Hey, pull in that gut. Nobody's gonna hold it in for you." She circled around him, buzzing with a feverish energy, squeezed his triceps and then patted a quadriceps.

"Not bad. Not bad. You gotta start taking take of that fine carcass God gave you. Starts slipping in your thirties, you know." It was good humored and playful, along with the running commentary. "I do personal training. I could work you out. Make you beg me to stop. Yeah, cop, you're fine, but you're on the edge."

Her brown eyes danced in a lean face. The smile displaying white, white teeth was wide and lopsided. A force field of energy glittered around her, along with an eager sexiness.

"I got half an hour until my next appointment. Gotta fuel up. C'mon." She led off with a bounce in her walk around the side of the house into the kitchen.

"Put a little scoot in your get-along. I'm in a rush here." Stafford couldn't help but laugh out loud when she patted him on the ass.

She shoved him down into a chair at the table and leaped up at the counter to swing open a high cupboard. It gave him a fine view of her ass and long muscled legs. She looked over her shoulder at him, catching him looking and grinned. She jacked open a can of tomato soup, stabbed buttons on the microwave and poured a few crackers on a plate, all the while chattering at him staccato. He was an expert at tuning out chatterers and isolating the one thing that was important to hear. His glance took in the kitchen, decorated in a slapdash fashion, and needing a few basic repairs. Someone running a business didn't have the time to take care of chipped linoleum and peeling cabinets. No smell of animals at least. He looked out the window beside him onto a covered patio on which six older women were doing aerobics to a Jessie Jay song.

"So what can I do for you, cop?" Perfectly innocent people turned strange meeting a cop, figuring the cop knew every petty twist of the law in their unremarkable past. From the perfunctory check on her background, Sanders had a clean criminal record. This whirlwind of an energy that could power a nuclear plant made him feel old.

She hollered out *No, you haven't seen the best of me/I'm still working on my masterpiece,* which Stafford recognized as the lyrics of the Jessie Jay song playing outside. He stared at her. She was dancing so hard he thought she'd wet herself.

"Hear that? *I'm ferocious, precocious/I get braggadocios.* I love that song. Don't you?"

"Could you sit down, please?" He pointed at the kitchen table and sat down himself to get control of the interview.

"I'm not much good at sitting, but I can see you're going to go all serious on me." The microwave pinged and she took the bowl of soup from it and perched on a chair at the table.

"We learned you were married to Don Farrow who is recently deceased," he began.

"Oh," she said, "It's about Don. I saw it in the paper. Made me sad." She slurped tomato soup off a spoon. "That's too slow. Sorry." She picked up the bowl and held it to her lips, her dancing brown eyes intent on his over the rim. "I got no manners. Never did."

"What can you tell me about him, Ms. Sanders?"

"Oh, call me Tingle. My mother had all these notions because here's a girl after three boys so she named me Tiffany before the name got popular and poor Mom tried to get me in ballet. I was the original ADHD kid bouncing off the walls. I guess you can tell, huh?" Her teeth gleamed in the tanned face. "She always said she didn't know what was going to become of me till I got into sports and dramatics. Seems like

I'm more Tingle than Tiffany. Know what I'm sayin'? So call me Tingle." Her body had gone through an array of jerks and gyrations, everything said at a holler volume accompanied by a blinding white smile.

"Oh. Well, it may not have been clear Mr. Farrow died under suspicious circumstances. We're trying to understand whatever we can about him to find out who may have killed him."

"Killed him? Oh, that's terrible. Oh, my. Who would kill Don?"

"Why do you say that?" Stafford asked.

"He was a wuss. Sorry, I know I should only say good things." She slapped her wrist, shrugging her shoulders. "I used to get mad the way he'd never stand up for himself. He'd always find something good to say about somebody, even if they were awful. I wish I could be like that but, hey, I'm shallow, one millimeter deep." She leaned forward and her thick silver pony tail wound through with ribbons fell over her shoulders. She glanced out the window and leaped to her feet. "Don liked me because I was fun. Pepped him up. For a while at least."

"Suck those abs in, Megan," she hollered through the open window.

The instructor, a tall, willowy beauty in lavender hollered back, "Whose class is this Tingle? Yours or mine?"

"Yeah, well."

He heard her mutter, "Man, I hate women."

She turned back to Dex and thumped down in her chair again, running her hand over his shoulders as she passed him. He flinched.

"What happened to Don?"

"We don't know yet. When was the last time you saw him?"

"Oh, it must be five, six months ago. We met up on the steps outside going into the Black Angus in Bakersfield one night. I was with some match.com loser. Don was with some people. Chitchat, you know."

She didn't act sad. But then did this whirling dervish, ditz ever get sad? He could imagine Don's attraction to her fine body but after five minutes she was wearing him down.

"We were hoping you could help us track down his financial records, things like that."

This brought a smile to Tingle Sander's face. She leaped up and slung the empty bowl of soup in the sink. "Don was hopeless with records. He'd throw his hands up in the air, then he'd get a paper bag and throw all the mail in there. We would laugh and laugh. I'm just like him. Maybe that's why we got along as long as we did. You seen that house of his? Can you imagine me living there?"

No, he couldn't. Her perching that lovely ass on those maple chairs around the Sears dining set with flowered cushions tied on each seat? No. What did they ever talk about?

"You have a key to his place? I heard you were friendly."

"Not that friendly."

"How friendly?"

"Oh, we'd run into each other once in a while in town, have coffee. Nothing big."

"So you'd have no idea who his lawyer might be?" The humming bird energy made him nervous.

"I never had anything to do with his business. He had dealings with people in LA, but it was years ago. Hey, where do you work out? Know any cops who might want a personal trainer?" She put both hands on the back of a chair, swung one perfect leg to the side at an angle he thought was physiologically impossible.

"We've got a gym at work." He stood up. She seemed eager to help, but it had been so long since she'd seen Farrow, he figured there was nothing there. "No kids then?"

"No. I don't think he had kids with anybody else either. I don't think he ever married again, did he? Not that I heard."

"You know anything about a bunch of kids who lived next door to him at one point? He was good to them apparently and they think they're written into his will."

She shook her head. "Must have been before my time. He was always doing things for people. I wonder if he left me anything in his will. He always said he would."

"Mind me asking where you were last Friday night? It's a formality."

"Oh, you're such a silly. Okay. I was with one of my clients, over at her place for dinner. What else?"

Stafford made a note of the name she gave him and the phone number. He was tired. He faced a long drive home and wanted to have time to practice mandolin before his next lesson. And Holly would soon be hounding him for time together. He couldn't imagine this woman focusing long enough to pull off a murder.

"Let us know if you think of anything," he said, looking around the kitchen one last time. He cast a sneaking glance at her body.

"When do you think his estate will be settled?" she asked, bouncing from one foot to the other in the doorway.

"Soon as we find the will. Or it goes to probate."

He picked up his notebook. "Nice business you have in back there."

"Gossipy women all day, if you like that kind of thing."

"Women gossip? Hunh," Stafford said with a grin. "Never met any bigger gossips than cops. Calming Mind. I could use some of that,"

"Come back sometime. I'll give you a facial and a massage. Give you a workout." The double entendre was clear.

He wondered what it would be like to take that twitching, live wire body to bed.

CHAPTER TWENTY-SIX

The trip back from Taft to the major highway leading to Bakersfield lay on a route through a desert landscape that could have been Martian. Stafford drove. Harry stayed on the phone most of the way, pushing along their other cases. He also took a call from one of his financial guys who were pestering him all the time. He swiped the phone closed and said, "I could hire somebody to shit for me I'm so rich. I thought I could pay somebody to handle the money, and it's still eating me alive."

"Hard to feel sorry for you, Harry," Stafford said. "Here, have one of these peaches I bought at the stand. They're wonderful."

Harry took a peach and a napkin and bit into it, looking out the window into the desolate landscape. "The ex-wife give you anything on the will?"

"Oh, man." Stafford threw his hands up finally, trying to describe her to Harry. "A piece of work."

"When were they divorced?"

"Didn't ask."

"Find out. You get anything on the $10,000 withdrawal Peach Bryson made?"

"Not yet," Dex said, concentrating on the long straight road back to Bakersfield.

"I put in a request for the maker of Don Farrow's will in all the Southern California legal newspapers to contact us. Something should pop soon."

"You hope," Dex said.

He got Shanko on the phone. Shanko complained it wasn't easy getting information about the guys who did work at Peach Bryson's cat rescue. For one thing, it was the cops asking, the same cops who periodically did a blitzkrieg round up of everybody on the street corner.

"I've been out at 6:00 every morning at the Home Depot on Ming near the Maui Pho, and as soon as they see me coming they run," Shanko said. Sniff. Sniff.

"Try the other Home Depots in town," Stafford said unsympathetically, terminating the call. He was sick of Shanko's whining. He wondered if the day workers knew Shanko's reputation for taking in a suspect the hard way.

Admittedly, Peach Bryson's description had been generic. The workers were smaller than average, brown men with black hair, like most of the Latino day worker population. These were people who lived in the shadows with no reason to make themselves available to the police. Finding these guys who worked for Peach would be plain dogged police work, talkin' to guys, movin' on, and talkin' to other guys. No glamor. Shanko liked chasing guys down alleys and bringing them in hard, not talking to people and getting information.

That was hard work.

Dex wanted to do everything at once: run down the Latino seen fleeing the crime scene, get the financial records, track the day laborers, link Bryson to the hoodie. Maybe Harry with his millions could *forget* Peach's $10,000 withdrawal, but Stafford couldn't. He could imagine a $100 withdrawal dribbling through his fingers, but not $10,000. He mused over Tingle Sanders, smiling to himself thinking of her. Considering her and Farrow in bed. What on earth had they ever talked about?

Doubts about Peach's innocence were beginning to grow. The Sarge had stuck Shanko with them for a few days longer until something else popped. Then there would be new bodies, new cases. None of the teams wanted Shanko full-time.

Shanko and Skip Bryson—Tough Mudders. Now there was a pair.

⊷ ⊶

Shanko had amazed Price and Stafford by getting off his ass long enough to turn up one of the crew of *jornaleros* Peach hired to do heavy work around the cattery. Shanko had an address and insisted on being in on the interview, driving on his own out to Pumpkin Center. Stafford drove Rodriguez, a native Spanish-speaker, who knew how to go in easy. His own Spanish wasn't good enough yet to do a tricky interview. Afterwards Stafford and Shanko would interview Peach Bryson's daughter, Marcy.

Stafford drove the I-5 highway that cut through the flat San Joaquin Valley unwinding in a straight line, the pink and white oleanders on the median on his left whipping away in the wind. He thought about Holly Seabright as he drove, tuning out Price, who was arguing on the phone with his wife. He thought about Holly a lot. She was different from his former girlfriends, less clingy, more independent. He didn't know if he liked that or not.

The two cars arrived at the address for the day worker. No green truck visible outside a crumbling stucco bungalow on the edge of the fields in a dusty brown and taupe landscape south of Bakersfield near Pumpkin Center, a strung-out, dirt-poor agricultural settlement. Lots of junkers and oil stains on the dirt lot, but the residents were all at work now. You didn't work. You didn't eat.

An old *campesino* answered the door after determined knocking. He claimed not to speak English, but behind him was a kid about ten years old who needed his face washed and a haircut. A pot of pinto beans bubbled on the stove and the fridge hummed. Judging from the number of rolled-up sleeping bags in a corner of the kitchen, a lot of people bunked there. From the front door Stafford glimpsed a scrap of meat on the counter that hummed with flies.

Lot of dancing around with the old fellow in rat-a-tat Spanish Stafford couldn't follow. Their guy Carlos was there, Rodriguez finally established, but he was sick. What kind of sick? Sick in his foot, Dex understood him to say.

"What the hell's that mean? Sick in his foot," Stafford muttered to Rodriguez.

"He got a bad cut while he was working," Rodriguez muttered in an aside to Dex and Harry. "The labor contractor sent him home. No health benefits."

Rodriguez spent another ten minutes convincing him they weren't Immigration. Finally, he stood aside and Shanko, Rodriguez, and Stafford entered the kitchen. The old guy stumped in front of them past a bathroom and closed the door on two bedrooms in which three sets of bunks lined the walls papered with posters of Tijuana bullfights and Tejano bands. Somebody kept this place clean. The three-layer bunks were unoccupied except for one in the bedroom at the back.

Their guy Carlos lay covered by a sheet with his bandaged foot jutting out. Once again they had to go through the whole song and dance about Immigration. The old guy talked to him from the doorway and finally Carlos beckoned them in.

His foot stank, a raw mass of infected flesh. His Spanish was a lot slower and Dex got the sense of it. Sure, he remembered the last day he'd worked for the nice lady. They'd left about 7:00 that night. They took a load of trash to the dump before leaving town. But the dump wasn't open, and on their way back through town, Carlos realized he'd left his jacket so they turned around and went back to the cat place.

"And what happened when you got there?" Rodriguez asked, nice and slow.

"I went in the back way through the loading dock and I heard arguing. Two men."

"Could you hear what they were saying?" Rodriguez asked, then translated his answer for Stafford. "They stay out of things."

"Ask him if he saw the two guys. See if you can get a description."

Carlos shook his head no, no, no. The cops glared at him silently doubting this, but he didn't break.

"Push him," Stafford said. "Tell him we're not saying he had anything to do with anything. Mrs. Bryson says she heard another man out there with the victim. She's not saying it's you."

Carlos hitched himself further up in the bed using his good foot and spoke quickly. Rodriguez translated. "He says the other guys will tell you he ran in there, grabbed his jacket off the hook inside the back door and ran back to the truck. A minute was all it took. They had another job to get to."

Good luck getting them to testify, Stafford thought. Something about the guy had the ring of truth about it. Apparently Rodriguez felt the same way. He looked at Dex. *¿Algo más?*

"Ask him if he'll set us up with the other guys to confirm what he's telling us? Tell him we'll get a doctor for his foot."

Carlos shook his head back and forth. Rodriguez translated. "They stayed in the truck. He don't need a doctor. They've got maggots growing on meat out in the kitchen. They'll take care of his foot."

Stafford had heard of the maggot treatment before. He shrugged. The boy spoke up.

"It's our way," he shrugged and scuffed one toe in the worn carpet. Perfect English.

"I know," Dex said. "It works. There's even hospitals and doctors that use maggots now to clean the wound." He wondered how many patients elected that treatment.

The kid smiled shyly. He went over and stood at the end of the bunk beds.

"You tell Carlos Mrs. Bryson asked about him," Dex said to the kid in English. "How about a phone number where she can reach him? See how he's doing? She's got more work waiting for him."

The kid denied anybody had a phone, which Dex knew was a damn lie. He grabbed Rodriguez. "Tell him again we're interested in the argument he heard. Nothing else."

"Stafford, I told 'im that three times."

"Tell him again."

Stafford thought it through. Not speaking English often rendered Carlos invisible. That didn't make him blind, deaf, or stupid. No one paid him any attention except to order him around. Peach Bryson would have mentioned if one of the men yelling had a heavy Spanish accent. Surely. Still Dex wanted to check out his story. Carlos wasn't going anywhere for a while. Not with that mess of a foot.

On the way out Shanko walked into a yellow jacket nest at the edge of the driveway. Leaping and dancing, a plume of wasps followed him as he ran for his vehicle. Rodriguez quickly slid inside the car and slammed the door. Stafford and Rodriguez drove off laughing.

"I wish I'd got a video of that to show around," Stafford said, looking back as Shanko danced and swatted an invisible enemy.

"It'd go viral in the station."

CHAPTER
TWENTY-SEVEN

The next step was an interview with Peach Bryson's daughter in Sierra Mountain Village. Price and Rodriguez went back to the station and Stafford picked up Shanko. On the way up Shanko bragged about the Tough Mudder events he ran, challenging Dex to join him. Dex had no interest whatsoever in proving his manliness—nor did he want to give Shanko any opportunity to beat him. Shanko was one of those guys you never asked an open-ended question. He also had a tendency to sweat, which left the scent of hair gels and aftershave in any vehicle he occupied.

Shanko had beat the subject of Tough Mudders to death and had no interest in Stafford, not that Stafford would ever share anything personal with him. Lauren, his wife and Stafford's old girlfriend, was not a subject of discussion, and Stafford had no interest in hearing about their baby. They talked who was getting promoted, the smell in car 52, and the rumors about body cams.

"You got the address?" Shanko asked when they pulled into Sierra Mountain Village.

"Of course I've got the address," Dex snapped.

"I've been thinking..." Shanko said.

"I've heard that the first time is the hardest," Dex said before he could stop himself. He smothered a grin. Nobody could get more mileage out of an insult than Shanko. Cop banter could be brutal and Shanko was oddly sensitive. He drove past Artworks Community Gallery, his head whipping around observing they had a new show of local painters. Wonder if Harry and his art-buyer wife knew about this place.

The Marcy Bryson-Fetterly home Peach's daughter shared with her husband and five children had one of the few lawns in Sierra Mountain Village. The small green expanse looked as though it had been edged with manicure scissors. The house gleamed with new paint and trim, and a pretty wrought-iron fence circled the lawn. The place looked as though it had been set down on the lawn yesterday under a clear plastic dome. Did they wax the driveway to make it so new looking and shiny? Five kids lived here?

Marcy Fetterly bustled to the door to greet them in a long skirt and high-collared white blouse. She dressed so modestly it was as if she were trying to hide a skin disease. Welcoming them, she had her mother's graciousness and easy manners. She led them past a great room where the children were playing a board game into a kitchen and dining area that spanned the back of the house and looked out into the forest. Someone had recently raked the dirt in the back yard. Marcy sat them at a long dining table and brought over a plate of dessert breads and cookies, explaining she'd had the girls over for Bunco night. Marcy was better dressed than most mountain folk who spent the day in sweat pants and T-shirts. Stafford looked around and saw a prayer book lying on the arm of the couch. The five children were so quiet Dex wondered if the Fetterlys drugged them. When the chitchat between Shanko and Marcy got around to whether or not Lauren should join the Red Hat Society ladies, Stafford stopped it. And Shanko didn't like it. There was rapport-building and there was wasting time.

"We're trying to get a read on Don Farrow."

Marcy Fetterly put her hand in the air. "Poor mother. I've never seen her so happy, and now this happens to Don. Do you have any idea who did this?"

"We're following some promising lines of inquiry," Stafford lied. He led her through her movements on the day of Farrow's murder.

"Can you tell me where your husband was last Friday night late in the afternoon and early evening?"

"He does our big shopping on the way home from work." She flounced out of the chair to fetch receipts and fling them at Stafford. He passed them to Shanko to check out.

Marcy's sweet face turned flinty hard when Dex asked about her brother. "My brother has a bad temper. The Lord knows I struggle with my faults too, but He never gives us more than we can handle, does he?"

Dex privately thought the Lord gave a lot of people more than they could handle. Like the ones who turned to drugs and alcohol, using their fists and tongues like knives on other people. Still he smiled to keep her talking. He listened for anything useful as he looked around the pastel room. Sunday school pictures of Jesus looking like a surfer dude, a stack of devotional books, places marked with ribbons on the counter, Christian kids' books.

"I don't know what the arguments between Don and Skip were about exactly. Mother tries to keep a good face on everything, you know. I know Don thought Skippy is too dependent on Mom. Skip thinks he's a big business man. First mother sets him up in a solar business that failed. Then he tried a dry cleaning business, but honestly! He finally did something sensible and got a teaching credential and now he's doing really well. On the job front at least."

"So your mother has funded your brother in several businesses?"

"Oh, it's been a whole string, bless his heart. Skippy doesn't…."

A kid got up and came to a stop in the kitchen doorway and said, "Momma, can we…"

"Darren. You are to play inside until 10 o'clock, and then you can go outside. Did you not understand that?"

"Yeah, but the kids are outside and …"

"Ten o'clock," Marcy Fetterly said firmly. "Pray for patience if you find it hard. Jesus will help you."

The kid hung his head, pivoted, and went back into the quiet family room.

"You must put children on a schedule. Otherwise, it's chaos," she said, pinching her mouth into the narrow line of a woman who tipped the waitress a dollar. "Now, as I was saying, Skippy's wife…Arielle's been in school for ten years and never had a job. She and Skippy, honestly, those two. No children. What do they spend their money on? Mom's always helping them out."

"Your brother doesn't sound fond of the cat rescue place," Shanko put in.

"Well, I can't say I am either. Don tried to get mother to see reason and dump all those cats on the pound. What a nice guy Don was, bless his heart. Over the years I can't tell you how much mother has spent on her cats. Don wanted to marry her and travel while they were both still able to get around. We were all for it. But he wanted her to close the cat place first. I think he'd almost convinced her, you know that? Almost."

"Why would you think that?" Stafford asked.

"Well, I just do. Nothing that was said. Maybe the Lord whispered it to me, you know. Skip was jealous of Don. He doesn't want to share any part of mother—or her money—with anyone. Even with me. My husband and I have needs too. It isn't easy with five kids, but Skip is always first in line with mother."

CHAPTER
TWENTY-EIGHT

The O'Malleys across the road from Peach Bryson had been bad boys. One of the deputies spotted their old beater and sidled up behind, lights off, seeing Dwayne and his brother Leroy reel out the door of the town's redneck bar. Dwayne got behind the wheel. Things got pissy in a hurry. Dwayne couldn't keep his mouth shut about Deputy Alvarado's national heritage. The deputy called in backup and before long had both O'Malleys sitting cross-legged on the sidewalk. Both deputies were searching Dwayne's old beater when Stafford and Shanko drove by after Marcy

Fetterly's interview. The search turned up a rudimentary lockpick set. Another DUI would sit Dwayne's ass in jail for a good while. The O'Malley brothers had been a problem in town since they were little shits, and with them off the streets, things would quiet down a while for everybody else.

Bill Madison at the substation in Frazier Oaks passed the news along to Dex and Shanko who were writing reports. They didn't have enough to hold his brother Leroy. Mama O'Malley had picked up Leroy in the company of Dwayne's girlfriend and howling baby. Dwayne O'Malley went to a holding cell in Bakersfield.

"Dumb bastard. You could buy a snap gun lockpick for fifty bucks on the internet," Stafford grunted.

"Even with that," Bill Madison chuckled, "I don't think Dwayne O'Malley could pick the lock on a little girl's diary."

CHAPTER TWENTY-NINE

Dex had bought an anniversary card for Harry and Rosalie Price at a CVS store on his way into work that morning. He drove through the ass end of Bakersfield to the station: thrift shops, cut price gas stations, recycling setups, places to sell your plasma, carnicerias. The Prices were having a party to celebrate 35 years together at the mini-Versailles Palace Rosalie kept redecorating. He wondered why there were no *Congratulations on your Divorce* cards. It also made him wonder about Shanko's marriage to Harry's daughter. From there, a thought popped in his head.

"We ever see divorce papers on Farrow?" Dex said later, swiveling his office chair to gaze at Harry Price who had the cubicle next to him.

"I don't remember. Look it up. I'm busy."

"And I'm just sitting here polishing my nice badge and gun? Is that what it looks like I'm doing?" Stafford said, swiveling his chair back and forth to make it squeak. He turned back to rummage around in his files until he found the list of documents in the Evidence Collection list.

"Who did we have on that? Was it me?"

"It doesn't matter," Harry said, his brow furrowed. "Check it out."

Things got dropped all the time because they were moving so fast.

Beatrice O'Malley ripped the pin on a tantrum with Stafford. She shouted at him through her front door. "What the hell is this? You bring my boys in and cost us all this money to get them out? Nothing but persecution. Those boys weren't driving drunk and now you tell me their fingerprints were found over there at that cat place? Well, why not? We're neighbors."

O'Malley jutted her chin out in a challenge to Dex and Harry. "You might as well come in since you're here to harass me. My feet hurt. I have to sit down."

"Mrs. Bryson says she never hired your boys," Stafford said, pulling out a chair at the kitchen table and looking at the seat carefully before he sat down.

The barking of the five Chihuahuas behind closed doors gradually stopped.

"We were there at a party in June, weren't we? I know you heard about that."

"She says they had no reason to go back into the kennel areas."

"She says! Why do you believe her and not my boys?"

That didn't even deserve an answer from Stafford.

"Well, they mighta snuck over to look around," she admitted. "Boys will be boys. If anything happens to my Dwayne, you're responsible. You've got no right draggin' him off to jail. What is this, communist Russia? You're worse than Nazis. You're all terrorists."

"Yes, ma'am," he said with a sigh.

"Always harassing us," she muttered. "You can't keep me in custody. I'm gonna sue the dog piss out of you."

"Hey, lady, we're sitting in your kitchen. Are you in handcuffs? Do I look like I've got you in my custody?"

She snorted.

"We hear you're a couple of payments behind on the mortgage and you might need money. I wonder if your boys were over there just before Mr. Farrow died. You might have thought Mr. Farrow, since he was such a nice guy, would give you the money."

"Oh, blow it out your ass. He never gave us nothing. Her! Nothing except aggravation and traffic all day long with her damn cats." Beatrice O'Malley was permanently indignant, glad to have them in her kitchen because here was an audience for venting her spleen.

"And him? He was a pussy. Did whatever she said. The reason we have no money is because my husband is such a shit-for-brains. Stupid useless brainless idiot. He spent every cent we could get together at that casino they built. He can't even go out on jobs anymore because he pawned all his tools. I wonder when the leg breakers are going to come around and kill us all."

Her last sentence rose to a falsetto, which strained her throat so much she broke into a phlegmy cough. The five chihuahuas started barking again.

"Then maybe the only option you had left was to hit Don Farrow up for the money."

"Then you're another idiot. I didn't kill him. My boys didn't kill him." She looked so downcast and beaten that Dex felt sorry for her. Then he remembered the sight of Don Farrow.

"Besides, he's not my husband, the lazy good for nothing. I divorced him but he's still hangin' around. He still spends anything he can get at the casino. You think he might have a gambling problem? You think?"

This was said so loud it startled an old dog sitting at her feet. The dog got up and moved away to flop down near the kitchen door. She eventually looked up at Dex with a defeated expression, took a swig of water out of a bottle and sat back, exhausted from her own vitriol.

"I kicked him out even though it's his name on the deed. My boys and I have to have a place to live, don't we? Then there's the boys beggin' me all the time to let him move back in because he's supposedly got a bad back. It's okay for me to go breaking *my* back cleanin' rooms at that fleabag Holiday Inn though." She heaved herself up. "I got things to do around here, you know, to keep this place up. Not that I get any help from anybody."

"Well, thanks," Dex said, slapping his notebook together and standing up. Harry said the usuals and they left her there muttering. It occurred to him she loved her sons, even if they were useless louts. Just as Peach loved Skip Bryson. Hard to figure, mother love.

He and Price did knock and talks again at every address on the street. The other houses on the road were owned by weekenders and vacant during the week. No hope there.

⬦

Holly made a pass by the dog park and found Chloe sitting with Boz at a picnic table. Christy had told her they'd broken up and Leroy O'Malley was now Chloe's boyfriend. Huh. And there she was with Boz with a shiny new golf cart parked next to them.

"Where did this come from? Is it yours?" she asked Chloe, who shook her head, adjusting her earbuds, and pointed to Boz. His earbuds were firmly screwed in, his head bobbing.

Holly didn't think Mike Jarvis would spring for a golf cart for Boz who'd lost his license because of a joyriding charge. Brenda said Mike didn't have two nickels to rub together. Stolen? Holly made a note to check. Brenda and Mike were still hot and heavy. He'd taken her for a night on the town down to the Crystal Palace in Bakersfield and dinner at the Padre Hotel. Holly could see he had his charms.

She meandered over to the Paws thriftshop to see how things were going, thinking about Dex Stafford, thinking about the shrine, trying to think of somebody else who might know something. The store was dark and small, cluttered to the rafters. Doreen was at the counter doing paperwork. The store got enough jeans donated that nobody in the Western world ever needed to go out and buy new ones—ever again. Or T-shirts. Doreen Spears, the manager, pointed to a box filled with stained pillows, Beanie Babies, and jeans. Holly picked up the box and shouldered it through the back room filled with furniture, pillows, mirrors, framed paintings, and lamps.

Volunteers weren't showing up at the store, even the long-term ones. Few people relished the hard work of grubbing through smelly black plastic bags of old clothes and dusty boxes left over from a garage sale. Maybe it was a link to the rumors about Peach and Don Farrow's murder. Doreen held the back door of the thrift shop open for Holly. They went into the yard they tried to keep hidden from customers.

"They find out anything about Don?" Doreen asked, her round face curious.

"Not as far as I know. It's a damn shame, isn't it?"

"Yeah, wow." Doreen sank down on a clear plastic bin filled with bedraggled Christmas ornaments. "Heard your new boyfriend is going around getting everybody stirred up."

"That's his job."

"You think Peach is going to close down Paws?" Doreen asked with a sidelong glance. "Everybody's asking me." She ran her finger through her half-inchlong gray hair. "Somebody told me she was getting ready to sell to one of the big animal organizations in LA." She mentioned a name anybody in the animal rescue community would know.

"Hmmph. Well, I don't know. That's the newest rumor, huh?"

"I'd be very disappointed in Peach if that's true. Letting Paws go without telling me. You know we're close, don't you?" she said.

"You and Brenda and Peach. Yes, I know that."

"Not so much Brenda. More me and Peach," Doreen said, looking smug. "Peach said she would leave the place with me in charge."

Holly made big eyes, wide with surprise. "Oh. To you." This sounded like a real setup for conflict.

One of the volunteers raced out the back door and shouted, "Holly, Peach is in the back of a police car along with your honey. People are saying they're taking her down to Bakersfield to arrest her."

"Was she in handcuffs?" Doreen asked, standing up and rushing to the side gate to look out.

"Somebody said she was."

"How would they know?" Holly argued. "Could they see in the car?"

"You know people are talking about all the vandalism at the shrine," Doreen said, peering out into the street. "They're tryin' to tie it to Paws because of Don's murder."

"That's crazy, Doreen. Maybe they wanted Peach to identify somebody, something like that." Surely Dex would have told her if he was going to arrest her. Wouldn't he? Holly went out in front of the thrift store onto the street and called him, but once again the call went to message.

She could already see posts about Peach's arrest on all the Facebook groups. She drove back to the office. Ed looked up with a sour expression, and tapped a pen on the log sheets as she slunk in the door past him.

"What are you doing about this vandalism, Seabright? See these calls? I want progress. So does the town council."

The paper reported on the story of how Peach had killed her first husband. Peach had given the reporter an interview, but they printed what they wanted.

Don Farrow was still dead. And now Peach was riding in the back of a police car.

CHAPTER THIRTY

Peach had scheduled an exec meeting at Paws for late that afternoon. Several times during the morning, Brenda and Doreen checked in with Holly to see if anybody had heard anything yet from Peach. Then about noon, Peach called Holly.

"What happened? People saw you with Dex."

Peach's voice trembled. "They asked me the same questions all over again and my lawyer told me what to answer and then it was all over. They let me go because there's nothing to find. Nothing. It's all over so let's not talk about it anymore. I'd like you to tell the others not to question me about it."

Holly heard the firm, soft voice of command and raised her eyebrows. "Sure, Peach."

"Let's go ahead with the meeting this afternoon. We've got things to talk about."

Four hours later the four of them were talking about a new grant possibility sitting in the kitchen, which smelled of freshly-baked carrot cake muffins. Skip Bryson burst in, slamming the door in the face of his sister, Marcy, who was behind him lugging a cat carrier. Inside a cat yowled. Marcy crashed the cat carrier down on the kitchen counter.

Peach stood up, a wary smile on her face. "Hello, dear." She looked over at Skip who was thunder-faced, pushing aside his sister.

Marcy shoved him back and marched over to her mother, "You gave Skip $10,000. How could you do that, mother?" Her voice was high and strained.

Peach looked stabbed in the heart. "How, how…do you know that?"

"Because he told me. He rubbed our noses in it. He told us you gave it to him in cash so nobody would find out. How *could* you, mother?"

Skip smirked. "She didn't give it to you because your husband would have spent it on his train set like a five-year-old kid."

Marcy puffed herself up, her face scarlet. "The trains are for our children too. My husband drives 200 miles a day to a job he hates to take care of us.

Those trains are his only relaxation, the only thing he spends money on. He has *responsibilities*, unlike you. And speaking of five-year-olds, how in the world do you think you can move to New York City and become an art dealer? I never heard anything sillier. Mother, make him give that money back."

"It's her money, little sister," Skip said, looming over Marcy. "Her money. You want to rob her of every cent she's got."

"You have two children, mother. Not one. Think of your grandchildren." Her voice was rising, words coming faster.

"Oh, low blow." Skip danced back.

"He's always manipulated you to give him money," Marcy shrieked. Peach backed up against the counter, her head in her hands.

Holly didn't know where to look so she kept her head down, cleared her throat, and straightened the budget papers. Two seconds longer, and she would get up and flee through the living room out the front door.

Marcy's voice shrilled. "And Barry heard it down at the hardware you're giving away the land you bought to one of those animal places."

"Stop this, both of you," Peach said sharply. "I can't stand any more of this. Both of you leave. I'll deal with you one at a time, and when I'm ready. I am so tired of both of you badgering me for money." She pushed Marcy toward the door.

Marcy slammed a hand down on the cat carrier. "Wait. Wait a minute. You have to take Roxy back. She pees on the floor and I can't have that."

"That cat's been with you since she was a kitten. She's twelve years old. She can't help it," Peach pleaded. "You can't do this to the kids. They love her. There's ways to help her."

"Give the cat to Skip then. He has no responsibilities. Give the damn cat to him!"

Skip lurched toward his sister with open hands as if he wanted to grab her by the throat and shake her. Marcy grabbed the carrier off the counter and hurled it at her brother. He stepped back and the door of the carrier cracked open when it hit the floor. The cat shot out and tried to climb straight up the wall, slipping and sliding back down with claws extended. It leaped on the counter, landing on a stack of mail, and scrabbled at the screen in the window trying to escape. Peach rushed to the window with the carrier in hand and stuffed the big tortie back in, snapping the door closed, turning back to her squabbling children.

"You always loved those damn cats more than you loved me," Marcy said, sobbing. "You can't give that land away. You can't. What about me and my children?"

"Now who sounds like a five-year-old?" Skip said, laughing in Marcy's face. Marcy fled and Skip followed her out the door, still laughing.

Holly could hear them bickering as they stumped down the stairs to the parking lot. She had a feeling where that cat would land up. Her house. One more peeing, unadoptable cat at her house.

She couldn't look at Peach. She shoved the grant application papers into a folder and slid out the door. Brenda and Doreen had already fled.

CHAPTER THIRTY-ONE

Peach called Holly back later to sign checks. Routine stuff once, but little else was routine at Paws now. Peach looked rundown and distracted and neither of them mentioned Skip and Marcy.

Holly closed the gate behind her on the section of the compound where they kept the new feral cats in a quarantine area, looking for Brenda. Many of them would run up into the pines and the cat trees when people walked through the grounds. She had to get going to take care of her own stuff. She found Brenda in the shed where they kept birthing mothers and kittens. As Peach had predicted, the volunteer pool dried up with the paper fanning the flames and without the spark of her cheerful bustle, her energy animating the place. The ones who had stuck with them were working so hard they couldn't ask them to do this for long. Today the kennels smelled because there weren't enough of them to keep the boxes clean.

Brenda looked over her shoulder at Holly and grimaced. "Did you ever? If I'd talked to my mother like that, she would have smacked me. 'Course we never had ten cents to argue over."

"Horrible, isn't it?" Holly agreed. "Peach say anything to you afterward?"

Brenda shook her head. "I think she was embarrassed."

"Say, how's things going with Mike?"

Brenda's face pinkened. "He's a fabulous guy. I'm so lucky. Everything's great."

"I saw his grandson with a new golf cart. Mike buy him that?"

"Hardly. Mike's got big bills. Soon as he takes care of that, we're talking about moving in together," she beamed. "That's if Boz gets his ass out of there."

"Where would Boz get the money for a new golf cart then?"

She lifted her shoulders in a big shrug. "Beats me. Maybe he borrowed it. Boz lies, you know."

Everybody lies.

A big, confident man wearing a Stetson and cowboy boots sauntered down the stairs from Peach's kitchen and walked toward a gleaming black Range Rover. Holly spotted him as she closed the gate, coming back to the main building with a dolly stacked high with boxes of kitten formula.

She couldn't help curling her lip as an already horrible day curdled even further. Larry Zentner was the outside hustler for a big land development company. She knew Zentner from public meetings the company staged to brainwash the local yokels about their new housing plans. Sure, development would bring a few minimum wage jobs and up property values for anybody living close by. But there was no water to support 600 new homes. Wells were going dry all over the mountain. She paused, pretending to read the label on a box of kitten formula until he drove away. Before getting in the Range Rover, he took a handkerchief from his pocket and polished a spot on the mirror of the big SUV, then swaggered over to her.

"I don't know why you people are afraid of anything new," he said in his booming politician's voice. "Developing her land is a good thing for construction jobs, this whole community. People around here need this. Why don't you talk to her?"

"Larry, the town Council would bring in a toxic waste dump if it meant enough taxes to buy one golf course improvement. Hey, you could build a nuclear waste storage facility if you can get her to sell? That would mean even more jobs, doncha think?"

He climbed in his Range Rover, tilting his hat to her as he drove off. Holly watched him as he turned onto the road. Was Peach courting them for a donation? Or was she really going to sell?

The thing to do was ask.

Peach sat at the kitchen table holding two kittens in her lap, a half-filled cup of coffee in front of her, no makeup, yesterday's clothes on. Holly picked up the mama cat from a box near the pellet stove. Peach stared out the window into the parking lot and didn't even say hello to her. Holly sat down in silence, the marmalade mama cat in her lap.

Peach pushed the latest edition of the local paper across the table. "Look. It's about my first husband."

Holly grimaced and shoved the paper back at her. "I saw it."

"Along with everybody else in town. I met Beatrice O'Malley in the grocery store yesterday, and she screamed *killer* at me. Right in the produce aisle."

"Peach, everybody knows that O'Malley creature is a crazy woman. Her kid is in jail. Her husband's a waste of space. She isn't important."

"Those foundation people that support us talk to each other. They'll all know."

"It hasn't happened yet. Don't borrow trouble from the future, Peach. The animal community loves you. The volunteers. We all do."

"Everybody except my own children." She gave a long sigh. "No matter what I give them, it's never enough." A Maine coon jumped down from a cat tree near the window, stretched, blinked at them, and stalked out of the room.

"Not much you can do about that." The nicest people sometimes had awful children. "What's that snake Larry Zenter doing here? I saw him leave."

"He wants my ten acres plus that piece I bought. But of course he doesn't want the cattery or the outbuildings. He'd demolish everything. And you know Best Pals, the dog place, has been calling me too." Her shoulders slumped. "Holly, I don't have enough energy to get up and do the dishes, much less take on a huge operation like we planned for taking in dogs. Everybody's badgering me now. Skip wants me to sell and give him the money. My daughter wants to move back to the city, and she wants big money to do that. Everybody's got his hand out. Don used to get hit up all the time. He was so generous to people, and it was never enough." She looked up. "I admire you, Holly. You need more money so you set up a business and do dog grooming. Why can't my kids be more self-sufficient? What makes them think I should give them everything I've worked for? I just want everybody to go away and leave me alone."

"My parents never had it to give, Peach. Maybe I'd be there with my hand out too if they had. I'm not that damn wonderful. You're not really considering selling to that sleazy developer, are you?"

"I can't help thinking about it. He's so forceful and they're offering such a good deal. I don't know about anything anymore. I wish Don was here to help me." She sighed and gave her a long, considering look. "Holly, I need you to give me a break and run Paws for a while."

Holly looked at her in surprise. "But Brenda thinks you've asked her to do that. She expects that. And so does Doreen? Now you're asking me?"

"But I never formally offered it to either of them. I was only thinking out loud."

"But they think you did, Peach. That's what's important."

Her face collapsed. "Don and I were so awful about management and so forth. I don't know if I can go on, Holly."

"Peach, you have to. None of us can raise money like you do. All we'd do is have a bake sale or a car wash, and that wouldn't keep Paws going."

"If I could only sleep..." Peach was crying again. "I keep hearing noises at night. I don't even want to tell you what goes through my mind. Holly, it's such a mess."

"Yep, it's a mess. But we can't sit here in the kitchen and make it any better. So why don't you change clothes and freshen up? Let's go out and see what's going on with the cats. The volunteers need to see you making an effort. And it will make you feel better."

Slowly she collected herself. "Okay. Give me ten minutes."

"Have a shower, Peach. You need it," Holly said. "Don wouldn't like to have seen you like this."

A look of horror swept across Peach's face. "Oh, my heavens! You mean I smell?"

Holly nodded, smiling. Peach fled up the stairs.

While she waited for Peach to return, Holly went out into the cattery to thank the volunteers who had showed up today. Chloe closed the gate in the fence at the outbuilding where they isolated the cats with feline AIDS and leukemia. A glint of silver at her throat caught Holly's attention.

"Chloe," Holly said, leaning in the doorframe. "What's that you're wearing around your neck?" Holly reached forward to touch the object on a silver chain.

"Boz gave me this. It's nice. It's a kitty and a heart."

"Where did he get that?" Holly said. "I've seen that before."

Chloe reared back, a red line of emotion spreading across her face, which went from surprise to anger to a flush of resentment. "You have not," she spluttered. "It's mine. Boz got it in Los Angeles just for me."

"I think I've seen it before. Funny, huh?"

"No, you haven't. It's mine."

Where had she seen it? Chloe had to know something about the shrine, but if Boz and the O'Malleys had anything to do with it, she wouldn't get anything out of her. She tucked the idea away and ran for her Jeep to check in for her shift. The boss insisted she watch the turnoff which led up to the shrine. The homeowners wanted to see action. She snorted, thinking this was a stupid idea, but she would do what she was told.

She made it to the Security office with minutes to spare. She was stopped in the lobby of the town hall by Caryl Hellman, the office manager, who whooshed out of the door in her wheel chair to alert her to a feral cat with a litter of kittens under the deck at the side of the building. Do something about this. Sigh.

Between mandolin lessons and now the Spanish class, nights together with Stafford were even fewer. "So if you're not coming over tonight, will you at least tell me where your case is at with Peach?" Holly badgered Dex on the phone. "Please, please. This is agony."

"Holly, Holly, Holly, you know I can't do that," he laughed. In the background she could hear the chatter of police radio.

She loved the way he laughed. It made her wriggle in the seat of her Jeep. "Yeah well, a hint?"

"I can't." Then he went silent.

She took another tack. "I happened to be there when Marcy and Skip had a big fight. Did you know Peach gave Skip $10,000 not that long ago? In cash, mind you."

Stafford whistled. "So that's where it went. We were looking for that $10,000."

"I bet you thought she used it to hire a hit man, didn't you? I told you she had nothing to do with Don's death. C'mon, tell me something. I gave you something. Okay, I'll torture it out of you. When can we get together again?"

"You're not free all that often either, babe," he pointed out. They compared days off and this weekend didn't look good either. The costs of a geographically undesirable relationship were becoming apparent. Dammit. She couldn't blame him for playing it close. If she were in his shoes, she would have done the same thing.

CHAPTER THIRTY-TWO

Late that night when Holly got home and was cleaning her own cat boxes, Peach called, her voice shaking.

"I heard noises downstairs, Holly. Then I heard a truck door slam and drive away."

"You sure? I looked the other night and there was nobody there when you called. Never mind. I'll come over."

"Thank you, thank you."

Tired and exasperated, Holly drove over to Paws. Peach's old dog Lily, supposedly the outside watch dog, shambled up to greet her. Peach unlocked the kitchen door, pulling her white chenille bathrobe tight around her waist. She had lost weight, mostly in her face, which had sagged into a pale and gaunt look. Absent-mindedly, she reached down and petted Lily. A tic had started under Peach's eye. She reached up and held it still with her fingertips.

"Did you see anybody?"

"I swear I heard somebody downstairs."

"Lily didn't bark, did she?" A thought occurred to Holly. She got behind Lily and clapped her hands and shouted Lily's name. The old dog didn't turn.

Peach flushed. She met Holly's eyes and nodded. "I know. She's gone deaf too. I know she's no watchdog."

"Wouldn't you feel more comfortable with an alarm system?"

"Yes, but Skip says they're so expensive…"

Holly took a big breath and zipped her lip at the mention of Skip Bryson. She believed Peach. The O'Malleys? Or was it Don's killer poking around looking for something? For what, though? Holly cleared the downstairs, checking windows and locks. She went out the front door onto the deck. Peach followed her, two steps behind. There was a cigarette butt crushed into the floor. Holly shone her Maglite on it.

"Peach, I sat out here this afternoon socializing that new litter of ferals. I would have noticed a butt on the floor where we were sitting. Nobody smokes here."

Holly went back in the house, Peach close behind her. One of the living room windows that looked out onto the deck wasn't locked. She pointed this out to Peach.

"See that." Holly hooked a finger under the sash and slid the window up. "Somebody could walk right up the stairs onto the deck, slide that window up, and step inside. Slick as shit."

"Oh Holly, no. That chair has been moved too. Look, you can see the marks where it was." She looked at Holly, aghast. "I hoped it was just my imagination. Since I started taking these pills the doctor gave me, I have terrible nightmares. Sometimes you don't know what's real, whether you're awake or asleep." She slumped into the couch and threw several throw pillows on the floor. "Come and sit by me, Lily." Peach pulled the old dog up on the couch next to her. "You're an inside dog from now on."

"Please check into a security system, Peach. And another dog." Holly caught Peach's look of alarm.

"I'll help you get the right dog. We found Lily, didn't we? It'll be okay. We need a dog with big teeth who's going to scare somebody."

"I can imagine what a barking dog will do to the O'Malley's. Of course, I have to listen to their dogs bark," Peach said with a wry chuckle. "Serve them right."

Holly looked across the road at the O'Malley place. "They'd complain if dogs were barking on the moon. Tell you what. I'll sleep down here the rest of the night."

"Oh, would you, Holly? I don't think I can sleep now knowing there really was somebody in the house."

"I'll also mention it to Dex. He'll want to know this."

Holly and Brenda were cleaning kennels in the cool of the morning when they heard raised voices outside in the parking lot. The two women exchanged a look and then ran down the corridor to the outside. Skip Bryson had a fist cocked back to hit a man Holly didn't know. She took the stairs down from the deck three at a time hollering, "Hey, hey, what's going on here?"

She'd had to break up a lot of fights in her time and knew how to do it the easy way. You're in a real fight for two minutes and you're winded. Bar fights, you let them wear themselves out first before stepping in and grabbing the biggest one. She picked her moment and came up behind Skip and grabbed his hand, twisting the knuckles up backward. She yanked his arm behind him, jerked it up good and hard so it hurt. Bryson bellowed, and tried to pull her over his back. She twisted her hip, kicked him hard behind the knee and he went down. He tried to get up again, but she leaned her knee on his back and put her full weight on him.

Behind her, she heard Peach shrieking, the other man muttering curses and breathing hard. Skip stayed down, screaming about his shoulder as though she'd permanently maimed him.

The other guy leaned forward, his hands on his knees, panting. "Lady, get this lunatic away from me." Blood dripped from his nose.

"What's going on here?" Holly demanded. "Skip, you touch me again and you'll be sorry."

"You're just a cop wannabe. A security guard."

"You're on the ground right now. And I'm not." She looked over at the other guy leaking blood on his nice suit.

"You all right?" Holly glanced up and saw Peach Bryson at the top of the steps. Peach came down the stairs slowly, her hand on the rail. She shook her head at her son.

"Skip, what have you done?"

"Hey, I saw this guy back in the kennels and he gave me attitude. He wouldn't tell me who he is," Bryson said huffily.

"Who is this jerk?" The other man looked to Peach Bryson. He stood up and wiped his sleeve across his nose and then held his head back, pinching his nostrils between two fingers.

"This is my son," Peach said wearily. "Honestly, Skip, I don't know what to do with you. Come inside, Gregory. Let's take care of that nosebleed." She looked at Holly. "Gregory is from Best Pals."

Oh. The dog sanctuary that wanted Paws. Holly let Bryson up. He took hard sweeps at his pant legs to shake the dust off, glaring at her. He would be a long time forgetting a woman had put him down.

Peach turned to her son. "Skip, I'll talk to you later. Go home, please."

"Mom, I was trying to protect you."

"Please, Skip. Go home." She turned to Holly. "Thank you."

Skip left, trailing the anger behind him like the odor of dead meat.

⊨⊩ ⊪⊨

"God, I can't believe you did that," Brenda squealed, beckoning Holly back in the cattery. "I saw Skip come at you and I thought, oh my God, he's going to kill her. I had just grabbed the axe to go out and defend you."

"An axe? Geez, Bren." Holly laughed but her shoulder hurt, the shoulder where she'd been shot four years ago in a drug bust clusterfuck back in Utah. She rolled it and hiked it up and down to make sure it wasn't going to give her more trouble. If Skip had got up off the ground and gone for her....she don't know what would have happened. Did she have any business thinking she was ready to work the streets again?

She and Brenda played the scene over and over again. Then she called Stafford to tell him as she drove into work.

"So Bryson likes to fight, does he? Doesn't surprise me."

"Peach always says Skip has an explosive temper and it isn't possible for him to control it. I figure he doesn't even try because he knows he can get away with it."

"Yeah, I've heard that story from a few mothers and girlfriends, wives too. The poor guy," Dex said with a snort.

"Do you know if there's been any incidents with Skip's wife" Holly asked quickly before Dex shut off the flow of information. "Don't you ever wonder what her life is like?"

He didn't answer. "You ever break his alibi for the night Don was murdered?" she said quickly.

"Yes and no. We tried. Believe me. We interviewed a whole string of people trying."

"Rats. I'd love to see you take him down." Holly laughed. "So when do I get hold of you again?"

"Sunday? Your place?"

"Sunday," she moaned. "I'm breathless with anticipation."

"That's if nothing else pops in the meantime."

"Right. What could possibly happen in the life of a homicide detective?"

"And thanks for telling me this," he added.

CHAPTER THIRTY-THREE

Stafford and Price had run out the investigation of the murder of Don Farrow as long as possible. There was also the budget, something TV cops never had to consider. If they forgot the budget for a minute, the Sarge was there to remind them. The will was still missing, despite the ads running in Southern California legal journals. Stafford had to interview a witness on a felony assault case in Taft and argued with Fields to approve a visit to Farrow's house to take another look through the mess of records he'd left behind. Harry Price stayed behind to work another case. They planned to attend Farrow's memorial service at a mortuary chapel later that morning.

He took a moment to leaf back through his notes and caught a reminder to nail down Don Farrow and Tingle Sanders' divorce date. While he had a moment, he opened public records and looked for the final divorce decree. Hunh. He called Harry.

"Never divorced?" Harry grunted into the phone. "Then his estate would go to the wife—to Tingle Sanders. Which would give her a damn good motive."

"That's what I'm thinking," Stafford agreed. He twisted and turned Tingle Sanders in his mind.

"She'd have a motive then along with Skip Bryson, Peach's daughter and whoever else we're coming up with," Harry said. "My money's still on the son. We just haven't nailed him yet."

"Is she savvy enough to know that?" Stafford considered. "She's pretty flakey. We gotta find that will. I still got stuff to look through here in his house."

"The way you describe her maybe she's dumb enough not to know. Get her in. Let's see what she has to say for herself."

"Will do."

No answer at Calming Mind Spa. He left a message.

Stafford made no further progress after a couple of hours pawing through the clutter of paper left in Farrow's ransacked house. He had an appointment while he was in Taft to meet Andrea Posner—the woman who'd called herself Don Farrow's daughter. She had been calling him, representing herself as the spokesperson for her seven brothers and sisters. If she had any claim on Farrow's estate, maybe she could give him a tip on finding the will.

Andrea Posner asked Stafford to meet her at her husband's law office. The location, furnishing, and general air of prosperity told the world Jerry Posner and his partners had a successful small town practice. There was always money in an oil town. Jerry Posner came forward and offered his hand. "You remember my wife Andrea?"

"Um, sorry about the other day," Andrea Posner said softly, tapping at the string of pearls at her throat. "I was a little upset hearing about my father's death."

"I understand," Stafford said. Upset? He was still wary. "Your father? We haven't established Don Farrow had any biological children."

"Please, sit down, Detective," Jerry Posner said. His wife went around the desk and stood behind her husband to establish her own authority.

"Well, not biological, but he always said I was the daughter he never had. I was his favorite out of all eight of us," she said. "Home wasn't all that wonderful, if you must know. He paid my way through nursing school and helped out some of my brothers and sisters, but I was his favorite."

Stafford waited while she went on about what a wonderful man Don Farrow was: understanding, kind, generous. She ripped out a tissue from the box on her husband's desk and mopped at tears Stafford couldn't see. "And that woman, that crazy cat lady. She's probably the one who murdered him."

Stafford sat back on the black leather couch. "Why would you say that?"

"She insisted he come and live over there at her place. Not that any of us live next door to him now. We're spread out all over the place, but you know what I mean."

"And the last time you saw him before his death?"

"Actually, a few months ago. Jerry ran for city council and we were just so busy, you know. He won, by the way. Isn't that wonderful?"

Dex nodded. He had combed through Farrow's phone records and Andrea Posner's name had turned up seldom in the past year. They'd never found Farrow's cell phone, on which Peach Bryson said he kept his business and personal calendar.

"But I knew about that woman, that Mrs. Bryson. He told me about her. We were close," she insisted, flushing.

"We're having a hard time finding his will," Dex said. "Would you know anything about that?"

"Have you checked around town? I would imagine Don would leave his business here," Jerry Posner said.

Stafford related everything they'd done to find the will, including his own searches through Farrow's records.

"He said he was looking into it one time," Jerry Posner said. "So the maker of the will hasn't come forward? There's been a lot of publicity about Don's death. You put in a notice in the *Daily Report*? That's for what's going on in the court…"

"Yes, we did that," Stafford interrupted him.

"Wills aren't registered until the maker dies. Then in California, whoever has possession of the decedent's will is required to file it with the Clerk of the Superior Court within six months. But I suspect you already knew that."

They did. "He could have made a will anywhere in California. Not necessarily around here. He had business in Los Angeles as well. For a smart man, Mr. Farrow left a lot to chance."

"That woman didn't even call me when she organized Don's memorial," Andrea Posner wailed.

"Maybe she didn't know how to reach you," Stafford offered.

"Hardly. My name and number would show up in his contacts."

"His cell phone was missing and that must have been where he kept his contacts. She put a notice in the Taft paper. That was the best she could do."

"Well, I don't think she tried very hard," Andrea Posner snorted. "And you know damn well she killed him."

"You bring me proof and I'd be glad to consider that, but for now she's pretty much out of the running."

Andrea Posner's icky sweetness, tempered with the mean streak he'd seen, made him suspicious she and her husband might have helped Don Farrow along his way. "Routine," he said, "but could you both tell me where you were last Friday from about 4:30 to 9 o'clock."

Andrea flew to her husband's side with a shriek of outrage. How could he, etc., etc. Begrudgingly both gave him an alibi. A good one if it checked out. Damn.

⇒⊹ ⊹⇐

Later that morning he and Price took a seat in the back rows of the mortuary chapel. So many people had shown up at Don Farrow's memorial that they couldn't find two seats together. Mournful organ dirges seemed to emanate from the pores of the old Victorian house, which smelled like flowery disinfectant. Peach stumbled as she sat down in the front row with Brenda and Doreen, along with other women they'd come in with—perhaps volunteers from Paws. He knew Holly couldn't get off work. Peach looked around and caught Stafford's glance. Her eyes were red and heavy-lidded.

She didn't react when Tingle Sanders Farrow flounced in wearing a short, tight jacket with a skirt made from black satin streamers that came to the top of her thighs on which she wore black fishnet stockings with garters. Sashaying down the aisle, every eye upon her, the ribbony skirt swung around her hips, revealing the shiny black panties she wore underneath. Eyes rolled. Tingle just grinned at everybody.

In the press of bodies surging out of the chapel after the memorial, Stafford lost Sanders. He left another message on her phone and he and Price swung by Calming Mind Spa to try and catch her. No luck. Doubtless she was out somewhere grieving.

CHAPTER THIRTY-FOUR

Holly watched Chloe sign out at the end of her volunteer shift at Paws. Brenda bent and gave the slight young girl a hug. "Thanks for coming in, sweetie," she said. "We really need you right now."

"Oh, you're welcome. I wish my mother would let me bring that grey tabby home. I really love him. Bye now." She jammed a big straw hat on her head and wiggled her fingers at Brenda.

"Say hello to Betty Anne for me," Holly called out as she went out the door.

Chloe ignored Holly. Betty Anne also wasn't talking to her, but another one of the shrine sisters she'd pinned down at the post office told her some of the women from the church had gone over to Betty Anne's place to attempt a reconciliation with the shrine sisters.

Holly watched Chloe go out the door and climb into Boz's shiny new golf cart. They paused at the edge of the parking lot, and Leroy O'Malley ambled out from the O'Malley house across the road to climb in the back, tossing his long black hair off his face.

"I know those three know something about the shrine. Or they probably did it themselves," Holly snorted, turning away from the window to Brenda. "Chloe and Betty Anne are fighting about Boz, you know. She's supposed to be grounded."

"I can see you've never had kids," Brenda said shortly. "Mike's isn't happy with him either. I know that."

Brenda had been irritable all day, inventorying vaccines in one of the tall cupboards that lined the room. "We spend way too much time talking about that little shit," she laughed bitterly.

She handed Holly a wad of cash from yesterday's donations. "Count this again. I'm making too many mistakes lately." She looked up. "And I spend more time correcting Chloe's mistakes, and telling her what to do next, than she's worth around here. That girl is dumb as dirt."

"What do you think she sees in that loser, Boz?"

"Somebody to get her out of that house with her crazy mother? Who knows?"

While they waited for the emergency executive board meeting to begin, Holly called up Carol, the church lady. Carol led the delegation to Betty Anne's house to reconcile with the shrine sisters.

"So, what happened?" Holly asked.

"Whole lot of nothing." Big sigh of exasperation. "Those nut jobs refuse to believe that we had nothing to do with their precious thingy. That's the last time I'm ever talking to her."

"Wait. Have you come up with any other ideas about who destroyed the shrine? I need something to go on."

"Betty Anne thinks the Sierra Club people did it but I can't imagine why."

"I can't either. Say, do you think Boz and the O'Malleys might have had something to do with it?" Holly suggested. If she could get them all suspicious of each other, somebody might talk.

"I would believe anything bad you told me about any of them," Carol said, "and I gotta go."

Instead of pastries fresh from the oven, Peach dumped half a bag of Oreos on a plate as the meeting began. No coffee. Looking at each other in an atmosphere of uneasiness, they settled themselves around the table, each of them with a cat. Were they summoned to preside at the funeral of Paws? Brenda and Doreen would be pitched back into hand-to-mouth minimum wage jobs, if they could even find one.

Tears rolled silently down Peach Bryson's face, silvery in the light from the window. She leaned her head against the back of the chair and closed her eyes. "I didn't even bother making up an agenda because we all know something has to be done for the sake of the animals and soon. Don's death has been worse for me than I'd ever imagined and all this rehashing about my first husband has been awful. Everybody knows Beatrice O'Malley screamed at me in the grocery store and made such a scene that now I can't bear to stick my nose out the door. I need to get away for a while. Then I need to make decisions."

Holly leaned forward and put her hand over Peach's. "We understand that, Peach. I'd like to wring her neck."

"I'll slash her tires, if you want," Brenda declared.

"If you're only gone a few weeks, I think we should be able to handle it, Peach," Doreen said.

"Well, I don't know," Peach said, fussing at the scarf around her neck while her hand stroked a calico cat in her lap. "I know I'm not myself, and I want to apologize for being such a drain on all of you."

Protest went up from all of them.

"Peach, we love you, "Brenda said. "You aren't a drain."

Doreen stuck in, "This is a terrible time for you. None of us think you're a drain."

Peach gazed around at all of them. "I think what's best to do is put Holly in charge of the operation while I'm gone. Would you be willing to do that, Holly?"

Holly sat back. "This I didn't expect, Peach. You know I've got my job and my dog grooming business. I'm not sure I could do it." She looked to Brenda and Doreen for a reaction.

"The reason I haven't suggested Doreen or Brenda is that each of their jobs are hard physically and they're at their limits. Well, isn't that true?"

"It's not that bad! And," Brenda protested, "I'm right here on the premises. I can do adoptions and make foster cat decisions. What else would we have to do?"

"It's the coordination with the board of directors, our funders, and events we've got coming up. Holly's got a nice way about her with the donors—not that either of you haven't—but the donors and the thrift store keep us going."

Holly looked down at the table. "What do you think of this, Bren?" she said.

Peach leaned forward. "This isn't a democratic decision, Holly. The biggest reason is Holly would do a better job of standing up to Skip. I can't stop him from interfering, and I know he's an awful bully. Brenda stands up to Skip, but it takes a toll on everybody else and the volunteers hate him. I know that. And Doreen, it's not good for your blood pressure dealing with him. So will you do it, Holly?"

Holly shook her head back and forth and ran her hands through her hair. "It's not like I'm going to be the big boss and throw my weight around. You guys both know that," she said looking at her two friends. "I don't really see it's going to make that much difference. We've always got along, haven't we?"

"I'm going to be available too," Peach added, eager to convince them. "I can't sleep here with all the worries, and calls I know I should be making, and things I'm plain not doing. And when I go to sleep I dream about Don being outside there in the treatment room. I've got to get some rest and sleep. So Holly, will you do it?"

Brenda shrugged. Doreen stared at me, her eyes sharp and searching.

"Well, it's for the animals and that's what we're here for, isn't it?" A nagging worm of worry gnawed away at her. "I'll take it on temporarily, and we'll make decisions as we go along. How about that?"

"Good. I hoped it would go this way so I drew up this document. It gives Holly signing authority. Sign it, Holly." She pushed the single half-page document over to her and she read it quickly. Brenda chewed her lip.

"Peach, you're not thinking of closing down when you come back, are you?" Doreen asked softly. "We'd have to know."

"I don't know what I'm going to be doing twenty minutes from now, sweetheart. The future looks like a white wall in front of my face. But you know how I feel about all of you. And I know you need this paycheck."

That was as much of an answer as they were going to get. They discussed a few details, adoptions in process, the foster cat network, deliveries expected, the next spay/neuter clinic. They made up a *To Do* list and eventually they all stood up to go, with a lot unsaid. Holly could tell neither of them was happy. Peach walked them to the door, talking fast, her voice nervously high, trying to convince them this was a great idea. A somewhat forced Kumbaya moment came when they stood together in the parking lot next to the thrift shop's pickup truck.

"I know this is going to work out. I just know it," Peach smiled, fondling the calico cat still in her arms.

CHAPTER THIRTY-FIVE

The next day was Adoption Day, the first day Holly was in charge—a responsibility she really didn't want. Peach left early in the morning for Santa Barbara. Holly loved the adoption part of Paws' work: seeing kittens and especially old cats off to their *furever* home. The kittens frisked around in a playpen charming potential adopters. The adoption room buzzed with eager families and excited children. A fit, older woman caught Holly's eye: gaily-patterned orange leggings and a rubbery-looking pair of tight black shorts worn over them, a midriff-baring, black tank top, and gladiator sandals. Her thick, gray hair was clipped to the back of her head with a coxcomb sticking straight up at the top, as though energy was spouting out of the top of her head. Holly hoped she would look so good swishing around in her 40's. Usually adopters were oooey-gooey cat lovers. This woman seemed to be checking everything out, as though she were going to buy the place.

"I want a kitten for a friend," she said, running her fingers decorated with big rings along the mesh on the front of the display cages.

"Cats have personalities, you know. Likes and dislikes. Maybe your friend should come in and choose," she suggested. "What if the one you choose isn't a good fit? We don't want the cats' lives disrupted by returning them."

"Oh, I'd never do that," she said, looking over Holly's shoulder.

Paws asked a lot of questions about previous cat ownership on the adoption paperwork and during the interview: vet care, indoor vs. outdoor, and particularly how former cats died. Holly gave her the adoption papers and left her darting from one kitten cage to the next. One of the volunteers distracted her with a question and ten minutes later she went looking for the woman to see if she'd filled out her paperwork. Brenda jerked her chin at Holly in the direction of those orange leggings heading back toward Peach's house where the public had no business.

"Can I help you with something?" Holly said, catching up to her in the hallway outside Peach's kitchen door.

The silver-haired woman turned and looked through Holly as though she were a window, the adoption papers in her hand. She smiled suddenly, a camera flash of white teeth. "Where is the woman who started this place? Is she around?" The questions came fast and hard.

"She's not here today."

"I was thinking of volunteering." She pivoted around to peer at Holly. "Actually, I'd love to meet her."

Volunteer? The magic words. Holly was now all smiles. They'd learned through hard experience not to take just anyone. Animal rescue work attracted passionate and unbalanced people. Volunteers all loved animals because they couldn't get along with people. A reliable volunteer who showed up, didn't steal, or pick fights with other volunteers was worth her weight in gold. Troublemakers all wanted to do things their own way, on their own schedule, and nobody else did enough, or didn't do it right. They didn't see the need for stringent sanitation measures and the reasons why Paws wouldn't adopt to people who had a bad record in cat ownership.

"Let me introduce you to Brenda then," Holly said, putting enthusiasm into it. "There's paperwork to fill out, stuff like that. We'd love your help." The interview would determine whether this woman was one of the unbalanced ones, which was Holly's initial cut in volunteer selection: crazy/not crazy.

Then a delivery truck drove up with a load of cat litter. Holly rushed out to meet the driver, crowding past other potential adopters. Their photographer, Pam, was taking pictures of adopters and their new cats to upload to the website and Facebook page. Paws played up big happy-ending stories, especially for a hard-luck cat. Doreen called in while they were unloading the truck to chortle about a near-record sales day at the thrift shop. All in all, a really good day for Paws, counting in adoption fees.

Shaking her gloves off, Holly took a look around for the woman who wanted to volunteer. She couldn't find her anywhere out in the cattery. Had she headed back again to the house? Suddenly her cop instincts began flashing. When she opened the unlocked kitchen door and stepped inside, she knew something was wrong. Something crashed to the floor in the living room. Picking a flashlight up off the table to use as a club, she called out, "Who's there?"

And waited. Of course the noise could have been made by a cat jumping up and knocking over a knick-knack. But things didn't feel right.

Holly eased into the living room the way she'd been trained. No one there. No cat washing itself energetically, looking innocent.

Downstairs bathroom. No place to hide in there. She yanked open the door of a closet where Peach kept cleaning supplies. The gaudy-looking woman who was supposed to be adopting a kitten for a friend stared out at her. Holly didn't trust anybody nowadays. Peach had suffered too much, and too many bad things had happened recently to ignore this.

"What are you doing here?"

"I had to go to the bathroom." Her face flushed.

"I don't believe you. Come out of there and sit down right over there."

The woman tried a jaunty, defiant look, but Holly wasn't having it. Hackles prickled the back of her neck. "I've been watching you prowl around. I'm calling the police and reporting you for trespassing."

"Oh, c'mon. I was only curious about this place," the woman said with waspish annoyance.

"I don't think so. People who are curious don't hide in closets. Come out of there." Holly folded her arms over her chest, blocking her way out of the room in case she decided to run.

"I don't have to take this." She held her purse in front of her.

"Yeah, you do." Holly took her phone off her belt and held it ready to call 911.

"Wait. Wait," the intruder said.

"Yes? What have you got to say for yourself? And let's see some ID."

"Who are you to ask me for ID?"

Holly put her hand on the top of the intruder's head and pushed her down into a chintz-covered recliner. "I'm the person who's going to call the police on you."

Instead she called Brenda who answered. "Yeah? What?"

"Can you come inside? Right now. I need you in the living room."

At this the woman sprang up. After all those hours in krav maga, the Israeli self-defense system, Holly was ready. Besides, the woman was off balance trying to get out of the chair. She swung her heavy purse at Holly who grabbed her arm and dragged her down to the floor. She twisted one arm behind her and had her knee on the woman's back without even breathing hard. Back in the day when she had been a real cop, she had to wrassle down people who smelled bad and nobody wanted to touch.

"Oh boy. Are you in trouble," her captor panted.

She heard the kitchen door open. "I'm in here."

Brenda stumped into the room. "What are you doing?" she shouted. "Holly!"

Holly grinned at Brenda.

"I found her in here snooping and hiding in that closet over there. Call 911."

⊷⊹⊹⊶

CHAPTER THIRTY-SIX

While they waited for the deputies to show up, Brenda went through the intruder's wallet. Tingle Sanders was the name on her driver's license. Holly and Brenda looked at each other and shrugged. Meant nothing to either of them, and the woman stayed mutinously silent, except for the occasional hissing curse. But she had an address in Taft where Don had lived before moving here. People didn't drive to Sierra Mountain Village from Taft 45 minutes away to adopt a cat. Holly left her wallet open on the red wing chair opposite the wood pellet stove.

"I'll let you get up if you promise not to run," she said to the back of her neck as her captive squirmed beneath her.

"You bitch!" she howled. "You hurt me."

"I can hurt you a whole lot worse." Holly declared, hearing her old cop voice. She wished Stafford had been around to see this. Brenda frowned, shaking her head.

"What are you doing?" she mouthed at Holly over Tingle Sanders' head.

"Get off me, you Nazi cow," Sanders screeched.

What do you talk about while you wait for the police to come?

━━◄╫ ╫►━━

Shavehead Deputy Jackson with the big muscles and no sense of humor showed up, barreling into the parking lot, scattering gravel and raising dust. Jackson must be hoping to apprehend an intruder with a long string of felonies to break up the routine. Holly still had the woman down but now it took real effort.

"Help me," Sanders screamed when the kitchen door opened and the deputy came in. "This beast attacked me."

Jackson knew Holly and had guessed her relationship with the Sarge and the detectives from Bakersfield.

"This woman showed up saying she wanted to adopt a kitten and started acting hinky. So I followed her in here and found her hiding in that closet."

"I wanted to use the restroom," Tingle Sanders shouted.

"Let her up." Jackson rested his hands on the equipment around his duty belt.

Tingle Sanders climbed to her feet and glared at Holly, who smiled back showing teeth.

"You first," he said to Sanders. Jackson held up a hand in a stop position toward Holly. "What were you doing in here?"

"I told you. I only wanted to use the bathroom." Sanders wriggled around, running her fingers through her hair, pulling her tank top down to show more middle-aged cleavage.

"Ma'am. You ignored the signs outside for the bathroom in the cattery and the sign on the kitchen door saying *Private No Entry.*"

"I didn't see them," she said gazing at him in challenge.

"Show me your ID."

Holly pointed at her black leather wallet, open on the arm of the chair.

"Take your driver's license out of your wallet, ma'am, and hand it to me."

Holly wouldn't undermine her position by arguing her version in front of Jackson. She stood there,

arms folded, watching this Tingle Sanders person protesting her innocence. With shaking fingers, Sanders
handed him her driver's license.

"You stay here," Jackson ordered Sanders. She
flounced into a chair. "You come with me, Seabright."

Denying herself the pleasure of smirking at
Sanders, Holly and Brenda followed the deputy into
the kitchen. Sanders was still rolling her eyes and
breathing hard, finger-combing her long silver hair.

"You know her?" he asked Holly.

"Never saw her before, but she's up to something.
Brenda can confirm she was outside sniffing around.
She told me she wanted to meet Peach and I told her
Peach wasn't here. Next thing she's inside the house. I
caught her hiding in the closet."

"I think I saw her at Don's memorial," Brenda
said.

They both swung around to look at Brenda. "Yeah,
I did. She was there."

"We'll find out soon enough." Jackson smiled
suddenly and gave Holly a slap on the back. "You
did good, Seabright. Hope she doesn't file charges
against you. Hey, maybe she's a reporter from the
New York Times."

Suddenly this all looked different to Holly. What if
she was? Or from some animal newspaper? Or PETA?
What if she was wrong? The deputy marched Sanders

out, running her mouth, her hands behind her in cuffs. Holly watched, now worrying.

—◄+ +►—

Stafford's head hurt. He was well into a long day of being lied to and nagging people to get things done. His head was exhausted trying to keep straight the details of the arraignments, hearings, and trials he had skidded in and out of during the morning. He yanked his tie off and crammed it into his pocket before sliding into his seat in the back of the classroom at Cal State Bakersfield. Sure he had some street Spanish. He knew how to say "Sit on the sidewalk with your legs crossed," and "Where does it hurt?" but anything else he had to think through word by word before he opened his mouth.

When the agonizing hour-and-a-half class ended, he threw the textbook into the back seat of the vehicle and headed to the lab to nag the criminalists, still thinking about Tingle Sanders. Alejandra Esquivel headed the forensics unit, and long after it was fashionable, she favored aqua eye shadow above her brown eyes. Her assistant with orange-red hair, freckles, and intelligent eyes looked up as Dex walked into the lab that smelled of strange chemicals. Esquivel ignored him. The tech's name tag read Perlmutter.

"Anything more on my boot prints?"

"Just the preliminaries." Perlmutter said with a scowl.

"Nobody's in a hurry except me, I guess," Stafford said, trying for a light tone.

"You know we had a multiple homicide in Oildale last night. I haven't had a chance to match the prints under the scope."

"What can you tell, though, looking at them? I mean, they have a tread. Can't you just look at them? Give me a hint?"

"With the naked eye?" Perlmutter said, as though considering some unusual new idea.

"C'mon, be a pal. Give me a break."

"You're not my pal, Stafford. Okay," he said with a long sigh. He glanced over at his boss who frowned and turned away. Perlmutter perched on a stool in front of the microscopes and stuffed his hands in the pockets of his white coat. "The print came up real nice." He paused, frowned and scratched his nose.

"And?" Dex tried to tamp down his impatience. Criminalists wouldn't tell you rain was wet unless they went outside and got a sample to test. "Did it match the boot we took from Bryson?"

"I thought you were going to get us that DNA sample from Bryson. The hoodie with the blood stain?" he said instead.

"We're putting together our case around it as fast as we can, but we don't want to tip him off yet by asking for a swab."

"And in the meantime we're processing that multiple from Oildale." Perlmutter looked over at his boss. "The boot print. Next week sometime?" She nodded.

"Fuck!" Dex exploded. "Next week?"

"You know we cast another unexplained boot print as well?"

"Yeah, but..." He and Price had pored over the crime scene photos again and again, trying to figure out how it had gone down. "You mean you didn't match it when you eliminated the paramedics and the rest of us?"

Perlmutter shook his head. "Not yet."

A window of possibility opened up. "Then this means somebody else was there at the scene?"

"Maybe. Maybe not," Perlmutter said.

That was a forensics specialist for you. Maybe. Maybe not.

⊶ ⊷

CHAPTER THIRTY-SEVEN

S tafford laughed to himself when Holly called him to say somebody named Tingle Sanders from Taft had been picked up for trespassing Peach's private quarters at the cattery.

"Oh yeah? Really? Sanders is Don's ex-wife."

"Whoa. You're kidding?" Holly burst out. "I can't believe Don was ever married to her. Geez. Have you seen her?"

"Yeah," he admitted with a laugh.

"What the hell was she doing here?" Holly hooted.

"You tell me," Stafford said. "I'll call you later."

His step was brisk with renewed optimism on the long corridor down to Field's office. "Hey, Sarge...." he said, standing in the doorway, slapping a file against his leg. "Did you hear about Farrow's ex-wife?"

"Yeah, Price told me. You think she's tied in?"

"Gotta be. Somehow…"

"So what have you and Price still got hanging?" Fields paced the office, squeezing a red rubber ball. "The other teams are bitching I'm giving you this long. I'm thinking of pulling you in on that multiple in Oildale."

"We haven't eliminated Skip Bryson. It looks like the old lady is out of the picture, far as I'm concerned. We need to pick up both Brysons and get a DNA sample. I want this over as much as you do. Forensics is stalling us…"

"Get outta here. Nothing I can do about that. The other teams are cryin' too."

How were they going to do everything at once? Sanders had been released by the time they tracked her down because Peach Bryson couldn't be contacted to press charges. Ah shit. Stafford decided to drive up to Taft to see if he could catch Sanders at home.

When he got to Calming Mind Spa, the wind chimes swung in the breeze. No answer. Stafford walked over to the young guy next door watering his dirt lawn.

"Oh yeah, her. She's a character. My wife hates her," he said, laughing and dragging the hose behind him. His big belly slopped over his khaki shorts and Stafford wished he wore a shirt.

"She's not home. You see her today?"

He moved the hose closer to Stafford. "Nope. She had a helluva fight with some guy last night on her back deck. Me and the wife were barbequing outside."

"Know who she was fighting with? Hear anything they were saying?"

The neighbor shook his head and his chins wobbled. "We were playing music. I'd tell you if I did. I'd like to get her out of here, her and all her customers parking on the street. Hell, I'd like to get out of this shithole town myself. Her car's gone?"

"Yeah, her car's gone," Stafford said.

While he was in Taft, Stafford took a dog leg side trip, and hit the principal at the high school which employed Skip Bryson. Les Aspinall was likely an affable guy in most circumstances, but not when a homicide detective turned up asking questions about their winning football coach. Aspinall sat behind his desk, one finger nervously tapping his desk phone, as though he were hoping it would ring and give him an excuse to flee. He summoned the Vice-Principal, Jerry Monroe. Monroe was introduced as the assistant coach who worked with Bryson.

"No, never any trouble with Skip," the Principal maintained stoutly. "Never any trouble. You ever see anything off, Jerry?"

Monroe thought long and hard and couldn't come up with anything. He looked like a deep thinker too.

"Funny, we hear stories about the coach knocking the kids around a little. He calls it motivating them. You know anything about that," Dex asked.

"Naw, there's none of that," the Principal assured them. "That would be illegal."

"And would you be able to confirm Mr. Bryson took inventory in the equipment room last Friday from four until about seven p.m.?"

"Well, that could be," Monroe conceded. "That's our regular track team practice. I saw him around then. You got his inventory report, right, Les?"

"That's true," Aspinall said, reaching for his inbox. He rummaged in it for a moment and came up with a memo attached to an Inventory Control sheet. "Yeah, yeah, here it is, dated last Friday." He passed it across the desk to Stafford.

"How long would it take for him to do this?" Stafford ran a finger down the sheet. "Number of basketballs, volleyballs, helmets," he read aloud.

Aspinall fielded the question to the Assistant Coach. "Depends on how thorough he was. A lot of stuff to go through and count, match inventory numbers and all that. At least a couple hours."

Stafford weighed timelines. Bryson could have started it at another time and showed up there just long enough to give himself an alibi. Would his wife even alibi him around 6 o'clock if a defense attorney decided to hit her hard?

"You mind if we talk to some of his players?" he ventured. "Maybe one of them could nail it down better."

The Principal and Vice-Principal frowned.

"I don't know," Aspinall said. "We can't be dragging kids in for no good reason to talk about their coach."

"I can see that," Stafford said, "but we've got a murder here. I'm sure you've heard about it."

"I don't know. You've met Skip, haven't you? Hard to figure him for that. He's a guy that what you see is what you get," Jerry Monroe said. "There's not much subtlety to him."

Stafford had to smile at that. "Subtlety, yeah. How about other people he works with. We need to work out a time line, figure out if anybody saw him in the early evening."

"I can tell you about that," Monroe offered. "I ran into him in the hall around 5:30. We talked about the season a little. You know."

"He say where he was going past that?"

Monroe screwed his face up into his thinking countenance. "Nope."

"Okay then, is Bryson liable to pop off without much provocation? Maybe against fellow teachers? You ever had to discipline him for losing his temper, anything like that?"

"No, not really. Can't think of anything." Both Aspinall and his Vice-Principal/Assistant Coach shook their heads vigorously.

"I'd think he's the kinda guy that'd be into martial arts. Is he?"

"Well, yeah, I guess so."

"Anything specific, Mr. Aspinall?"

"Oh, he'd mention it once in a while, but I've got no idea how serious he is."

"I guess we're done here then." Stafford rose to his feet. The two school officials got up as well and they chit chatted their way to the door.

As soon as he got outside, Stafford called Harry, laughing.

"Prince of a human being then, that's Skip Bryson. They were stonewalling, sure. But if there was anything official—or even off the record a little—Madison would have told us. He knows everybody here. Could be we're just after Bryson because he looks wrong."

"He's big and aggressive and mean," Price said.

"You mean he looks like me? Worse than me?"

"Ah, Stafford. You're a pussy. Squealing like a little girl."

Basecamp café was open and a good cup of coffee might lift his spirits. Maybe Holly could take twenty minutes off and meet him? He called her. Apparently not. She had paperwork to finish. He parked on the circle near the summer gazebo where it got so cold sometimes, the theater company handed out blankets at performances for those who came unprepared.

A family of girls with cocoa-colored skin held hands with their exotic mother, who got an appreciative second glance from Stafford, as they giggled their way past him. A bearded husband wearing a baby in a sling across his front and Jesus sandals on his feet strolled down the path toward him. Stafford gave him a smile. Life went on.

CHAPTER THIRTY-EIGHT

Stafford's heart clenched driving back to Bakersfield when he saw he had a call from the red-headed tech in the Forensics section. He pulled over by the roadside next to a barren field where almond groves had lined up mile after mile, that is, before the drought.

"Gimme something, please, gimme something," he pleaded.

First Perlmutter had to read the case number and check to make sure there weren't two Don Farrow homicides reported a week ago at the same time. Stafford stopped himself from climbing down the phone and tearing the head off the guy.

"If this is the correct case number and victim, you have a match on the blood we lifted from the item of clothing."

Stafford clutched the phone tightly, folded his lips in over his teeth and drew in a breath, letting it out with a polite "Yes?"

"Donald Farrow's blood. I can tell you that. But maybe you expected that since he is the deceased, is he not?" He read off the case number again and the item number on the hoodie.

Perlmutter dragged it out. "But we did get a match on the boot print. It matches to…" he paused to read off the case number and item number of Skip Bryson's Doc Martens. So Bryson had been there. "No blood found on the boot…"

"No blood? No blood?"

"I'm hanging up now before you start screaming at me…"

"Thanks. Appreciate this," Stafford said, swiping the phone closed.

Stafford brightened thinking about the boot print match. The lack of blood on the boot puzzled him, though. He called Price to relate the news. "The hoodie and the boot print is enough to get a search warrant on Bryson's house."

"We need a body warrant to take his DNA too. I want one for Peach as well, just in case they kick up a fuss. "

Stafford got back to the station and caught up writing reports while Price chased down the body warrants. He grinned triumphantly at Stafford, poking him in the shoulder and waving a document at him, as he passed his cubicle. "Get Bryson in. We'll do him first."

Stafford was already punching numbers into his phone.

"What in hell do you want?" Bryson snapped.

"Where are you right now?"

"I'm with my mother, you bastard. She's had a heart attack and they think she's going to die."

Ah, shit.

Stafford weaseled his way around the nurses as he and Price entered Peach Bryson's room. She lay pale and small in the hospital bed, tubes supporting her connection to life. They'd brought her back to Bakersfield from Santa Barbara where she was visiting a friend. She was conscious when they came into her room, but her lips were pale.

"Sorry to hear about this, Peach." Dex whispered, taking the hand which wasn't connected to an IV. She shook her head weakly from side to side.

A stocky Nurse Ratched marched in and stood, arms akimbo. They knew her from frequent visits to the ER.

"Out, Stafford. Out. I told you I didn't want you in here. Do I have to call Security to throw your cop asses out? Take your pretty green eyes somewhere else."

She wasn't smiling. Stafford sidled past her.

"We'll be in the waiting room."

"Don't bother waiting. My patient needs rest. She doesn't need to be bullied."

"Good Lord, woman. Talk about bullying. Who's pushing who around here?" Stafford protested, winking at her.

Skip Bryson paced the waiting room. His sister, Marcy, prayed, holding a devotional book in her hands. They looked up as Stafford and Price walked in. Other family clusters in the room paid them little attention, caught up in their own vigils. Dex called Skip Bryson out into the hall, removing an audience for his belligerence. His sister followed, the prayer book held tight against her chest

"I'm sorry about your mother. What do the doctors say?" Stafford wanted to start this on a positive note by showing his concern.

"What do you care?" Bryson got up real close to Stafford and sneered in his face.

"I'm getting a warrant to search your house," Stafford said, not intimidated. "We found a blood-stained Search and Rescue hoodie in the room where Don Farrow was killed. Wouldn't be yours, would it? We're expecting you at the station in two hours. Be there."

This set Bryson off. Screaming, yelling, and protesting his innocence. His sister dragged on his arm and he threw her off, so that she landed hard on a chair arm and began to cry. Stafford considered arresting him for assault. Bryson pounded the walls until the unit secretary stuck his head around corners watching. Security swung into the room in moments, and hustled Bryson out. It was instructive to see the guy provoked into the kind of rage it would have taken to kill Don Farrow.

Peach's old friend in Santa Barbara had been kind enough to notify Paws about Peach's heart attack. Gripped by fear for Peach and fear for the future of Paws, she still had to punch the clock to get a paycheck. No way to take time off to visit until her shift was over.

She stood with one hand on the roof of the Jeep in the parking lot of the community center, listening to Brenda sniping at Doreen. Since *Holly* was in charge *she* should do something about Doreen's crappy record keeping. As soon as that call ended, Doreen called complaining Brenda interfered in the running of the thrift store. This was *unacceptable,* completely *unacceptable.* Holly was supposed to do something about it. She'd known they were competitive, but she thought for the good of the cats—and Peach—that they would get along. Now the animosity was naked and *her* job to deal with. She got into the Jeep and drove away, needing some mindless patrolling to calm her nerves.

The back-to-the land people who kept chickens reported a bear destroyed their flimsy chicken coop. Burglars hit three empty cabins on a steep curve high up on the edges of Sierra Mountain Village, big news that flashed around town. Robbery was unusual and brought in the deputies from the substation down the hill. Holly hoped to run into one of them and get the inside scoop. The local online paper was all over it, trumpeting a crime wave, which it was for SMV.

The boss barely looked at her now since she hadn't come up with names, dates, and video of the vandals in action. The GM ignored her when he walked past her in the office. For him everything was an unending *nightmare.* She hit Stafford's number wanting to hear his voice, just wanting to connect for a moment.

Leave a message.

Unsatisfied, Doreen called back in another high mosquito whine of complaint, now demanding an emergency board meeting to settle it with Brenda.

306

Two busloads of Red Hat Society ladies alighted from a chartered bus as Holly parked to buy a pastry from the bakery. The ladies were looking for retail therapy in the gift shops in the village and somewhere to graze on trans fats and spend their money. High-spirited and boisterous, they streamed across the parking lot of the town's gas station dressed in red hats and purple dresses. Holly smiled at the old gals who liked each other and got together expressly to laugh and have a good time. What an idea! Maybe she'd join them one of these days—in a couple of decades or so.

CHAPTER THIRTY-NINE

Skip Bryson thumped himself down in an orange plastic chair at the station an hour later. Just enough time for Price and Stafford to get a strategy in place. No lawyer with Bryson and his superior smirk firmly in place.

"What's this about?" Bryson said after Stafford and Price had the recording equipment running and all the protocols in place.

"It's the matter of your alibi the night Don Farrow was killed. Or your lack of an alibi. Nothing checks out for you."

"Who did you talk to? I told you everything."

"Like I said, you don't check out," Price commented. He sat back in his chair and watched Bryson. Stafford stood by the door, his arms crossed, legs spread—the cop asshole stance.

"Try harder," Price pushed.

"How do you explain this then? We got a Search and Rescue hoodie with Don Farrow's blood on it." Price shoved a photo of the clear plastic evidence bag with the hoodie in it at Bryson. A sheen of sweat appeared on Bryson's pale forehead.

"That's not mine," he sputtered.

"A DNA swab will determine that," Price declared. "See, we've got a body warrant here to take your DNA." He waved the kit he'd taken out of his briefcase. "The tech swabs inside your cheek with a popsicle stick thing. If you want to do it the hard way, then it's a forced blood draw and that's okay too. We strap you down to a gurney and the tech takes the blood intravenously from your arm. They don't get much practice so they're not real good at finding the vein. So what's it gonna be?"

Bryson folded into himself, sweatier by the moment. "I didn't kill him. I don't know where you got that jacket. It's not mine." He lurched to his feet. "I looked this up. I don't have to talk to you, and unless you're going to arrest me I can leave. I'm getting a lawyer."

"You can leave, sure, Mr. Bryson," Price said. "But first we'll take care of the DNA swab. You make a call to your lawyer. I'm sure he'll tell you all about a body warrant."

Bryson already had his phone out and was making the call. The swab got done, Price and Stafford watching. Bryson ploughed past Stafford on his way out the door as though he didn't recognize him.

He and Harry shared a small smile. "We'll know in a couple of days," Harry said. "Come on. Let's roll on the search of his house, see if we can beat him home."

"And there's that other boot print. Somebody else danced around in Farrow's blood."

"There's always some detail you can't fit in. Don't fall in love with that," Price said.

"I'm tired. You drive," Stafford said.

An hour or so later they pulled into the driveway at Bryson's home. Stafford fumbled for the folder containing the search warrant. Bryson's SUV wasn't there. A couple of deputies from the local substation parked and came up the stairs behind them. The search warrant was limited to knives of any kind and blood-stained clothes.

"If we're lucky he'll have kept the knife," Price said to Stafford. "I don't know why you're so hard-headed about this," he said, pausing at the top of the stairs to knock on the screen door. "He's the only one with motive."

Stafford went pffft! "So far. I'm not signing off on him." He looked out into the mountains. "Beautiful place. Gorgeous. C'mon, c'mon, somebody answer the door."

Bryson's wife wore a long white robe and had her hair wrapped in a towel. "I thought I heard something. Hmmm, what brings you here again, Detective Stafford?"

"We have a search warrant. Please take a look at this."

She took it from him and began to read. They gave her a moment. She looked up. "This is a search warrant. You're looking for knives and blood-stained clothes? Here? In my house?"

"Right."

"Then you really think Skip killed Don? No, No. I don't believe this." She went back to reading the search warrant while they stood there, her face coloring as they shifted from foot to foot, anxious to get started.

"Ma'am, we don't need your permission to come in," Harry said. Dex was glad to let him be the bad guy.

"Skip's meeting with a lawyer right now," she whispered. "You've got him really upset. He told me about the blood on the hoodie. There must be some explanation. But Skip should be here for this. He can tell you....I mean, my husband is an asshole. No argument. But he's not a killer, I don't think." Some hesitation there. "You can just come in?"

"That's the way it works," Harry said.

The deputies came forward and she stepped aside. "The house is a mess. I'm preparing for my final orals. Um, all of Skip's stuff is downstairs. He lives down there." She pointed to the stairs.

"We need to search the whole house," Harry said. He snapped off orders in a low voice to the deputies.

"Take it easy with things, guys," Dex said. The residence of a meth cooker didn't matter. This was a nice house, messy with books and papers, but clean and sweet smelling with bowls of potpourri on polished furniture.

"You take the kitchen, the rooms up here, Stafford," Harry directed. "You want to get dressed, Ms. Bryson. Call your husband if you like."

"I'm calling him now." She disappeared into the back of the house. He heard her talking on the phone, then the whine of a blow dryer and doors opening and closing.

Dex gloved up and started in the kitchen drawers and cabinets. Real cutlery freaks and gun nuts had weapons everywhere. Soon enough he found a Glock 40 in a drawer in a cabinet beside the kitchen door. Right. For the intruder coming up the steps. He was absorbed in what he was doing, knowing it was unlikely he'd find the knife back in the rack or in the kitchen cabinets. He didn't hear Arielle Bryson return.

She went to the stove and put the kettle on a burner, flicking the burner into life. She reached up and took down a box of teabags. As the kettle hissed, she crossed her arms and perched on a stool at the table. "He's got guns, I know that. They're not mine, you know."

Dex nodded as he searched the kitchen drawers.

She got up to make her cup of tea and returned to the stool at the table. "I talked to my husband. He says his lawyer's going to sue you."

"Yeah, we hear that a lot. Hardly ever happens. People get mad and then they get over it. The innocent ones at least."

"Innocent, huh?" She watched him with cool eyes. "You really think my husband killed Don?"

Dex didn't answer. He tried to stare her down.

She leaned forward and put her fingers over her eyes as though to hide a vision of what could happen. Then she got up and went into the bedrooms at the back of the house.

Harry and the two deputies came back upstairs later, smiles all around. They handed Dex a list: recovered were a complete set of kitchen knives and assorted killing knives kept nice and clean and separate in long, white athletic socks. His collection had been found in a wooden box in a bedroom he inhabited downstairs. Forensics and the autopsy report could tell them if one of the blades was a match.

"Whole bunch of other stuff too. Guy's a serious hunter," Harry muttered to Dex.

"Hear him tell, he runs Search and Rescue and everything else."

One of the deputies in earshot gave a snort. He picked up a magazine off the coffee table. A search in a John Q Public residence was something out of the usual. Here they read actual books with hard covers.

"You guys keep your mouths shut about this," Harry said, watching Deputy Jackson leaf through a *Smithsonian*. "We don't know what we've got yet, and I don't want it all over town. Bryson's a local celebrity. Winning football coach. Put all that stuff in the trunk of my car, will you? We'll check it in back at the station."

Bryson's wife came out as they were ready to leave. She looked around, gritting her teeth. Stafford wanted to tell her how lucky she was they didn't take the place apart.

"Thank you for your cooperation, Mrs. Bryson," Price said.

"My name is Cartwright, not Bryson," she snapped, shutting the door on him.

Stafford and Price stood a moment talking by their vehicles after the deputies drove off.

"So?" Dex said, palms up.

Harry shrugged. "Imagine yourself telling the DDA what we've got is a guy who's got enough knives and guns for a small war." He held up a finger, "No witnesses. His boot print…"

"As soon as we get the DNA swab we can be sure."

"That's good enough to start hammering on him, but we need more, a lot more."

"Maybe," Dex said, unconvinced, getting in the vehicle and pulling out his phone to check his email on the long drive back to the station. "But if we get a DNA match on the boot it's all over."

Sgt. Gordie Fields made a skeptical face when they laid it all out before him back at the barn. Fields took off his glasses, folded them up and stuck them in the pocket of his shirt, preparing to go to lunch. "What do you think of Sierra Mountain Village? Wife wants us to buy a cabin up there to get out of the heat in the summer."

"Not much to do. Hang out in the geezer bar maybe at the community center. Bang the ball around in the golf course, which is mostly sand now," Price said. "Whole place closes down at 8 o'clock at night. Beautiful, though."

"They don't even have streetlights," Stafford said, heading for the door. "And people think it's the Paris France of Kern County. I don't get it."

Price gave him a strange look. Fields went hmmph, grabbed a stretchy band from a desk drawer and setting his hands close together, pulled the ends apart. "Well, get out there and knock on doors.

You've got enough to interview the people he works with, his Search and Rescue buddies. You might get something there."

CHAPTER FORTY

Dex should have been thinking about making love to Holly, now they finally had the chance. He looked down into her flushed face and frenzy of blonde curls and thought about Don Farrow's killer instead.

She caught the drift of his attention and gasped, "What?"

His mind fizzed with a thought, then died. Her hips danced beneath him. He forgot everything. In the morning he watched her making coffee in her kitchen, the cats circling her, miaowing. She set the coffee filter down on top of the coffee pot and began opening cans of cat food and filling the water bowls.

"Hey, coffee. I'm dyin' here," he groaned, sinking down at the table.

She scowled over her shoulder at him. "The cats won't leave me alone until they're fed. I presume you've made coffee once in your life before?"

Truth was, he liked being waited on by his mother. The women at the station, the civilians at least, catered to him. The women officers didn't bring anybody coffee. News about his involvement with Holly hadn't filtered down yet, so he was still regarded as a hot property on the loose. So he got up and made the coffee and put bread into the toaster, and scrambled a few eggs. Holly wasn't a talker in the morning. The silence in the small kitchen was comfortable. He pinched off a leaf or two of parsley from a pot growing on the windowsill, chopped it up and sprinkled it on the eggs and lined up the toast. It looked good on the plate and he was proud of himself.

"You might actually be a keeper," Holly said, smiling. "When I see you emptying cat boxes, that is."

"Is that a test?'

"I don't know. Maybe."

He was getting the impression he liked her more than she liked him. Something else to think about.

Peach's house smelled good on Sunday, the day she insisted on being released from the convalescent hospital. Holly patted the gerbera daisies she'd put in a ceramic cat vase on the kitchen table. Skip brought Peach home. He scowled when he saw Brenda, Doreen, and Holly at the top of the stairs waiting. Damned if Skip would drive them off with his ugly attitude. Peach sat down at the kitchen table and immediately wanted a cat to cuddle. She looked tired and moved slowly, but the old fire glowed in her eyes.

"Tell me about the cats. What's going on?" She snuggled a mama cat in close.

"Mother. Never mind the cats," Bryson protested. "You should rest."

"Oh piffle, Skip. I want to hear about the cats. Tell me everything. Did Jasper get adopted?"

Brenda and Holly tumbled all over each other catching her up with news about adoptions, the current population, and the signups for the next spay/neuter clinic. They showed her the latest financials from the thrift store, donations from the website, and mentioned a couple of new volunteers who were working out well. It was a celebration, but Peach was tiring. They didn't mention Tingle Sanders, and she didn't either. Holly wanted a chance to talk to Peach alone and insist she press charges against that woman, not that it was any of her business. Skip banged around the kitchen, investigating cupboards, opening and closing the refrigerator.

"Are you looking for something, Skip?" Peach said over her shoulder, reacting to a loud crash. He was pulling ceramic casserole dishes out of the cupboards and acting like a little kid making noise to get his mother's attention.

"Just making sure you have enough to keep you going here," he barked.

"Well, it looks as though the girls thought about everything. Thank you so much." She leaned across the table and took Holly's hand. "As soon as the doctor says I can drive, I still want to get away for a while." Meaning Holly was still in charge?

"Mom, you're not fit to drive anywhere. I'll take you wherever you need to go."

"You have a job, Skip," she reminded him. Peach stood up and took a deep breath. Holly winced seeing her move so carefully.

She had a job too, she reminded herself, her own animals, her grooming business, and now making sure Paws stayed on track.

As they left Peach, Doreen pulled Holly aside to ask her for a loan of $100 till payday. Holly had the money to lend her, thanks to the dog grooming business. She gladly wrote her a check, ripped it off and handed it to her.

"I always thought I'd marry a rich man and have kids, and I wouldn't have to work," Doreen said with her mouth twisted up into a forlorn smile. Her thirties were passing fast.

"How would you ever think that's going to happen around here?"

"Well, it could."

"Probably not, sweet stuff," Holly said drawing a breath in through her teeth.

"You think I should move to Bakersfield? Maybe I could be a vet tech. What about you? Are you going to marry Handsome?"

"Stafford? I don't think so." It was the first time she'd thought it out loud.

CHAPTER FORTY-ONE

Stafford carted the last box of papers he'd brought back from Don Farrow's cabin in Sierra Mountain Village through the station. He looked around for a place, and then set it beside his desk. Nobody to release Farrow's effects to without a will. He could kick people who left their affairs in a shamble. Then the picture of the stack of mail on his kitchen counter his mother nagged him about flashed through his mind. He decided to go through the box of Farrow's papers one more time. Bills from vendors for scientific equipment, an invoice from a plumber. A receipt from Home Depot, all the odds and ends of paper that made up a life. He paged through looking for anything dated the week before Farrow's death. He examined them one by one and put them in two piles upside down: one for business, one for personal. He'd seen the yellowed separation agreement before, dated twelve years ago.

This time when he set the separation agreement face down on the desk, he saw a penciled note on the back of the last page.

Tingle: 11:30 the 12th. He scrambled back through his notes. Jilly Peters from the restaurant dated Farrow's lunch with a woman on the 12th.

He got Harry Price on the phone. "I might have something." He told him about the penciled note and the conversation with Jilly Peters, the hostess at the restaurant. Peters had led him to the bride-to-be and the photos of her engagement party. He'd emailed her twice and no response. Another loose end to tidy up.

"Tell me again what this is about," Harry said impatiently. "Yeah, okay. The 12th. That's the date he met with this woman. Could be something. But you got nothing to say it's this year. And you think it was Sanders? Don't get your hopes up. Why haven't you got her in yet?"

"I've been trying," Stafford exploded. "I put out a BOLO on her. She's not answering the phone or her email."

"Get a deputy to sit on her place till she comes home."

"That's not gonna happen, Harry. They don't have those kind of resources. She's gotta come back sooner or later."

The task of matching fingerprints to the renters who had been in and out of Farrow's cabin felt fruitless to Stafford. Other murders, other killers, had pushed it way down on the list of priorities. He'd explained to burglary victims hundreds of times that it wasn't always possible to get fingerprints, no matter what they saw on television. One woman even wanted the crew to fingerprint her cat because the boyfriend who had cleaned her out had picked up the cat.

"And we never figured out who tossed the place," Stafford said, his spirits sinking.

"The same guy who killed Farrow. Maybe it's those vandals Holly's after. Like they hear Farrow's dead and they decide to go over and see what they can rip off. We have no idea what they might have taken."

"This guy is pissing me off, whoever he is," Stafford said picking up his keyboard and smacking it down on his desk. Like that helped.

CHAPTER FORTY-TWO

Judith Cassill, the bride-to-be with the engagement party photos, returned Stafford's call as he headed out from his condo to go to work early on Monday morning. He had to be reminded who she was. Recognizing the name, he answered with an eager, "Stafford here."

"Sorry I didn't call you back. The wedding you know. Jilly Peters said you wanted to look at the pictures we took at Mimi's at my engagement party. We'd be glad to help. I've got thirty-eight shots."

"Could you email them to me? It would be a big help."

"You don't want me to identify the guests or anything like that, do you? My fiancé wouldn't like that."

"No, I'm interested in the people in the background."

"You didn't catch the guy yet, I guess."

"Not yet." He wanted to get off the phone and hit a diner he liked for breakfast, and talk sports with the guys. She wasn't done talking.

"You really should call her. She's nice."

"Who?" There were too many names swirling around in his head.

"Jilly, at the restaurant."

"I'm pretty tied up with somebody right now," he said, thinking fast, and suddenly appreciating Holly Seabright.

"Well," she sighed. "If you ever need a wedding planner, call us. We have the sweetest person—and she saved us a bundle. "

"That's a long way off," he said. "You think you could send me those photos now?"

By the time he got logged into the computer, the email arrived with photos attached. He had the answer.

Ha! Tingle Sanders. Gotcha, Tingle. Gotcha.

Stafford dialed the whole case back a few notches to see if he could get a fresh perspective. He'd run background checks on Tingle Sanders just after he'd interviewed her. No criminal record, which baffled him because he'd turned his sights on her when he'd learned she and Farrow were never divorced. Time to turn up the heat, which meant another trip back to Taft to see if he could catch her. She was conniving something. For one thing she'd lied about not seeing Don Farrow recently. Why was she trespassing in Peach Bryson's house? Was it the simple curiosity an ex-wife felt for her successor? Looking for something? Proof Don Farrow had married Peach? She was just crazy enough to want a look—just because. Lots of people did crazy, impulsive things—just because, whether it was panic, stupidity, bravado. He got up for a cup of coffee and passed Shanko's cubicle. Shanko was looking at baseball scores.

The ride up the hill to Taft was way too familiar. Nobody home at Calming Mind Spa. The day was hot and bright, the sky so blue it hurt to look at it. To not waste the trip, he started out on Sanders's block hitting the neighbors, sweat running down his sides. Walking up one side of the street, then the other, he felt as if his hair might ignite under the blazing sun.

He'd already spoken with the people on one side of Sanders' place. The house on the other side was a rental; they left for work in Bakersfield at 7:00 a.m. They were young and after work hit the gym, getting home well after dark. Catty-corner across the street he knocked on a door which was opened so fast he took a step back. He held his badge up and the scowl disappeared. The woman had the prim, severe face of an eighth grade teacher disgusted by her student's hormones.

"I've been watching you. I was about to call the police."

"And here I am. So what can you tell me about the lady who lives across the street in the yellow house?"

"Oh her. The spa outfit. Well, I'd never gossip about my neighbors."

No, of course not, Stafford thought.

"No parties. I'll say that for her at least, though from the look of her she's a good times gal. A lot of women in and out of the place. Too much traffic on the street. There is that man she lets park in her driveway, not on the street."

"Could he be a client?"

"And stay all night?"

"What does he look like?"

She wrinkled her brow. "Big, a stomach on him. Fiftyish. I tried to get a Neighborhood Watch going on the block but these people, they think there's no crime around here. You and I know different, don't we?"

Stafford nodded politely. She wanted to play on his team. Great. Always room for good citizen's eyes and ears. "We really appreciate citizens like you, Mrs?" he said, hamming it up for her.

"Mrs. James Elloway."

"Right. Mrs. Elloway," he said, noting her name down.

"I watch all the cop shows on TV," she said. "And I'm a birder."

Stafford's hopes went way, way up. Photos. Ah yes, there were photos.

"I happened to see an acorn woodpecker in her tree over there. They're not so plentiful around here."

Stafford nodded politely again. Nope, he hadn't seen that many, whatever they were. Thank God for old ladies. She kept him on the porch outside while she got her photos, surprising him by returning with the latest model IPhone, which she handed to him.

He looked away from her phone to ask: "Is there a sign or lettering on the van anywhere? I only see the back end here. Can you email this to me?"

"Certainly I can. But you can figure out the owner from the license plate, I would think. Can't you?"

"Yes, of course. Thank you." Put in his place.

Sweet old lady stereotypes are gonna kill you someday, Stafford.

A quick license check back in his vehicle gave Stafford the name of Michael Edward Jarvis and an address in Sierra Mountain Village. The name tugged at him. He let the thought percolate as he drove back to the station. He paused, fingers over the keyboard of his laptop, thinking. The air buzzed with detectives talking on the phone, hollering over the cubicle walls to one another, phones ringing, keys clacking, bursts of male laughter. He finally placed the name. The cremation guy Mike Jarvis?

Really? The same guy? How about that?

He knew Jarvis slightly from visiting the cattery: He was Brenda Viglen's boyfriend. Holly didn't like him. Yeah, he was big, paunchy, fiftyish. How did he connect to Tingle Sanders?

Hope flared up. Jarvis had gone to gangster college in county lockup a couple of times, short term. Years before he'd been a locksmith gone wrong and had been charged with receiving stolen goods. After that, they'd picked him up on petty beefs in LA County. Suspicion of a lot of things, no charges. A check on business licenses confirmed Jarvis had set up his dead animal pickup business eight months ago. Stafford did a fist pump in the air, and went to search for Harry. Price had set his sights on Bryson, which had never completely convinced Stafford. He printed out Jarvis' info and his known associates.

CHAPTER FORTY-THREE

"I got something," Price said when Stafford found him shooting the breeze with the desk sergeant. He followed him back to Price's desk and filled him in on what he'd found in Taft.

"Skip Bryson said he was at the school doing inventory," Harry said, shoving aside a pile of paperwork to perch on his desk. "Remember? One of the gals in the school office tipped me she saw him driving past her place, which happens to be at the turn off to the cat place around 7 that night. So he was in the area around the time Farrow was killed."

"Why'd she come forward with that? Why now?" Stafford asked, puzzled.

"She doesn't like cats," Harry said with a snort. "And he called her fatso."

"Does anybody like him?" Stafford laughed, a buzz high in his blood. They were chiseling down Bryson's alibi. A few more swipes at it and they'd have him if he was their killer. "But we can't pull Jarvis in just because he connects to Tingle Sanders," Stafford said, taking a seat in the desk chair. "It could be anything."

"Hey, Tingle knows him. Overnights at her place? She wants Farrow's money. She doesn't want to get her hands dirty. She enlists him?"

"I like the way you think," Stafford said.

"It comes from seeing the world from the ass up."

Another detective passing by stopped behind Stafford. "Hey, you talking about Mike Jarvis? Lives up around Taft somewhere?" He had his jacket off, sleeves rolled up, shirt pitted out, and carried a heavy box. It was 108 degrees outside in sunny Bakersfield.

Stafford wheeled his chair around. "Yeah, what do you know about Jarvis?"

"Girl Scout cookies. You want to buy some? Harry, you got money from what I hear. Help my poor little girl out. Can I put you down for a dozen boxes?" He set the box down on the corner of Harry's desk.

"Sure," Harry said reaching for his wallet. Harry was used to being hit up these days. Rosalie also wouldn't let him keep sweets at home. "Gimme a dozen boxes of Thin Mints. What about Mike Jarvis?"

"He's related to the Wexler boys that run the paint store in Taft. Mike's the black sheep of the family."

Stafford leaned back in his chair. He tapped the background printout on Jarvis. "Related how?"

"Half-brother, if I remember right. Younger than the rest of them."

"You figure him for a murder?"

The beefy detective who worked property crime tilted his head from side to side. "Be a stretch. He's small-time as far as I know."

Price ripped open the Thin Mints. Food was an attractant to both flies and detectives. Soon Harry's desk was surrounded and the second package went fast. Stafford got up and pulled the cookie detective aside.

"You got anything outstanding on Jarvis that could help me out?"

"Hey, man, I got cases of my own. Do your own work."

"Think the Sarge would give us surveillance on Tingle Sanders?" Stafford said to Price when the feeding frenzy subsided.

"No. Not for a weak ass connection like this. He wants to clear the Oildale multiple. Everything's going there."

The Tingle/Jarvis connection kept nagging Stafford after lunch as he headed back to Taft. She still didn't answer his knock on the kitchen door. The longer he knocked, the more his certainty rose she was involved in Farrow's murder right up to her neck. He strode around in back to the deck outside Calming Mind spa. Two women in halter tops and leggings who would never look as good as Tingle, waited, and none too patiently. He introduced himself and told them he was looking for her.

"Well, so are we," the one wearing turquoise cried. "We had appointments, me for a massage and Beverly for nails and hair. None of the girls in the salon are there."

"Any idea where Ms. Sanders is?" Stafford asked.

The older of the pair shrugged, and heaved herself to her feet, no mean accomplishment with the weight she carried. "Why can't she tell us if she can't be here? I mean, I love her to pieces but she's getting to be such a ditz. Like this is not the first time, is it, Suze?"

"I would have quit her but she's so fun," the one wearing black glitter said, groaning as she bent to pick up her purse. "See ya, Bev."

"She's not much fun lately," Bev said. "She sometimes acts like she hates us. We have the money to pay her and she resents us for having the money to pay her."

"Yeah, I wonder. Oh well, I'm off."

Stafford sat down in the low chair she vacated. "So why do you say that? You see anything different about her lately?"

"I noticed her nails bitten down to the quick. That's new."

"What do you know about her background? You mind telling me?"

"Oh, why the hell not? Over the years I've got to know her pretty well. She grew up in Alpaugh, little bitty crossroads up north in the San Joaquin Valley. Her mother did hair in the kitchen and Tingle couldn't wait to get away from the stink of home perms. She wanted to be a dancer."

"Yeah?"

"But she couldn't learn the moves fast enough. She's still got big ambitions, I know that." Bev stood up and spanked the seat of her baggy sweats. "She wants to live in a hotel and be waited on the rest of her life. She talks about that all the time."

"Sounds good to me," Stafford said. "Where's she going to get the money to do that?"

"She seemed pretty confident lately."

"Hey, she ever mention Don Farrow?"

"He the one who was her sugar daddy? She was way younger than he was. Long time ago?"

"Maybe," Dex said.

"She says he was still after her. Why you asking?"

Stafford wondered if that were true or just Tingle's version. "He was murdered."

"Wow. That must be the guy they found over in that place with all the cats in Sierra Mountain. And you think she did it? Oh, c'mon." Bev's face split in a wide smile. She reached over and slapped him on his hand. "Remember that movie *Clueless*? One of the lines was the aerobics instructor couldn't have done it. Too many endorphins."

He forced a laugh. "She teaches aerobics too, does she?"

"She'll do anything to make a buck. She'd suck off a dog for money." She fanned her chest with a hand pretending to be shocked at herself. "I can't believe I said that." She looked him over.

"Say, I'm hungry. How about a coffee?" Bev stood up with a slow smile, and swayed her hips in front of him.

He sniffed the scent of cougar in the air and excused himself.

He had eyes everywhere in law enforcement watching for Tingle's old Mercedes. What good would running do her? Did she think he would forget about her? He stuck another card in her door asking her to call him, then dropped in on the Wexler Family paint store, the business owned by Jarvis' stepbrothers. A gray-haired clerk directed him up a flight of wooden stairs to a loft area. The old building that housed the family business looked as though it struggled to hold its own against Ace Hardware. The loft area looked down on the main floor. He found Mike Jarvis' step-brother scratching his bald head over a set of directions to a cell phone he'd taken out of the box.

Stafford introduced himself. Steve Wexler shook his hand warily. Stafford noticed he had no eyebrows and a long, gaunt frame. Ah, chemotherapy. Radiation.

"What's Mike got himself into this time?" Wexler sank back into his chair at a wooden desk piled high with paperwork.

"Maybe nothing. A lot of police work is asking questions, seeing where things go." Stafford began, keeping it vague. "I'm looking for background, that's all, seeing what his link might be to a few people."

"Not like I'm close to Mike," Steve Wexler said cautiously. "See, my father married again when most of us were teenagers and Mike was the kid he had with his last wife. So he's quite a bit younger than the rest of us. There's four of us, all boys, and we all work in the store here. You can see it's a small operation and we branched out a bit as each of us came into the business. But Mike was the baby of the family and my father pampered him. Hell, we all did. I don't suppose it did him any good." He fell silent, shifting a pile of invoices, his eyes on the paperwork.

"Yeah?" Stafford said, to prompt him.

"He's lazy," Steve Wexler said. "Born that way maybe, or maybe we made things too easy for him. "But he was no use in the store and frankly, there's not enough money now in the business competing with the big box stores to support all of us."

"So he's got this pet cremation business now."

Steve Wexler rolled his eyes. "Yeah. Actually it's not a bad idea, but you have to work at it, get there when the vets call, line up new customers. That's what Mike's not good at. Followup. Consistency. What's he done now?"

"Like I said, background."

"Yeah?" Wexler stood up, looking as though it hurt. He jammed his hands in his pants pockets and went over to a file cabinet and leaned against it.

Stafford consulted his notes. "He's got a sheet here. Bad checks…"

"I know. We covered up a lot of stuff for him. Paid people off. Me and my brothers are tired of him sponging on us."

Stafford made notes. "You know anything about a Tingle Sanders?"

Wexler gave it a moment's thought and shook his head. "Her." He laughed, a wheezing huff. "Don's ex-wife. Surprised she held on to him as long as she did. She was jealous. Big spender. She thought she'd have the high life, but he was a lot more involved with his inventions and all that stuff. She wanted to go places.

He was a homebody. You getting anywhere on figuring out who killed him?"

"You see a lot of Mike?"

"Only when there's a free feed, barbeque, things like that. Truth is, I don't know why he comes around. He's resentful of all of us. Always commenting on things we bought, the way our wives look good. Always noticing we've got something he'd like, as though he expects us to give it to him. You think this store runs itself? You think it isn't hard work?"

"No, I don't," Stafford said.

"He does. Like when he was in the Navy. He got into the Navy Seal program, which surprised all of us, but then he was stupid enough to steal diving equipment and he got caught selling it. The Navy threw him out, which he twisted around somehow to blame on us. Like the way everything's Obama's fault. Right? Say," he said straightening up, "Is this about that murder in Sierra Mountain Village? The one at the cat place? I think that's one of Mike's clients. You think he was involved?"

"I don't think anything yet, Mr. Wexler. Like I said, I'm only asking questions." Stafford finished up with him, then took the steps down to the main floor liking the way the store smelled. Outside, next to a row of new wheelbarrows, potting soil, and water hoses, Stafford debated. Mike Jarvis was the kind of guy with big needs. Big enough for murder?

He wiped his forehead. The pavement shimmered in a heat wave that refused to lift. Bakersfield often hit the 110-degree mark and more during the summer. But up here, the heat bothered him more. People complained about the heat, then in winter complained about the cold. Because it was so hot, everything took longer, more effort. Everybody he ran into knew what the weather report said and wanted to hash it over as a real topic of conversation. A broken air conditioner was now a major tragedy. He'd seen the on- air talent on Bakersfield TV go crazy.

He got back in his vehicle and swung by Calming Mind Spa again. Nobody there so he called the woman that Sanders gave as her alibi. A Margie Trask.

"She got to my place around 6 and was there until 9 o'clock or so. I remember that night because she brought over this bottle of wine I swear she bought at the dollar store. I told her to take her cheap ass wine home." Trask gave a bubbling giggle. "Like she thought I wouldn't know?"

Stafford ended the call, telling her he'd be over later to get a statement. They dicked around a while fixing the time she'd be home. She was a very busy woman and he was just a cop.

CHAPTER FORTY-FOUR

Stafford had a satisfied grin on his face as he knocked on the front door of Calming Mind Spa and this time heard loud headbanger music inside. Sanders opened the door wearing a spangly halter top and leggings that outlined every line of her lithe form.

"Why are you harassing me?" she hissed.

Stafford took a step backward in the entranceway, his palms up. "Harassing? Hey, no hot fuzzies today? I'm calling on you as a member of the public asking for information. We're interested in a friend of yours, and I thought you'd want to help us. Guy named Mike Jarvis?"

"Wrong." She closed the door in his face. He knocked again and it opened an inch or so. "I have a client coming who's very important to me. I can't talk to you now," she said fast and hard. No beaming grin today like a cheerleader on uppers.

"I'm here now," he said smiling. "It will just take a minute."

She edged away from the door. "Okay. Come in."

"Let's see," he said. "You were married to Don Farrow from when to when." He already knew when they'd married and now knew they'd never divorced.

She barked out a date at him.

"What do you think his murder was all about?" he said.

"Search me. Ooooooh, I'd like it if you searched me," she said, her eyebrows flicking up. Now the smile with all those blazing white teeth. "Go ahead."

"Know something, Tingle? Let's quit fooling around. Don never filed the final divorce decree. That means you're still married. Bet you knew that, didn't you?"

"No," she said, eyes wide, teeth gleaming. "Really?"

"Tell me you didn't know that? C'mon, Tingle."

Again, the big, wide eyes of innocence, a twitch of violent energy. "I moved on and I didn't think about him any longer."

"But you thought about him later when he told you he was planning to marry Mrs. Bryson."

"Hey. So did he leave me all his money?" That laugh again.

"Don't lie to me, Tingle," he shouted in her face. He kept back the photos of her with Farrow and the engagement party. He and Harry wanted to get her into the station where they had control over the interview. Wanted to provoke her to see what she'd do.

She pivoted to look out the window. "Here's my client. She's fussy and you gotta go." She placed both hands on his chest, smiling hard, and pushed him toward the door. "You gonna arrest me, cop? Go ahead and arrest me. If you're not, I'm getting a lawyer before I talk to you again. Go on, handsome. Get outta here." Her brown eyes were so bright they were throwing off sparks.

"Call me and set up an appointment for tomorrow or I'll have the deputies pick you up and bring in you into the station in the back of a car. You won't like that."

He grinned at her and allowed himself to be pushed out the door. It slammed shut behind him. He tucked his business card in the screen door and drove down the street and parked out of sight of the house and waited. In the movies Tingle would pull out of the driveway and lead him to the bad guy. It could be Mike Jarvis. Tingle might also have some other guy on the string to kill Farrow for a sniff of her pussy. That was entirely possible.

Too bad waiting for her to lead him to the killer didn't work here. An hour later nothing had happened and he had to pee. But not before visiting his teammate, the nosy neighbor across the street, asking her to keep an eye on Calming Mind and let him know if she saw anything suspicious. Oh, she loved that. He wished all the dog-petting, tax-paying citizens were as helpful.

They had no reason to put a tap on Sanders's phone. The law was funny about that.

He and Price convened later at the Knotty Pine for a late lunch, a restaurant not far from the Sheriffs' station. Price put on his glasses to read the menu. When the food arrived, Stafford stared at his partner as he dumped half a salt shaker on his hamburger. When Price lifted his eyes to him, Dex pointedly rolled his eyes and said nothing. Harry had all the ills of an aging cop who got no exercise. And didn't care. Stafford had decided to go for it and have the Volcano special and it was slung in front of him, hash browns slopping over the edge of the plate. Forget his vow never to become the paunchy detective in the cheap suit, rooting around his teeth with a toothpick at a crime scene.

"So we've linked Sanders and Jarvis, whatever that means," Stafford said, eager to convince Harry. The mountain of food slowly disappeared from his plate. He was loading up on carbohydrates and trans fats, Mother Earth's own antidepressants, to deal with his frustration at the stall in the Farrow case. "No trespass charges, though, so she's hanging in the air. Madison tried to talk Ms. Bryson into it, but she said no because she already has too much stress in her life. I might give it another try, dog her a little more."

Price waved his knife in a circle in the air. "You got nothing, Stafford."

"I know you like Bryson but we only got his boot print and Forensics is still backed up on the DNA. Say, how do art dealers even get started? Don't you have to go to school for that? I mean, look at this guy. Does he look like he likes art?"

"How the hell do I know, Stafford. Ask my wife. She's got art people calling her all the time since we got this money, but back to Bryson. He's got a motive. He kills Don off so he doesn't get his hands on his mother's money. He owes Farrow money and can't pay. For all we know Farrow was raggin' on him about it. People kill over this stuff every day. You know that. Why are you so blind to him?"

"I don't see it, Harry. He's a high school teacher. A football coach. This guy's got somewhere to be, things holding him in place, a life, responsibilities.

He's a John Q. Public. Even if he's crazy. My money's on Sanders. Maybe Jarvis. The neighbor says he does overnighters at her place."

"Okay, I'll bite. What's her alibi?"

"She says she was with a girlfriend having dinner at the girlfriend's place."

"You check it out?"

"I talked to her on the phone but I haven't got a statement yet. I didn't have time to get back to her and make it for the briefing with the Sarge," Stafford admitted.

Price raised his eyebrows. "Get the statement done. And bear down on Jarvis. Tingle's got motive," Price said, mopping up egg yolk with a piece of toast. "She must be about ready to bust right now anyway waiting to see if Don made a new will. As long as we don't say anything to her about it, she figures she's home free. Her and Don Farrow were never divorced. You ask her about that?"

"Of course I did!" Stafford said, louder than he intended. Two patrol guys from the station turned to look at him and he glared them down.

"What did she say?" Harry pawed through the fake sugar packets for the one he liked.

"She insisted she didn't know."

"You buy that?" Price said, wiping ketchup off his chin. He held his finger up in the air to snag the waiter who passed with a pitcher of iced tea.

Stafford shrugged. "Not for a nanosecond."

⊷⊶

Stafford was surprised to get a call from Dwayne O'Malley's public defender. Dwayne O'Malley wanted to deal. Cops didn't make deals. They took it to the deputy DA.

"Is he blowin' smoke?" Stafford asked the PD.

The guy shrugged. "Maybe not."

They both looked at the deputy DA. It all depended on how bad he wanted a charge to stick on O'Malley. It was penny ante, but Don Farrow's murder wasn't. They got a deal.

The jailer brought O'Malley into the interview room. Price and Stafford introduced themselves and sat down along with the PD. O'Malley kept wiping his nose with the back of his hand, then scratching his stomach.

"Um, I might know something about that guy getting killed across the street. You know."

"Then tell me. I got other things to do." Price made his face wooden.

"Me and my mom, we both saw the Mexicans driving away from that cat place."

"Yeah, we heard that. And?"

"But it was afterwards…Like about fifteen minutes later, we're sitting there and somebody else comes out

347

of the place and goes tearing down the road toward town. He was in a big hurry, right?"

"Yeah? And you're just telling me this now?"

"You know how it is. Ma said to keep our mouth shut. She doesn't want us to have anything to do with that place."

"Like you might have done a little vandalism, a little burglary there one time?" Dex suggested.

The kid looked outraged. "Me? Us? Never."

Stafford laughed. "So what did this guy look like?"

"For one thing his shirt was all bloody."

Stafford sat up. "How could you tell? It was dark."

O'Malley waved that away. "Like the dude dropped his hat in the road. Ma and I talked about it. She said keep out of it. We don't want anybody in our business. You guys pick on us. We can't do nothing. And it wasn't like we knew what happened over there. Not then. Not till about half an hour later when all the cops started coming. Anyway, just for the hell of it, I walked over and picked up the hat because nobody else saw it, one of those good Tilley hats. They're worth about ninety bucks. I always wanted one."

"What happened to that hat?" Price said, his voice tight.

"Ma grabbed it. She wears it all the time."

Stafford made a note, suppressing his eagerness. "What else?"

"Hey, man. Isn't that worth something? How about you talk to the judge and get me reduced time. This place is driving me crazy."

Price snorted. "First you tell me what this guy looked like."

"He was just a guy. It was dark, man. He was wearing a light-colored shirt, and Ma and I both thought he was covered in blood. But that was when we were talking about it afterwards. Maybe he ran through the sprinklers," he smirked.

That was worth precisely nothing. "And where did he go?"

"Down the road toward town, walking."

"Walking. You didn't see him get in any vehicle?"

"No. It was dark. I told you. You gonna talk to the judge for me?" he whined.

"Doesn't work like that, O'Malley, but I might be able to do something. Gimme a day or so. And you're willing to swear to this, sign a statement?"

"Yeah, whatever. I got this rash." He started hitching at his pants as though he wanted to pull them down and show them his ass. "They won't let me see the doctor. Ma says I should tell you this. You'd maybe get me out early."

"Okay, okay. Maybe I can do something for you." Stafford was impatient to get going. Go after Beatrice O'Malley.

"You stay put. I'll be back."

"Like where do you think I'd be going?"

The PD shrugged and was on to his next case already. Stafford and Price gave each other a half-hearted fist pump outside the door. Well, it was something.

CHAPTER FORTY-FIVE

S tafford and Price headed out to see Mama Bear
O'Malley. Of course, she wasn't home, to make a
frustrating day worse. They tucked a business card in
the screen door and left phone messages for her to get
in touch. Stafford saw Holly's truck parked across the
street at Paws.

"Gimme five minutes, will'ya?" he said to Price. "I
want to talk to Holly."

Stafford wanted to make this work with Holly. He
did. He really did, he assured himself. When things
settled down he could put time into it. Yeah, when's
that gonna be, he asked himself, thinking of all the
cops he worked with who had divorces behind them.

Holly must have seen him coming because she waited on the deck, a welcoming smile on her face. His day brightened.

"Hey, babe," he said. "Gimme a kiss."

"Not here." She pulled him around the back of the cattery and was all over him. He was ready to ignite like a teenage boy.

"When? When?" she said breathlessly.

"Tonight," he said, pulling away from her.

She pushed him away. "I work nights for the next two weeks. The boss is on vacation. I told you that."

"Shit," he said. "I start days off tomorrow."

"Yeah, shit, crap and corruption. This weekend?"

"Absolutely. If I can wait that long…Hey, I want to talk to Mike Jarvis," he said. "The dead animal pickup guy."

"I know who he is. What's he been up to?" Holly said, looking at him skeptically.

Price got out of the car when he saw Stafford coming back. "Madam O'Malley just pulled in. Let's go," he said, jerking a thumb at the ramshackle house.

Beatrice O'Malley yanked open the door and peered at them. Willie Nelson sang a sad tune inside the house. She looked tired and empty, and frowned as she recognized them.

"What do you want now? Haven't you done enough to ruin my piss poor excuse for a life? Now there's nobody to fix the back door so the axe murderer can come in here and kill me and steal what little I got left to last me out. And what do you people do?" The initial look of weariness faded. Now the belligerence was back.

"Your son Dwayne called us in and gave us a story. Something you saw the night of Don Farrow's murder."

She twisted her head to one side, looking at Stafford from one eye, then came out on the deck in front of their house.

"So why didn't *you* tell us this, Beatrice?" Price said.

"I don't want anything to do with that old lady."

Stafford looked away, suppressing a smile. If anything, Beatrice had a few years on Peach Bryson.

"She's nothing but trouble. Ever since she moved here, her and her fancy friends. First she gets her boyfriend killed—that is if she didn't kill him herself. Then we find out she's already killed one husband. Why don't you go arrest her? It's like my boys are black. You're just out to get them." She slammed her coffee mug down hard on the deck railing. Some of it slopped over. She reached forward and mopped it up with the long sleeve of her sweatshirt.

"So your boy Dwayne told me a story," Stafford said, when she'd settled down and the vein in her forehead stopped throbbing.

"It's more than a story. That's what happened that night! We saw some old guy running away."

"So he's old now, is he? I thought it was dark." Eye witnesses were notoriously unreliable.

"We could still see enough," she insisted. "I might even recognize him again. There was something familiar about him."

"Why would we believe you, Beatrice?" Harry said. "It's been more than a week since that night and now you and your son all of a sudden remember something? You going to stand up and tell that story and expect a jury to believe you?"

"It's the truth!" she shouted at Price.

"Okay, okay, calm down."

"What about the hat your son told us about?" Stafford interjected. He got up and stood across from her, hands in his pockets.

"What hat? Okay. You want to see that hat? I got it." She half lifted herself out of the webbed aluminum deck chair she'd plunked down in.

"And you're willing to swear your boy found it in the road after the guy you allegedly saw dropped it?"

"Wasn't no alleged. I saw it with my own two eyes." Her face filled like a balloon with hot blood, ready to explode. On her feet now, she stomped into the house. "I'll show you."

She beckoned them to come in and they followed. Stafford gloved up. She marched over to a coat rack near the door. She yanked a hat off the stand: green with a mesh panel and leather loops. She threw it across the room at Stafford, who caught it on the fly.

Stafford turned the hat in his hands and looked inside. The label read "Tilley."

Price raised one finger and pointed it at Stafford. Stafford didn't need telling. DNA.

Stafford took it to the lab and for once he made it nearly to the head of the line. They promised results in two days.

Brenda Viglen's old Volvo took the turn at Freeman too hard and screeched into the lot at the SMV grocery store where Holly had pulled in. Brenda barreled out of the car and marched into the store, not even noticing Holly who followed the flapping tail of Brenda's old red checked flannel shirt into the store. Holly found her, head down, rummaging in the ice cream freezer. She and Brenda had shared many a happy half pint of Hagen Dazs at the end of a hard day's work at Paws.

Brenda looked up at Holly. "What?"

"Nothing. You were driving pretty fast."

"Yeah, so what? You gonna arrest me?"

Holly shrugged. "You feel like sharing? We could go down to the pond. I'll bring my own spoon."

"Oh, I suppose."

It was a fine day, as most days were during a drought. Lots of sunshine, the golf course hanging on. The golfers were still out there banging balls around in the dirt. The town council would fine residents who used more than a glass of water a day so they could irrigate the golf course. Priorities, right? They called the pond a lake, but it *was* water, and in the middle of a drought, a pond of water with cattails and ducks was a pretty sight. The bravest of the coots floated over looking for a handout while Holly waited. Brenda drove in with a long face and parked next to the patrol Jeep. She got out of her Volvo, slamming the door with her hip and sat down heavily next to Holly on the bench.

"Did you call him?" When big competent, independent, women like Brenda get knocked off course, it's usually a man.

Tears filled her eyes. Holly had never seen Brenda cry. Whine, holler, stomp around, dance her ass off, raise hell in the bar on Friday nights? Sure, but not cry. She took the ice cream tub from her hand, and pulled the top off.

"I haven't seen him in a week. I think he's dumped me."

"That's a pisser. You sure?"

She shook her head and yanked a handful of tissues out of her pocket and blew her nose. "No." She put her hands up to her face. "He's probably back on match.com looking for somebody thinner." Her face was blotched and haggard, her eyes small behind swollen lids. "It's okay. He has a bad temper," she said, sliding a sideways glance at her.

"What do you mean?" Holly said, even though she knew what Brenda meant.

"He liked to hit." She looked away.

"Ah, geez, Bren. Why didn't you tell me? I would have pinned his balls to the wall."

She shook her head. "I was so glad to have a boyfriend. I had these stupid dreams…" She put her head down and howled with grief. "Now he's got all these excuses. He can't leave because he has to wait up for Boz, etc. etc."

"Can't you go over to his place, knock on his door? Get it settled once and for all?"

"I hate that slimy little shit grandson of his. And he hates me right back. Sometimes I think Boz is just an excuse. I am *so* grateful I never had children, Holly." She mopped at her forehead with a bandana she took from around her neck. "Now the hot flashes are starting to kill me. If I'd known I wasn't going to have children, I would have had the whole business yanked out twenty years ago. And he's blind, Mike is. I saw Boz driving Mike's truck. When I told Mike, he said it couldn't be because the truck was home all night. But I know damn well it wasn't."

"Boz is tight with Pete," Holly stuck in.

"And the O'Malleys. Think I don't know that? They're all riffraff."

"Hey, Stafford was asking me about Mike? Any idea what that would be about?"

"I don't think I know a damn thing about him. Not really."

Just then the radio Holly wore on the belt of her black uniform crackled. She listened, grimacing, while the caller demanded that somebody from patrol should go over to her neighbor's house and get back the snow shovel the neighbor stole. "Gotta go. Is there anything I can do for you?"

"Kill that weasel, Boz."

Holly left Brenda with her long legs stretched out in front of her, worn-out Keds on her feet. Worried and discouraged. Just like Peach. Her own love life wasn't much better. Stafford was involved in his job. He was a mama's boy. Frantic sex when they could meet. Then, either he had to go to work, or she did. Every once in a while she'd catch that whiff of disdain. His caseload was murder and big felonies. She was charged with sniffing out vandals. Murder trumped vandals any day.

At least he didn't hit her. Was this what they called romance nowadays?

CHAPTER FORTY-SIX

On a fine late spring day, one of those days that lied and said snow and icy roads would never come, Ed Bradley and Holly took a drive up past the burglarized cabins. Holly had been storing up a piece of information she'd had for a while and figuring how best to drop it in. A couple of people she knew told her they'd seen Pete sleeping on graveyard shift, tucked in behind the church in the village. The big lighted cross illuminated the windshield of the Jeep. Dumb bastard.

"I noticed the burglarized cabins were ones on our Vacation Check log," she said giving Ed a sideways look.

"Yeah?"

"I've got my suspicions. You know that."

"You complaining about Pete again?" Ed had a blind spot about Pete. Maybe it was because it was so hard to hire a new patrol officer. Applicants knew they had to pass a drug test, yet they'd light up on the way down to get tested. Maybe it was the pitiful salaries. So Ed was loath to fire Pete, despite the complaints of his being heavy-handed with the homeowners. Holly didn't know about the guys working other shifts. Maybe they liked him.

"You know Lanny, the maintenance supervisor? I heard him telling the GM he was missing a whole bunch of new building materials. Somebody had to have a key to the maintenance shed because he had the stuff stored inside."

Both of them waved at the Chumash Divas, a group of older women who gossiped their way two-and-a-half miles up the road every morning, summer or winter. Holly had to admire them, and would have sooner had a spinal tap than do what they did. She turned back to Ed who was looking grim and dyspeptic. Problems so close to his retirement made his stomach rumble and explode with gases. Ed shot her a quick glance. "So, whose key do you think?"

"Pete's."

Ed rolled his eyes. Pete again. "Better have proof for an accusation like that."

"I know." She'd kept an eye on the terrible trio: Leroy O'Malley, Pete, and Boz Jarvis. Their Facebook posts were a chore to read—beyond stupid and illiterate. She knew from the sly references each of them made that they were the vandals. The senseless vandalism of the shrine was some mix of showing off for each other, some grudge she had no idea about, or whatever. Just for fun maybe. Who knows how they thought?

After work Holly and Christy went out for a few beers to rehydrate at Crazy Al's, the biker bar in town. At least Christy would have a few beers while Holly stuck to Coke. Stafford said he'd drop in if he got back in town at a decent hour, but she didn't have much hope for that. The bar looked out over the parched golf course and the soaring peaks beyond, dimming from lavender to purple in the twilight.

They climbed the wooden stairs and said hello to the pariah smokers on the deck outside the bar. The smell of hot oil and fried meat came from the restaurant downstairs Al had to keep open to maintain his license. The bar inside was crowded, people stacked up three deep clamoring for beer. Stepping inside, the noise was like an assault, shouted conversations, music from the band, laughter—like a party in progress. Christy surveyed the crowd. She had a taste for men, and an inclination for all the bad ones.

Holly's eyes stuck to Chloe, standing there with Leroy O'Malley, chewing on a skein of her hair. He had his hand down the back of her jeans and was fondling her ass. She was showing a bump. Ah Jeez, Chloe being pregnant would kill her mother.

She whipped around to hiss at Christy. "Leroy? I thought it was Boz Jarvis who was her boyfriend."

"He's a kid."

"Yeah, but Leroy's subhuman."

"Heard it from Beatrice O'Malley herself. She's been telling anybody who'll listen that Leroy and Chloe damned well aren't going to be living with her. You know they already got Dwayne and his girlfriend and their baby living in the garage."

"I almost feel sorry for Beatrice," Holly said.

Christy rolled her eyes. "That's how it is with these people. They've got nothing better to do except do each other."

"And do drugs."

"Where do they get the money?" Holly said, thinking of the golf cart.

"Pete's got a job."

"I can barely make it. How could he have anything left over from his paycheck to share? Wonder if he's also sharing her?" she said, tilting her glass at Chloe who was wearing that silver cat on a chain around her neck. It looked so familiar yet she couldn't place it.

"Peach used to have one like that," Christy said, her eyes fixed on the necklace

"Wonder if she's still got it."

The weekly newspaper kept fanning the flames of the vandals' path of destruction, and now they had the robberies at the three cabins to catastrophize over. The vandalism and broken windows in vacant houses got rehashed in every new edition. People in town were scared, excited—and pissed off too. Holly was tired of saying that village patrol couldn't do anything, call the Sheriff's deputies. The patrol department enforced the town charter and couldn't do a damn thing about domestic abuse, or neighbor-to-neighbor disputes.

It was too hot to sleep, especially with cats climbing all over her. Holly kept reading the stupid Facebook posts of the O'Malleys, and Boz and Chloe, waiting for them to post something she could take to Stafford. Instead it was all hints: Chloe posing in new clothes; Leroy putting chrome wheels on his pickup; a day at Magic Mountain on the roller coasters. Magic Mountain for the four of them would have cost real money.

Everybody was mad at everybody. It was hot and the weather predictions said it was going to get hotter.

⊷⊷ ⊶⊶

Stafford did a backgrounder on Margie Trask, the woman whose name Tingle Sanders had given as her alibi for the night Farrow was killed. She wasn't home at the time he'd arranged to meet her, and hadn't answered his messages. One more obstacle in a long, unfulfilling week since the murder. He leaned back from the keyboard with a whistle of surprise.

He leaned over and pounded on the wall of Harry's cubicle. "Sanders' alibi? Task has a record as long as your arm. Petty crimes. How'd she think we wouldn't find out?"

Harry snorted, tilting back in his chair "Maybe Tingle didn't know."

"You kidding? My money's still on her," Stafford said.

"And I like Bryson."

"Wouldn't be the first time you were wrong, Harry. Remember that kid out in Lamont? The one you said shot his mother in the foot, then the knee, then the hand? You liked him too and it turned out to be the father, not the kid."

"Yeah, well. Even if she's telling us a story, we got no evidence tying her to the scene."

"What about her buddy? Mike Jarvis?"

Price tilted his head to one side and looked up at the ceiling. "Bryson looks a lot more likely."

"Stay tuned." Stafford took a walk down to the vending machines and got a Snickers bar. It helped him think. When he got back Price was all smiles.

"Don't bother getting the statement from Sanders' alibi. Guess who's here? Your favorite aerobics instructor?"

Dressed in a short, flouncy skirt that showed a lot of fine leg, Tingle bounced from foot to foot as Price led her back to an interview room. Ahead of her she shoved along a second-rate lawyer Stafford knew from the courthouse, somebody who always looked as though he needed a shave—and the stubble wasn't a fashion statement. Everybody got introduced and he and Price took a seat opposite them in the mirrored interview room.

"You got something to tell me, Ms. Sanders?" Stafford said.

"Maybe. I'm tired of you harassing me," she burst out, twitching her important little self.

"Harassing you? I thought you might be happy to talk to me about somebody who killed the guy you're married to."

"Yeah, yeah. See this?" she said dramatically, making her eyes wide. She pushed a manila envelope across the table. Stafford took it and removed a document titled Last Will and Testament.

"Sooooo," he said, scanning the document then looking up at her. "You found a will. Where did you find it?"

She was all pissy defiance, fizzing with energy. "Yup, I finally found it. In a storage place in Taft. I just remembered it, and dug out the key. I didn't think Don could have been paying the rent on it all these years, but good old Don, he was."

Stafford and Price exchanged a quick look. Dex knew what Harry was thinking. Was that the reason to toss Farrow's cabin? It might even be the reason Tingle would take the risk of trespassing in Peach Bryson's property. And the noises Peach heard at night Stafford hadn't quite believed. Had Tingle been on the hunt for the will at Peach Bryson's?

"And leaves everything to his dear wife. That's me. See there." She pointed with a finger and the corded muscles danced in her tanned forearm. "It's all legal. Look at the dates. We were married then. Have you found a will cancelling that out, cop?"

Stafford grinned at the sheer outrageousness of her. She grinned back at him as though she were impervious. Price tilted his head toward the door and got up out of his chair. Stafford followed him out of the room.

"Get Shanko on her financial records and you write the search warrant for her premises," Price said.

"Gotcha." He made the call to Shanko then headed back into the interview room to pull up the search warrant template on his laptop.

Tingle grinned at him, all perky when he sat down at the table.

"And it's a happy accident he was killed before the final divorce papers were signed and you inherit everything?" Price said.

The lawyer dragged Tingle's head closer and began whispering in her ear. She ignored him. Stafford noticed she had purple pouches under her snapping brown eyes.

This was the cue for the lawyer to loose off five or six thousand words while Tingle Sanders nodded and yupped through it all. Stafford leaned back from him. His breath was rancid enough to gag a maggot. The upshot was that the detectives should remember the tender feelings of the grieving widow of Don Farrow. Stafford laughed out loud.

Something had built up Tingle Sanders' confidence. "I had nothing to do with his murder. That Bryson woman killed him."

"One thing we've been wondering," Harry said, "What's your connection to Mike Jarvis?"

"Why are you asking me about him?" she said, jutting her chin out. "I've got nothing to do with him. I met him on match.com. So what? We dated."

"Yeah? Match.com?"

"Yeah, and unless you're going to arrest me, cop, I'm leaving." She capered over to the door, the lawyer trailing after her. She paused to look over her shoulder, stuck out her tongue, then tilted her ass saucily, and laughed at him.

Writing the search warrant, Stafford looked up, amused. Price banged his fist down on the table the moment the door closed behind her. He lumbered to his feet.

"Stafford, what the fuck are you laughing about?"

The door opened and the Sarge walked in, his hands in his pockets. "You figure her for it, Stafford?"

Dex went serious. "I do and I don't. Finding the will? What makes her so cocky?"

"That's what I can't figure. How did you miss an ongoing charge to a storage bin?"

Stafford's immediate thought was Shanko, but then he had looked at the financials as well. He knew who had been responsible for signing off on Farrow's financials. Him. Oh shit.

"I'll check into it." He stood up as well, three big men in a small room. Harry wouldn't look at him. Harry picked up the envelope off the table and followed Stafford and the Sarge out of the room.

"If she did it, she had help," the Sarge said. "Jarvis might be ready to move up from penny ante to big time murder. For a price. A cut in the inheritance. A piece of her ass maybe."

CHAPTER FORTY-SEVEN

Price organized the search warrant on Tingle's premises. While he was putting that in place, Stafford swung over to the lab and caught Alexandra Esquivel who headed the forensics lab. Her purse over her arm, she had her hand on the doorknob.

"No, Stafford. I'm leaving for lunch. I've been here since 6:30 this morning and I'm leaving."

Only one thing left to do. Stafford fell to his knees on the linoleum and held his hands in a prayer position. "Please, Esquivel. Please."

"Oh, for heaven's sake. Get up. I checked. Nothing yet."

"Please, check again. You know I love you, Alexandra. You are esteemed above all women."

"Well, I hate you, Stafford."

He lowered his chin on his folded hands and looked up at her with puppy dog eyes. Sometimes it worked.

"Alright." She set her purse on the floor and marched back to one of the many computer screens in the lab and tapped her way through a few screens. He got up and followed her.

She smiled over her shoulder at him.

"What? What?"

"Beg. I want a Starbucks every morning for a week. Tall venti latte."

"You have my first born and Starbucks. Tell me."

"Who wants more kids? You got a match. It's the Bryson guy's blood on the S & R hoodie, but talk to Perlmutter. He might have something to say about the spatter pattern analysis."

Stafford picked up her short, dumpy body and whirled her around whooping and hollering.

"Put me down, you animal," she giggled.

The big hopes on getting incriminating evidence from a search warrant on Tingle Sanders home and spa premises crashed. She did have a fine collection of sex toys, which amused the deputies; however, nothing they could take to court on Don Farrow's murder.

＝＋ ＋＝

Holly couldn't let go of the idea Boz Jarvis was the ringleader of the merry little band of vandals—and now burglars—who were amping up the fear quotient in Sierra Mountain Village. People told her Boz was smart, a lot smarter than the O'Malleys. Pete had to be plain stupid to take part in their jolly pranks. But then, Pete *was* plain stupid. She already knew that. She was also pissed at Mike Jarvis for dumping Brenda and ready to believe anything bad about him—and his grandson.

She drank a bottle of water sitting outside Chloe's house, watching the pretty gambrel cabin with Adirondack chairs on the deck, thinking. Betty Anne's car was gone which left Chloe alone. When she got her head prepared, she ambled up the path to the deck and knocked on the front door. The bottom half of the door was set with small square window panes, handy for a burglar, which gave a view into Betty Anne's country cottage living room.

Chloe opened the door and gave her a startled look. "What?"

"Can I come in?"

Chloe flung the door open and slouched over to the couch and picked up a cigarette. Her laptop was open to her Facebook page. Holly perched on the ottoman facing her.

"My mom will be back any minute."

"Oh good. She know you smoke?"

"I'm 18 years old. I can do what I want."

"Yeah? Must be nice doing whatever you want. Wish I could. I'm just thinking about you and Leroy. Guess you and Leroy are going to be parents now. Or is Boz the father?"

Chloe's jaw actually dropped in a classic look of surprise. "How do you know?"

"Think I read it in *People* magazine? You're showing a bump."

"Well, you don't have to be nasty."

"I'm not being nasty. I just wonder what you're going to do."

"We're going to get married. That's what."

"Oh yeah? White dress and everything. Your Dad in a tux?"

Chloe dropped her eyes.

"So you set a date? Can I come?" No answer. Taunting Chloe was cruel, like shooting fish in a barrel. Holly changed her tone. "See why I'm here is, I'm wondering what Boz is up to with the O'Malleys. First Boz was your boyfriend. Then I see you with Leroy. What was all that about?" There was no reason she'd tell her anything, but Chloe *wasn't* smart. Holly put on her older sister face and leaned toward the girl, radiating good will and interest. "What's goin' on, Chloe?"

"Leroy was my boyfriend for, like a minute. I was mad at Boz. I'm back with him now. Leroy's horrible."

"Yeah, I've seen him stuffing french fries up his nose like he thought that was funny. So what's your plan?"

"Well, we're going to get a lot of money soon and raise our kid right, not like our parents. We're going to be around for our kids." She took a pillow from behind her on the couch and folded it across her middle protectively. "I'm going to stay home with my baby and breastfeed and…We've got ideas….and stuff," she added.

"So where's the money coming from? Your mother?" Not likely.

"Boz has money and we're going to get a lot more. And he's coming over soon and you shouldn't be here. He doesn't like you."

"I'm crushed. I may burst into tears any second."

"Nothing you do is going to stop us."

"You're pretty sure of yourself, aren't you?"

"I got Boz and I got my baby and things are going to be different now."

Holly looked at her. So young. So dumb.

"Okay, Chloe. Where did he get the money for the golf cart? And your necklace?" She leaned forward and touched the silver cat hanging on a chain around her neck. "Nice. Looks pricey."

"That's not your business. You have to leave." Chloe lurched herself off the couch. "Don't let the door hit you in the ass on your way out," she said, smiling with the smugness that came of youth.

"Wow, there's an original line," Holly said as she passed her on the way out the door. "And you shouldn't be smoking if you're pregnant." What gave the girl this confidence all of a sudden? And did her mother know all this? Poor Betty Anne.

The wind chimes turned in the sunshine as she went down the stairs and got in the Jeep. The Jeep wouldn't start. Piece-of-shit junker. She had a Tourette's moment and hoped the neighbors didn't hear her. She had to sit there waiting for Christy to pick her up.

CHAPTER FORTY-EIGHT

Stafford had court that morning and sat at the back of the courtroom studying the righteous-looking defendant with a fresh haircut and thrift shop suit: a guy who had branded his girlfriend with the red-hot bottom of a cooking pot. His four-year-old son annoyed her while she was making spaghetti, so she flung the pot of boiling water on the kid. The child had died. Stafford reviewed his notes, hoping to get out of there by 1:30 to meet with Bryson and his lawyer.

Driving back to the station, his mind pinged between the Farrow case and his neglected life. So the little vandal troop Holly was chasing had money coming in? He choked down a 7-11 tuna sandwich one-handed at the 58 and 99 interchange. Tingle Sanders, still his pick. He needed to hit the bulletin board to see if anybody had posted a boat for sale. Skip Bryson, firmly in the running. Take Holly out on Buena Vista Lake in a boat. Could he afford it? What did Perlmutter find on Bryson's hoodie that was unusual? Follow up.

He was in time to catch Harry before starting the interview with Bryson. They strategized, moving aside as a deputy dragged a kicking, screaming felon down the hall. The coach had got himself a lawyer, some local slimeball who modeled himself after Gerry Spence and loved the camera. But competent. Bryson had chosen well in engaging John Anthony Bannerman, who was linked to a firm the cops called Lucifer and Faust.

Bannerman shoved his client into a chair. "I'll do the talking," he growled.

Stafford hoped Bryson wasn't going to be smart enough to keep his mouth shut: random thoughts about Tingle Sanders. Was she smarter than she seemed? Maybe. Maybe not.

"My client is here voluntarily. And will answer the questions I tell him to," he said. Bryson was dressed in a white polo shirt and khakis, freshly shaved and combed, and looking apprehensive.

"Sure. Sure," Harry Price said, his manner brisk and serious. "It's the matter of his alibi being slippery the night of the victim's death. And the appearance of having a good motive. These are matters of concern to us."

"Naturally," Bannerman said. "And are you planning to charge my client with the death of Mr. Farrow?"

"That depends on his answers to our questions," Price said. "Perhaps he can clear up his movements on the evening of Mr. Farrow's demise?"

"Ah, demise." Bannerman chewed the word in a mocking way and Stafford's blood jumped. "Mr. Bryson has divulged information that may shed light on this case."

Bryson sat straighter, his jaw set. A melodramatic pause from the attorney.

"I will relay his information. Mr. Bryson did indeed visit Mr. Farrow at the location where he later met his demise. He and Mr. Farrow had a brief conversation, and Mr. Bryson left him alive and well."

"At what time was this?" Price said.

Bannerman looked over at Bryson who had pinched his lips tight, his hands clenched tight around the chair arms. "He cannot say with any exactitude, but again, when he left, Mr. Farrow was alive and well."

"And how does he explain Farrow's blood on his jacket?"

"Nothing ties it to the time of Mr. Farrow's death. He thinks he left it there that day. Or alternatively:

It could have been deliberately placed there by the killer."

"You're telling us he's not the killer?"

"Yes." Bryson's voice came out high and squeaky. Both Price and Stafford swiveled to look at him. Price let a silence cook. Bryson bit at a cuticle on his right thumb, darting glances at his attorney.

"And what was the subject of his conversation with Mr. Farrow?"

"Certain debts owed by Mr. Bryson to Mr. Farrow."

"And was Mr. Bryson offering to make good on these debts?"

"Mr. Bryson was offering to make good on the debts."

Stafford let his disbelief show. That was the loud voices Peach Bryson had overheard. And Carlos with the cut foot. He caught Bryson's eye. Bryson looked away. He'd be a terrible poker player.

Bannerman capped his Mont Blanc fountain pen with a flourish and closed his IPad with its leather case. He shot his cuffs. "Unless you're charging Mr. Bryson, this terminates our interview."

Bryson smirked, now that it was over. He lurched to his feet.

A long silence filled the room after they'd left. Finally Harry gathered his folders together and stood up. Stafford remained in his chair, looking across the table at him.

"You still think it's him?" Stafford asked.

"Yeah, I do, but we still gotta go through the motions with Jarvis."

"Look, Harry, we've got Jarvis' bank records and a match to Tingle Sanders' cancelled checks. She wrote a check for a $4800 purchase of a used golf cart on Craigslist. Why would Tingle pay for Boz Jarvis' golf cart? Like a lot of your small businesses, Jarvis was only making enough to feed himself and the kid, and meet expenses." He ran out of breath, trying to convince his partner, his face a question.

"Both Jarvis and Bryson had legit reasons for being at the cattery," Harry said, thinking. "We need a DNA sample from Jarvis. He was last arrested before they started taking routine DNA samples. The Tilley hat could be the whole key to the case."

"If the O'Malleys can be believed," Harry said.

Dex shuddered at the picture of Mama Bear O'Malley on the stand. To ease the tension between them, he changed the subject to another case they were trying to inch forward.

Peach Bryson opened her kitchen door, looking between Stafford and Price.

"Oh," Her hand went to her throat. Had her son told her about his session in the interview room?

Stafford couldn't tell. What kind of terms were mother and son on these days?

"We're looking for a fellow you employ. Name of Mike Jarvis? He does your dead animal pickup," Price said.

Relief filled her face. "Why would you want to talk to him?"

"He may have been involved in Mr. Farrow's death," Harry said, taking a step back and straightening a framed photo of a Persian cat.

"You're getting somewhere then? You still think my son had something to do with it?"

"No," Stafford said confidently. He hoped he was right. And he knew he shouldn't have said that. Price crossed his arms over his chest, scowling at him. Harry thought they were wasting their time on Jarvis when Bryson was nailed down. Teams argued all the time because cops had confrontational personalities, but he and Harry were smooth together. Most of the time. But Harry was lead. Stafford could disagree all he liked, but he still followed the strategy Harry laid out.

"Let me take you out to Brenda, then," Peach said. "She had more to do with that fellow than I did. In fact, I think, well, never mind what I think."

Brenda Viglen wasn't happy to see them. Even less happy when they started asking about Jarvis. "I haven't seen him lately." Her eyes welled with tears and Peach moved closer to her. "We had to call another cremation company."

CHAPTER FORTY-NINE

Holly ran into Chloe's mother, Betty Anne, at the transfer site where unwanted items of varying value left on top of the trash compactor made every trip to the dump an adventure. Wearing her denim overalls, Betty Anne was picking through the day's offerings when Holly pulled up next to her in a patrol Jeep.

"You still up there at night, Betty Anne?"

"I got other things on my mind," Betty Anne said, giving Holly a sharp look, picking up and examining a colander, then a VHS tape.

"You know Chloe is still seeing Boz, don't you?" Holly said. "He's a nasty, scheming little shit."

"I know that," Betty Anne snapped, eyes flashing, her lips pinched into a tight knot. "And he's got her knocked up and everybody in town knows that too. Short of nailing her feet to the floor what do you suggest I do? Put a GPS on her? Hunh?" She slammed into her antique Subaru. "She wants to go and live with her father and take Boz with her, and her father doesn't want her." Betty Anne peeled rubber on her way out of the transfer site and sped past the equestrian center. The horses looked up as she passed.

Holly sighed.

She'd been watching Jarvis' place, driving past whenever she had an excuse to swing by. She never saw Mike there. The bastard. Brenda had gone into a slump. She wasn't even bothering to fight with Doreen. Stafford had gone cagey when she asked him what was going on with the Tingle Sanders thing. Peach didn't have the push left in her to press charges, which Holly insisted was a mistake, but she couldn't *make* her do it. Peach hadn't seen the venom in those glittering brown eyes the way she had.

Holly pulled up facing Stafford and Price as they emerged from the community center. Hunh. Did they have lunch without asking her? Harry waved and went back to his phone. She only had a few minutes; there was a welfare check to do up on Yellowstone Drive which sounded serious.

"Chloe told me she and Boz were going to come into money soon."

"Yeah? Did she say where it's coming from?" Stafford asked.

"No. She believes everything he tells her. I got this tip from one of her friends that Leroy O'Malley and Boz were fighting over her and she loved it. For now she's with Boz. Seems like Mike Jarvis is floating money around too. I heard he paid off his bar tab at Crazy Al's and the grocery store."

Stafford's eyes narrowed. "Have you seen him? I'm looking for him. Real hard."

"Why?"

Stafford looked around, as though somebody might be listening. "I've got a link between him and Don Farrow's murder."

"Good news, Stafford." She knew he wouldn't tell her what it was. He'd gotten so close-mouthed and careful that it wasn't even fun flirting with him anymore.

"Keep your eye peeled looking for him. We want him."

Holly didn't bother trying to set up a date when she'd see him again. She said to herself she didn't even care that much. That is, until she got her hands on his hot body. Then she'd care. She also missed plain talking to him, hanging out, doing stuff. He was goofy and fun—away from the job.

She remembered a time before Don Farrow had got himself murdered. She had dinner with Dex and his parents, and spent the evening at his condo listening to BeeBee's stories about her job at JoAnn's Fabrics and getting to know his father. BeeBee turned in early, his Dad went back to his house, and she and Dex hustled into his bedroom shutting the door softly behind him. Holly flung herself in his arms and pulled him down on the floor. His bed squeaked. They had giggling sex on the floor while the hated Persian cat watched them from his bed.

The next morning she couldn't get the smirk off her face. She knew it wasn't his fault he had to keep his mouth shut.

Stafford had left several messages with Perlmutter, the forensics tech who worked on Don Farrow's blood on Bryson's hoodie. Finally Stafford caught him on the phone as he negotiated the I-5 and 99 interchange.

"Sure, it's Farrow's blood, but see, I found this paper on bloodstain pattern analysis that describes research on the difference between impact spatter and pressure transfer."

"Yeah, and..."

"The bloodstain pattern analysis has to explain the fluid mechanics of blood and the mathematical formulas to aid in reconstruction as well as understand how blood reacts with various targets or substrates on which blood is deposited. I've had the basic courses, but..."

"But? I'm driving, Perlmutter, and talking on my phone, setting a bad example for the civilians."

"Well, see, it doesn't look as though it's spatter..."

"What does it look like?" Stafford was beyond impatience.

"Alexandra and I are still talking...and I want to consult with my old prof, but ..."

"Tell me, Perlmutter." Stafford exploded.

"In layman's terms, it looks as though somebody used Bryson's hoodie to mop up the blood... the transfer pattern is all wrong...denim fabric.... contact, pressure, and projected bloodstains. The stains are all wrong." And on and on.

"So what's your conclusion?"

"Oh, I could never make a conclusion from this," the red-headed tech spluttered.

"Perlmutter, you're not on the stand. Tell me."

"You might say, it could be possible...maybe somebody swiped his hoodie through the blood and pressed hard to make sure the blood was absorbed. Like it's not a natural pattern."

"Like somebody was trying to implicate Bryson using Farrow's blood?"

"It's possible. I could never testify to that, though. It's too inconclusive. The literature on pressure transfer on fabrics just doesn't support it."

Stafford ran his hand over the top of his head to keep it from flying off.

Something had to connect to something in this mess of a case. Margie Trask, Tingle's *alibi* for the night of the murder, could be the key to nailing down Sanders. But really all it proved was that she had not been in Taft. They still had nothing connecting her to Farrow and the cattery. Still it had to be followed up. From Sierra Mountain Village, Price and Stafford took the connector road heading toward Taft. Following a steep ridge, the road rolled out spectacular California mountain scenery. Deep canyons unfolded, ridge after ridge rippling down and down to the flatlands of the Central Valley. In the purple distance lay Bakersfield, a hopscotch of square green fields marking out the edge of the city's sprawl and Big Ag territory. The road wound through the Los Padres National Forest, a splendor of coastal mountains rippling away to the left, through the Bittercreek Wildlife Reserve where they released condors into the wild.

Price and Stafford found Margie Trask in an upscale, three-bedroom home in the foothills section of

Taft where she lived with her newly married oil executive husband. Trask gave a worrying glance over her plump shoulder at the county vehicle parked out front as she shut the door behind them. Her face took on a look of alarm as they pressed her to confirm Tingle's alibi for the night of Farrow's murder.

She went red from the cleavage up to the hairline. "You mean to say she was connected to that old guy's death? Really?"

"We're not saying that," Price said carefully, following her into a well-appointed living room. "We check everybody who's involved in something like this. Routine. She says you were with her the night Don Farrow died. The 19th?"

"I remember her asking me to say that," Margie Trask snapped. "I didn't realize it was *that* night. She told me she wanted to do some guy she met and she didn't want Mike to find out. I'm not covering her for a murder. No way."

Stafford smiled.

Trask sat forward on the new-looking couch, her jaw stiffened, her posture combative. "You're not going to tell my husband, are you? He doesn't know about all that stuff I got into. It was all way before I met him."

"Don't see why we'd have to," Price said.

How do you marry somebody and know nothing about them, Stafford wondered, watching her, yet people did it all the time.

Trask stood up and tried to herd them toward the door. "Tingle actually thought I'd lie to the police for her? After watching her prance around in her bikinis and act superior to the rest of us. Ha ha."

Revenge of the fat woman scorned. So much for female solidarity.

CHAPTER FIFTY

Holly was patrolling that night when she saw Mike Jarvis' truck parked in front of his apartment building overlooking the basketball court across the street. A group of older guys had a game going under the big lights and she waved to them.

Curious, she pulled up behind Jarvis' truck, got out and looked around for him. Lights on in his apartment, the other two apartments dark. She had a look in the back of his truck. He'd taken a camper shell off and the bed of the truck was piled full of cardboard boxes: she spied clothes, kitchen stuff, and an old-fashioned desktop computer and TV.

She called Stafford who was leaving the substation down the hill, a stroke of luck. "Looks like Mike Jarvis is moving. I've got him parked in front of his building."

"Excellent. Thank you, Holly. Don't do anything. Nothing! You hear me. Leave it alone. I can be there in 15 minutes."

"Alright. Alright. Hands off. Jeez," she said, offended. "What if he drives away? You want me to watch him leave?"

Stafford hesitated. "Just tell me what direction he's headed in. I'll put out an APB on him."

"Like with who? There's only the deputies and they're 18 miles away," she said logically. "And there's only one way in and out of the village. You better get here soon."

"I'm calling them in for backup now."

Whew, boy. Action. Holly was jazzed. Then she got a call on another bear sighting. Pete was working nights too. She went silent on the radio, waiting, waiting. Finally Pete picked up the bear call.

The lights went out in the front bedroom of the apartment Mike Jarvis shared with his grandson.

Stafford hit the gas hard, all the Christmas lights on, heading back to Sierra Mountain Village. The road in his headlights showed a tunnel of trees, tossing their branches in the sudden wind. A road sign warned of twisty roads ahead as the road snaked back and forth on the downhill slope into the valley floor where the village lay. On the left it was steeper, clinging to the side of a sheer rock wall. His headlights picked out the dead and dying orange trees among the still living. His cellphone rang.

"He's coming," Holly said in an excited rush. "No wait, he's going back to the apartment."

"I'm five minutes out, just past the abandoned camp. Wait. Don't do anything. Jackson is on his way in from Lebec. He's five minutes behind me."

"Maybe I should try and stop Jarvis? Chat him up?"

"No, no. Stay away from him. He's dangerous. Holly, the last thing I want is you getting hurt. Please don't do this."

"I'm not going to get hurt. Stafford, I know what I'm doing."

She ended the call and his heart started beating double time.

Jarvis came down the steps carrying a cardboard box with one shirt sleeve dangling out of it. He saw Holly and came to a halt, a shit-eating grin on his face, a jeans jacket open over a hairy belly. What the hell did Brenda ever see in him? Women!

"Hey, Holly, how ya' doin'?"

"Hi, Mike. I got a call down the street. You hear any loud music? Dogs barking?"

"No, I've been inside all night." Bulbous, piggy eyes. Wide nose marked with enlarged pores.

"You going somewhere?" Holly asked.

"I got work in LA. New job. Great pay."

"Yeah? Good for you. You tell Brenda?"

He slapped his pockets. "Aw, Brenda. You tell her for me, will'ya? Where's my phone?"

"Tell her yourself. You in a big hurry? I grew up in Hollywood. Have you already got a place?" She was making conversation now, chattering away, listening hard for Stafford to slide up. She chanced a quick look at the open door of Mike's apartment. "Traffic's awful there. Where you going to live? What part of town?"

"Don't know yet. I'll see when I get there. I forgot my phone." He headed back into his apartment.

"I'll wait for you." She hit Stafford's contact number. It took him an age to answer.

"Where are you?" she hissed.

"I'm almost there."

"Drive faster."

"Where's Jarvis?"

"He went back in his apartment...shit, he's coming." She hung up and swiveled around to greet Jarvis with a smarmy smile on her face. "Say, how about a coffee before you go?"

"No time, Holly. No time."

Made her sick, but you gotta do what you gotta do. "My place for coffee?" She made her meaning clear.

He hesitated.

Where are you, Stafford? Don't make me do this.

CHAPTER FIFTY-ONE

Stafford hit the S-curves just outside the village going 70, way too fast. Ahead of him in his brights, a deer froze half way across the road, a delicate hoof raised, eyes gleaming green. He screeched to a stop with inches to spare. Hitting a deer would not only slow him down: he'd have to explain it to Holly. One deer often meant more and sure enough, two more deer darted across the pavement in his headlights. He pounded the steering wheel in frustration and gunned the engine when the herd had passed. Minutes later he reached the edge of the village, house lights pooling in the darkness. He looked for the turn off. Hesitated. Nothing looked right in the darkness.

He'd checked Jarvis' address on the way, but his onboard computer map display now flashed green and black, green and black, green and black. The signal had gone wonky. Everything looked different in the darkness with only a thin slice of crescent moon.

He was lost. Lost in a village of 3000 lots.

He watched the road, groping for his cell phone and its GPS software.

The brightest thing in the village was the glaring white lights from the gas pumps in the center of town.

Jarvis' place was to the south of that, one or two streets off the two-block long main drag.

Or was it on the frontage road near the golf course? Shit. Shit. Shit.

He was running fast on the main road through town, hitting the corner hard at the new fire station, the siren off. Taking it on two wheels. The red light over the heliPad glowed in the darkness, the lights blazing nearby in the fire station windows.

He recognized the big green Victorian house on the corner opposite the community center and tennis courts. Okay. He was on the right street. Finally. He tramped the brake and killed the headlights. A radio call told him one of the deputies from the substation was still behind him, now six minutes out, running lights and siren.

⊷⊷ ⊶⊷

Mike Jarvis opened the truck door, looking antsy to get going. Holly made another desperate attempt to stop him. She slinked close to him and made herself look down and pat his arm. Was that her batting her eyelashes?

"Hey, Mike, I always thought you were hot. Maybe it's not too late."

"Yeah? Me? You sure never acted like it."

"Well, there was always Brenda. You know."

"I donno, Holly. I'm in a rush."

"Big guy like you could please me in ten minutes." She gagged as she said it. *Stafford, where in hell are you?*

Behind Jarvis she could see somebody standing in the doorway of his apartment.

Jarvis leaned in the back of the pickup and his shirt rode up showing a gun in the waistband of his pants.

Holly's eyes widened. A gun. What the hell was he into? It wasn't as though she didn't think there weren't guns around the village. But why was Mike Jarvis carrying a gun?

"I mean, Brenda's great, but I don't wanna settle down. New job, new life, you know." He looked around at her, his face taut and ugly. He smoothed his shirt down and pulled his keys out of his pocket. Jarvis was armed and she wasn't. Stafford wanted him and it was probably for some damn good reason.

The gun. The gun.

He was about to leave. Desperate to think up an excuse to call Stafford and warn him about the gun.

⊫ ⊨

Stafford was fifty yards down the roadway on Siskin Drive. He stepped off the gravel onto the pavement when he heard his footsteps crunch in the gravel by the side of the road. Ahead of him he saw Holly talking to Jarvis in the faint light cast by the overheads on the basketball court across the street. She had her hands on his shoulders in a way that looked tense and intimate.

What the hell is she doing? Jarvis pulled her hands away. A flash of movement caught Stafford's eye. Somebody was coming down the stairs from his apartment.

Tingle Sanders.

He stole closer. Then close enough to see Holly twist close to Jarvis.

He yelled out. "Hey, Jarvis. Mike Jarvis. I want to talk to you."

He drew closer. When she saw him, Seabright's face took on a look of relief. She stepped away from Jarvis, whirling her arms in the air, mouthing words he couldn't catch.

"Who are you?" Jarvis growled.

"Detective Stafford, Kern County Sheriff's Department. Just wanted to have a talk with you." He made his tone easy.

"Oh yeah, what about? I'm in a rush here."

"How about we go over to my car and have a conversation in private?"

"We can talk right here."

Seabright was semaphoring some kind of message behind Jarvis' back. Stafford looked at her blankly. Jarvis shrugged and took a pack of cigarettes from the pocket of his jeans jacket. He bent his head out of the wind and lit the cigarette with a match, flaring blue and yellow in the darkness. He took his time about it, giving Stafford time to wonder if he could drag this out until his backup arrived.

"It's kinda private like."

"Yeah? What about?"

Stafford nodded his head toward his vehicle parked down the road. The lights on the basketball court switched off as the game came to an end. Manly claps on the back, handshakes all around, shouts and guys leaving. Then car doors opening, engines starting, doors slamming.

Tingle Sanders sauntered toward them.

Holly danced with impatience, seeing Stafford didn't understand about the gun Jarvis had jammed in the waistband of his jeans. She'd stepped well away from Jarvis' grabbing distance and had her hand on her baton. Fat lot of good that and pepper spray would do against a gun.

The woman who had broken into Peach's house was approaching.

What the hell was Tingle Sanders doing here?

She and Mike Jarvis. Oh yeah? Really?

One of the guys who had been playing basketball stepped into the headlights that suddenly blinded her. "Hey, Holly. Got a minute?" he called from across the road.

Oh shit no. Holly gave him *go away* body language. "Kinda busy right now, Roger. Give me a call later?"

He stepped across the road, all open friendliness. "Just take a minute."

She sidled close to Stafford and muttered out of the side of her mouth, "Gun. Jarvis. Gun."

Stafford's eyes were on Tingle Sanders in a black tank top, shorts, and gladiator sandals. Over his shoulder Holly saw Chloe pounding down the stairs past Sanders sauntering over, taking her time approaching them. Chloe knew who Stafford was. She'd seen him at Paws asking questions.

"Noooooo. You're not doing this to me," Chloe screamed, racing toward Dex and Holly.

Holly, Stafford, and Roger the basketball player, turned to look at her. Jarvis took off running past the line of juniper bushes around the back of the building. Around the corner was a side street of darkened houses.

Holly smelled fury in the air. The glazed, wild look on the girl's face startled her. She swung around to face her.

Stafford bolted after Jarvis. She was on her own in the dark facing a screaming banshee.

"Hey! Hey! Hey! Chloe. No, no, no."

Chloe came at her screeching like a jet engine. "You're not doing this to us. I won't let you."

Holly bent and gave her a shoulder. Chloe spun and fell on one knee and was up again and coming at her, howling. Roger stood transfixed. Sanders crossed her arms over her chest and watched, smirking.

Jarvis took off as though he were in the race of his life. Stafford figured since he was younger, leaner, and didn't smoke, he could take him quickly. Ahead of him, Jarvis crashed through a lilac hedge and headed up a hillside, showing no inclination to slow down. Stafford was dressed for court and his shoes slid on the pine needle duff and fallen pine cones. He fell headlong, cracking his chin on a rock. He stumbled to his feet and in a rectangle of illumination cast by an outdoor light saw Jarvis vault a low fence and knock over a barbecue set up at the side of a house twenty feet off the road.

He was right after him. And then he lost him in the darkness.

Branches, like the outstretched limbs of the desperate, grabbed and slashed at Stafford as he lurched forward. A cloud had gone over the crescent moon and ahead of him was blackness. Every dog in the neighborhood barked.

Lights flicked on from darkened windows around him, but nothing shone with enough illumination to see where Jarvis went. He thought he heard Jarvis panting, and a slide of rocks tumbling down the hillside. He shoved aside a prickly scrub oak bush, which snapped back and clawed him on the forehead.

"Jarvis. Police. Stop. I want to talk to you."

No answer.

A screen door opened above him and an old man in a ratty bathrobe stuck his head out. A big dog shoved past him and pranced on the deck barking so hard the dog began staggering around in circles.

"What's going on out here? Get the hell out of my yard."

"Please go back inside, sir. Sheriff's Department. Police business," Stafford panted. Bent forward, he placed his hand on his thighs and paused to catch his breath.

"You don't look like no cop to me."

Stafford pulled aside his suit jacket where he had his badge hooked on his belt.

"Sir. I need you to go inside and stay there." Below him, back on the road, he heard shouting and a siren wailing into town.

A scraping sound caught his attention ahead in the darkness. He spun off after it, instead of waiting for back up, his weapon in hand, one round in the chamber, his thumb on the safety. He recognized the massive thump of adrenaline when it hit him, the taste of copper in his mouth, and heard his nervous system screaming *Holy shit. Holy shit.* Time stretched and whoo-whooed around him.

His head jerked up as a shot zinged past him—too close.

He flattened himself against the hillside, then zigzagged for cover beside the nearest house. Ah, shit. Gunfire. Everybody would be sticking his nose out to see what was happening. A sudden wind shook the tree branches overhead. The ringing in his ears rose to a screeching cacophony.

"Jarvis. Don't do this. Don't be stupid. Throw your weapon down. C'mon. I've got backup coming. You can't get away. We can work this out."

"I'm not falling for that, cop."

Stafford heard branches cracking and then Jarvis crashing through the scrub oak. He'd lost his radio off his belt somewhere in the initial fall he'd taken. He crouched and circled back to where he'd initially fallen but didn't want to light himself up with his Maglite. Scrabbling around in the dirt for his radio, he wiped blood off his chin. Shooting in the dark was the quick way to get yourself killed. Or your backup. Or civilians.

Probably only one deputy, one vehicle, would be near enough to respond. The other two deputies could be clear over on the other side of the coverage area. The deputy might call in the CHP to assist. But how long would it take a CHP to get there?

Too long.

Procedure said he should go back to the car to communicate his position and coordinate the action. The radio was his lifeline. But he could almost smell Jarvis.

CHAPTER FIFTY-TWO

Chloe did her best to wriggle away from Holly who had ten inches and forty pounds on her. "What are you doing, Chloe? Stop. This is crazy. I don't want to hurt you."

Out of the corner of her eye, she heard Sanders laugh triumphantly, then sashay back to the house.

Holly wrestled the girl down to the ground but she had no cuffs. Chloe blubbered, crying hard, snot running down her face.

"You can't take this away from us," she said, still struggling.

"What? What are you talking about?" Holly panted.

"Mike is taking us to LA. We're going to get our own place to have our baby."

Roger, the basketball player, watched, mouth agape. "Roger, get in your car and get out of here."

The basketball player blinked hard. "You sure? I mean, I could..."

Yeah, right? You could what?

"I'm sure. Leave. I can handle this." Holly already had Chloe, arm twisted up behind her, so close she smelled fear sweat and cosmetics. She pushed her toward the stairs, back inside the apartment.

Then she heard the shot. Holly's heart went bam, bam, bam.

Who fired that shot? Stafford or Jarvis? Was anybody hit? What was Sanders doing?

She had to lock her knees to keep from falling and keep her grip on Chloe.

"Boz! Boz!" Chloe screamed. "They're taking Mike away. Don't let them."

She caught Holly by surprise, twisting away from her. She turned and bit Holly hard on the cheek.

Instinctively she shoved Chloe away. Chloe ran towards the stairs. Holly put one hand to her cheek which was wet with blood.

"Ow. That hurts."

A human bite was like being cut with something fished from the bottom of the sewer. If she'd still been a cop Holly would have cuffed her up and slung her in the back of her vehicle, but she wasn't.

The long wail of a siren approaching went silent. Jarvis would have heard that too.

She saw Boz Jarvis backlit in the doorway of the apartment. His hand was in the pocket of his black hoodie. He glared at her holding Chloe, eyes tiny slits.

Gun?

Stafford pressed himself against the side of a house, his weapon still on safety. He couldn't see a damn thing in the darkness.

A siren wailing toward town. Easing along the side of the house, he stumbled into a woodpile, giving away his location. He froze, then called out.

"Jarvis, I'm pulling out now. My backup is here and you don't have a chance. We can wait for daylight if we need to, and your time is running out."

Silence.

"Hey, Mike. Tingle put you up to this? Did she kill Farrow? You get yourself killed here and she'll roll over on you. You know that. That what you want? You want her telling your story?"

Silence.

"We can still work this out, Mike."

What a load of horseshit. He peered through the darkness, alert for movement, noise, breathing. The shouting below stopped.

The house he was pressed against faced Birchwood. The deputies, or the one deputy, would set a perimeter and stuff curious homeowners back inside. Good luck with that.

Creeping around in the dark looking for somebody with a gun was an excellent way to die. Anything he heard in his vicinity was Jarvis.

Then he heard the crackle of radio traffic from the street. Closer.

Jarvis must have heard it too. He crashed away in back of what sounded like the other side of the house Stafford was hugging. He strained his ears listening, pivoted, and edged back along the lower floor, the windows dark, cursing himself for dropping his Maglite.

He couldn't let Jarvis get away, knowing the guy had plans to run.

A scuffle ahead caught his attention as an upstairs light flicked on, shining into a back yard. Jarvis vaulted a fence not six feet away from him. Stafford launched himself and snatched at a pant leg disappearing over the top.

Jarvis slipped out of his grasp. An earthy odor waved up from the yard, a curling vapor of well-seasoned garbage and something else. A chuffing sound.

Jarvis screamed and fell back against Stafford who had come over the fence after him.

Stafford was about to say something profound like gotcha and reach for his cuffs.

Bear. Garbage. Cubs. A roar as the bear lifted her head and opened her mouth. The teeth in her jaw looked about six inches long.

He flung Jarvis aside and with Olympian speed ran for the fence across the back yard. Knowing he wasn't going to make it.

The bear charged with a scream of primal rage. All 300 pounds of her hit Jarvis like a freight train. Jarvis went oooof and catapulted against the wooden fence like a sack of shit.

Stafford wasn't there to see it. His foot hit the cross bar of the fence and he vaulted to the top, then made the mistake of looking back over his shoulder.

His feet twisted, and in a balletic move which cost him his balance, he went down and down and down like Alice in the rabbit hole, landing on his left hip and torqueing around. His head bounced and then, tumbling through an ocean of stars, his head cracked hard against a tree.

CHAPTER FIFTY-THREE

After the shot the world went still for Holly.

Boz Jarvis was at the bottom of the stairs. Chloe was still in her grasp. She stopped howling at the sound of the gunfire. Then she was all spitting, fighting, clawing, threats. Deputy Jackson launched himself out of his vehicle leaving the lights spinning, the doors open, radio chattering. He and Holly exchanged a look. Jackson barked into the radio on his collar. Backup. Backup.

"What about Stafford?" Holly shouted.

"I'm not going back there alone," Jackson muttered, not looking at her. He twisted his head, looking into the darkness, his neck engulfed in the fat of past donuts. Boz was running towards them.

"Get him," Holly said pointing at Boz. "Put her in your car. Stafford wanted the both of them for questioning. We can't leave Stafford out there…"

"I'm following procedure," Jackson said. "Communication…"

Holly shoved Chloe toward the deputy and turned to run. "You are so weak, Jackson. I'll go."

Stupid. Stupid. Boz immediately started arguing. He punched Holly hard in the left breast She clutched at herself in agony, the pain making her gasp for breath.

While Jackson stood there citing protocol, Boz and Chloe ran toward the stairs leading up to Jarvis' apartment.

Then came the roar of the bear from the darkness behind one of the houses up the road. People shouting. Barking dogs gone ballistic. Every outside light on the street flicked on.

Aghast, Deputy Jackson looked at Holly. "What the fuck was that?"

"Bear."

A high-pitched yelp. Horrible rending noises. A human scream. A forest creature's rage. Holly wanted to cover her ears, fall to her knees and howl.

What a godawful way to die. No way could a human fight against a mother bear defending cubs. Stafford. Stafford.

"I'm going back there. Get that pair and watch them. He might have a gun. Call Fish and Wildlife."

"You don't give me orders, Seabright."

"Jackson, you're pathetic." She couldn't wait.

The door slammed in Jarvis' apartment, barricading Boz and Chloe inside. Tingle Sanders sauntered past the deputy, sneering at Holly. She got in Jarvis' white truck and drove away.

Holly's mind spun with a thousand different scenarios. Decisions. The terrible screams were dying away.

She saw the headlights of the patrol Jeep barreling down the road toward them. The Jeep took the corner too fast, skidding sideways on the loose gravel at the side of the road and slewing off into the juniper bushes.

The Jeep crashed into the stairway to Jarvis' apartment. Pete fell out of the driver's side door, and struggled to his feet, his baton in hand.

"What? What? Everybody's calling me." If he'd hurt himself in the crash into the stairway Holly didn't care.

"Come on." She left Jackson, still babbling into the radio, walking around in a circle. Grabbing Pete by the arm she took off at a run, dragging him.

A guy she knew from the archery club was running down the street toward her.

"Bear," he panted.

"I know. Show me."

"She took off back of us. Saw her go over the fence into the forest. You wouldn't believe. The cubs right after her."

"I know. Show me."

He whirled around and Holly followed him, not trusting the bear wasn't still around.

"Harry Edward's place. In the backyard," the archer said, gulping, turning away to vomit in a stand of rabbit brush.

By then other people had come out of their homes shouting and pointing. With her heart going whumpity, whumpity in her throat and flashlight high, she ran, smelling blood.

"The bear's really gone?" Holly shouted to the people standing on the deck of the house next to the Edwards.

One of the lacemakers from the community center nodded, her chins trembling. The old guy was clutching his chest.

She had to know for herself. She slid down the passageway between the two houses, listening hard. Pete hung back.

Nothing. Bears breathe loud and they stink. They make a funny chuffing sound when they're agitated. Holly took in a lungful of air. Blood. She didn't hear anything.

"Stafford, I'm behind you," she shouted.

She reached up for the latch on the gate and rattled it. Still nothing. Pushed at the gate but it was blocked. Shoved harder and an arm in a jeans jacket flopped into view.

Jarvis was wearing a jeans jacket.

Holly tilted her head back and took a breath of relief, then realized the bear could have gotten both of them.

She shoved the gate wide and forced her way in, shining the light around the yard strewn with garbage. Idiot lazy homeowners. A fed bear is a dead bear.

No Stafford. She didn't want to look at Jarvis. It was too awful.

"Dex. Dex! Where are you?"

Nothing. She walked the perimeter of the fence and heard a groan. Human. Not bear. She ran to the gate at the back of the property and lifted the latch, stumbling into the forest behind the row of houses, Maglite held aloft, baton ready for anything.

Long legs in grey suit pants. Stafford's face and white shirtfront was covered with blood. The sleeve of his suit jacket was torn at the shoulder. He wasn't moving. Shot? Dead? Mauled?

If he was dead, Jarvis had shot him. Only one shot.

Stafford opened one eye, at least half way, and she ran to him, skidding in on her knees.

"Dex? Dex? You're alive?"

"I think so." He grinned but it was a sideways, goofy grin and his eyes had gone funny.

"Move something."

She leaned in and he grabbed her breast, fortunately not the one Boz Jarvis had punched.

"You're alright," she said kissing him on the non-bloody part of his face.

"Cracked my chin. Cracked my head, I think. It really hurts." He closed his eyes.

She heard shouts, big boots and hollers. She jumped up. "Back here."

The paramedics from the fire station a quarter mile away had arrived. Along with chickenshit Deputy Jackson. The ambulance took a lot longer. Holly paid little attention to the team working on Jarvis. Stafford was slurring his speech and had obviously taken a hard bonk on the head.

Holly missed the part where the deputies from the substation pried Chloe and Boz Jarvis out of the house. Boz had a handgun and only one magazine so the standoff didn't last long. Pretty damn dramatic for Sierra Mountain Village. They'd be talking about this for years, the story getting bigger and bigger, and she'd missed it.

Deputy Jackson was running his mouth to the paramedics as they loaded Stafford into the ambulance.

"We told the kid that the SWAT team was coming. Who knows how long that wouldof taken, so him and her come out of the apartment. I've got my taser ready and he sees the red light on his chest and the kid busts out crying, 'Don't shoot me. Don't shoot me.' I'm about to start laughing. He thinks my taser is a gun? I only wish all the low life did."

At the hospital later, Holly ran into Price and his wife Rosalie outside the ER. If she squinted and looked at Rosalie through one eye, she recognized her. Rosalie had new cheekbones, new face and neck, breasts, and had starved herself down to the size of a TV anchorwoman.

"Uh, hi, Rosalie, you look great!"

"Big difference, huh?" she preened, twirling. She had no ass left.

She wanted to say, "Man, you look spooky," but of course she didn't. Holly gushed and said the right things and exchanged an eye roll with Harry behind her back. She was surprised Rosalie was there. Dex thought she hated him.

Stafford would most likely be released the next day or so. His mother would pick him up and take him home. *His mother.*

CHAPTER FIFTY-FOUR

S tafford slept most of the next day between tests and visits by his buddies and the brass. His concentration wobbled in and out. Price brought him the news they had Tingle Sanders in custody. He opened his eyes wide to concentrate on the two versions of Price that stood by the side of his bed.

"....didn't have much of an escape plan set in place...a ticket to Costa Rica in her purse ...sunning herself on a white sand beach until Farrow's estate was settled," he thought Price said. He closed his eyes for a second and woke later while Price was still talking, but it seemed like hours had passed.

"… run for the I-5 interstate twenty miles away down the mountain in Jarvis' truck…CHP who brought her back was ready to gag her…" Price's belly laugh.

Late in the evening he woke to find himself alone and more clearheaded. He asked for something to eat and the nurse brought him a cold cheese sandwich that may have been the best thing he'd ever eaten. A headache made him squint and think hard before he moved anything in an effort to control the nausea. They woke him up what seemed like seven or eight times in the night.

The next day his mother kept turning the TV up so he wouldn't miss a single mention of his name on the local news. TV news was going crazy with Jarvis' mauling by the bear. A ping pong ball rattled loose inside his head and he had a purple bruise on his hip where he fell off the fence. The doctor brought the news he'd suffered a mild concussion, but he could be released. BeeBee was there to drive him home and hover over him. When he got in her car, he insisted on going into the station, BeeBee arguing with him the entire way.

Harry was at his desk and he swung around in his chair, seeing Stafford. "What the fuck you doing here?"

"I'm okay. Back to normal."

Price raised his eyebrows half an inch. "Normal, huh? Okay, cowboy. I got some of the paperwork out of the way. About nine thousand reports due."

Stafford turned as one of the guys walked past fast and slapped him on the back, almost knocking him over. Everybody would have heard about the bear by now. He could hear it already. The start of endless stories. He would be a legend.

They had Boz Jarvis in a cell downstairs. His arraignment had come and gone. The standoff with Boz shooting wildly at the deputies was enough to charge him. Jarvis was in critical condition. Tingle Sanders had lawyered up and was harassing the corrections officers. Maybe they could put her on trial for being a pain in the ass.

Price laughed and made a stack of manila folders. "The Jarvis kid wants to talk. Says he don't need no stinkin' lawyer. He figures we'd think he was guilty if he asked for a lawyer."

Stafford's spirits brightened. "I thought he was smart."

Price snorted. "I already called the lawyer. He and Jarvis are coming in at 2 today."

"What about Bryson? Do we need to grind him at this point?"

"It's Jarvis' DNA on the hat for whatever that's worth, so...*if* the O'Malleys are credible on the stand—" Price said.

"Yeah, if..."

"Then we can place Jarvis at the scene at the right time. Maybe. Bryson was there, we know that, but proving it? Pffft. A defense lawyer could say the blood got on his hoodie at any point. We've got Perlmutter's idea that the blood appears to have been soaked up, but then he won't swear to that in court."

"Don't they now have techniques that can age date a blood stain?" Stafford said. "I thought I read that."

"In Kern County? That stuff costs. C'mon."

"I never though Bryson killed him," Stafford interjected, getting out of his chair, grabbing up his coffee cup.

"You think you're smarter than me? You're still green as grass, Stafford."

"Yeah, well, if Farrow's blood got on his jacket during the stabbing, how come he was able to leave the scene without stepping in blood? There's no blood on his boot, remember? We need a confession. Make Jarvis and Sanders start snapping at each other."

Price clapped his hands together, picked up a manila folder and jerked his chin down the hall toward the prized interview room that didn't smell of farts and vomit. Pausing at the door, Harry said, "I'll lead. You look like shit. Let's hope Ms. Sanders might be polite and want to cooperate with the nice policemen after a night in a holding cell."

They had a deputy bring in a round of Starbucks to soften her up. They met a snarling hellcat, indignant over spending the night with smelly drunks, and homeless people, and of all things, skanky prostitutes.

"How awful," Stafford said with a shake of his head. "We should have put you up in a hotel. We heard you like hotels." He pushed a coffee across the table at her and flung a handful of creamers and fake sugar on the table. She snatched at the coffee.

"Now, see how nice we are," Price said, shaking his head.

"The breakfast was terrible. Cold pancakes and…." she spluttered.

Stafford turned to Price who sat himself down at the table in the interview room. "Did you hear that? We ought to file a petition. Cold pancakes."

"Now you've got a taste of how badly we've let things slip in the way of accommodations, let's talk about Don Farrow. See, we've been real busy here. You told us you spent the evening with Margie Trask the night Don Farrow was killed. Margie Trask? Guess what? She rolled over on you. She denies it now. Maybe it was your cheap-ass bottle of wine she didn't like." Stafford gave her a grin.

He caught Tingle's look of surprise. "Oh, I guess you didn't know her as well as you thought. You didn't know she had a record of bad checks and shoplifting? Makes me think you were up on the hill murdering Don Farrow instead of enjoying Margie's very pleasant company."

Tingle blinked, then the bravado roared back. "Cop, if you had one bit of evidence, you would have arrested me. So arrest me or let me go."

"You hear that, Harry? She wants to leave. After we fixed the place up so nice for her."

"It must have been the soft furnishings. I told you that shade of taupe was off."

"Ha. Ha. Funny guys." She drank down the last of the coffee. "Get me another cup."

"No please and thank you?"

"Fuck you, cop. I'm not going to beg." She crossed her arms over her chest. "And it's cold in here."

"Oh, Tingle. You disappoint me," Stafford said. "You and Mike, huh? Just can't see it, myself. Now why would you hook up with a guy like that, somebody that hauls away dead cats? Where would you even meet him?"

She pursed her mouth. "Match.com," she said grudgingly. "That's illegal all of a sudden?"

"So it's a love connection?"

"Hardly! Friends. You ever heard of friends?"

"He must be a good enough friend you wrote him a check for $4800."

"You have no right to go snooping in my life. I haven't done anything." She leaped to her feet. All that suppressed energy sprang up with her.

"Sit down."

"I can't sit still," she said, all huffy. "Sitting still hurts me."

"You want me to shackle you to the table?"

She sat. "Bastard," she hissed.

Stafford laughed. "Why'd you give Mike $4800?"

"He did work for me around the place. Prove he didn't," she smirked, drumming her hands on the tabletop, brown eyes glittering with triumph.

"We just got started on you, babe," Price said, standing up. He walked to the door and called out "Take her back."

"Wait. Wait. No, don't put me there. I can't go back there."

Price put his hands on the back of the chair and gave her the flat cop eyes. "Sorry we can't arrange private accommodation."

"Likes her creature comforts, doesn't she? We hear you'd like to live the rest of your life in a hotel being waited on," Stafford said, steepling his fingers under his chin. "Hey, Harry. Show her the pix we got of her with Don Farrow at Mimi's. Didn't you tell us you hadn't seen him for weeks? Look at the date."

Her mouth worked as she took in the photos. "Maybe I forgot." Her eyes flickered here and there. "Wait." The panic looked genuine. "I'll tell you."

Price sat down, tapping his pen on his notebook. "Go."

Her eyes, cold with speculation, swung to him. "Okay. Mike. It was all his idea once he heard I was still officially married to Don. I met Don for lunch that day at Mimi's, yeah. He told me he planned to send in the final filing for the divorce. Mike went crazy when I told him that. He killed him for me. He thought I would inherit and we'd get all this money and go to Costa Rica. Ever been there? It's nice."

Both cops said nothing.

"Honestly! It was all his idea." Her brown eyes were wide, all the freshness and innocence of a little bunny. "I didn't know he would actually do it. I thought it was all big talk. Honestly! Honestly."

"He had quite a story to tell us. I spent all day with him yesterday," Price lied. "He says you set the whole thing up."

"He never told you that. I know him." She gave Price a withering look.

"And you were going to take off with him, looks like? At least that's what he thought."

"Don't be so stupid. When do I get out of here? I need to wash my hair. Besides I didn't do anything," she said looking around, preening her red-tipped fingernails through her long silver hair.

"Resisting arrest and conspiracy to murder might be a start," Price said. His voice was hard and flat and swiveled Tingle's head around.

"You can't prove anything!" she screamed with an edge of panic. "They told me Mike was dead."

That was exactly what Stafford and Price had suggested the deputies leak to her.

But it wasn't true.

CHAPTER FIFTY-FIVE

The town was still buzzing with the excitement of the so-called gun battle between the sheriff's guys and the killer of Peach Bryson's boyfriend. One caller after another was on the line to Holly hoping to get the inside scoop. There was Pete in the office, his feet up on the desk. Why couldn't Price and Stafford have arrested Pete and Leroy while they were at it? Holly burned that she still had no way of proving anything against them.

She chortled with glee when somebody other than her reported Pete for sleeping on the couch in the lounge on graveyard shift. That was a no-no, but it was the first time he'd been caught and Ed was only allowed to give him a warning. She was going to get Pete, no matter what.

⊷⊶

It was taking plain old shoe to pavement, pen to paper, fingertip to mouse, ear to telephone, as well as footwork for Price and Stafford to nail down the case on Tingle Sanders and Mike Jarvis. The bear had inflicted considerable injury to Jarvis, but she hadn't killed him. He'd been patched up and stuck back together again. Stafford and Price dogged his doctors and had been allowed brief moments to interview him in his hospital bed where protocol kept him shackled to the bed. This morning he was sitting up when they hit his room. He didn't look pleased to see them.

Stafford regarded Jarvis who was trying to sip broth. An untouched breakfast tray lay in front of him. He was all taped up: more gauze than skin showed.

"Where's Tingle?" he asked.

"We've got her in a cell with a bunch of alkies and prostitutes."

"She won't like that," Jarvis smiled weakly, using a thickly bandaged hand to pat at the gauze wrapped around his head. He picked up a fork and poked it under the wrapping to scratch the stitches.

"Did she kill Farrow?" Stafford asked. He wanted to see Jarvis' reaction.

Jarvis' gaze skittered around. "You bet she did."

The nurse came in and shooed them out. Not before Price asked, "Then give us something to help us get her."

Jarvis closed his eyes. "Why should I help you? She's gone. I know that. I go back to a rented apartment. My truck's got 200,000 miles on it. I listen to a Sony Walkman and I earned $21,000 last year. I don't give a damn anymore. Take your best shot, asshole."

That afternoon he developed an infection, a bad one. It gave them the time they needed to work on Sanders.

People couldn't shut up about it and Holly took part in her share of gossip too. The bear, Mike's hospitalization, Tingle, Jarvis, and Boz's arrests, were spun and respun in the local weekly and even made Bakersfield TV. It was the most interesting thing to happen in Sierra Mountain Village since the mayor was beheaded. She was glad for Dex and Harry, sure. But it left the vandalism hanging in the air.

Mulling over a problem at Paws, Holly drove in behind Pete at the maintenance yard where they gassed up patrol vehicles. Suddenly, as though somebody poked her in the butt with a needle, she had an idea.

Three days before the end of the month and she knew what was left of that month's paycheck.

When it was fully dark she drove back to the maintenance yard, pulled up a few straw bales and made a hiding place near where they parked the snow plows. She lay on her back on the straw bales and looked up at the millions of stars winking overhead. It was a beautiful sight. She thought about how much she liked living in Sierra Mountain Village: knowing everybody, feeling useful, Peach and the cats, the silence, the peace, the astonishing beauty she delighted in every day. She fiddled with her camera until she was sure it would take good pictures in the dark and settled back to wait.

Late in the night she heard the gates open and saw the headlights of Pete's patrol vehicle coming in. The fool pulled up to the pumps and took four 5-gallon cans out of the back and filled them up. Holly got it all on camera. There was a honk at the gates. Pete swaggered back to open them and Leroy pulled in his old Corolla. He unloaded a few propane cylinders and by the way he slung them around, she knew they were empty. Not when they left.

She got it all on camera. The next morning she took the photos in and dumped them on Ed Bradley's desk. Ed actually apologized to her. They saw the GM and he called out the deputies.

Pete was fool enough to let the deputies search his truck and his house. "May I search your car?" yields tons of dope and burglary arrests. Why people say yes, knowing they have a dozen kilos of coke in the trunk, amazed Holly. They didn't find coke, but they did find roofies and bath salts, and more importantly, items on the lists provided by the owners of empty cabins that had been burglarized. Pete, Leroy and Boz's gummy fingerprints were all over everything.

The blood spatter pattern and crime scene photos had told Price and Stafford that Don Farrow's killer was at least six inches taller than Farrow who hardly topped 5 ft. 7". The height differential had kept their interest in Bryson as long as it had. Jarvis, too, was tall and beefy and had martial arts in his background.

"But Jarvis didn't think this up alone. You know damn well Sanders was up to her neck in the shit," Stafford insisted while he regarded the whiteboard where facts about the case were noted down. A confusing set of arrows in different colors linked facts, time lines, and question marks.

"She was the brains behind it." Price declared, pacing in front of the whiteboard, jingling the change in his pants pockets. "Neither one of them is an intellectual giant. We're going to have to let her go, probably today. We don't have enough evidence to charge her and her lawyer's yammering at me," Price said. "Hey, cheer up, we got the search order on Jarvis' place," he said, slapping Dex on the shoulder. "We'll find something."

Once again, they made the long, familiar drive up the hill to Sierra Mountain Village. Stafford called Holly while Price drove. He had days off coming up and he wanted to spend them with her.

"What's up, babe? How's about lunch today?"

He heard delight in her voice and it cheered him.

"Hey, we got Pete and Leroy on the burglaries I told you about," she said, happily. "Big stuff."

He poured on the congratulations and warm praise. "Madison is gonna love you clearing those burgs for him," he said. Maybe they'd actually get together that evening to celebrate at Café Silva Bella, Holly's favorite restaurant in town.

Jarvis' place looked like it had been ransacked in his haste to leave with Tingle. Stafford's spirits soared when they found a pair of hardly worn boots in the back of the closet. He figured he'd found a match to the unidentified boot print. He'd bet the farm that dark spot on the still new treads was blood. And that the blood would be Farrow's. How could the guy be so damn dumb? Didn't he watch *CSI?* Boz Jarvis had too many toys: two IPads, a computer setup Dex envied, and a flat screen that crowded the edges of the walls, along with five remote controls. Price followed Dex into the room snapping on blue latex gloves.

Minutes into the search Stafford heard the faint sound of a recorded voice followed by a shout.

"Bingo!"

Dex made for the bedroom where Harry stood looking smugly at a cell phone on which Jarvis had kept a series of files recording planning sessions with Tingle. If he was going down at any time for Don Farrow's murder, he was taking Tingle with him.

The deputies dug until they found out Leroy, Boz, and Pete had sold the building materials stolen from the town yards on Craigslist, leaving a mile-wide paper trail. The three of them together had enough brains to make a half-wit. Holly was enjoying being the hero around town because of her part in seeing them charged. Dex was good about giving her credit. Sgt. Madison at the substation told her he'd send in a letter of commendation to add to her application file.

No raise of course.

CHAPTER FIFTY-SIX

A few nights in the cells convinced Tingle being charged with accessory to a murder wasn't such a bad thing after all. She bragged to her cell mates who reported right back to Stafford through the deputies. As long as there were men on the jury, Tingle figured she could walk out the door ready to start her life over with a big book deal. But there would be women on the jury, and it didn't seem to Stafford that a lot of women were ready to play on Tingle's team.

Jarvis hadn't trusted Tingle any more than she had trusted him. He had kept every piece of paper connecting them that he could. The evidence was still circumstantial so far. They could prove the connection between them, but it had to go further than that.

Boz Jarvis nailed down the links to save his own neck. The little gangster in training had sharp ears.

The Deputy DA assigned to the case was the Dudley Do-Right with the Brooks Brothers suits and good haircut. He tapped a pencil, skeptical, picking holes in the case he had to take to court. The Sarge and the new Lieutenant of Operations made notes on yellow legal pads, IPads, and laptops while Price outlined their case against Jarvis and Sanders: the evidence, time line, proof of the collusion between the two as the motivation for Farrow's killing. Forensics was solid on Jarvis: witnesses were iffy. They had to tell a story to take to the jury. Sometimes the story was as important as the evidence. Juries liked motivation.

"So how did they pull it off?" the beefy Lieutenant of Operations asked.

"Sanders led Mike Jarvis around by the dick for years, like she had him on retainer for when she needed him. Which one of them thought of it first?"

Stafford eased himself up from his chair in the conference room, intent on his partner's overview. He still ached from the fall off the fence.

"Tingle was desperate to get out of Taft but she didn't have the means. When Farrow told her he was finalizing the divorce and marrying Peach Bryson — he may even have mentioned his will, we'll never know — but Tingle saw her chance. Killing Don before he remarried would bring her in line with more money than she'd ever see in her lifetime doing massage and dealing with women all day. So they cook up this scheme," Price said.

Stafford interrupted, swiveling back and forth in his chair. "Jarvis hung around Paws and heard enough from Brenda, the manager, he figured he could lay Don's murder on Skip Bryson. And letting all the cats out would create confusion. Somebody who wasn't familiar with the operation wouldn't have even thought of that."

Harry paused. "Sanders passes on the rumors Don and Peach were getting married, or had got married. She didn't know for sure until she met Don at the restaurant. So that starts their clock ticking."

"Think they knew about Bryson's IOUs?" the DDA asked.

"Maybe. Maybe not. But Bryson was a convenient fall guy. Tingle shows up with the will at exactly the right time. Not too early. Not too late. That woman has moxie in spades." Stafford laughed, shaking his head. "She waited to hear from us about the will and when she learns we haven't found one, in she comes waving it in our faces and thinks she's pulled it off."

"Bryson admits he was there just before Farrow was killed," Price said. "Tingle and Jarvis were right down the road shitting their pants when Bryson shows up. But then he leaves."

"Maybe Bryson went in to hit him up for more money. We're not getting his story on that so far but we're still digging. Skip leaves. Mike's been waiting his turn. He goes in and kills Farrow. And he drops his hat in the road and doesn't realize it until later."

"Talk about shitting his pants," Price said.

"Maybe not. He figured he could have dropped it anywhere."

"Too bad we've only got the O'Malleys as witnesses. And all this time Skip and Jarvis are in there with Farrow, Peach is on the phone?"

"Yeah, a phone call from 7:10 to 7:35. That's enough time. Mike is smart enough to see Skip's Search and Rescue jacket he left there and swipe it through the blood to implicate Bryson."

"Wife doesn't really alibi him. Girlfriend can't remember if she saw him." Stafford got up and started pacing, his voice rising. "What I wouldn't give for a chance to hear Jarvis' story," Stafford said.

If he could be believed, and that was a stretch, Boz Jarvis cast a light on Mike Jarvis. The nasty little shit was led into the interview room, so short and slight the shackles around his waist seemed to be wearing him rather than the other way around. All the piss and vinegar had been kicked out of him. He greeted his public defender with a smirk. They had a brief consultation and Boz was ready to lie his head off, sing any song he thought might be a hit.

His words tumbled over each other. "I heard Mike telling Tingle what happened the night he went over to kill Farrow."

"You just happened to overhear this?" Stafford snapped. He tilted back in his chair.

"I keep track of things that involve me. My grandfather got so crazy I didn't know what he was gonna do with me, whether...whether he was gonna throw me out or what. So yeah, I keep track. For me and Chloe." He flung back the flop of blonde hair that fell over his forehead. He was still young enough to have pimples.

"Oh, yeah, your girlfriend. Chloe."

"She's got nothing to do with anything," he protested.

"Except she's hanging out with you. That's the only thing wrong with her."

"Hey, man. Why are you busting my balls? What'd I do? I'm telling you stuff, aren't I?" His public defender looked pained.

Stafford scoffed. Boz would have learned how to reinvent reality, changing its shape at will in his short life and criminal career.

The kid strained forward in his seat. "No, really. Mike got Tingle to call up that old lady and keep her on the phone. Tingle called her from a pay phone in the village."

Price shot Stafford a look. If she made the call anywhere near the cattery, there were damn few phones to check. One outside the grocery store. Maybe someone had noticed her. Tingle stuck out.

"I swear I'm telling you the truth."

"Yeah," Stafford said in a bored flat voice. "The truth. Right."

"Mike was a Navy Seal for about a week and he learned stuff. It's not like him and me talked about it." The kid looked at him sharply. "I heard him and Tingle talking. What a laugh. They were going to run away to Costa Rica. Eeeeuw, sex between old people."

He thought this was funny. Neither detective nor the public defender laughed.

"Yeah, well, I'm gonna be a father. I would'na said anything if it was only me, but I gotta think of us. Mike's got money and I'm figuring the only way he's getting money is from Tingle. Tingle has to give him more than pussy to get him to kill that old guy. I know he bled her for everything she had. So I hint and he starts giving me a twenty here and there."

"So you blackmailed him?" Stafford said, shifting in his chair. The bright lights in the room were making his head pound again.

Boz didn't like the word. "Tingle's funneling him money because she's scared he's gonna talk. Mike's not stupid—only stupid about her. But he doesn't trust her and at least that was smart. Chloe and me both want to live in LA. That's the place for somebody like me."

"Somebody like you, yeah. Something else bugs me," Stafford said, Holly crossing his mind. He leaned forward, fixing Boz with a hard stare. "Why did you pull down that shrine thing up there on the meadow? What was all that about?"

Boz smirked with self-satisfaction. "Just to teach Chloe a lesson. I caught her with Leroy. So the bitch needed a lesson."

"Who shot at that bunch of women? Was that you?"

"Not me. Not me," he protested.

It was one of them for sure. You could look and look and look for something that made sense when these losers didn't have a thought in their head or any purpose beyond what felt good in the moment.

"So when do I get out of here?" Boz asked, bobbing up and down in his chair, the shackles rattling.

"You're not going anywhere for quite some time."

"What'd I do?" His shackles rattled and shook.

His public defender spoke up. "Mr. Jarvis, I know you're aware of the consequences of the charges."

"Yeah, but you're supposed to get me off. I've got places to go."

Stafford stood up, yanking his tie loose. "We got lawyers slavering to get hold of you with about a thousand more questions, but right now I got a headache and you're making me sick."

Price would stay behind and be the good cop. Maybe he could get more. He paused at the door, watching.

"Hey, hey, hey," Boz said. "I didn't do nothing."

Price took over. "Yeah? We searched your place last night. That surprise you? We found a lot of nice stuff in your room. Most likely you didn't know it, but burglary's another no-no."

"You searched our place? You have to have my permission to search our place." His conception of the law lay beyond Stafford's imagination. And Holly had told him Boz was the smart one.

"Grow up, kid. Most of that stuff was on an evidence list we got from the property crime guys. Stuff missing from cabins broken into. Stuff like an antique sled. What the hell would you keep that for?'

Boz Jarvis' voice went high and shrill. "No, that was Mike. He brought that stuff home. Not me. Not me."

"Thing is we didn't find Mike's fingerprints on that stuff. Only yours and your pals. Tell it to your public defender. He'll tell you all about felonies."

Boz Jarvis gave a long wail. Cases had been made on less.

CHAPTER FIFTY-SEVEN

Holly drove by Chloe trudging home from the post office. She dragged a plastic bag of groceries, shuffling along in flip-flops. She still wore the silver cat in the heart around her neck. Her belly was getting big now and Holly slowed, but didn't stop. What was there to say? She felt sorry for her. And for Mama Bear O'Malley. Both her sons were in jail and she was stuck with Dwayne's druggie girlfriend and their baby.

Last week Beatrice had sailed into Holly at the grocery store, as though it was all her fault. "Dwayne's girl would sell her own mother, sell me for drugs. The hours I've spent worrying about my sons being on drugs and now she's the real poison we injected into our own house."

Holly let her go on for a while with her long list of unfair things. Then she made an excuse and left her muttering to the wilted lettuce at the produce counter. She felt sorry for Betty Anne too, stuck with Chloe, and soon a new baby. That shrine up on the meadow, a spiritual comfort for some people, was also a magnet for craziness.

The likelihood of another homicide in Sierra Mountain Village was pretty dim, so maybe she'd be seeing more of Stafford. Or maybe less. Shifting the Jeep into low, she considered that. She'd driven down to Bakersfield last night, deep into the poisonous air to meet him and look for things about the city that she liked. Trader Joe's and a Whole Foods. Movie theaters. A college that offered forensics classes. Places that stayed open after 8 o'clock at night. Lush fruit trees lining the streets. The old downtown. They went dancing. Dex was a good dancer. Another plus.

Peach was almost back to her old self. No more talk about closing Paws. She had insisted Brenda and Doreen call a truce and have a hug at the last board meeting. Both of them now talk as if they're enthusiastic about enlarging Paws to take in dogs. Holly was too, but oh, the work that lay ahead. Turned out the silver cat in the little heart belonged to Peach. She recognized it around Chloe's neck and had said nothing.

Skip Bryson had swaggered around town bragging about being a suspect in a murder investigation until he received an offer to work in an art gallery in Los Angeles. His move made everything easier at Paws.

Holly pulled into her driveway, thankful that her shift was over. She was still scuffling to make it to the end of the month with her patrol job and dog grooming. No word yet from the Sheriff's department.

The older she got the less certain she was about the way things would turn out. Stafford had quit pretending. It was clear he hated it up here in the village. And she didn't know if she could hack hot, polluted, horrible Bakersfield. There were her cats and his allergies. And his mandolin. And his mother. How far was she willing to bend and twist to meet him in the middle?

Life would unfold no matter what, wouldn't it? The world was not always bright and new and she was just along for the ride. All in all, it was a pretty good ride.

Tomorrow was another day. Something good was bound to happen yet. She grabbed her mail out of the post office box and flipped through it. Bills, flyers and an official looking envelope with the return address of the Kern County Sherriff's Office.

Yes. Or no. Maybe?

Jostled aside by a young mother with wet hair, and kids fresh from the swimming pool, her hand froze.

Then she tore the envelope open to peer inside.

Thank you for reading *The Most Dangerous Species*

The kindest thing you can do for any author is to leave a review on Amazon and Goodreads

The initial book in this series is *Payback (2014)*

Read the Dave Mason crime fiction novels set in Santa Monica
in either eBook format or paperback version available on Amazon:
(2015) *A Very Private High School:*
(2013) *On Behalf of the Family*
(2012) *Rip-Off:*
(2011) *No Dice*

———————————————————

Website: http://marpreston.com
Facebook Author Page: https://www.facebook.com/pages/Mar-Preston/136299239777273
Twitter: YesMarPreston

I invite you to email me at marpreston@frazmtn.com